Epithymy

T.D.Cloud

Illustration by Y.Dan

Book One of The Duskriven Chronicles

ISBN-13: 978-1976420412

ISBN-10: 1976420415

Acknowledgments

Another book, another universe, and another foray into the unknown. I'd like to thank my amazing readers and fans who continue to support me, for without you there would be no more adventures to be had.

To NIL for putting up with my persistent mistakes. I swear that one day I will learn how to use a comma.

To Linden, for surviving a hurricane and still helping me whip this book into shape.

To Daphne, for your indomitable excitement. You keep my spirits high when they they want to be no such thing.

To Sun, for helping lay this out while still recovering from Petrichor. Your reward is coming. Be prepared.

To my mom, who I sincerely hope chooses this to be the book she doesn't read. You're amazing but killing me.

To my dad, who has never (and will never) read my books. Thank you for showing me how to skin animals. It's finally come in handy.

To Yougei, for making this journey with me. This story really is our brainchild, and the art you've done is absolutely breathtaking. You're my reason for reason and always my beloved. Thank you for taking the leap with me. I can't wait to see what we do together next.

Contents

Prologue

The tavern was crowded when Sorin managed to shove his way inside, filled with smoke and bodies and the stink of sweat and ale. It was better than the storm outside but only just. Sorin let the door slam shut behind him, nose wrinkling but too used to this sort of environment to bother complaining. He had a job to do. He could complain after.

"What'll you have?" the elderly man asked from behind the bar, bushy eyebrows blending with his wild mane of white hair. He was polishing glasses with a dingy rag, keeping up the veneer of productivity while accomplishing little at all. "Look like a drowned mire rat, you do."

"Feel like one." Sorin grunted, waving off the proffered glass to lean against the grimy bar. Water sloughed off his cloak, the rain matting the fur trim. He'd be in for a miserable night if the weather didn't calm itself. He really didn't want to pay for lodging in a place like this.

The old man hummed and went back to his pointless cleaning. "What brings you to these parts?" he asked, seeming desperate for conversation. Sorin's father was the same way, always eager to talk someone's ear off if they stayed still for too long. "Don't get many with that accent 'round here."

"Here on business," Sorin said gruffly, knowing better than to tell the old timer he was a bounty hunter. Even if he wasn't on a job just yet, it tended to make any known or unknown criminals in the vicinity twitchy. "Meeting a client."

"Ahh, yer waitin' for someone," the man said sagely as he tapped the side of his nose, blinking his bushy browed eyes.

1

The rag in his hands paused. "Say, you wouldn't be lookin' for that shady bloke back there?" he asked, gesturing to the furthest corner of the bar where a single figure stood out against the lively background of the bar. "Been sittin' there all night, he has. Been tellin' my boys to keep an eye on him. Doesn't feel right, if you get my meanin'. Best not to bother yourself with bad news, son."

"I make my living on bad news," Sorin sighed, pushing away from the bar. He pulled a silver piece from his pocket and dropped it onto the bar, nodding at the man evenly. "Thanks for the warning, old man."

"You'd be thankin' me more if you listened, but I'm not your pa," the barkeep huffed, palming the coin and turning away to go tend to the other customers. A Dwarf banged his goblet on the top of the bar, growing violent in his need for a refill. "See that you keep that trouble to yerself, son," he called, leaving Sorin to his work.

Sorin rolled his eyes, turning around to face the tavern at large. First order of business when meeting a new client was always the same no matter the venue, no matter the client. The room was large and crowded with carefully segmented groups that bespoke of regular customers. A card table was set up in the middle of the tavern, its occupants ranging from a hard-eyed Halfing to a brutish looking boar of a man losing handsomely to her. A few onlookers were gathered around betting on the outcome, and around them sat individual tables of lonely drinkers, adventurers worn out from the day's travels, and old men and women regaling each other with stories in between drinks of their bar swill.

His first perusal told him that there weren't many visible weapons, which Sorin considered a boon. He couldn't count the number of times he'd been dragged into a bar fight while in the middle of hammering out the details of a new contract. It was always a possibility in this type of setting, and he'd learned long ago that exposed weapons only added to the carnage. He may have relished it in his youth, but these days, all it did was add to his growing collection of scars, scare off more customers than it brought in, and get him kicked out of the tavern for the night. He certainly didn't need that, especially on a night like this.

And that brought him to the shadowy figure tucked into the corner. If this were indeed his client, and all signs pointed to him being just that, then he was far smaller than Sorin had anticipated him being. Even from across the room, Sorin could see he was just a little slip of a thing wrapped up in his cloak as he was. He hardly looked like he would come up to Sorin's chin if standing. Small gloved hands were wrapped around a steaming mug. The hood didn't move an inch even when the stranger sipped from the cup. Sorin observed for another few moments, trying to read the stranger, but there simply was nothing left to garner. This person could be armed to the teeth or be as harmless as a child, and Sorin wouldn't know the truth until he got within striking range.

Sorin let out a sigh, blinking tiredly. He had walked into worse, so there really was no point in prolonging it any longer than he already had. Shifting his axe higher onto his shoulder, he cut through the oblivious drinkers, glaring at the eyes that followed him until they went back to their mugs. He could already tell which were the 'boys' the barkeep had been referring to. It really didn't bode well that his prospective client had already garnered enough attention to be watched like a hawk in somewhere as innocuous as a tavern.

"I take it you're the one who contacted me?" Sorin said by

way of greeting, coming up to the table slowly, assessing as he went. There was an empty seat across from the solitary figure, but he was hesitant to take it. It was one thing to get within striking distance with minimal information. It was another thing entirely to willfully sit across from the stranger as if they were old friends.

The voice that replied to him was entirely unlike anything he expected to hear. "I suppose I am," the stranger said in a soft, melodic voice. "Are you the feared bounty hunter Sorin?"

"You sound surprised," Sorin grunted, dragging the chair out and sitting down. The stranger didn't sound older than twenty, and that, in itself, calmed Sorin's distrust. But just to be safe, he unslung his axe from his back and rested it against his leg. "Were you expecting something different?"

A gloved hand tugged the hood of the stranger's cloak lower, obscuring his face but for his cheeky little smile. "I suppose I expected someone a little less wet," he teased, his lips parting to showcase a row of sharp, white teeth. "But I shouldn't poke fun. It's a mess outside. It doesn't rain like this where I'm from."

Sorin hummed, narrowing his eyes. "You're the one who contacted me?" he said, trying and failing to catch a glimpse beneath the cloak. "I expect to look my employer in the eye when discussing business."

"Ah, well," he began, his hands fluttering nervously around his cloak. Upon closer inspection, it looked shiny and slick, almost as if it were treated to repel the elements. Expensive. "I'm trying to avoid attention. Don't take it personally."

"That's not how I operate." Sorin made a move to pick up his axe, lifting himself from the chair. "Thanks for wasting my time."

Quick as lightning a slender hand shot out to wrap around Sorin's wrist, holding him in place in a desperate move. "Please don't leave," the stranger said, biting his lip with his perfect, sharp teeth. "My name is Khouri? Khouri Lucifin. At least hear me out first. I can make it worth your while."

He let out a sigh but sank back into his seat. The alternative was going back out into that rain. "Khouri?" he repeated, rolling the strange name on his tongue. "Where are you from?"

Khouri let go of Sorin's wrist, settling back down into his own seat with a nervous little shuffle. Carefully, he peered around at the bar behind Sorin, tugging up his hood just a bit to show his dark, dark skin and his pointed ears. "It's just easier to show you, I guess," he murmured quietly, meeting Sorin's gaze with a pair of eyes so deep that just looking in them induced the sensation of drowning. "Please don't leave. It really was a lot of work to get in contact with you."

Drow. Sorin's lip curled in distaste. That answered that question. He had only ever dealt with them sporadically and usually never in such a public setting. They were notorious for keeping to themselves, especially aboveground like this. Sorin supposed that was probably do to the stigma more than anything. Drow certainly weren't well received here. "You're a long way from the Duskriven," he observed gruffly, letting his arms fall from his chest so he could rest a hand on his axe beneath the table. "I'm surprised they let you in here."

Khouri's polite smile grew tight. His small nose wrinkled as he pulled his hood down lower. "Yeah, well," he began, looking about as uncomfortable as a Drow above the earth should look. "There's a reason I kept my hood up. Is this going to be a problem?"

Sorin didn't know how to answer that. He certainly didn't

5

want to *work* for a Drow. The added risk it presented was far more than he would ever willingly accept on any other job. "That depends," he drawled, leaning back in his seat to better take in the potential customer before him, "on what you're wanting done. I'll tell you right now I don't kill for less than five hundred."

"I don't need you to kill anyone," the Drow huffed. "I could do that myself if I needed it done so badly. I just need you to escort me for a bit. Or do you charge five hundred for that too?"

Escort? If there was one thing in this world Sorin hated, it was escorting some helpless sap somewhere he patently didn't want to go. "I'm a bounty hunter, not a babysitter," Sorin said.

"I'm aware," the Drow replied, furrowing his brow.

If he were so aware of that, then why bother coming to Sorin? There were plenty of others around that could handle something as simple as an escort contract. What a waste of his time. "It'll cost you." Watch this brat have barely two gold to rub together. "I don't do charity work." Even for the pretty ones.

The Drow rolled his dark eyes. Sorin hadn't met many Drow in his time, but he knew that this one's coloring was odd for their race. Everything about him was dark, muted. Black hair as shiny and sleek as the feathers on a raven's wings peeked past the edge of the hood. His eyes were a midnight black, at odds with Sorin's memory of brilliant red or burning pink. As Khouri shifted to reach for something beneath the table, Sorin drank in his petite figure. No, this was certainly something different. In both behavior and appearance, it seemed.

A thick, rough sack hit the scarred tabletop with a metallic rattle. "Is this enough?" Khouri asked, leaning forward to push the money closer to Sorin. His fingers were slender, the

6

dark color of his gloves stark against the tan of the sackcloth. "It's not quite five hundred, but I think you'd be an idiot to refuse it either way."

Sorin dragged over the sack and loosened the drawstrings, his eyes going wide when he looked inside. It was full of not silver or bronze but pure gold coins. There were dozens of them, all neatly stamped with the Imperial crest for the region. He lifted a coin from the bundle and bit down on it, testing its authenticity.

"Oh, come on," Khouri huffed, crossing his arms over his small chest. "It's real. I just traded for it all earlier this evening."

"You can't blame me for doubting you," Sorin retorted, a bit rankled that it was in fact real.

"If you're going to be like that, I can take my business elsewhere. If me being what I am offends you then I don't want to trust you with my safety."

Sorin rolled his eyes and dropped the bent coin back into the sack, closing the bundle with a sharp tug to the drawstrings. "It won't be an issue," he said, fastening the payment to his hip. "I'm a professional. Where are you wanting escorted? Back to the Duskriven?" He hadn't been that way in a long while, and the thought of traveling downwards made his skin crawl.

He hadn't expected to make the Drow laugh. If Sorin were being honest with himself, he hadn't thought the race capable of something like humor unless it were directed at something foul or sadistic. Khouri wiped an errant tear from his dark, dark eyes and smiled at Sorin brightly. "Oh, absolutely not. I don't want to go anywhere near there," he said, leaning forward to rest his elbows on the table. "What I want from you is a little unorthodox."

"More unorthodox than a Drow who doesn't want to go back to the Duskriven?" Sorin posed. It just earned him another laugh, one that he begrudgingly had to admit sounded rather pleasant.

"I guess when you put it like that…" Khouri looked off at the bar, turning back quickly when the lumbering brute at the card table caught him staring. "What I want from you is to be more of a… companion to me. I get dragged into conflicts more than I'd like to admit, and while I can take care of myself just fine, I thought it might be smart to employ some help. I don't have any destination in mind. I don't need you to escort me like chattel. I just want to accompany you and count on you for help if something does happen."

As if this Drow couldn't get stranger. Sorin stared at him, searching his odd, comely face for any sign that he was lying. It had to be a trap, right? Or some sort of deception. Sorin had heard the Drow bred themselves to be pretty to make duplicity easier for them. Who spent so much gold on hiring a traveling companion?

"I have work to do," Sorin said, resting his hands on the tabletop. "I have bounties to collect. You say you can take care of yourself but what guarantee do I have that you can protect yourself while I'm on a job?"

Khouri cocked his head and blinked slowly like a cat. He leaned forward, off his chair to loom into Sorin's space. "Trust me," he whispered, Sorin's attention stolen by the way the Drow formed the words with his full lips. "I won't be what slows you down."

The moisture disappeared from Sorin's mouth. The rumors he'd heard of Drow, the ones he had studiously avoided thinking, roared between his ears unbidden. *They're so tight,* one bawling drunkard had bellowed during one of Sorin's tavern stays. *Soft skin, hot mouths, tight, tight, tight. If you can get past the thought of what you're fucking, you'll never regret the nights you keep one in your bed.* There were a lot of things said about Drow, but for the life of him, Sorin wasn't entirely sure what was true and what wasn't. The uncertainty of it all was a bit daunting. He hardly needed a distraction at his side, even one as attractive as the one before him.

"Are you amenable to that?" Khouri continued, shattering Sorin's reverie by batting his eyes in a way that Sorin distrusted immediately. "If not, I'll have to ask that you return my money."

He leaned back instantly. Was it worth it? He couldn't say he wasn't at least interested in this strange, pretty Drow. The weight against his thigh was too much to ignore, and he would be loath to lose it now when he had only just gotten it. "There will be rules," Sorin growled out, meeting the Drow's eyes carefully.

Business. This was just business as usual. Nothing more.

Khouri sat back in his seat with a self-satisfied smile. "But of course." He looked too happy. It just made Sorin's gut burn hotter.

"I expect them to be followed to the letter."

"Naturally," the Drow murmured. "Cross my heart and hope to die."

Sorin gritted his teeth. "Else, I'll take your money and leave you in the woods."

"I would expect nothing less," Khouri said with a smile. He clapped his hands in front of him and cocked his head. "With that settled, I think there's only one more thing left to do."

Sorin was getting a headache already. "And what would that be?" he asked, running a hand through his long hair, his jaw tight. He should have taken up the offer for a drink. How long had it been since he had last traveled with another? This job better be worth the pay.

Instead of answering him, Khouri just raised a hand and pointed somewhere over Sorin's shoulder with that damnable smile still on his face. "Well, it would appear that I've been found out," he said cheerfully. And when Sorin followed his hand, he saw that the card game had been abandoned, the men approaching their table with weapons in hand and foul looks on their faces.

"I think it best if you get to protecting me," Khouri said, making a little shooing motion with his fingers as he settled in with his mug of tea. "I did just pay you, after all."

As Sorin stood, wrapping his hand around the wrapped handle of his axe, he tried to swallow back the instinctive urge to lash out at his newest employer. This was definitely not worth the money.

Chapter One

When it came to bar fights, Khouri had a couple of rules of thumb. They were simple rules, really. Almost more like universal truths than actual guidelines. The first was to avoid them at any costs; the next to get out as quickly as possible. When both of those failed, he had only one rule left to deal with the aftermath: Don't fall asleep anywhere without a lock.

This rule had come about over the course of the past month, and if Khouri were asked why, he would have to answer that it was frankly just common sense. Bar fights led to grudges. Grudges led to ambushes. Perhaps it wasn't the same for conflicts between surface dwellers, but Khouri had walked these grassy lands far too long to trust that anyone up here might stay their hand should they find him defenceless and vulnerable in some field or communal area.

It was because of all of those reasons that when Sorin limped his way out of the bar, Khouri in tow, and decided to make camp in some clearing not even a stone's throw from the wrecked bar, Khouri had vehemently put down his foot and told him in the kindest possible way to think again.

"Oh, it'll be *fine*," Khouri muttered under his breath, sitting with his back against a tree, so he could keep an eye on as much of the makeshift camp as possible. "You worry too much. No one would walk the five minutes towards the woods to kill the Drow lurking in their midst."

Sorin let out a muffled snore, not awake but somehow still seeming to know that he was being mocked. The hunter had collapsed into his bedroll the moment they stopped moving, a bit bloodied around the knuckles but boasting not a single injury of his own. Khouri had no idea what to think of this man he had attached himself to, but at the very least, he worried him an idiot if he fell asleep so easily after downing half the bar's men in a fist fight started on Khouri's behalf.

Khouri sighed, closing his eyes to the darkness that seemed as bright as day. It had been hours since they had settled down to rest. Hours of nothing but hooting owls, rustling leaves, and the other performers in the night's orchestra. Exhaustion didn't cling so heavily to Khouri's bones as it did to Sorin's, but he could admit to the day taking its toll on him regardless. It was hard to brush off instinct and caution. This new world above the loam didn't trust him, and Khouri would be hard-pressed to trust it in return.

Sorin was shifting now, his breath coming a little faster. Probably on the verge of waking up, if Khouri had to hazard a guess. Sorin was definitely the first human to lower his guard so easily in front of him. Trusting a Drow to sleep at his side… What an odd man he was. Odd but waking. Khouri bundled himself tighter in his cloak, finally letting himself give in to the sleepiness tugging at his eyelids. It was an unspoken guard shift, but it was enough to help him relax enough to rest.

There was a resounding of pops and cracks as Sorin forced himself up, and then the shifting of fabric as he stood. Khouri slowed his breathing and let the quiet sounds soothe him, proof as they were of Sorin being awake.

He was on the verge of sleep when he felt Sorin's eyes on him. Khouri kept his breathing slow, trying not to let it bother him. He had just been watching Sorin too, so fair was fair he supposed. Grass crunched, and Sorin let out a tired sigh.

"Still asleep? Figures."

Well, that was a little rude, all things considered. A flush of light teased Khouri's eyelids as Sorin stirred the dying fire. Its warmth soothed Khouri. It would be alright to sleep now, right? Just for a few hours. Sorin made no move to shake him to his feet, so Khouri took it as a yes.

The soft breeze carding through his hair made it all too easy to give in. Khouri drifted off, chin tucked against his chest, letting Sorin do whatever it was he did when he woke up. With his eyes closed, it seemed like Sorin was pacing. Perhaps he was cleaning up the camp? The quiet hiss of a drawstring being opened was nearly buried in the shifting and cracking of the fire.

Khouri's ears twitched at the sound of clinking glass. That was an odd sound to be hearing now. Did Sorin have some in his bag? It was hard to imagine given the man's work that he might carry something like that around with him. Khouri did, and he could attest to it being one of the more challenging things to keep from being jostled, especially in fights. Sorin was muttering to himself, his voice tugging Khouri from his doze.

"Gotta be something here," the hunter was saying under his breath, punctuated by another round of clinking glass and furtive, shifting sounds. "Where are you from, brat? You have to have something on you."

Who was he talking to? The only one here was Khouri, and there was no way… Khouri opened his eyes, angry beyond words. He looked through the darkness, knowing instinctively what he would find in front of him. Sorin was on his knees, wrist deep in Khouri's satchel. Brow furrowed and mouth tight, the human looked intently into the depths of Khouri's bag, rooting around inside as if he had a right to invade a person's privacy any time he so chose.

13

What did he think he would find in there? Khouri narrowed his eyes and let his hand fall to his thigh, fingers brushing over the six daggers sheathed in their small pockets. He pulled one loose and palmed it, letting his cloak fall to the ground in a silent heap. Sorin was holding one of the small vials up to the wane light, taking in the clear liquid inside. He was going to get himself killed if he didn't stop rooting around in things not his.

In one swift motion, Khouri stood just behind Sorin. With one hand he snatched up the vial, and in the other, he held the small dagger to Sorin's throat. Sorin went stiff, his hands letting go of the bag to let it fall roughly to the ground.

"Good morning, Sorin," Khouri murmured, turning the blade to follow the movements of Sorin's head when he twisted slowly to meet Khouri's eye. "This isn't how I envisioned our first day starting."

Sorin managed a tense smile and, in the next moment, had Khouri's wrist seized in his iron grip. He yanked hard and threw Khouri off balance. Khouri rolled with the fall and took Sorin down with him. The dagger and vial fell harmlessly to the grass, narrowly avoiding being crushed in the scuffle.

"What do you think you're doing?" Sorin hissed, using his considerably size to his advantage. Khouri was fast, but it didn't mean much when off his feet. Sorin snatched up his other wrist, rolling himself to hold Khouri down with his body. He was warm, nearly burning against Khouri's skin. After nearly a month of being on his own, Khouri could barely handle the proximity.

"What do you think *you're* doing?" Khouri gasped, shelving that thought for never. He tugged at his wrists but, failing to free himself, met Sorin's eyes instead. His face felt so warm. He hoped the human couldn't tell. "I certainly didn't pay you for this."

Sorin gritted his teeth at that. "You attacked me," the human grunted as if that excuse was justification enough for pinning his employer.

"You were digging through my things," Khouri bit, narrowing his eyes into a pointed glare. "Is this how you treat all of your clients? Get off me before I hurt you."

Scoffing, Sorin did just that, letting go of his wrists first and then climbing off of Khouri. The moment he could, Khouri sat up and rubbed at his wrists, feeling bruises already beginning to bloom. "You couldn't hurt me," the mercenary muttered, leveling himself onto his feet to go kick out the meager fire, extinguishing the thought of breakfast with it. "Fucking brat."

What a pompous ass. "I heard that," Khouri said, grabbing his bag and checking inside, making sure everything was safe and accounted for. His clothes were a bit rumpled, his poison vials out of order, but thankfully, none of them had been cracked by Sorin's rough touch. Biting his lip, he pushed them all to the side, ignoring the disorganization for the moment. Was it still safe? Khouri dipped his fingers past the flat inner pocket, feeling for the hard shape hidden just out of sight.

"I didn't take anything," Sorin said, jolting Khouri from his thoughts. "So if you'd like to get your shit together, I think it's past time we get moving." Khouri looked up. Sorin glared back down at him, his bag and weapon already shouldered. All that was missing was his foot tapping to show that he thought Khouri was wasting his time.

"I don't appreciate being spoken down to," Khouri muttered, gathering up his bag and bedroll, wrapping himself in his cloak. The morning was cool, if it could even be called morning yet. Darkness still outweighed the light, but if Sorin thought himself able to see enough to progress, then who was Khouri to argue? It wasn't as if Khouri couldn't go a night without rest. The grass was still slick with dew, anyway. Laying down would be uncomfortable, even if they did linger. Shouldering his bag, Khouri wrapped his arms around himself and glared at the human.

"You paid for protection, not conversation," the hunter grunted, stomping out the remains of the fire.

"I paid for a partnership," Khouri interjected, walking in front of the hunter to glare at him properly. "Not for you to treat me like an idiot you can push around."

Sorin laughed. "I work alone," he said, shaking his head as he shouldered his large axe. "No amount of money can buy yourself a place as my partner. You're a tagalong, if anything. I don't plan on restructuring my life around you, so get used to being disappointed."

Maybe embroiling Sorin in a bar fight so soon after meeting hadn't been the best way to endear himself to the hunter. Khouri frowned and kicked at the dirt, letting the conversation die.

At least the rest of the world wasn't as inhospitable. Khouri could travel the surface three times over and still never quite quantify the amount of green the world held. Burgeoning light climbed up the far horizon, painting the sky with pinks, golds, and purples; the sun warmed his chilled skin in a comforting wave. Birds sang, insects chirped, and despite the clinging, lingering darkness, morning took root as it always did. Khouri smiled softly as he walked, counting out his footfalls in time to his breaths. Not even the hunter's sourness could spoil the

16

joy he felt in the wake of all before him. There really was nothing quite like this down below. The Duskriven stole its color where it could get it, but up here, beneath the sun, the surface overflowed with abundance.

Not many of his kind ever saw this kind of beauty. Khouri had to wonder how many of them cared or if they even thought about the loss. Probably not many.

The sun had risen high in the sky by the time Sorin saw fit to break the silence his rudeness had imposed.

"So," he began, startling Khouri from his thoughts with a gruff voice. "What is a Drow doing above ground anyway?"

Khouri wrinkled his nose and held tighter to the strap of his satchel. "You sound like you've been holding that in for a while now," he observed, noting how Sorin's jaw went tight. "Did your little rummage through my clothing not give you the answers you wanted?" The human didn't balk though, holding his head high and glaring back at Khouri without much heat. Defensive, really.

"I'd think anyone would be curious," the man said, hefting his axe higher onto his broad shoulder. The metal shined dully in the mid-morning sun, the worn engravings along the head Dwarven in design. "I can count the times I've seen a Drow on one hand and still have fingers left over. You're a rarity up here."

"Careful," Khouri sighed, "or you'll make me blush."

"Just answer the question." He slowed his quick pace a little, angling towards Khouri once they were abreast of one another. "You wanted to travel with me. The least you can do is be a little forthcoming about yourself."

Khouri raised a brow. "And how forthcoming have *you* been, Hunter Tolgrath? I hardly know much about you outside of your reputation. Why don't you give a little first, break the ice as they say."

"There isn't much to say," Sorin said in a way that told Khouri he was purposefully being obstinate. "I'm a hunter. I go around hunting bounties."

"Yeah, but where are you from?"

"Around," Sorin grunted.

Khouri frowned. "How old are you?" he tried asking, crossing his arms. "I can't tell if you're old or not. You humans age so weirdly."

"You can't tell?" Sorin laughed a little, giving him an odd sort of look. "I guess I can't tell your age either. I'm forty."

Only forty? Khouri cocked his head in disbelief. "That's not old at all. I'm way older than you if that's it," he murmured, his eyes narrowing as he thought on it. "Is that old to you?" How long did humans live, anyway? It would be a problem if he just wasted his money on a human who would keel over if a stiff breeze rolled through. It would probably be too late for a refund at that point. What a bother.

Sorin shifted his pack higher onto his shoulder, letting out a tired sigh. "It's old enough to feel. Are you going to answer my question now, or are you content to bother me about my age for awhile longer?"

"Why?" he chuckled, nudging Sorin's arm with his own. "Are you sensitive about it?"

"Don't get cocky, brat. I'll knock that grin off your face

18

in a heartbeat," the hunter warned, cold blue eyes flashing dangerously in the bright morning light.

Khouri couldn't help it. He laughed into his hand. "You are!" he exclaimed, dodging the wide swipe Sorin made for him easily. The man's reach was certainly impressive, but Khouri was small and fast. It took no effort to evade. "You're so sensitive. What a treat. It's good to know I didn't hire a gargoyle instead of a partner. What a waste of money that would have been."

"How many times do I have to tell you that we aren't partners?" Sorin said stonily, stomping off ahead of Khouri, making him jog a little to catch up. "You aren't working *with* me. The way I see it you're just a client I have to put up with until you get bored of this."

This again? "There's not much you can to if you don't plan on working with me," Khouri huffed, glaring at the man's broad back. "I'm not going to just sit patiently and wait for you if you feel like running off to chase a bounty."

"You will if you expect to keep traveling with me. There are rules I expect to be followed. Rules you agreed to abide by when I took your money." Sorin's eyes were heavy when they landed on Khouri. "I'm in charge. What I say goes. That means that if I tell you to sit and wait for me to finish a job, you will stay put. I'm not a babysitter. I'll leave you behind if you can't keep up, and I'll ditch you if you refuse to listen."

"I can see why you don't do these sorts of jobs more often," Khouri scoffed, sending a stray pinecone flying with an annoyed kick. It soared up ahead, skidding along the dirt and grass and disappearing in a patch of weeds. "You're actually a beast, aren't you? No concept of proper etiquette in you."

"I don't want to hear that from a Drow." Khouri startled a little when another pinecone went shooting past him, traveling much further than his own had. He turned and stared at the smug looking hunter. Sorin didn't grin, but it was a close thing. "And there are more rules. No sassing me is another. Don't test my patience. Don't try to get chummy with me. I'm not being paid to be your friend."

Khouri grimaced. "You don't have to worry about that," he simpered, batting his lashes just to make the human scowl. "I wouldn't dream of befriending a man like you. Even I, a dastardly Drow, have better taste than that."

Sorin's face was hilarious, frozen in some mixture of shock and anger as it was. Khouri laughed and kicked another pinecone. A hand snatched him by the collar and yanked him back before the kick could connect. "What did I say about sassing?" Sorin asked tersely, holding Khouri by the scruff like a disobedient cat. "I'll charge you a fee for every infraction. Don't think I won't."

Khouri shrugged his hand off his collar, fixing his cloak around his shoulders with a frown. The cool air teased his bare shoulders beneath it, and he hurriedly covered back up, the morning air too crisp for that just yet. "As if I couldn't afford it," he huffed, rolling his eyes. "How much would I have to pay to change your temperament entirely? Another hundred? Two?" He shot Sorin an unimpressed look. "You don't intimidate me. If you think that's how you're going to deal with me, you're very mistaken."

"Rich brats like you are exactly why I have rules in the first place." Sorin upped the pace even more, passing Khouri with nary a backwards glance. "You think you can do what you want, that nothing applies to you so long as you've enough money to throw at the problem until is disappears."

"I'm not rich," Khouri shot, jogging after him, refusing to be left behind.

"Then, how did you get the money to pay me?" Sorin slowed up a little but not much. His curiosity seemed to do it or his disbelief, at least. "Did you steal it?"

Khouri held his bag closer to his side. "I've things to sell," he said stiffly, dearly wishing Sorin would drop it.

A pale brow raised. "So you did steal it." He chuckled. "No wonder it was real gold."

"Excuse you," Khouri shot, stopping in his tracks. "My lover likes to spoil me, and a lot of the gifts he gives are worth a lot of money. Some pawnshops don't care where they get their wares, even if that means dealing with a Drow. So, stop making assumptions. You don't know anything about me."

Sorin gave him a look, one that Khouri wasn't quite sure he liked. "Sounds like quite a lover."

"He is. He's a far more impressive man than you are." Khouri looked at the dirt and rocks along the road. "He's skinned men alive for daring to look at me let alone speak to me the way you're doing now."

Sorin gave a mirthless laugh, not intimidated in the least. "Why did you leave if you had all of that down below?" he asked. "Seems to me I'd stay down where my lover has all the power instead of trusting all my safety to some rude human hunter."

This really was the last thing Khouri wanted to be discussing today. "Because for all the gifts he's given me, he still doesn't seem to understand what I really want," Khouri said sharply. "Can we change the subject? I don't want to talk about him right now." Not to some human who looked at him so judgmentally. "And what of you? Do you just go around killing people for money, then? Don't judge me for how I get my coin when you took it eagerly enough."

"I don't kill them unless it's more profitable," Sorin said, failing to rise to his bait. "And it's almost never more profitable. I'm no saint. I don't care where you get your gold so long as its real."

Khouri took in Sorin's rugged appearance. The way he moved was slow but purposeful, no waste or excess to his stride to suggest he ever did things that went against his habits. It showed conviction. Intent. Sorin caught him staring and returned it evenly, his jaw going a little tight at whatever it was he saw.

"If you've got something to say, then say it," Khouri said evenly, wondering what he could be fixated on now. His gaze wasn't on Khouri's body. It stayed upwards, not quite meeting Khouri's eyes but close. "Something wrong with my ears?"

"What are your earrings made of?" Sorin asked flatly, walking a step closer to Khouri to get a better view.

Khouri frowned, his hand coming up to cover the one closest to Sorin. "Why?" he shot back, curling his fingers around it carefully. "What business is it of yours?"

Sorin's look was patently unimpressed. "I'm curious. Humor me."

"Turquoise," Khouri said in a clipped tone, wondering if he should've taken them off. No one had bothered to look too closely at them, usually too focused on them rest of him to bother. "They were a gift."

"From that lover you ran from?" Sorin asked, his voice breezy in a way that Khouri didn't like one bit.

Before Khouri could reply, the sound of muffled voices filtered past them on the wind. Given the distance they had traveled from the last village, Khouri hadn't expected to see others on the road, but a look forwards showed him the outlines of just that up ahead. He wrapped himself all the tighter in his cloak and tugged the hood over his face when Sorin gave him a pointed look. Annoying but probably a good idea to avoid attracting attention.

Khouri followed Sorin towards the side of the road, giving plenty of room to let the group pass. "I don't see how it's any of your business at all," Khouri grumbled, crossing his arms to look at Sorin, keeping his face away from the people nearly upon them. "I'm not selling them."

"I wasn't going to say you should," Sorin said, arching a brow in annoyance. He kept glancing at the oncoming travelers, stepping forward to meet the travelers first as he put a hand in front of Khouri to push him backwards. There looked to be five of them, adventurers if their weapons were anything to go off of.

Khouri glared down at Sorin's hand and pointedly shoved past it, walking at his side nearest to the men. He lowered his voice, but he didn't bother softening his frustration. "Then, what were you going to say?" he asked, ignoring the men even as their voices began to grow closer, their raucous laughter rending the air.

"I don't know, brat. Maybe if you stopped assuming the

worst, I'd be able to tell you." Sorin glanced at the oncoming men but sighed, moving back to Khouri. "They're too fancy to be flaunted like that," he said, his words muted. "Don't wear them up here. Or at least take them off when you take off your cloak."

Khouri could feel the brush of someone's cloak against his leg, but he ignored it. "They're not even that rare," he argued, gesturing with a hand towards his covered ears. "Don't people walk around in far fancier things up here? It can't possibly be that out of place t–"

A hand fixed itself over Khouri's mouth before he could finish his tirade. He let out a smothered cry as he was torn from his feet and into the arms of one of the passing men. The others converged like vultures on a corpse to brandish their weapons at Sorin.

Despite Sorin's gruff, cantankerous personality, Khouri had to give the man credit for being all business when it came down to it. The axe was off his shoulder and swinging before Khouri had gathered his wits, hewing through one of the bandits as if they were made of paper. The man crumpled in a spray of gore, his companions flinching in the face of Sorin's brutality.

"What the hell do you want?" Sorin shot, brandishing his axe to keep them at bay. "You picked the wrong group to rob if you want an easy mark."

A chorus of laughter rose up around them. Khouri struggled, twisting and fighting against the one holding him. "That's cute," the man holding him chuckled, punctuating his jeer with a knife against Khouri's throat. "Exceedingly cute, but I think we're going to be the ones getting what we want today. Try to behave, old man. I'd hate to make you watch your little friend here bleed out."

"We'll take your money now," another said, his long, greasy hair bound into a ponytail at the back of his neck. Khouri couldn't see his face from this position, but he had a startling notion that the man was as ugly as his personality suggested. "All of it. Toss it down in the dirt with that axe."

"That goes for you too," the one holding Khouri crooned, his tone painting him as the leader. "Don't do anything stupid now. If you try, I'll slit your throat before you have time to regret it."

Cutthroats and bandits. The surface really did hold so many attractions. Khouri gritted his teeth and tried to keep his face pointed down. "I don't have any money," he murmured, tucking his hands beneath his cloak as slowly as he could.

The leader clicked his tongue, tapping the blade teasingly against Khouri's skin. "Somehow, I doubt that," he said. He wrapped his arm around Khouri and shoved it beneath his cloak, patting along his body as if in search of a money pouch. Khouri went stock still and flushed, meeting eyes with Sorin. Panic was becoming hard to avoid.

Khouri's cloak must have jostled somewhere along the way, because a moment later, one of the men was staring at him, his eyes going wide with something more malign than just glee. "Is that... Holy shit. I think it's a Drow, boss!" the ginger man crowed, his ruddy cheeks flushed with shock. "This geezer is runnin' around with a fuckin' Drow!"

The leader let out a grunt of surprise. His hand stopped its groping; he peered around, trying to see beneath Khouri's downturned hood. "You're shitting me," he breathed. "What the fuck is one of those doing up here?" When he failed to

25

see under the cloak, he resorted to just tearing the hood from Khouri's head. Khouri closed his eyes to the bright light, but the man was already braying out a laugh, his knife tracing Khouri's cheek with glee. "So it is!" he declared. Khouri opened his eyes when the hand that had been on his hood dropped to his ass. "And such a pretty one, too. We don't see many of you around here, do we, boys?"

There was a general murmur of assent nearly overtaken completely by Sorin's furious growl. "Get away from him," Sorin ordered, his voice so low that it rumbled like thunder.

All of the blades turned towards Sorin but the one aimed at Khouri's throat. "Don't get cocky," the ginger snapped, his sword pointed at Sorin's spine. "You're out of your league, old man. Don't be an idiot."

"It's fine, Sorin," Khouri told him, teeth clenched as the hand moved a little higher, skimming along his bare lower back. "Stand down."

For a moment, Khouri didn't think Sorin would listen. He glared daggers at the leader holding Khouri, his hands tight around the shaft of his axe. Khouri held his breath and shook his head, imploring him not to get himself killed. Sorin closed his eyes tight and let his axe drop to the ground, his shoulders hitched tightly from his barely contained anger.

The bandit's hot, rotten breath coated the back of Khouri's neck as he laughed. "There's a good man. Smart of you to stop. Are you paying him, beautiful? Bet you aren't paying him enough to risk his life for you." The blade dug into Khouri's throat as the man began to drag Khouri backwards and away from Sorin. His companions stayed on Sorin, keeping him from following.

"What do you want?!" Khouri hissed, struggling despite the pain. Blood trickled down his throat but he didn't care. "I've done nothing to you people!"

"Ah, but we happened to overhear you two chatting," the bandit explained. When he buried his nose in Khouri's hair and inhaled loudly, Khouri shuddered. "You've got some pretty earrings there. Why don't you be a lamb and hand them over along with any other valuables you may have?"

"Just do it, Khouri," Sorin called out, his tone clipped and his fury muted. "We're outnumbered."

"You heard him, beautiful," the bandit laughed, tapping the flat of the blade against his clavicle like a warning. "Listen to the old man, and don't make us do something nasty."

"My... My lover gave me those," Khouri said shortly, staring at the ground. "There's no way I'm giving them to scum like you."

The man's fingers were hot as they toyed with an earring, tugging on it gently in a way that made Khouri's ear twitch. "Is that so? A lover who buys you turqouise earrings. Gold mounted too by the look of it." He glanced over at Sorin with a grin. "Are you the lucky man? You don't look the type to be able to afford this sort of thing. Or, you know," he said, his free hand wrapping around Khouri's hip in a grip that was far too friendly, "someone like this."

Sorin let out an angry growl, his fists tightening at his sides. "No," he bit, looking ready to break someone in half. "I'm not the one he's talking about."

The leader let out a knowing laugh, squeezing Khouri's hip. "That's certainly interesting, but who am I to judge. Your

27

lover must be awfully worried about you, beautiful. Probably worried sick if you're expecting someone like this to keep you safe." The bandits all looked at each other with glee, an unspoken agreement passing from the leader to the others. "A rich lover would pay a pretty penny to have you back too, wouldn't he? Boys, I think we've found something a right side more valuable than a few shiny baubles."

Khouri stopped breathing. This was a complete nightmare. "I'll bite my fucking tongue off before I let you take me," he swore. Sorin was staring, his lips curled into a snarl. "You're going to die if you don't let me go right the fuck now."

"You think so?" the man mused, holding tighter to Khouri as he addressed his men. "You guys hear that? This little Drow thinks he can kill us." They all laughed. Khouri's mind went blank when a warm, disgusting tongue licked a stripe up his cheek. "Just you try it, beautiful. Think your lover will mind if we rough you up a little? Pretty as you are, he probably won't care much so long as you still end up back in his bed."

They didn't know Navidae at all if they thought he would be okay with them breathing Khouri's air, let alone touching him. "Your fucking funerals," Khouri whispered, narrowing his eyes at Sorin. They would only have one shot at this, so he hoped Sorin was ready to fight. Khouri wrenched his head away and stomped down on the bandit's instep. He ripped himself from the man's arms before he had time to react.

"What the fuck–"

The bandit went down when Khouri aimed his next kick for his groin. The others near Sorin made a move towards Khouri, weapons drawn, but Khouri was in no mood to play. His daggers were in his hands in an instant, snatched up from their customary place on his thighs.

"You little bitch!" one shouted. "How dare you–"

Khouri didn't bother to wait to hear what he was daring to do. He flung out a dagger and watched it fly, embedding itself in the man's throat before he made it more than a step away from Sorin. Unlike the leader, Khouri didn't waste his time with naked blades. The poison worked faster than the penetration. A thick white foam coursed out of the man's mouth as he dropped like a stone. His companions balked at the sight of his twitching form, but their hesitation just made them easier targets.

"Sorin, feel free to help!" Khouri spun and threw another dagger, this time hitting the ginger bandit in the thigh. He swore under his breath and backed up, the poison needing longer this time to work. A sword pointed at him, and Khouri nearly tripped in his struggle to evade. He closed his eyes and heard a wet, bone-chilling sound. When he opened them, he saw the ginger sans his head, Sorin panting over the corpse with his cheeks flecked with blood.

"You little *bitch*," the leader hissed behind Khouri, rallying from the blow he had already been dealt. He rose up from his pained slump, face contorted with rage. "You think you can just do what you want, a Drow bitch like you? You've got another thing coming."

Poison was too kind of a way for this man to go. That much was clear.

"Take care of the rest of them, Sorin," Khouri said, not bothering to take his eyes off the man before him. "I've got this."

"Oh, do you?" the leader jeered, his pockmarked cheeks flushing. "Let me see it then. Let me see what you can do."

Khouri tossed the dagger aside. He had plenty more where it came from, and he wouldn't need it anyway. Not yet at least. They stared at each other for the span of a breath, and then Khouri was darting towards him, ducking under the man's lunging arms to cut away at the distance between them. Brawling was as common as breathing on the dark lit streets of the Duskriven. This was nothing new. Evade, distract, strike– Khouri delivered a sharp blow to the man's ribs and then struck him beneath the chin, sending him to the ground in a gasping, stunned heap.

"How's that?" Khouri snarled, kicking the man onto his back. He straddled the man's chest to keep him down. "You like that?" He balled up his hand into a fist, hitting the bandit leader in the nose, feeling the bone break against his knuckles. "You disgusting excuse for a person." He drew back and hit him again and again and again, losing track in his need to hurt, in his desire to make the man bleed. He thought he could drag Khouri back to the Duskriven? He had another thing coming entirely.

"Khouri," a low voice called out from across the road, Sorin wiping the blood from his axe on the grass. "Khouri, you need to stop. He's unconscious."

Khouri pretended not to hear, pulling out another dagger and readying it to slit the man's throat.

"Goddammit, Khouri! I said get off him!" Khouri bared his teeth and stabbed downwards, the blade just barely kissing the leader's skin before Khouri's hands were torn away. Sorin grabbed him in a grip as firm as iron bars, refusing to let him kill the disgusting creature between his thighs.

"Get off me, Sorin," Khouri hissed, trying and failing to shake off the hunter's hands. "I'm going to kill him."

"Normally, I wouldn't give a shit what you did with scum like this, but if you want to waste a thousand gold, do it on your own time," Sorin shot, his hands tightening around Khouri's wrists and making no move to loosen. He let out a rough breath and lifted Khouri bodily away from the prone man.

Khouri protested the moment his feet left the ground. "Let me go!" he ordered, shoving at Sorin until he deigned to set him down a few feet away. He ripped himself free of the hunter's hands and tried to fix his clothing, his breath coming too fast to really calm down. "Don't do that. And don't tell me what to do. If I want to kill him, I will!"

Sorin loomed over him, crossing his arms in a way that was meant to intimidate. "You won't," he argued. "That man has a bounty on his head, Khouri. One I intend to claim."

"Then we can turn in his corpse," Khouri hissed, refusing to be cowed by a man who did next to nothing that whole fight.

"And get half the reward? Like hell I'd let you lose me that much gold." He dug into his bag for a moment and drew out a crumpled piece of parchment, shoving it against Khouri's chest before turning back towards the prone man. "I don't care if he hurt your pride or insulted you or whatever it is you're feeling. This is business, not vengeance. Learn the fucking difference."

Khouri glared at the hunter but unfolded the parchment, seeing it as the bounty Sorin was talking about. It had a vaguely sketched likeness of the man lying in the dirt along with a bulleted list of his various crimes. Thief, highwayman, drunkard, murderer. The list went on and on punctuated with a large set of numbers that boasted the reward for his capture. It was a lot of gold. Almost as much as Khouri had blown on hiring Sorin.

Looking up, he saw Sorin already binding the man with rope from his bag, looping some sort of manacles around the man's limp wrists. "And you think that it's better to just give this man to the authorities than end him for what he just did to us?" he demanded, stomping over to give the unconscious thief a good kick to the ribs.

"If I held a grudge for every time I had someone try to cut my purse or rob me on the road," Sorin said, looking up with a put upon air about him, "then I would never turn in a single bounty. He'll get what's coming to him when I sell him to the sentries. What happens to him after that doesn't concern me."

Khouri bit his lip, the logic of it all warring it out with everything he his mind was telling him to do. Perhaps it was easy for Sorin to separate himself from the situation, but the feeling of that man's tongue against Khouri's cheek was burned into his flesh. Blood might not wash it clean, but he bet it would help.

"That's not how Drow do things," Khouri said quietly, taking a step back as Sorin hefted the bandit onto his shoulder, standing up with a muted grunt. "If we were in the Duskriven, we would flay him alive for trying to do what he just did."

"Then I'm glad we're up here," Sorin huffed, nodding towards his axe still on the ground. "I'd hate to have to deal with the clean up that would entail. Taking things personally won't get you far, Khouri. You don't have to be better than them, but you have to put the reward first. Grab my axe, would you? Unless you'd rather carry this guy's fat ass all the way to the nearest guard post."

"You're really doing this," Khouri said flatly, his eyes widening when he grabbed the axe and hefted. His muscles strained as he struggled to lift it from the ground, dragging it up and nearly tipping himself over when he tried to settle it on his shoulder the way Sorin carried it. How did Sorin make it look so easy? This thing had to weigh more than Khouri did.

Sorin laughed a little, smiling as he watched Khouri sweat. "I really am," he said, nodding his head in a seemingly random direction. "Now, come on. We need to get away from these bodies and get you someplace off the road."

Khouri took a step and then another. He tried to make a rhythm with his movements to keep him from unbalancing under the foreign weight. "Aren't we going to the sentries?" he asked. The unconscious bandit was hanging like a limp doll, jaw slack and temple bloodied. What an ugly sight.

Leading through some tall grass, Sorin slowed down a bit so Khouri could catch up. "No," he said slowly, enunciating as if speaking to a child. "*I* am going to the sentries. *You* are going to sit your ass down and wait for me to get back."

The axe thumped to the ground, Khouri giving up on trying to lug it. "Excuse me?" he asked. "You're not leaving me behind. I told you that already."

"And I told *you* that there are rules to this arrangement," Sorin said, turning around to glare at him. He wrinkled his nose irritably when he caught sight of how Khouri had dropped his weapon. "You think I can just walk up to some armed sentries with you in tow and expect them to hand over gold to me?"

Khouri felt his lips curl into a pronounced frown. "I'm not a burden for you to abandon at will," he said, glaring hotly at the hunter. "I held my own against them better than you did. I can keep up with your precious work."

33

"This isn't about that," Sorin said, and Khouri's anger stuttered for a moment at the almost begrudgingly proud look Sorin wore. "You held your own. I was surprised by it, sure, but you did. That's why I'm not throwing a fit about leaving you alone here. But I'm serious. I can't walk up to some sentries with a Drow. They'd kill you on sight and then move on to me for not doing it myself the moment I saw you."

The grass was thick beneath his feet. Thick and green and speckled with wildflowers. Khouri stared down at it as his ears burned. Praise was the last thing he expected to hear up here, let alone from someone like Sorin. He looked up when Sorin cleared his throat impatiently. Khouri swallowed. He didn't want to stay behind. He didn't, but it wasn't a bad call to make.

"Fine," Khouri sighed, plopping himself down onto a patch of soft grass. "Don't think this is going to be a common thing, though. I'm not going to let you leave me behind all the time."

"Whatever, brat." Sorin bounced the man higher up onto his shoulder and reached down for the fallen axe, navigating it onto his back. "Don't do anything stupid while I'm gone," he said in lieu of a goodbye, turning on his heel and making off towards the road.

He was acting like he knew well enough where he was going. Hopefully, that meant it wouldn't be a long wait. Khouri watched him leave, letting out a breath once he disappeared over a hill.

Waiting had never been Khouri's forte. He wasn't patient and wasn't accustomed to being kept waiting. For a moment, he pondered following Sorin anyway, but in the end, he decided against it. As rude as Sorin had been in saying it, the fact that the sentries would kill him on sight wasn't an exaggeration. Being on the surface had taught Khouri a few things, and near the top of that list was not to trust people to be kind when they had no reason to be, especially to someone like him.

It was just so boring to sit here. Khouri kicked at the dirt and let out a sigh, throwing himself down onto his back to stare at the clouds as they rolled by. That at least was something novel, the clouds. He had never really seen them before this trip to the surface, not that he could remember clearly. They looked unbelievably soft like spun spidersilk wound in airy little tufts. Khouri reached up a hand as if he could touch them, smiling to himself. If he managed to hold one, he doubted it would feel like spidersilk. That was something for below. The sky deserved better.

Hours passed slowly, Khouri giving in to the urge to doze. Lights danced behind his eyes, the soft breeze rolling over his bare skin like a cool, considerate touch. He shivered a little and bit his lip, rolling onto his shoulder as if he could shake off the thought. His hips ached a little from Sorin's rough grip, his shoulder from the bandit's yanking. It seemed like every touch he got up here was mean. Every touch but the wind's. What was Navidae doing right now, he wondered. It didn't take much imagination to think about what he would *want* to do if Khouri were still in his arms.

It took awhile, but Sorin arrived without much fanfare eventually. He made his presence known loudly enough to jostle Khouri from his partial rest, at any rate. Sorin stomped his way into the makeshift camp, axe balanced on his empty shoulder; a weariness about him that looked a bit more pronounced than what a simple hike should have prompted.

Khouri sat up straight and looked at him. "Did it go alright?" he asked. "Did he stay out the whole time?"

"Unfortunately," Sorin said, rolling his eyes. "I would've made him walk himself there if he had. Lazy bastard." He grumbled under his breath like the grumpy man he was and approached Khouri. As he walked, he reached into his pocket and pulled something out that was nearly hidden in his large hand.

"Here," Sorin grunted, dropping a small pouch into Khouri's lap. It jingled when it landed, heavier than he expected it to be.

"What is this?" he asked, lifting it up. He tugged at the drawstrings while Sorin took in the grass around them. The hunter tossed down his bag and then himself with a groan of exhaustion. The pouch opened up, and the sunlight reflected off the gold in a blinding display. Khouri's jaw fell open.

"Your cut," Sorin called out from his slumped spot, dragging his bag under his head as a pillow. "For the bounty."

"My cut? I get some?" he breathed. "But I thought this was your job, not mine."

Sorin grunted and rolled onto his shoulder, turning his back to Khouri. "Yeah, well, you took down those men. It'd leave a bad taste in my mouth if I took all the reward for a job I didn't fuckin' do." He sounded rueful as if he hadn't expected Khouri to be capable in a fight. "Now, shut up. Don't say anything about it. I'm going to take a nap. Keep watch, would you?"

"Yeah," Khouri laughed, emptying the pouch out into his hand. As the money settled in his cupped palms, he had to smile. "No problem."

Perhaps this arrangement could work after all.

Chapter Two

It was all rather exciting, Khouri thought, to be involved with hunting bounties.

Prior to coming above, the most Khouri had ever done resembling an occupation had been stealing or perhaps assassinations, though he had only ever tried the one. It certainly wasn't something he ever considered a job, but it had been his way of making a living down on the inhospitable streets of the Duskriven's inner city. Down there, it had been something fairly lucrative. Nobles were always looking for underlings to do their bidding, and with that level of trust came plenty of opportunities to steal. But up here where everything worked so differently, Khouri found it a little harder to make money through his usual means.

When it really came down to it, Khouri was a Drow without skills traveling in a part of the world that ran on money, connections, and the exchanging of goods and services. The bits and baubles he had taken with him wouldn't last him forever, and because of that, it made perfect sense to seek training in the one occupation he had within arm's reach.

"No," Sorin cut in, shaking his head emphatically. "Absolutely not."

Khouri had just anticipated Sorin being a bit more forthcoming when asked. Given his limited experience with the man, Khouri might have been a bit foolish in assuming as much.

"What do you mean absolutely not?" Khouri walked faster to get ahead of Sorin, cutting him off before he could end the conversation before it had even really begun. "I practically handed you that bounty on a plate the other day. I think you owe me this for getting us through that situation with our wallets full."

"Keep walking backwards like that, and you'll run yourself into a tree," Sorin said dryly, side stepping Khouri to carry on as if nothing had been said to begin with.

Glowering, Khouri turned back forward, walking abreast of the hunter instead. The forest around them was pretty dense, and Khouri had to think that running into a tree probably would hurt his chances of convincing Sorin. "Come on, Sorin," he tried. "You said it was good work. Let me help."

Sorin met his eyes with a look that was anything but impressed. "You don't know the first thing about my line of work. How are you supposed to help me if all I can count on you for is acting like bait?"

Khouri frowned. "I can do more than that—"

"Oh, of course you can," Sorin interrupted. "I forgot you're also a bloodthirsty little thing. Did you think I had forgotten how you tore into that mark? I suppose that means I can count on you to slaughter my targets, too. Yeah, thanks, I think I'll pass."

"I can hold back," Khouri said pointedly. That had been a fluke yesterday. How else was he supposed to react to threats of being dragged back down to the Duskriven? "I can do anything you can do."

"Really?" Sorin said, his tone flat and decidedly disbelieving. "Can you track? Can you hunt? Do you know how to take down a person without causing them irreparable damage? You may not know this, Khouri, but not all bounties are for criminals. Sometimes you only get paid if you treat them gently."

Khouri slowed a little, biting his lip. "I can... I can be gentle," he said, hating how Sorin grinned. "What? You think something funny?"

"Yes," Sorin answered, "the fact that you completely ignored my first two questions. If you can't track or hunt, then you're of no use to me."

Khouri grabbed Sorin by the arm, forcing him to slow down and look at him. "Then teach me," he said evenly, staring Sorin down. "Give me a test. Tell me what to do, and we can see if I've got what it takes."

There was a quirk to Sorin's frown that betrayed his annoyance. "You really are desperate to learn, aren't you?" he muttered, yanking Khouri's hand off him. He looked around at the forest for a moment before sighing. "I can tell you won't drop this if I don't humor you. Persistence isn't always a charming quality, brat."

Khouri grinned, bouncing on the balls of his feet with nervous excitement. What would the test be? Would Sorin hide and make Khouri hunt him? Would he make Khouri track down a bear? A wolf? What sorts of surface creatures were there up here? The mystery was intoxicating, especially when Khouri knew he was going to get his way.

Sorin let out a put upon sigh and began to head off into the woods, abandoning the rough path they had been walking for about two hours now to take to the brush instead. Khouri rushed to follow. "Where are we going?" Khouri asked when Sorin didn't say anything more. "I thought you were going to

39

test me."

"I am," Sorin grunted, stomping through the undergrowth as if it were nothing. Khouri kept to Sorin's footsteps, letting him clear the way ahead. "We just can't do it here."

Khouri didn't bother asking where. It didn't look like Sorin would answer anyway. Instead, he focused on keeping up. The ground was strewn with all kinds of branches and detritus, enough that it took every ounce of focus he had to navigate it without falling. The earth sloped downwards in a gradual decline, taking them down a hill and towards what looked to be a clearing nestled in the center of a thick patch of trees. Sorin aimed for the clearing with clear intent.

It was almost too idyllic to fight here or whatever it was Sorin planned on having him do. The grass was as soft as fur, the scent of wildflowers a lilting, teasing note on the faint breeze carding through Khouri's hair. He forgot about Sorin for a moment entirely as he was struck by the colors. A small winged bug fluttered past his cheek with wings speckled and painted like a stained-glass window. A butterfly, perhaps. He had only ever read about them in books, and those hardly did the beauty justice.

"Quit daydreaming, brat," Sorin said, his voice cutting through the reverie like a blade through paper. "First test: Bring me a rabbit."

Khouri blinked, thinking he had misheard the man. "A rabbit," Khouri repeated slowly, narrowing his eyes. "And what happened to hunting people? What possible crime could the rabbit have committed?"

"Don't think of it as a rabbit," Sorin pressed, tossing down his big backpack and axe in the center of the clearing.

Were they making camp here? They must be since Sorin was already going to the tree line for firewood. "Think of it as a mark. A mark who will bolt the moment you show any sign of being on its tail. A mark that will disappear forever if you fuck up your one shot at snaring it."

Khouri let out a sigh. "You just want me to get us dinner, don't you?" he murmured, rolling his eyes. "I've never hunted things before, so you'll have to tell me how to go about it."

"What do you mean you've never hunted things before? How have you been feeding yourself up to this point?" His tone was a little harsh, but Khouri was learning that it was probably just the man's natural sound. "You can't have just walked up to a store and bartered for your bread."

Khouri felt his cheeks flush with indignation. "You found me in a tavern, Sorin. Sometimes, people are halfway decent towards me." He kicked at the dirt with arms crossed. Or sometimes he just got lucky when hiding his face as he ordered. "And I know what sorts of things are edible out here. There are plenty of berries and mushrooms and things like that to eat."

Sorin stared at him like he was an idiot. "You can't just live off bird food," he said derisively as if the thought of eating nothing but vegetation were horrific.

"You're just picky," Khouri sniffed. He watched Sorin stand with his armful of wood, the man scanning the ground for something Khouri couldn't see. "Come on. Are you going to teach me or not?"

"First lesson," Sorin said after a moment of silence. "Everything leaves its mark." He cocked his head down at the ground. Khouri moved over to where he was, seeing nothing

41

but grass and bits of leaves. "Tell me what you see."

"Not much of anything." Khouri knelt down to get a closer look, hoping this wasn't some kind of joke. The grass wasn't as soft here as it was in the center of the clearing. It was a bit curly, portions crushed while others stood up to catch the light of the sun. Khouri cocked his head and furrowed his brow, knowing this was a test of some sort. "Was… did something pass through here?" he guessed, touching the broken pieces of grass.

Sorin nodded, stepping out of the woods and back into the clearing. "Follow it. Rabbits are like men. They leave tracks, and they have their habits that can be exploited."

"Like what?" Khouri didn't know many men, and he knew even fewer rabbits. He carefully stepped over the grass and tried to follow the line of broken, bent blades. It was hard not to feel like an idiot when he barely knew what he was looking for.

"Scat, footprints, trash," Sorin listed off, watching him progress. "Leftover meals, warm firepits, the remains of camps."

"Doesn't sound like a rabbit," Khouri muttered, getting even closer to the ground. He moved another few feet forward and nearly stumbled when he saw the pellet-like scat next to the barely perceptible trail. His heart beat a little faster. Was he getting closer?

Without a word, Khouri began to move faster. He wove through the brush with his eyes locked on the trail, taking the course the rabbit had, no matter how convoluted it became. Within a few minutes, he had looped around the clearing and towards what looked to be another one. Was Sorin following him? Khouri could just barely see their clearing through the trees.

"I'm right here."

Khouri jumped, his heart pounding somewhere in his throat. Whipping around, Khouri glared at the hunter leaning against a tree. "What the fuck, Sorin," he hissed, clutching his chest.

Sorin has the audacity to look smug. "I'm monitoring your test," he said breezily. "You should've expected me to stick close."

"You're such an ass." Khouri let out a breath and glared for a minute before looking back down at the trail. It led right into the next clearing, some hundred feet away. "I think it's in there," he said quietly, eyeing the fresh scat by his boot. "What do I do now?"

"You sneak up on it. It's not that hard."

Khouri had a sneaking suspicion that Sorin wasn't going to be much help with the rest of this. "Well, be quiet then," he muttered inching closer to the clearing. "You'll scare it away."

Sorin snorted. "Then you'd have to compensate. The real world won't be quiet for you when you ask, so don't expect it to now." He trailed Khouri silently despite his words, his footfalls purposefully masked in the tufts of soft grass that managed to burst through the thicker undergrowth. Khouri noticed it and began to copy him, keeping low to the ground as he neared the edge of the tree cover.

"It's gotta be eating somewhere close, right?" Khouri breathed, looking up at Sorin who was looming just over his

43

shoulder.

"Don't charge in recklessly. You have to be ready to fight for your life at any moment. Your prey will do whatever it can to keep itself from being captured." Sorin tapped his foot impatiently. "You can't let your guard down for an instant."

"I've had my fair share of fights." Khouri crossed his arms and focused all of his attention to the sounds around him, listening for the telltale sounds of rustling grass. It would be a lot easier if Sorin would shut up for five minutes. If he closed his eyes, he could just make out a crunching down in the undergrowth.

"And I'm sure those fights were as elegant as that bar fight you dragged me into," Sorin muttered behind his back. "I'm not talking about some brawl, Khouri. I'm talking about a fight between you and a wild animal."

Khouri looked over his shoulder, raising a brow. "And here I thought we were hunting rabbit-people," he murmured.

"Take this seriously. A man is just a man until he's cornered." Sorin met his gaze head on, a shadow passing over his face. "You've fought plenty of people? You've never fought one backed into a corner. You've never fought one who preferred death than capture at your hands."

A shiver ran down Khouri's spine despite the warm day. He looked back forward, swallowing. "You must have a lot of good stories to tell," he said, eyeing the tree beside him. He needed to think like a hunter, not a brawler. Direct approaches would probably get him killed. Or he supposed in this case, it would leave him with an empty stomach and a lecture.

"It's impossible not to when you've done this as long as

44

I… have…" Sorin trailed off as he watched Khouri consider the tree. "What the hell do you think you're doing? You can't climb that. The branches are too high."

They were, but creative thinking could overcome anything. Khouri pulled out a dagger and twirled it in his hand, stabbing it into the base of the tree about two feet off the ground. With a smile tossed over his shoulder, Khouri stepped on the flat of the blade, lifting himself up with a jump to grab the branch that had been just out of reach a moment before.

"Oh, do carry on," Khouri laughed, heaving himself up with a muted grunt. "Please, by all means, keep telling me what I can't do."

Sorin glowered up at him as Khouri found his footing on the thick tree branch. "Shutting up is apparently out of your purview of skills," he snapped, stomping over to the tree to yank the dagger out of the wood. He took in the make, testing the weight of it in his hand. "Is this Drow-made?"

"Yes, and it's also coated with enough poison to take down a mountain troll," Khouri called down to him, already making his way down the tree branch and towards the meadow that lay just at the end of the bough. "So don't cut yourself with it. I'd hate to have to skin this mark myself."

Sorin promptly stopped testing the tip of the blade. He held it at a distance from himself, looking at it warily. "Poison is for cowards," he said judgingly.

Khouri rolled his eyes. "It's for people who have better things to do than trade blows with an opponent. Some of us would rather not swing around a massive axe until we accidentally lop off an enemy's head." His voice lowered the further he moved, becoming increasingly aware of the stillness of the forest around him. He had a feeling the rabbits were ahead. Adrenaline sang between his ears, urging him to move, but Khouri held tightly to his control, slowing his breath instead.

"If that's how you feel about fighting, then why are you so determined to learn this?" Sorin asked, resting his hands on his hips as he watched Khouri progress through the trees. "Spoiled little rich boy like you, you don't need to work for anything."

Khouri huffed out a breath and looked down to glare at the hunter. "How many times do I have to tell you that I'm not rich?" Having a rich lover did not make one rich. Navidae would probably say otherwise as indulgent as he was, but Khouri didn't quite see it the same way. "Everyone should know some skill, right? No time like the present to make myself more marketable."

There. Through the break in the leaves, Khouri could just make out a soft patch of brown meandering through the green grass below. His cheeks flushed and his breath hitched a little in his chest. Was this how hunting always felt? Khouri could get addicted if so. It felt an awful lot like gearing up for the assassination had. But this time, he supposed, there was less chance of losing his life in the process or of getting distracted.

"With that outfit you call clothing, you're already plenty marketable."

Khouri's foot nearly slipped on the branch. He caught himself with a muted grunt, his previous thrill shattered. He looked down through the boughs to pin the hunter with a look. Sorin didn't even look embarrassed by what he had just suggested. "If that's some sort of surface humor," he said icily, "I don't appreciate it."

Sorin scoffed and held up his hands placatingly. "I didn't mean anything by it." He jerked his head towards the target. "Stop focusing on me and get to it before your window closes."

"You most certainly did mean something by it," Khouri growled, turning his attention back forward. He carefully moved across the steadily narrowing branch, keeping his focus on the target and nothing else. His shirt was cropped. So what? That didn't make him any less dangerous. "You think I don't have other people making those insinuations? You think that bandit's behavior yesterday wasn't the norm? I don't need it from you too, Sorin. Don't treat me like that."

There was a moment of silence as Khouri moved directly overhead of the target. The grass was thick here, nearly obscuring the soft brown bodies below. "You have to know what is said about your kind," Sorin murmured, and Khouri froze when the rabbit's ears perked up at the sound, its small nose twitching as it searched for danger. "You have to know that what I say won't be remotely as bad as what a mark might throw at you on a job. I'm not doing it now to offend you, Khouri."

The intent behind it hardly mattered. Not when the stigma followed him everywhere he went up here. "And you must know what is said about yours," Khouri shot back at Sorin in a harsh whisper. "Greedy, lying, backstabbing. You're as distrusted as I am." The only difference was who held the majority up here.

"And?"

Breathe. Just breathe. Khouri closed his eyes and exhaled, letting the rabbit's quiet chewing fill him before the frustration could. Sorin was doing this on purpose. He knew he was. There would be worse yelled at him on these jobs. Khouri couldn't afford to let himself be distracted by slurs and goading barbs.

"And," Khouri breathed, crouching down on the branch as he pulled another dagger from his hip sheath, "you don't see me holding it against you."

He dropped from the tree before Sorin could muster up a reply. With the dagger pointed down and the element of surprise, there was no time for the rabbit to look up or even think of bolting. Khouri forced himself to keep his eyes open as he severed its spinal cord cleanly. Blood stuck to his hands and matted the fur, but he had to smile. Perfect. Absolutely perfect.

"That knife better not have been poisoned too," Sorin grunted, cutting through Khouri's celebration without a backwards glance. "And I thought I told you to capture it. You've lost yourself half the bounty by killing it."

Khouri rolled his eyes and lifted the rabbit by the ears. "It's not, and I thought I was getting us dinner, not another handful of gold. If you're accustomed to eating your meat alive, then perhaps I'm keeping the wrong company." He really couldn't be this critical. That was a flawless assassination. "Besides, like hell I'm grabbing a wild rabbit. Look at the claws on this thing."

Sorin really couldn't argue with that. His eyes narrowed a little as he took in the sharp claws, and when he huffed, Khouri knew he had won. "You won't have a choice in a fight," he warned him, taking the rabbit and heading back to the makeshift camp. "A person with a weapon is still a person you have to take down alive."

"Sure, sure." They entered the clearing within a minute

or two as the sun began to make its westerly trek towards sundown. They had a few hours left, but it probably had been wise to stop here where they knew a good camp spot was. Khouri crouched down to rest on his haunches as Sorin pulled out his big hunting knife, beginning the process of breaking down the rabbit. All of that stalking had woken up Khouri's appetite. He couldn't wait to dig in.

"Where did you learn to cook?" Khouri asked, a little bit jealous of how easy Sorin made skinning the thing look. "You aren't going to throw it on the fire and call it good enough, are you?"

"You making assumptions about me? Fair enough, I suppose." Sorin chuckled, gutting the rabbit and piling the entrails off to the side. "I've been on the road for awhile. You learn a few things as you go, and one of those things is how to make something taste bearable."

Khouri hummed, wrinkling his nose at the gut pile. "You still never told me where you're from," he murmured, resting his chin on his knees. "Are you making something from your hometown?"

Sorin met his eye briefly as if assessing Khouri's intention by asking. After a moment, he let out a breath and looked back down, separating the rabbit into quarters and then eighths. "They don't eat much rabbit where I'm from," he answered once that was done.

"Why not? Do they not like it?" Khouri hardly had it down in the Duskriven, but it wasn't bad. There was no reason to turn one's nose up at it.

"I'm from a port city," Sorin said, gathering up the chunks of meat and tossing it into the hot pot. It immediately began to sizzle, the camp filling with the scent of cooking meat. "We ate a lot of fish and seafood there. Hand me that, would you?" Khouri handed Sorin his pouch when prompted and watched the hunter toss in some spices, shaving salt off a block with his knife once that was done. "The rich families got to eat real meat. The rest of us ate what we could catch from the sea. Or chicken, I guess, if you had them."

Khouri blinked and cocked his head. That sounded a bit bitter. So, Sorin had been poor growing up. That certainly explained the constant rich-boy barbs. Sorin ignored him to prod at the meat with the tip of his knife, making sure it didn't burn. "Do you have family there still?" he asked, leaning back when Sorin poured in water from the canteen, a cloud of steam rising up in a wave.

In went more spices as well as a few of the bigger bones Sorin has set aside. He put the lid on top and leveled Khouri with a look. "Why do you want to know?" he asked, rising to his feet to take care of the still-warm gut pile.

"Because I'm curious?" Khouri didn't bother to stand up and follow. He lingered close to the pot, the scent already mouth-watering. "Living by the sea sounds amazing. I can't imagine why you'd want to leave unless you were all alone there."

Sorin snorted and disappeared into the woods with the guts, returning about ten minutes later with empty hands and a wet face. Khouri figured there must be a river or a creek nearby. "You would think living anywhere that's not beneath the earth amazing," Sorin said, eyeing Khouri's hand and the lid of the pot. "Don't you dare go picking at that until it's done. I swear, you're as bad as a toddler."

Khouri pouted and wrapped his arms around his legs. "I'm

hungry. When will it be done?"

"Give it twenty minutes. I'm sure you can survive until then."

Twenty minutes? Khouri groaned, staring at the pot forlornly. "Tell me more," he murmured, rocking a little to occupy himself. "Tell about the sea. Is it big? What does it look like?"

Sorin settled down into a comfortable sprawl, sighing. "It's big, blue, and wet," he said dispassionately. "And if you try to drink it, you die."

Khouri broke away from his staring contest with the pot to take in Sorin. "Die?" he asked incredulously. "What would you die? Is it poisonous?"

"You really don't know much of the surface, do you?" Sorin stared off into the trees for a minute. "It's saltwater. It dries you out. The more you drink, the faster you die. We would go swimming sometimes when the surf wasn't so rough. A wave would swipe your feet out from under you, and you'd get a mouthful of it and be spitting for the rest of the day." A gentle smile teased his stern mouth. "I use to throw my sisters in just to make them complain later."

Khouri held his breath and tightened his fingers in the laces along his thighs. "Sisters?" he posed lightly, hoping Sorin would share more. "What were they like?"

"They're brats like you." The hunter fell back onto the ground and pillowed his head with his arms. The sky was blue and clear of clouds. Awfully boring to look at, Khouri thought. "With half a dozen smaller brats between the two of them now, I guess. More incentive to keep on the road, I tell them when they write. Children are exhausting."

"I wouldn't know," Khouri said quietly, feeling a little out of his depth. "Children aren't all that common where I'm from." He had certainly never been around them. Most didn't take their offspring out in public. The streets weren't safe, and the public sphere was for the adults alone. For the people worth seeing.

Sorin raised a brow at him and smiled. "Trust me. They hang all over you and want picked up constantly. Last time I went to visit Mastha, her youngest wiped his nose on my knee and had the audacity to laugh about it."

Shrugging a little, Khouri smiled back. "That doesn't sound that bad to me. At least the kid didn't try to stab you."

"I can't tell if you're joking or not," Sorin huffed, closing his eyes.

"I am. At least, I think I am. I don't know children and what they will or won't do. Where I'm from, they don't tend to have more than one if they can help it, and I've never been around kids to know what they're like." Khouri looked back at the pot, wondering if it had been twenty minutes yet. He really didn't want to talk about the Duskriven. "Can we eat yet?"

Levering himself back up, Sorin let out a groan. "You're so impatient. It'll taste better the longer you let it cook, you know," he grumbled, moving over to lift the lid. The scent grew tenfold, Khouri inching closer eagerly. Sorin dug through his bag for a spoon and stirred the stew, checking the doneness of the meat.

"So?" Khouri asked, nearly vibrating with excitement.

"Still a little thin," Sorin answered, digging into his cavernous pack for a small pouch. Khouri inched closer to watch, nearly touching Sorin as he poured what looked to be flour into a small dish. Sorin drew back his elbow and nudged Khouri in the chest, pushing him back. "Would you give me some space? You act like you're starving."

If Khouri whined, Sorin didn't seem to acknowledge it. Instead, he took up the canteen and mixed the flour with a little water to make some thick, white paste. Before Khouri could ask what he intended to do with it, Sorin was pouring it into the stew.

"There," Sorin said as he stirred in the ribbons of white, the broth thickening like magic. "That's better. Now you can eat."

"You're amazing," Khouri murmured, eyes locked on the stew. "Absolutely amazing."

"Get your damn bowl before I spoon it into your lap."

Khouri rushed to dig out the extra bowl from Sorin's pack, holding it up before Sorin could make good on his threat. His eyes widened as the food filled the bowl, Sorin giving him extra before he could ask. He settled down with his legs crossed, bowl balanced on his knee as he looked up at the hunter. "Thank you," he said with a smile as Sorin served himself a portion too. "It really does smell amazing."

"Don't go giving me credit before you've eaten it," the hunter warned, looking a little flustered by all of the praise. He lifted up a spoonful and eyed it carefully. "Who knows what that dagger of yours could have done to the taste."

"I already told you, I didn't use a poisoned one for that," Khouri laughed, spooning some of the rich broth into his mouth. The flavor burst across his tongue, thick and heady and more than satisfying. If he had to wager a guess, he would say Sorin thought so too. "See, no poison to ruin the taste! It tastes just as good as it smells."

"Yeah, well, beginner's luck."

Khouri smiled around his next mouthful. "Guess I'll have to bag another one and prove you wrong. The first was easy enough to catch. I bet you've never seen such skill before."

"You're a far cry from a master hunter, so don't get cocky. But, as much as it pains me to admit it, you did good," Sorin said, smiling wryly. "Maybe there's hope for you yet."

"Good enough to be your partner?" Khouri asked hopefully. The warmth from the bowl warmed his hands. It felt good. Really good.

Sorin rolled his eyes and took another bite. "Don't push it. There's still a lot left for you to learn. Hurry up and eat. There's still daylight enough to teach you how to snare."

They were just words to him, Khouri told himself as he took another bite of the food he helped make. The human had no idea the weight of what he said, but for a moment, Khouri was content to pretend that Sorin did.

Chapter Three

It was strange –stranger than strange– having to restructure his life around Khouri.

Sorin was not accustomed to traveling with others. If he ever did, it was for a job and therefore on a very limited and professional basis. He didn't need to worry about his companion's skill level; he didn't need to think about how best to utilize another's skills to hone them into something sharper. But traveling with someone like Khouri meant that everything Sorin knew about traveling companions was garbage. Khouri was a Drow, who, for whatever reason, wanted to become a bounty hunter.

They took it slowly because nothing else could be done to combat the sharp difference in their worldviews. Jobs that Sorin would have thought easy suddenly became difficult. He couldn't simply wait for the mark to enter a tavern. He couldn't just go about things with Khouri in tow. The Drow's appearance wouldn't allow it. Sorin found himself employing more creative thinking than he ever had before combined.

And the awful thing was that it worked. It worked *well*.

Khouri was quick and clever, and even with the sizable difference in their skill levels, Khouri kept up. He listened well in a fight and made his appearance an advantage. Not many up here had ever seen a Drow. The sight was shocking enough to inspire an opening, and Khouri was certainly good at making the most of those opportunities. Sorin would be the last one to admit it aloud, but he had to think every now and again that perhaps Khouri wasn't the deadweight he had thought him to be when they first met. Just because Khouri looked like a young upstart certainly didn't mean he was one.

Worst of all, Sorin knew, was coming to terms with the growing realization that Khouri was a thoroughly enjoyable person. The brat was beautiful; of that, there was no argument. Sorin had known that from the start, really. But he was also clever and funny and viper-tongued enough to always give Sorin a run for his money. Khouri wasn't afraid to knock him down for some ill-mannered barb, and that was certainly teaching Sorin how to shape his speech better. Separating the truth from the rumors came quickly with Khouri. It was probably the first time Sorin had ever met someone so evenly matched to him. They worked well together, and they traveled well together. It was a dizzying thought, truly.

But, even with all of that factoring in, Sorin still couldn't quite swallow the stab of surprise he felt every single time he turned around, thinking himself alone, only to find the Drow tagging dutifully along behind him. It was one thing for the closeness while they were hiking. It was another thing entirely when Sorin was consulting the map.

"Shit," he cursed, jumping when he caught sight of Khouri out of the corner of his eye. The Drow was peering over his shoulder, his breath tickling the back of Sorin's neck. Sorin shoved him away and glared at Khouri, hastily folding the map back up. "What the hell do you think you're doing?"

Khouri had the audacity to raise a brow, crossing his arms over his chest. "You were taking so long, so I thought I might come over and help you," he explained, rolling his eyes. "At first, I thought you had forgotten how to read. I guess you're just slow today. Took you ages to notice me, but then again, you're pretty old for a human." He smiled like the brat he was. "Maybe it's just to be expected."

He easily dodged the swipe Sorin threw at him, dancing back with a grin on his perfect face. "Oh, come on now, Sorin," he laughed, avoiding the half-hearted blows with ease. "It's just a joke."

"What's got you so unbearably bubbly today?" Sorin asked, still stalking towards the Drow, map clenched in his hand. He didn't know what he would do if he caught Khouri, but that was hardly reason enough not to try.

Khouri hooked a hand around the narrow base of a sapling, using it to spin himself out of Sorin's range. His every move looked like a dance as smooth and as skillful as his speech. "What's not to be happy about?" he asked, smiling brightly. "The sun is shining, the birds are singing, and you're still as grumpy as ever. Not to mention the thick stack of money we have now. It's exciting! I've never earned money before."

Sorin paused, gaping a little. "What do you mean you've never earned money before?" How did that even make sense? "Aren't you older than me? How did you survive?"

Jumping onto a fallen log, Khouri threw out his hands and walked along it like a child balancing on a beam. "Stealing, mostly," he said, looking over his shoulder and keeping balance easily. "Navidae took care of the rest after I met him. It's novel, isn't it? It feels rather nice knowing I've earned something the way everyone else earns things."

Sorin didn't have the heart to tell him that not many people made their livings by capturing other people. When it came down to it, the how didn't really matter. He'd let Khouri have his moment. "Yeah, well," he began, unfurling the map and going back to his previous task, "good on you. It's going to be a lot of work if you want to keep at it. Apprehending them is the easy part. It's finding them that takes time." Not to mention building information networks, laying traps, and all the other facets of the job Sorin hated to think about right now.

Khouri skipped off of the log and landed with nary a sound, moving back towards him as quietly as the wind whispering through the treetops. "I'm glad I've got you to learn from then," he said, cocking his head as he looked at the map over Sorin's arm. "Where are we going next? Do you know?"

Shrugging, Sorin's eyes wandered along the parchment. There were a few villages within a day's hike but none big enough to boast a bounty board. "Wherever there might be work," he said, chewing the inside of his cheek. The Drow's soft scent filled his senses, Khouri standing too close but not seeming to care.

"No leads?" he murmured, his hand resting on Sorin's forearm as he peered at the map too.

Sorin couldn't focus on the map with Khouri touching him. His small hand was a negligible weight on his arm, the curve of his pointed ear peeking out from behind his dark, silky hair. "No," Sorin said gruffly, tearing his gaze away from the Drow and back onto the map. "We need to head towards a bigger town, but there aren't any within a day or two of here. It's just a matter of picking which one to aim for."

"Oh," Khouri murmured, letting go of Sorin's arm. "If that's how it is…"

The map was gone before Sorin processed it had been stolen from him. Khouri's sleight of hand was too quick for the eye to follow. He made a grab for it, but Khouri just darted out of the way, unfurling the parchment with a wave of his hand.

"You... You brat," he snarled, chasing after Khouri. It was aggravating how the Drow didn't even need to look up to evade him. "What do you think you're doing?"

"Well, since you don't know where to take us next, I figure it's only fair that I be the one to pick," Khouri answered, spinning around with a smile, tapping at the map's wrinkled surface. "It's all the same to you, isn't it? You only had the one bounty, so there's no point in heading towards any one area in particular."

"That's not the point," he growled, taking another swipe but catching nothing but air between his fingers. How was Khouri so fast? "You don't get to call the shots. That's my job."

Khouri hummed, smiling smugly at Sorin. "Ah, but I'm helping you with your work now. It's only fair that I get a turn," he said, hopping back up onto his log to balance and read at the same time. Like this, Sorin couldn't easily reach him. Not unless he wanted to risk falling on his face trying.

"Fine," Sorin grunted, throwing his hands up in the air. Better to give the Khouri what he wanted than risk looking like a fool trying to stop him. "Pick a damn town." Not like it mattered much anyway.

The Drow laughed and shot him a grin. Sorin was a little surprised when it didn't inspire another flare of irritation. Khouri perched himself on the edge of the log and looked at the map, tracing lines and paths with his fingertip as he did. Sorin sighed and stared up at the sun through the trees. Everything was calm for the moment, but that didn't mean they shouldn't hurry and get a move on.

"You almost done?" he asked, raising a brow as Khouri

peered at him from over the top of the map. "We don't have all day."

"I think so," Khouri answered, turning the map around to face him. His long, dark finger pointed at a small speck of black on the left, a good three day hike from their present location. "This is Mardeau, right? I've heard good things about the merchants here. It's probably big enough to have bounties."

Sorin leaned in and looked closer. He had heard of the town before but never been there himself. It probably did have what they needed as well as being a large enough town to have a decently sized rumor mill. Running his hand through his hair, Sorin shot Khouri a look. "Yeah, I think that will work," he said, holding out his hand for the map. "Get down from there. We need to head out."

Khouri rolled up the map and handed it over, hopping down beside him with a cheerful expression. "So impatient," he murmured, hitching the strap of his bag higher up on his shoulder. "Lead the way. I'm ready to go when you are."

Glancing up at the sky again, Sorin shouldered his own bag and hiding the map away. "Yeah, let's move," he said, heading west, tearing himself away from the thick clouds off in the distance.

So long as they made good progress today, it wouldn't matter where they went.

Letting the Drow pick was the worst decision Sorin had ever made.

"Move faster!" he shouted over the wind, grabbing

Khouri by the shoulder and shoving him forward. The clouds overhead churned more and more with every passing second. The rain wasn't threatening to fall so much as it was readying itself, stray flecks of moisture cutting through the wind to warn them to hurry. It promised to be one hell of a storm.

And Khouri, the complete idiot, seemed to think it a better idea to gawk and watch the clouds roll in rather than move towards shelter.

"Hey, don't shove!" Khouri complained, pouting as he wrapped his cloak around him and tried to move through the oncoming wind. His hair was a mess of inky tangles, the wind whipping it in his face and over his eyes. "Where are we going? Do you know?"

Sorin grimaced and put himself in front of Khouri, acting as a windbreak so the Drow wouldn't be swept away, cloak and all. "Of course," he shouted, though he really didn't. Khouri had pointed them off in a direction away from any near villages, and Sorin had never traveled these parts before. It certainly didn't look as if there were any homes or other manmade structures nearby from which to barter shelter for the night.

He let out a scoff that was lost in the cry of the wind. As if they would be able to barter shelter with Khouri being what he was. That left them either the forest, a markedly bad idea, or the open air. Both were awful prospects. There was no winning when the choices were be crushed by falling trees or be pelted by rain and hail all night.

A tug on his sleeve had him looking down, Khouri at his side. Be it the rain or the wind, Sorin didn't know, but the Drow looked far younger than what he was. "I think there's a cave near here," he said, Sorin reading his lips more than hearing him. "I saw it on the map." He pointed out a hand towards the west and tugged at Sorin's sleeve.

A cave? Sorin didn't remember seeing that on the map, but with the wind and rain as hard as it was, it would be idiotic to try and check it now. He bit his lip and looked at the sky, seeing no break in the clouds in sight. "Lead the way," he shouted, knowing they had no other options. Khouri nodded his head and set off, only bowled over a little from the force of the wind. He seemed confident, which was somewhat reassuring. With the weather like this, Sorin would take any optimism he could get.

Within twenty or so minutes, the sky turned from gray to an eerie sort of orange, the clouds backlit by the sun as the teasing, light rain continued to spit at them from on high. Khouri kept moving, guiding them forward, occasionally pausing to look in either direction before carrying on. If Sorin had any clue what he were looking for, he might have helped. It was a bit hellish having to sit back and follow, especially when he had no idea if Khouri knew where he was going.

Another ten minutes of walking, and the rain stopped teasing them. A crack of thunder echoed overhead, tearing through the air with strength enough to jostle them both. The mud turned rocky, the dark, orange-tinged light revealing a rocky outcrop a quarter mile to their left. It wasn't huge, certainly no mountain, but as the only landmark in sight, Sorin welcomed it all the same. He wrapped an arm around Khouri and practically carried him forward, searching for the break in the dark stone that might prove to the be the cave Khouri had spoken about.

"Hey!" Khouri squirmed, fighting the hand around his waist. "I can run on my own!"

Sorin opened his mouth to snap at him, but another peal of thunder cut him off. It wasn't worth wasting breath on, he decided, tightening his grip and charging forward. Khouri grasped his arm in shock and held tight as his feet left the ground. The moment the distance between them and the rocky hill closed, Sorin set him back down, eyes narrowed through the rain for any sign of shelter.

They found it just as the rain began to come down in sheets as opposed to the light trickling that had been with them so far. The cave was nestled between the eastern facing side of the stone formation, entrance nearly obscured by bushes and thorny bramble. It looked like the sort of place a dragon might call home, but Khouri was already racing towards it, hood held close to his head as he ran off. Sorin let out a groan and began to run too. There wasn't much time to check for beasts or animals, and Sorin made sure to go first as they ran beneath the outcropping of rock, ducking inside just as the torrent opened up behind them.

Khouri let out a peal of laughter, the sound nearly lost in a rumble of thunder in the distance. He wiped the water from his eyes and tossed his bag down, plopping down beside it. "That was close," he said, slicking back his hair with a smile. "Are we going to stay here for the night then?"

Sorin couldn't bring himself to be so chipper. He threw down his own bag and stared into the darkness at the back of the cave, trying to listen for the telltale sounds of kobolds or mountain lions or any of the hundreds of things that could be lurking inside a random cave. Axe in hand, he narrowed his eyes, barely able to see five feet ahead of him, let alone into the rest of the inner darkness.

"There's nothing back there," a voice whispered in his

ear, and Sorin jumped for the second time that day, nearly dropping his axe. He whipped around and glared at Khouri, wondering how the Drow could be so light on his feet.

"How can you tell?" he demanded. "It's as black as pitch."

Khouri raised a brow and tapped at his temple. "Drow? I live beneath the ground, Sorin. I can see in the dark." He rolled his eyes and turned away, sitting back down beside his bag after kicking aside a few rocks. "We should build a fire, right? It's chilly in here."

Sorin let out his breath, loosening his hold on his axe. "Yeah." They were fortunate that the inner part of the cave was littered with dried brush and broken branches, probably swept in by winds from other storms. Propping his axe against a near wall, Sorin set to gathering up enough for a fire, building it near enough to the entrance to filter out smoke but deep enough to avoid the inevitable water. With a few strikes of his flint, they had a fire blazing, filling the cave with its warmth and light.

"That's better," Khouri sighed, scooting close to the fire to warm his hands. "It's so damp in here. Reminds me too much of the Duskriven."

Damp and cold was right. Sorin shrugged off his fur-lined cloak, tucking it under him to spare him from a night of sleeping on the heat-sapping stone. "Can't say I've ever been," he grunted, debating whether or not he should kick off his boots as well. It would be more comfortable, but some part of him had trouble shaking the worry that they could be ambushed while asleep.

Khouri didn't seem to have any such compunction. He tugged off his tall boots and rested them beside his satchel, casting off his own cloak to bare his shoulders completely. Sorin couldn't help but stare. "You're lucky for that," the Drow muttered, stretching like a cat, all lithe muscle and careless grace. Even rain spattered as he was, it was hard to think of him as anything but beautiful. "It's awful. Boring and cold and you can't trust a single soul you meet."

If Sorin were being honest, that sounded like half the towns he had visited in the last few months. All the port cities were like that, though perhaps not quite as cold as Khouri meant. He couldn't count the times he had been thought a troublemaker from just walking through town with his sisters in tow as a youth. Perhaps that was what it was like being Drow. On second thought, it probably wasn't even close. Khouri had it a lot worse, really. Sorin probably couldn't understand. He nodded along despite the realization, reaching for his canteen. "Any place you Drow call home must be a special sort of hell."

Khouri laughed a bit wryly. He folded his legs and propped up his elbow with a knee, resting his chin in his palm. He looked out at the rain wistfully. "You can say that again."

When Sorin managed to find his canteen, he was met with a woefully empty rattle. "Have you got any water?" Sorin asked, loath to stick his canteen out into the rain and wait for it to fill that way. He should have filled up that morning. Today really wasn't his day.

Khouri perked up, blinking for a moment before moving for his bag. "I think so; let me check." He rooted around inside his pack, shifting onto his knees to scrounge. As he dug, he tossed out a few clothes that were in the way and then a book and then a small bundle that rattled when it hit the stone. Khouri didn't seem to pay much attention, too busy digging to look up.

A glint of silver caught Sorin's eye however, and he leaned forward, plucking up the bundle of cloth before Khouri could catch on. It was heavier than he expected it to be, the cloth slipping away to reveal some sort of jewelry. His eyes went wide when he saw the rubies, but in the next moment, a dark hand cut into his field of view, snatching the piece away from him before he realized what had happened.

"You dropped that," Sorin said quickly before Khouri could accuse him of stealing again. "I wasn't trying to take it."

Khouri frowned at him, shoving the half full canteen into his chest as he cradled the jewelry close. "I... I know," he mumbled, trying and failing to keep his expression level. "I just don't like people touching my things."

Sorin untwisted the cap of the canteen and took a drink, sensing they were heading into sensitive territory. He gestured towards the thing with the canteen, swallowing his mouthful before speaking. "Is that what you were so protective of before?" he asked casually. "Back when you thought I was rooting through your bag."

"You *were* rooting through my bag," Khouri delivered pointedly, opening his hand to stare at the trinket pensively. He let out a tense breath, lifting his gaze slowly. "But, yeah."

"Another one of those gifts from your lover?" Sorin guessed, setting the canteen on the ground. "What is it supposed to be?"

"A bracelet," he murmured. "He gave me this a few weeks after my earrings." Khouri held the shiny silver bracelet up to the light, showing Sorin but making no move to let him hold

66

it. "It's the last one I have left," he said ruefully, stroking over the inscribed links, his thumb pausing on the blood red stones inlaid in the silver. "I couldn't bear for it to be stolen."

"But selling it is okay?" Sorin asked, not understanding at all. The earrings were a gift too, but Khouri was still wearing those. "If you care so much about them, then why bother pawning them? There has to be other ways for you to get money."

"There weren't," Khouri said succinctly, meeting his eye. He cradled the jewelry between his palms, his look almost forlorn. "It's one thing for me to give it up on my own. Something I've come to terms with losing, I guess. Having it taken from me is completely different."

"Do you…" Sorin began, keeping his voice level. "Do you want to wear it now? No one's around. If you like it so much, you might as well wear it while you can."

For a moment, Khouri looked like he was considering it. His hands went tight on the bracelet and then loosened, his head hanging as he sighed. "No," he decided, putting the bracelet back in the deepest part of his pack. "The less I have to remind me of Navidae right now the better."

Sorin hummed. "How did you even meet a Drow like that?" he asked. "You said he's rich, right? And you aren't. I wasn't under the impression your social classes mingled much."

Khouri glanced at him as if to judge his sincerity. "They don't," he murmured. "He's rich enough to have enemies. I was just fodder in some grudge. It all worked out in the end, so I don't ruminate on it."

That didn't answer much. "Do you miss him?" As soon as Sorin asked the question, he regretted it. Khouri looked up, his expression miserable. The Drow scrubbed at his eyes and then looked at the wall, lips curled into a pout that made him look anything but his actual age.

"That's... a hard question to answer," Khouri said sourly, hands balled up tightly in his lap. "I've spent the last fifty years of my life with him. I don't have anyone else on this earth I'm as close to or as intimate with. It's... odd being away from him. From our home."

Sorin could sense there was a lot Khouri wasn't saying. Instead of calling him out on it, he simply raised a brow and waited. Khouri frowned down at his hands, continuing after a moment of silence.

"But he's also insufferable and pushy and clingy," Khouri huffed, falling back to prop himself up with his hands. He glowered at the rock over their heads. "He doesn't let me do anything. I used to go everywhere. I used to come and go, and I always came back!" He looked at Sorin animatedly. "But I guess he didn't trust me. That all stopped and I was trapped in that mansion."

Khouri sighed, kicking at a loose piece of rock. It rolled along the uneven floor, clinging its way to a stop against the far wall. "But for all of that, yeah. Yeah, I miss him. I'm antsy without him. I never had to worry when I was with him. He knew how to provide for me, no matter what I needed. No matter whether I knew what I needed or not." A small smile settled along his full lips, his eyes meeting Sorin's warmly. "He has so many pet names for me. For all he has, I think I'm the most precious thing he can call his own."

The firelight flickered off the stone walls of the cave, and when Sorin looked at Khouri, he saw the same light turn the Drow into something ethereal. His cheekbones sharpened. His eyes were hooded and inviting. Every inch of bare skin glistened, Khouri's cropped shirt and slitted, laced trousers baring far too much of him. Sorin swallowed and looked back down at the burning logs, ignoring the warmth forming in the pit of his stomach. Why was he even affected by it? Khouri had looked like that since they met. There was no reason to be getting so worked up by it now.

"Those are some pretty words for a man you left behind," Sorin said, directing his words to the fire where it was safe to look. "If you felt so safe there, then why did you bother coming up above?"

Khouri sighed, leaning against his bag. Sorin took a quick glance and regretted it immediately. Draped along the pack and his bundled up cloak, his spine curved and hip bare, he looked like a forlorn angel begging to be worshipped. "I suppose," Khouri breathed, unaware of what he was doing or aware and not caring, "that I wanted to make sure there was nothing better up here." His ebony eyes cut across to Sorin, smiling gently. "I still like Navi just fine. I just wish he would move somewhere else."

That seemed too simplistic to be the truth. Sorin propped his arm on his bent knee. "So you decided to run away from home without a backwards glance?" he prodded, noting how Khouri frowned. "How much can you like him if you run off on him?"

Khouri shoved himself upright, his eyes hardening into a glare. "Well, obviously it's not as cut and dry as that," he said defensively.

"I think you're hiding something," Sorin huffed, banking

the fire with another handful of wood. A spray of sparks lit up the cave, dissipating like the rain outside wouldn't.

"I think you're too interested in my private affairs," Khouri muttered, crossing his arms. "It's really none of your business why I left Navidae. And it doesn't matter anyway. It's not like I belong to him. He may think I do, but he knows I'm my own person first. I can do what I want." He gave Sorin a once over, one that wasn't subtle at all. "I can... I can have other lovers, if I wanted them."

Sorin stared at him, wondering if that could possibly mean what he thought it meant. Khouri stared back, his dark cheeks flushing indigo in the firelight. The world was still, the only sound the crackling, whispering fire and the pelting rain outside. The tension was stifling. Sorin didn't dare breathe.

"Just because you're maudlin..." Sorin began, and Khouri bit his lip, body as tense as the strings of a lute. "Are you... Do you *want* me?"

Khouri looked away first, wrestling for his cloak, his pack, his bedroll. Whatever bravado he had held disappeared the moment it was pointed out. "I'm... Just..." he began, his voice cracked. "Nevermind. I'm going to bed. You can keep the first watch."

"Khouri."

The Drow froze, meeting Sorin's eye carefully. His teeth worried at his lip, his chest rising and falling quickly. The movement drew attention to his neck, to the tight little top he wore and how it just barely covered his gorgeous skin. Sorin's mouth went dry, pinning Khouri in place with just his gaze.

"What do you want me to say?" Khouri asked, trying to

play off his gamble with a forced laugh. He drew his hand behind his head, tangling his fingers in his thick hair like a nervous habit only half broken. "It's been over a month since I left the Duskriven. No one wants me up here, and if they do, they don't want *me*. They want some... some disgusting fantasy. You're... You're a brute and you're vulgar, but you at least like me." He tugged and yanked at his hair, meeting Sorin's eyes slowly. "I'm not asking you to. Just ignore me. I'm going to bed."

With the offer out in the open, the words all but unsaid, Sorin couldn't just *ignore* it.

Sorin reached across the space between them, grabbing Khouri's slender wrist in his hand before the Drow could shift away. Khouri froze like a rabbit caught before a fox, eyes wide and his body already trembling just from the simple touch. Sorin had wanted it for awhile now. He wanted to touch Khouri. He wanted to feel every single inch of Khouri's soft skin against his own. If it were within his reach, of course he would take it.

"Don't run. Please," Sorin said, conveying every ounce of want, every single drop of desire he held for the Drow before him. "I... I do like you." Khouri looked stricken, drowning in the weight of Sorin's spoken need.

It took a loud, sharp snap from the fire to tear the tension to pieces. Just one crack to set them loose on each other. Khouri reached Sorin first, knotting his hands in Sorin's long hair, dragging him into the most painful kiss of his life. The Drow kissed with every inch of his body, his teeth nipping, his hands roving, his hips rolling desperately against Sorin like the dancer he so resembled.

"Are we really doing this?" Khouri gasped between kisses,

his warm, lithe body plastered to Sorin's front. "I don't want some pity fuck. Do... Do you really want me?"

Sorin took him by the hips and dragged him to the floor, laying him out on the fur mantle. Khouri was built entirely of smooth, gentle curves and sharp, pointed need. His hands were already grasping for Sorin, his thighs spreading to welcome the hunter against his body. Were they really doing this? The question came a little too late for the answer to matter.

"Shut up," he growled, laying his hands on hips too perfect to resist. Khouri was beautiful, and he was competent in a way Sorin wasn't accustomed to seeing. Respect wasn't something he was used to feeling for another, but looking at Khouri, looking at the knives he wore and the sharp glint in his clever eyes, Sorin felt it. He felt it, and it made him weak. "I want you so much I could break something."

"Oh, thank the gods below," Khouri gasped, hands fisted in Sorin's shirt, nearly ripping it off his body. Sorin shucked it before he could, the Drow's touch burning his skin with its desperate heat.

When with a new lover, Sorin tended to take his time to acclimate himself to their body. He would test and play, touching all he could while searching for the places that made his lover sing. He wanted to savor his intimacy when it came to him, if it came to him. But now, with this Drow, there was no time for any of his usual habits. Khouri's berry dark lips were parted on a moan, a sheen of sweat glistening across his soft, dusky skin. Sorin didn't need to ask to know that the Drow wasn't in the mood for niceties.

He didn't want intimacy from Sorin; he wanted to get fucked.

"Isn't this against one of those rules of yours?" Khouri gasped, his dark eyes laughing even as Sorin released his hands to begin unfastening the snaps that held shut the front of the Drow's shirt. They parted easily, opening up Khouri's chest to Sorin's eager, assessing eye.

"Those rules are meant for you to follow, not me," Sorin grunted, lowering his head to lap at the dark bud of Khouri's nipple. Everything about the Drow was made to entice from his abyssal eyes to his tight, lithe body. His chest was smooth, his nipples pierced with simple silver bars. Those were certainly different, definitely not something he expected to find on the Drow, but like hell was Sorin about to complain. Not when the look sent fire straight through his veins. He merely cupped what his mouth couldn't touch with a hand, his other slipping down to tear at the laces running down Khouri's shapely thigh.

Slender fingers carded through Sorin's hair a moment later. Khouri's laugh echoed through his chest, his mirth tinged with want. "Hypocrite," he said, lifting his thigh to make Sorin's search for more skin easier. "You're lucky it's been awhile for me. Usually I'm very picky when it comes to lovers."

Somehow, Sorin doubted that. He bit down gently on Khouri's nipple, tugging at the warm metal until the Drow cried out. God, but it sounded good. Were those another gift from Navidae? The man had good taste, that much was true. With one last soft lick, he abandoned Khouri's chest entirely. "Oh?" he went, giving the laces a hard tug that loosened them enough to yank down Khouri's tight leather trousers. "So I should be thanking you for this, is that right?"

"I'm not saying you *have* to, but a little gratitude wouldn't be out of place," Khouri teased, lifting his hips to help Sorin peel off the leather. They weren't eager to be parted from him, but given how good the Drow tasted, Sorin could hardly blame the trousers for lingering. Khouri preened beneath his gaze, his dark cheeks all the darker for his blush. He was so cocky now that he knew he wasn't being rejected.

"You look like you want to eat me alive," he murmured, smiling as Sorin stroked his bare legs. "Is that how you show gratitude?"

"It's how I shut you up," Sorin murmured, entranced by how soft the Drow's legs were. His skin was as smooth as satin, hairless and perfect beneath his hands. Khouri gasped prettily as his legs were kissed, Sorin trailing his lips along the mindlessly soft skin.

He stopped moving entirely when he spread Khouri's thighs.

Aside from the obvious, perfect shape of Khouri's sex against his thigh, what greeted Sorin first and foremost were scars, old, silvery and raised just a little. They lay in uneven clusters, some more ragged than others.

"What are these?" Sorin asked sharply, trailing his fingers along the numerous little crescent moons littering the inner portions of Khouri's thighs. Most were faded, but a few were still sharply prominent, made all the more visible by the light of the flickering fire beside them. Not fresh wounds but still young enough to feel rough beneath his fingers. Someone had been here not that long ago. A few weeks. Maybe a month at most.

Khouri had the audacity to look confused. He peered down his body and through his parted legs, smiling sheepishly as Sorin traced the shapes cut into his thighs. "Oh," he said, blinking his dark, dark eyes. "Those are from my lover. You can just ignore them."

If that wasn't the biggest load of bull he'd ever heard. Sorin was a lot of things but an idiot wasn't one of them. "I can't just ignore these," Sorin said, trailing off as a leg hitched itself around his hip.

"Yes, you can." Smiling sultrily, Khouri arched a little, dragging Sorin's attention away from them and back onto the rest of him. It almost worked. Sorin took him by the thighs and dragged him closer, utterly entranced by the perfect picture the Drow made beneath him. Or, he was right until he caught sight of similar marks on Khouri's shoulders too, the soft fan of his hair not doing enough to keep them covered now that his cloak was off and his shirt gone. Sorin growled lowly and rutted his clothed cock against the swell of the Drow's ass, bending him in half to get a closer look at his already claimed body.

It didn't take a genius to realize they were bite marks, and it took even less to know that Sorin was about to fuck some other man's pet. "Your lover doesn't treat you very kindly, does he?" Sorin huffed, wondering why he even cared enough to bring it up. "I thought you said you liked him."

"Maybe I like it when he's rough," Khouri said, his eyes hard, his teeth a little bared. He was defensive of the markings and obviously unbothered by them. Sorin just rolled his eyes, turning Khouri onto his stomach. Leave it to the Drow to enjoy pain and bloodshed even during something like sex. "And I don't like that judgemental look of yours," Khouri muttered, dutifully lifting his ass as he made himself comfortable on his folded arms. "Don't act like you know better than me. I'm a lot older than you."

Well, he was probably right about that. Sorin didn't know

many Drow, but he knew plenty of Elves, and if the two were anything alike in that regard, then Khouri was probably twice Sorin's palty forty years, if not three times that. But Khouri didn't look it, Sorin mused, trailing an appreciative hand down the Drow's smooth, full ass. Khouri looked no older than twenty, and with a body as beautiful as his, Sorin could keep his mouth shut and take what he was given. If Khouri wanted to defend some violent, biting lover, then who was he to say otherwise? Khouri was an adult, and Sorin wasn't in the business of caring.

A cursory touch told him that Khouri was tight. Too tight to proceed recklessly. "Have you got oil in that bag of yours?" Sorin grunted, entertaining himself by tracing his thumb over the Drow's entrance, eliciting shiver after shiver from him.

"Yes," Khouri gasped, throwing out his hand to snag the strap of his satchel. He dragged it over and rooted around inside, pulling the small bottle free and tossing it blindly back at Sorin. "Don't waste it all," he muttered, burying his face in his arms. "It was a gift."

If Khouri kept bringing up his lover, his Drow lover who apparently was also *extremely* rich given the quality of the oil, Sorin might just lose his patience. He poured a considerable amount onto his fingers and down the cleft of Khouri's ass, using more than he needed but not quite all of it. "Stop thinking about him when you're with me," Sorin ordered, dipping his fingers inside without warning or preamble. Insult to his pride aside, if Khouri was running from his lover, thinking about him at a time like this wouldn't help anything. Sorin leaned over Khouri's back, pinning him down with his bulk. "I'm going to fuck you blind for getting me caught up in that bar fight. The least you can do is pay attention as I do it."

He felt more than heard Khouri's answering laugh. "Still hard up about that?" It came in a breathless keen, his shoulders shaking from the effort of trying to support both his and Sorin's weight. Sorin slipped inside another finger and Khouri yelped, eyes closed tight in concentration. "Fair enough," he managed, fucking himself back onto Sorin's fingers eagerly. "Fair enough."

Though his voice was cracking around the edges, Khouri took the intrusion beautifully. Sorin could feel how his muscles clenched and loosened around his fingers, riding them with all the confidence of one more than accustomed to being pleasured this way. It wasn't that surprising, given his talk of his Drow lover, but Sorin couldn't help but be in awe. Sorin hadn't fucked many men, but he could already tell that Khouri relished in this side of the act, his every movement geared towards submission.

"You really want me to fuck you, don't you?" Sorin breathed, crooking his fingers and prodding the spot inside Khouri that nearly sent him to the ground. His spine went ramrod straight, his long, slender limbs quaking with need. "Is that what you like? Being fucked raw by someone bigger than you?"

Khouri spread his thighs and whined. "Gods, yes," he moaned, his voice echoing off the cave walls, reverberating deep in Sorin's bones. "I want it. Be rough with me. Make it hurt."

Sorin swallowed, slowing his hand. With his free one, he yanked at his trousers, freeing himself as Khouri thrust abortively for more. He had never fucked a masochist before, and he wasn't sure if he was very interested in indulging Khouri in that kind of play. "Calm down," he murmured, removing his fingers entirely to coat himself in the oil. Whatever it was, it filled the cave with the heady scent of sex and pomegranates, mingling with the already rich scent of Khouri's skin. "I'm not going to hurt you like Navidae, if that's what you're wanting of me."

For a moment, Khouri stilled his desperate bid for more. Turning his head, he looked back at Sorin, his eyes dark and hazy. "I don't want you to mark me," he panted, his lips swollen from his worrying teeth. "That's not for you to do. I just want to hurt a little."

Lining himself up, Sorin rubbed the blunt head of his cock against the Drow's soft, slick entrance. In the glowing light of the fire, his skin glistened wetly, the puckered hole beckoning him inside as good as a pleading beg. "You'll get what I give you," Sorin said lowly, gripping Khouri's narrow hip to hold him in place, feeding him an inch and nothing more. Khouri bowed his head and choked, his cock dripping between his shaking thighs. "Don't get greedy now, brat. Not unless you want me to stop."

Khouri stiffened and looked back at Sorin desperately, pupils blown wide and locks of hair sticking to his sweaty face. "Please," he begged softly, biting his bottom lip when Sorin rewarded him with another inch. His eyes slid shut, his cheeks flushed dark.

One look was all it took for Sorin to bury himself to the hilt without another word. The rumors couldn't hold a candle to this. Sorin groaned and was moving before Khouri had a chance to catch his breath. Everything about the Drow pulled him in, dragging him forward to fuck into the tight, burning heat like a man who would die without it. Khouri took him beautifully too, spreading his thighs wide and rolling his hips, sincere in his wish for Sorin to hurt him, to own him, to make him cum in the dirt like a whore.

Whoever Khouri's lover was or had been, Sorin had to pity him. What a shame it must be to lose such a perfect fuck like this.

"Sorin," Khouri moaned, clawing at the cloak beneath him desperately. His shoulders trembled and he looked back with wet eyes, his expression so lewd that it made Sorin sweat. "Harder. Please."

Sorin swore and braced his knees, leaning over Khouri to mount him properly. They had only just begun, and already, he felt winded. He drew back his hips and thrust inside in sharp, quick motions, dragging Khouri back to meet him by the hips. Khouri's cries rose louder, rolling against the stone cave, filling the night air with his sweet voice. God, but it sounded good.

Khouri hadn't been lying when he had said he hadn't done this in a while. He was tight, clamping down around Sorin like a vice despite the oil and prep. If he were in any pain he didn't show it, or at least, he didn't complain about it. Khouri rolled back to meet every thrust he gave, delighting in all he felt. He spread his thighs wider, rested himself on his forearms to lift his ass higher for Sorin; Khouri knew what he liked and how to get it, and he didn't mind being used a little to get what he wanted.

God, and if that wasn't a heady thought. When was the last time Sorin had fucked someone so submissive? Ages, if he had ever to begin with.

It wasn't enough just to hear him and touch him. Sorin needed to see his face as he came apart. He gripped Khouri's hips tight enough to bruise and pulled out, ignoring Khouri's bereft cry as he shoved the Drow onto his side, lifting up a slender thigh and burying himself once again in the tight, wet heat. "Let me see your face," Sorin all but growled, the thrusts turning brutal as he neared his end.

The Drow looked at him, beholden to him no matter what he asked of him. Khouri looped his hands around Sorin's neck, bending himself in two as he dug his sharp nails into the meat of Sorin's shoulders. "H-Harder," he urged, scratching harder, the burn driving Sorin faster. "I'm so full. Gods, Sorin. So good. Please."

If Sorin fucked him any harder, they were liable to dent the stone beneath them. He grabbed Khouri's wrists and dragged him back down, pinning his hands above his head. "You'll take what I give you," he said, loving how his voice alone seemed enough to make Khouri shiver and shake. "Don't get greedy. You aren't in control here."

The words elicited another moan. The Drow tossed his head back and bared his throat, submitting like a well-trained pet to his touch. Sorin let go of his hands knowing they weren't likely to try scratching again and instead took up Khouri's hips, giving him every last ounce of strength he had left to give. Khouri scrambled at the slick fur of his mantle, at the stone above his head, his cock weeping when he found nothing to hold onto. Sorin wanted to watch him cum. He needed to see what Khouri looked like when drunk on his cock.

"I'm... I'm-" Khouri couldn't seem to get the words out, every breath he took punched out of him in the next moment from Sorin's punishing pace. His hands trembled, burying themselves in the fur above his head, his eyes staring but not seeing. "S-Sorin, I'm—"

"Do it," Sorin ordered, his voice low, rumbling through his chest as he drank in the sight beneath him. "Do it. Cum all over yourself. Cum like the filthy little toy you are."

Khouri closed his eyes tightly, his knuckles whitening as he clenched the mantle hard enough to nearly rip it. His lips parted, and he choked on a moan, his entire body trembling as he toppled over the edge. Cum coated his stomach and his chest, his muscles going tight like a vice around Sorin's cock.

The sight alone was nearly enough to send Sorin over. When Khouri opened his eyes, staring up at him in utter rapture, Sorin couldn't hold on, no matter how hard he tried. He pumped his hips in a frantic, broken rush, spilling inside the Drow with a low groan. He fucked himself through the white bliss, only stopping when Khouri began to whine and fidget in discomfort.

Sorin opened eyes he hadn't realized he had closed, taking in the beautiful Drow and the mess he had made of him. Khouri had his hands over his eyes, struggling to catch his breath. A thin sheen of sweat coated his body, his belly awash in release. Sorin bit his lip as he pulled out, wincing at the unpleasant feeling. With the frantic haze gone, a pronounced ache began to take root in his joints, his knees creaking painfully as he sat back on his haunches. There were several reasons why he didn't bother pursuing bed partners much these days, and this was definitely one of them.

"Are you okay?" he asked after he had managed to catch his breath a bit, shucking his trousers completely to avoid the mess covering Khouri's skin. "It makes me nervous when you're not talking incessantly."

There was a moment of silence and then a wrecked laugh. "Wow," Khouri gasped, splayed out on the mantle in an

81

uncoordinated heap. His cheeks were flushed violet, his hand shaking as he wiped at his brow. A smile split his lips, and he stared at Sorin with a look of utter glee. "I've never had a human before, so you certainly set a low bar high."

It was meant to be a compliment, and Sorin decided to take it as one instead of hearing it for the insult lying just beneath the surface. "Thanks," he said, falling down onto the mantle beside Khouri, muscles sore and hot. It had been awhile since he had gotten so wound up. "You sure don't hold back, do you?" he winced, feeling the scratches tug and sting across his back. "Are you always like that?"

Khouri hummed, rolling onto his side to trail kisses along Sorin's bicep. His lips were soft, his fingers even softer as they settled on his chest, playing gently with his chest hair as if he had never before seen the like. "Did you not like it?" he whispered, looking at Sorin through his thick lashes. "Navi never complained."

"I'm not complaining," Sorin frowned, narrowing his eyes at the mention of the spurned lover. There was a time and place, and neither were found while Sorin was still shaking off an afterglow. Certainly not when Khouri still bore the imprints of Sorin's fingers along his hips and wrists.

"Oh, I see," Khouri murmured, leaning in for a teasing kiss. "You just can't handle me. It's okay. I'm hard to satisfy. Navi would fuck me every day just to keep me sated."

"Now you're just trying to make me angry." Sorin took Khouri by the wrist, tugging him closer so the cheeky brat couldn't run away. Though, given how hard he had just been fucked, Sorin doubted Khouri would be walking, let alone running anytime soon.

Khouri leaned in and kissed his nose then his cheek. "Maybe just a little," he chuckled, inching even closer, slipping his bare leg between Sorin's to roll on top of him. "It has been awhile though, and maybe I got a little excited. I'm not used to going untouched for so long."

That sounded like a downright shame to Sorin, even if the thought of someone else seeing and tasting and touching Khouri like that sent a stab of envy through his chest. Something that erotic shouldn't be given to just anyone. Even now, Khouri was gorgeous; the firelight glistened in his shiny, dark hair and along his svelte form.

"Why are you smiling so much?" Sorin asked, giving in to the urge to stroke his knuckles along the line of Khouri's spine. His skin was so soft, and Khouri leaned into the touches like the most affectionate pet. "Fucking couldn't have put you in that good of a mood."

Stretching, the Drow smiled all the wider. "Oh, I don't know about that. You did do such a good job. It's been so long, after all. I missed it something awful." Khouri folded himself along Sorin's body, his bare toes brushing against his calf as his cheek nuzzled his chest. "I think we're going to have a great partnership if that's how you fuck every time," the Drow purred, smiling at Sorin.

"We're not partners, and we're not doing that again," Sorin said, frowning when Khouri's smile just got bigger. "I'm serious. That was a one-time thing. I don't fuck clients."

"You fucked this one," Khouri grinned, propping himself up on Sorin's chest with his crossed arms, looming over Sorin's lips like a cat waiting to pounce. "You fucked me so roughly too. You..." He trailed off, rolling the words against Sorin's ear like a lewd promise, his voice a moan. "You *marked* me, Sorin. I told you not to, and you just came inside me instead."

"It's… It's not like I scarred you," Sorin murmured, beginning to sweat, his over-tired body trying valiantly to heat back up.

"And yet here I am," Khouri teased, lapping at Sorin's ear, dragging his sharp fanged teeth along the lobe. "Dripping with your claim."

"That's not…" Sorin tried to speak, tried to argue, but he found himself distracted by a kiss. His hands fell to Khouri's hips as he melted into the Drow's lips, the fight leaving him just like that. Dangerous. It was dangerous to let Khouri get so close to him like this. Unprofessional, sloppy, a conflict of interests–

"Oh," Khouri breathed, speaking against Sorin's tingling lips, his soft hand wrapping around Sorin's hardening cock. "It looks like you agree."

Sorin wanted to argue. He wanted to insist on profession-alism, on some degree of separation, but then Khouri let out a sweet, needy little mewl in his ear, and Sorin's worries stuttered to an abrupt stop. What was the harm, he reasoned, rolling Khouri back onto his back and nipping at the Drow's enticing ear. Didn't he deserve a little release now and then?

So long as Sorin pretended it was his own idea, he could put up with another few rounds. Just until the storm let up. Then he would go back to how it had been before.

Chapter Four

The cave was far behind them by the time they neared the town Khouri had picked out. The days and nights were since filled with this new development between them. Every night was spent in something a right side better than arguing, and every morning in something tamer but only just. They weren't fighting as much now, which Sorin had to think was a good thing, but when the afterglow faded and reality set back in, nothing much had changed. Khouri was still a brat, and Sorin spent more time than he would like to admit keeping the Drow from doing something stupid.

Sorin just wished Khouri would stop being so... so...

"What do you mean I can't come with you?" Khouri demanded, crossing his arms and glaring up at Sorin, blocking the man from moving forward. "I helped with those bounties. That money is mine too, so why should you be the only one to spend it?"

Sorin frowned. Bratty. That was the word. He used it so much because there really wasn't a better way to describe Khouri's unique brand of obstinance. He listened up to a certain point and then willfully ignored Sorin's orders. For as much as the Drow argued that he wasn't nobility, he sure seemed to act as if he were owed that much consideration.

Sorin sighed, taking a step closer to loom over the small Drow. At least he still had that over Khouri, their height difference granting him some measure of influence. He wished it would grant him more. He towered over the Drow by a full foot, and it did little but make Khouri crane his neck when he pouted. "I told you already," he repeated, willing Khouri to back down. "You can't go into a town looking the way you do. No one would sell to us, and we'd be going without supplies if that happened. You want to eat, don't you? So just stay here and let me go do what needs to be done."

Khouri narrowed his dark eyes. Sorin had hoped sleeping with the brat would have won him some control or even just some measure of trust, but for as submissive as Khouri was, he certainly seemed to save that for the bedroom alone. "If food was all we needed, we could hunt," he said shrewdly, refusing to balk as Sorin grew closer. "You left me behind once already. If you make a habit of it, how are you earning your pay from me?"

"You paid me to keep you safe–"

"I paid you to *accompany* me," Khouri cut in, his hands coming down to his sides as he glared upwards at Sorin. "You leaving me behind in the forest isn't that."

Sorin let out a low sigh, too tired to be getting into this again. "It is when the alternative is taking you into a village of humans and who knows what else and expecting them to stay their blades the moment they catch sight of you," he growled. "Keeping you safe means getting food for us no matter what. I'll tie you to a tree if I have to, Khouri. You're not coming into town with me."

Khouri glared hotly at Sorin but, after a beat, wilted and looked away. "Fine," he grumbled, dropping to his knees to dig through his bag. "Fine, fine, go off without me. I'll get my own work done while you do yours, then."

As he spoke, he pulled out vial after vial, bottle after bottle, all filled with some manner of dried herb, insect, or liquid. Sorin took a half-step back. He wasn't the best with herbology, but he could identify enough to know that what Khouri held in his hands were poisons. "What... Have you been carrying all that around with you?" Sorin demanded, thinking of how close that bag had been to his head as he slept. Horror filled him soon after when he recalled the blind grab Khouri had made for the oil. How close had they come to using something other than oil?

Humming, Khouri peered at his various bottles with no sign of sensing Sorin's distress, pulling out a leather bound book and a pen. "Are you regretting digging through here that first night? Perhaps that will teach you to keep your hands off other people's belongings." He opened it to a random page and began to write, scrawling words in a looping script with his lip caught between his teeth. "Pick me up these," he said, tearing the page from the book, handing it up to Sorin. "The amounts are on there. Take it out of my portion of the bounty."

Sorin took it in hand and read the words quickly, eyes growing wide. Belladonna, amanitas, hemlock... "What do you plan on doing with these?" he asked, looking down to find Khouri sitting with his legs crossed, vials balanced on his knees as he pulled a mortar and pestle from his bag.

"Use your imagination, Sorin," Khouri sighed, glancing up at him tiredly. "You have your work, and I have mine. Or well, I have my hobby. Never got to do much with it before when I was with Navidae. He thought it unbecoming to play with poisons in the house."

For once, Sorin had to agree with Navidae. "Is that safe?" he asked, taking another step back as Khouri opened a jar of oleander, mixing it with some black, speckled beads that upon closer inspection turned out to be some sort of dried beetle. Khouri took up his mortar and pestle and began to mash them together, forming a thick paste.

Khouri chuckled as he worked. "Not to whoever tastes it," he said, giving Sorin a cheeky smile. "But don't worry about me. I'm immune."

"Immune?" Sorin said in disbelief. "Really. To all of that?"

Khouri nodded, carefully balancing the stone bowl on his knee as he reached for a vial of something purple and vaguely viscous. "Well, most things. Definitely most toxins. Paralytics not so much since those are more dangerous to immunize yourself against alone. If you take even a hair too much, you could suffocate, and there would be nothing you could do about it." He furrowed his brow at the thought. "I'm the first to admit to playing fast and loose with my safety, but even I have my limits."

He looked up at Sorin then, smiling. "But don't worry. None of what I'm doing today is capable of harming me."

For some reason, none of that gave much comfort to Sorin. Khouri noticed.

"If you're really worried," he said, smile angelic, "you could always let me come along into town."

Sorin frowned, shouldering his bag higher. "Absolutely not," he grunted, looking off through the trees. If Khouri ended up killing himself by playing with his poisons, that would be one less problem for Sorin to deal with. "Don't move from this spot. I'll be back in a few hours."

"Oh, don't worry about me," he said, rolling his eyes. "Worry about yourself if you don't get me everything on that list. Your blanket is the tan one over here, yes? Just checking."

Pausing mid-step, Sorin looked at the smiling Drow. "You wouldn't," he said.

Khouri's glee was beatific. "Oh, wouldn't I?" he pondered, tapping at his lips with fingers that couldn't possibly be clean of poison. "Perhaps the threat will teach you to be kinder to me. Or," the Drow grinned, eyes falling to half-mast, "perhaps we could just share tonight, so long as you apologize."

Sorin made a mental note to burn his bedroll once he got back, poisoned or not. Clearing his throat, he refused to let his thoughts show. "Don't do anything stupid," he said, walking towards the smoke he could see just above the tree canopy.

"Wouldn't dream of it, Sorin," Khouri called out to his retreating back, no doubt a smile on his face as he juggled his vials of poison as if they were toys. "I save the idiocy quota for you." It was small comfort to think that the Drow knew what he was doing, but either way, Sorin needed to move before any more daylight was burnt worrying.

It didn't take long to get to the village, but Sorin could admit to the silence making it seem longer that it actually was. Without Khouri chattering in his ear, the miles stretched on and on. So when Sorin finally came to the fenced in village, he put on an extra burst of speed, eager to leave the silence of the road behind him. He wasn't in any mood to ponder when that silence had become so unwelcome.

The town at least proved a good distraction from his thoughts. The main square was alive with activity, the early afternoon bringing with it a sense of productivity that Sorin found contagious. There wasn't time to be moping or gloomy. He had a list of things to get and an ornery Drow to return to, and he knew that the longer he lingered, the greater the risk there was of Khouri setting fire to the forest or poisoning himself.

It took only a few minutes to find a store that probably sold the things on Khouri's list. One of the perks of a larger, well-stocked town, Sorin supposed. He kept it in mind as he went towards the town's bounty board, taking in the broadsheets with drawings, descriptions, and rewards along its front. There didn't seem to be many takers around here, so Sorin helped himself to the sheets. He tore them down, folded them up, and tucked them all into his pack for later. Not much competition in this area for once.

Hopefully, they would be able to find all of the marks without issue. It would be nice to have that much money to burn. Good insurance in case Khouri ended up causing another bar fight, and Sorin needed to smooth things over with some locals.

The thought alone made him smile. Turning away from the bounty board, he looked for the apothecary he saw walking in. It wasn't likely he'd let Khouri goad him into taking him into a town, but it was reassuring to know they would be able to afford it should it happen. But, that was a long way off. They still needed to find the marks first, and for that to happen, they would need supplies.

The store was empty when Sorin walked inside or as good as. The only other occupants were the shopkeeper and a couple milling customers, who looked like they were just finishing up their own errands. Sorin brushed past them and headed towards the counter, glancing around at the wares on the walls and counters. He wasn't used to coming into apothecaries, not for anything other than health draughts or the odd herb here and there. He tried to look like he was well-versed though when the vendor gave him a once over. Sorin could tell with just a look that the man would overcharge him if he smelled even the slightest weakness in Sorin's herbology knowledge.

"Afternoon," the man greeted, his voice a bit rough but still hospitable. "What can I do you for?"

Sorin pretended to look around with a discerning eye for a moment. "I've a list of ingredients I need," he said, meeting the man's eye evenly. He pulled out Khouri's list and handed it off, keeping his expression steady even as the vendor's eyes went wide from the poisons he was asking for. "And I also need a few other things too. Standard provisions, whatever's freshest. Price doesn't matter."

The vendor swallowed a bit nervously, eyeing the list and then Sorin. "Of course, sir," he said, his tone far more polite now. "Will there be anything else?"

Blinking slowly, Sorin took another look around, this time actually seeing what the man had. Dried bundles of herbs hung from the ceiling interspersed with sacks filled with nuts, berries, and even bones waiting to be ground up for spellwork. The shelves were laden with all sorts of apparati for potion making, an entire section filled with tiny glass bottles boasting ingredients, completed potions, and empty vials waiting to be filled.

"What all have you got over there?" he asked cocking his head towards the potions. It had been awhile since he'd last stocked up, but it always did make a job easier when he dosed a bounty with sleeping draught during the final transit. Especially when traveling with Khouri, too. If a mark ever got loose while Sorin slept, it could be bad.

The vendor set down the list and walked over towards the shelves, pointing them out as he spoke. "Pretty much any sort

91

of potion you could need," he began, tapping a dull nail on the vials as he counted down the rows. "Healing, spell boosters, plague cures, disease cures, sleeping draughts…" He paused, taking a breath, smiling through his windedness. "You get the idea. If it's not here, I can probably make it within a few days."

Sorin hummed, taking in the numerous vials. "I'll take six of the sleeping draughts, three health ones, and…" he trailed off, eyes catching on a small vial off to the side in a line of potions that seemed to glow in the meager light. "What are those?" he asked, gesturing towards them. They were a bright pink, shining like gems more than liquid.

The man paused in gathering up the specified potions, looking over to where Sorin pointed. He smiled toothily, giving Sorin a look. "Oh, those just came in. Elven-made, even. Guaranteed to give you the best night of your life. For you and your, ahem, special someone, if you catch my drift, sir."

Realization flooded Sorin, and he had to hold back on the urge to smile too. Oh. "Well, I can't argue with a guarantee," he chuckled, lifting a hand, two fingers up. "I'll take a couple of those too. Whichever is best." Sorin could see it now: Khouri laid out on his cloak, naked and flushed and crying from the force of his pleasure. The pink would look good against his dark skin, and Sorin did need to make it up to him for leaving him behind in the woods. Sorin couldn't imagine a better way to make amends than to treat the Drow to the best night of his life, even if it were made possible through Elven means.

"Good taste, sir," the man said, his previous discomfort eased in the light of Sorin's mirth. "I'll get all of this together for you. It'll be a few minutes."

"I'm saying he saw it!" someone insisted behind Sorin, the voice soft and easily ignorable.

"Alright," Sorin said, leaning on the counter to wait. He was confident now that he wouldn't be taken advantage of, but he still had to wonder how much they were spending on frivolities. Sorin wasn't accustomed to traveling any way besides light, and he rarely allowed himself to splurge on novelties like Elven-made oil. One of the pitfalls of traveling with a gorgeous companion, he supposed, smiling a little despite himself.

"And *I'm* saying," a smarmy voice said, cutting through the quiet of the store, "that no Drow can just traipse around the surface in broad daylight! What you heard is patently wrong, and I won't stand to hear you spit such nonsense."

Sorin's ears pricked immediately. He looked away from the vendor already fumbling away to the back storerooms to find the source of the chatter, his eyes falling on a few browsing customers off to the side.

They must have come in while Sorin was haggling since he didn't recognize them from before. A Gnome stood beside her companion, waving her hands as she spoke. The Elf stood far, far taller than her, but their ears were as keen as they were long, hearing every word despite the distance between them. They both stood before a wall of herbs, the Elf barely paying attention as they plucked herbs from the bundles with a confidence that smacked of witch.

Normally, Sorin avoided gossip like the plague, but that was far too close to home to be ignored. Whatever gossip they had heard, if it involved a Drow, it involved Sorin.

Sorin crossed the shop in a few strides, smiling tightly at

them. "Excuse me," he said, hoping he sounded more pleasant than he usually did. "Did I hear you mention something about a Drow?"

The Elf's expression fell as if they had just smelled something foul. "Why?" they asked, raising a pale blond brow. "Have you seen the detestable thing, too? Great, another lout with broken eyes professing he's seen the impossible."

"No, I haven't seen anything," Sorin rushed, shaking his head. "I'm just a bounty hunter by trade, so talk of a Drow aboveground tends to mean business for me."

The Elf softened their expression a little at that, but the upturned nose seemed to be ever-present with them. "Oh," they said haughtily. "Well. Perhaps you could expect work then, if it were a real Drow."

"It *is* a real Drow!" the Gnome cried out, her hands balled up into fists at her side. "I heard it from Jaen! He works with the sentries, so he would know!"

The Elf let out a long, put upon sigh and looked down at their companion. "Did Jaen see it himself, or did he hear about it?" they asked, glancing up and meeting Sorin's eye as if to say *Look what idiocy I have to suffer.*

The Gnome flushed red at that. "He... Well, no, okay, he didn't see it himself," she admitted, gesticulating, "but he heard it from *another* sentry who heard it from one of the patrol guards!"

"Who in turn heard it from, what, a prisoner?" the Elf guessed, tossing their hand up elegantly to make their point for them. "I've heard all about that bandit they apprehended, dear Nicau. Spitting tales of some Drow who slaughtered his men and led to his arrest."

Sorin went pale. Given the dark complexions of the two in front of him, he hoped they wouldn't notice. "Bandit?" he asked, a weight in his gut telling him it was the same one from before.

"Yes, obviously one who is angry and embarrassed at his arrest and decided to spread false rumors to lessen the blow to his ego," the Elf reasoned.

"What makes you so sure, 'Tsylk?" Nicau demanded, crossing her arms. "Since when are you such an expert on the matter?"

"Because," 'Tsylk sighed, "I know well enough that Drow can't function on the surface during the day."

Sorin paused at that. "What do you mean they can't function?" he asked. Khouri had never shown any discomfort or sign of struggling at all, no matter what time of day it might be. "I've never heard anything about that."

'Tsylk looked ecstatic to have two ignorant people before them. They clapped their long hands together, smiling with glee. "Oh, you don't know either? Well, I suppose it can't be helped." Just a glance down told Sorin that Nicau wasn't in the mood at all for this. It was just a shame that 'Tsylk didn't seem to care. "You see," they continued, "Drow, scum of the earth as they are, can't function aboveground because they simply aren't built for it. They scuttle around beneath the surface like moles and insects; their eyes are keen to the darkness. Up above, they can't see a thing when blinded by the sun."

Now that the Elf said it, Sorin could see how it made sense. Or it did up until he applied it to Khouri. "Can they get used to the sun?" he asked, recalling that Khouri had been above for only a few months at most. "How do you know that Drow hadn't been here for awhile?"

'Tsylk furrowed their brow, wrinkling their long nose. "That would take years," they said flatly, lip curling in distaste. "Decades, perhaps, and it would not be a pleasant experience to get accustomed to. No Drow could go so long without being slaughtered, even if it were possible. There's no such thing as a Drow keeping a low profile."

There was silence as Nicau glowered at the floor, Sorin too stunned to find any retort. An Elf would know, wouldn't they? Sorin knew about Drow in passing, but Elves had been at war with them for centuries, so it would stand to reason that 'Tsylk would know of their weaknesses.

"What if it wasn't a full Drow?" Nicau posed after another moment of quiet, her brow furrowed as she tried still to win the argument. "What if it were half or a quarter? It's not like any of us would know the difference."

'Tsylk grimaced. "What a disgusting idea," they remarked, the earthy brown of their skin tinging green. "Any abomination like that would be hard-pressed to live longer than its full-blooded kin."

"But could they still see?" Sorin pressed, wondering why he cared to know so much.

Shrugging, 'Tsylk's look soured. "I suppose they might be able to," he muttered, hating having to concede an inch. "Half-breeds aren't common. The Drow tend to eat their weak offspring rather than suffer it to live and bring shame. The odds of that bandit having seen and been trounced by a half-breed are even slimmer than the chance of it being a true

Drow."

It was enough for Nicau, though. She grinned and punched the air in victory. "But it *is* possible!" she crowed. "That means there's no way for you to disprove it! Half is still Drow enough to me, so it counts!"

As much as he agreed with her, Sorin couldn't let them go around telling tales of Drow or half-Drow or any combination of the two. He cleared his throat and shook his head, gesturing to 'Tsylk. "I have to agree with them, actually," he said, ignoring how the pretentious Elf preened. "The chance of it being less than full Drow is miniscule. The bandit probably was trying to save face. You know how they get. The higher the bounty on them, the more they blame others when they get caught."

"Thank you," the Elf said pointedly, looking up at the ceiling. "Finally, someone speaks sense."

"I wouldn't go around spreading more rumors like that," Sorin said to Nicau, suffering her glare in silence. "It'll just scare people and spread the sentries even thinner trying to police the roads for some fictional Drow."

Nicau crossed her arms. "Fine," she bit, refusing to look at either of them. "I can see I'm outnumbered here anyway."

There was a clearing of a throat behind them, and Sorin turned to see the vendor had returned, the counter now piled high with vials and pouches. "Sir, I have your order," he said, politely. "If you'd care to check that I've gotten everything?"

"Come on, Nicau," 'Tsylk huffed, forgetting Sorin easily enough. "Surely, you'll listen to reason now. Help me carry these, would you? I think it's time we joined back up with the others."

Sorin left them to their grumbling, taking in his own purchases with a keen eye. All of Khouri's things had been bottled up, sealed, and bundled in a thick cloth to keep them from coming into contact with the food Sorin had ordered. There was a slab of meat, some jerky, some bread, and a few other foodstuffs. Everything looked in order.

"How much for the lot of this?" he asked, pulling out his money pouch. The gold was heavy in his palm, shining dully in the dim room.

Taking his chin in his hand, the vendor eyed the stack in front of him. "I'd say you've got at least six gold worth of goods here, and with the herbs and potions, it'll take it up to seventeen." He glanced at Sorin as if expecting him to balk at the hefty fee.

Sorin just counted out the coins, letting them fall onto the counter in a clump. "Thanks," he said, tying his pouch back to his hip. He swung his bag off his shoulder and began to pack away the goods, making sure that the poisons were well away from the food in case something broke along the way.

"Um, if you don't mind me asking," the vendor began, cutting himself off when Sorin looked up pointedly. Swallowing, he tried again with a smile. "It's just that you don't seem like the type to need herbs. So I was just curious–"

"You were curious why I bought so much poison," Sorin finished for him, hefting the bag back onto his shoulder. It was now considerably heavier. "It's not for me. Someone I'm traveling with asked me to fetch them for him. Don't think on it."

From the look on the man's face, that was easier said than done. Sorin decided to make it easier on him by turning on his heel and leaving, exiting the shop just as the sun began to dip below the edge of the trees encircling the village. It cast a shadow along the town. Sorin let out a sigh, adjusting the strap on his shoulder. It would be nice to stop for a drink too, but he didn't trust Khouri to stay put should it grow dark.

With that thought in mind, he turned away from the taverns and smoke and back towards the forest, walking twice the speed he had used to get here for fear of what might be waiting for him back at camp. The vials in his bag clinked as he moved, and the birds overhead serenaded him on his way. The way they sang spoke of pleasant things, but Sorin knew that rain was on the way from the chill in the breeze. It carded through his hair, sending a shiver down his spine. They would need to make good time tomorrow if they wanted to outrun the storm on its way.

Running a hand through his wind-swept hair, Sorin sighed and ducked into the trees, leaving the road behind. He never used to have to think about things like this. Before if he sensed the weather about to turn, he would hole up in a town or walk all night to avoid it. But now, with a companion to worry about and the added issue of his race on top of it, things weren't quite as simple any more. It was as annoying as it was charming in a sense. It had been a long time since Sorin had been forced to be so creative while he traveled.

When Sorin entered the camp, he expected to see flames, destruction, or at the very least, Khouri laid out on the ground, dead or dying from his poisons. Instead, he found destruction of a different kind. The camp had become a mess of vials, detritus, and junk, Khouri in the epicenter balancing a vial on his knee as he scribbled something down in his notebook. His dark leather trousers were speckled with a glimmering, purple dust, his fingers white with some other powder. Sorin had no illusions that it was safe, and he kept his distance as he approached, making sure to keep up wind in case the dust felt the need to move.

"I'm back," he called out, watching Khouri jump, the vial on his knee nearly tumbling into the grass.

"Shit," Khouri swore, catching it carefully before he glared at Sorin. "A little warning next time? I thought you were going to be back later. That didn't take long at all."

Sorin rolled his eyes, cautiously approaching but keeping to the edges of the camp to work his way towards the fire. He settled the heavy pack down and began to unload the purchases. "I told you I'd only be a few hours," he said, shaking his head when he saw that even the fire was a mess from whatever Khouri had been doing. The coals were scattered across the ground, just barely staying lit. "What the hell did you get up to while I was gone?" he asked, using a stick to gather the coals back up, coaxing them back to life.

Khouri turned to face him, a pout on his face that Sorin wasn't going to fall for. "I was working," he sniffed, lifting up the vial and holding it up to the sunlight, his free hand still writing furiously. "We all have our methods."

"Well, I can tell you right now that my methods don't involve trashing the camp," Sorin grumbled, eyes narrowed as the sun caught Khouri's lovely face. He didn't so much as flinch in the sunlight, bringing the words of the Elf back to the forefront of Sorin's mind.

"I can't help it if you can't understand my genius, Sorin," Khouri huffed, glancing past his work to raise a brow at Sorin.

Sorin stared until Khouri began to fidget. The Drow's hands fumbled on the vial, and he cursed softly, letting it fall into the grass instead of trying to catch it. Smoke rose up where the spilled liquid dropped. "What is it?" Khouri bit, looking up to glare at Sorin. "Why do you keep staring at me?" He looked down at his ruined poison, kicking at the coated vial. "You made me ruin it, you ass."

"Are you full Drow?"

Khouri froze like a deer before a predator. It was clear that he hadn't expected to be asked that. "Why?" he demanded, his face blank now, giving away nothing. "What makes you ask that now?"

"I heard some things in town. It made me curious. You're born and raised beneath the earth, right? I would think the sunlight would present more of a hardship. Not to mention your coloring. A Drow with dark hair isn't a common sight, is it?" Sorin rested on his haunches, arms crossed, keeping his tone light. "I'm not trying to out you or trick you somehow. I'm just curious why you never told me before."

Khouri was silent, his every muscle tensed. Sorin kept himself relaxed, feeling as if he were staring down a wild animal liable to attack should he show any sign of antagonism. "What prompted you to ask?" he demanded quietly. "What were people saying in town? Did someone see me?"

"What? No." Sorin looked off past Khouri into the trees. "I overheard some people talking about some Drow on the loose, one that's got a bounty on their head. I figured it was just talk spread by that bandit we turned in a while back since you're the only Drow he's likely to have seen. The Elf I heard it from made mention of it being odd that some Drow was up and causing havoc during the day." He looked back at Khouri, watching the tension slowly bleed from his figure. "So, I got curious how it is you're faring so well like this."

Crossing his arms, Khouri kicked again at the grass like a child. "You're pretty dumb if you only just started to wonder about that," he muttered, reaching out a hand to poke and prod at his potions and vials. A breeze went by, carding through his silky hair. Khouri tucked a lock behind his ear, glancing back up at Sorin.

"No," Khouri said sourly, a bit of poison smudged along his cheekbone. "I'm not full Drow."

"So?" he pushed when nothing else was forthcoming. "What are you then?"

Khouri rolled his eyes. "First of all, you shouldn't ask someone *what* they are. I'm a person, Sorin, just like you."

Sorin hoisted himself back onto his feet, moving closer, the poison still coating the Drow be damned. "You know what I mean," he sighed. "Don't give me an ethics lesson, Khouri. Just answer the question. Or don't. I'm not making you tell me."

He shot Sorin a look that said otherwise. "I don't know for sure *what* I am," Khouri sighed, falling back onto the grass in a loose sprawl. He stared up at the forest canopy, looking drained. "I wasn't born in the Duskriven, but I ended up there. I look Drow enough to pass as full, even if my *coloring* is off. It set me apart which isn't always good, but Navi liked it, so there's that."

"Does Navidae know?"

Khouri rolled his eyes. "He's not the type to care about such things," he said. "Blood, status, wealth– None of it matters to him. He cares about power above everything. I'm strong enough to keep up with him, and that's what matters in the end."

Sorin hummed, curiosity pricking him like a pin. "You said you weren't born there," he led, watching Khouri's expression carefully. "Did you have parents? How did you make your way below if you hate it down there so much?"

The Drow furrowed his brow and stared up at the sky. "That was a long time ago," he sighed, closing his eyes for a moment. A breeze rolled past, mussing his silky hair. "I suppose I must have had parents; else, how would I be here? I don't know them. I don't think I ever did. Some ratfolk took me in for a bit, but I bounced around a lot once I knew enough to take care of myself. Hopped on a caravan I thought would take me somewhere good but it turned out it was heading down."

He gave a bit of a shudder then, a grimace marring his pretty features. His eyes flicked towards Sorin, a smile sitting wryly on his lips. "It's a lot easier to go down into the Duskriven than it is to leave it. I was as good as trapped and as good as dead if anyone learned what I was, so I did my best to blend in. Learned the language, learned the streets, learned how the city operated. Stole for money, but you knew that already." Khouri fell silent and looked back up at the clouds. "I didn't hate it much at first, but it got so boring after a few decades. I wonder what my parents are doing, if they're even still alive. I wonder if they think about me at all."

There wasn't much to say to that. Sorin scrambled to think of something to say, but none of the words felt right. For a moment, he focused on the ratfolk part. Really? Those creatures were far more likely to eat a foundling than take one in. The curiosity really was too much for his will power and this conversation.

Khouri let out a little laugh at whatever conflicted expression Sorin wore. "Do you think I'm part human? I really haven't been able to tell," he asked instead, this line of questioning a but less weighted.

Sorin smiled, grateful for the change in topic. "You're awfully small," he teased. "Probably part Dwarf."

"But I don't have body hair," Khouri chuckled, crossing his arms behind his head. The next look he gave Sorin was smoldering. "But you knew that already."

The day was mild, but Sorin felt himself sweat. "Gnome then." He turned away from Khouri laid out so temptingly in the grass and set to unpacking the supplies he had just bought. "I'm going to start supper. Are your poisons cleaned up, or do I need to worry about killing us both if I use the cooking pot?"

Khouri's laugh flowed like honey along the warm summer breeze. He rolled onto his side and propped his head up with a delicate hand, his smile soft and innocent. "Both of us?" he wondered, tapping at his full bottom lip. "Last I checked, I'm immune. So, I suppose it's really up to your discretion, Sorin."

"I'm going to boil a pot full of water and dump it on you if you keep up those jokes of yours, brat," Sorin grunted. He went ahead and put the pot beside the fire coals, pulling out his knife and the meat he had bought in town. "Let's see how immune you are to that."

"You're so much fun, Sorin," Khouri sighed, pushing himself off the ground and back onto his feet. "But, that does remind me. I saw a river nearby, so I'm going to go bathe while you do that. Feel free to use the stuff I picked up today. It's over near my bedroll." He snatched up his pack and waved cheekily, blowing a kiss just to make Sorin glare. "I won't be long. Try not to poison yourself on anything while I'm gone. You'd probably die before you reached me for an antidote."

Well, that was certainly comforting. Sorin glared at Khouri's retreating figure, and then when he looked back at the heating pot, he wondered if it really was safe. It certainly didn't look poisoned, but he saw the types Khouri made. A lot of them were clear, indistinguishable from water. His frown grew more pronounced.

Taking a quick look to make sure Khouri really was gone, he lifted the pot and smelled it. It smelled like tinny metal and nothing else. Sorin figured he would have to content himself with the fact that Khouri wasn't in the habit of letting food go to waste. If it really were poisoned, it would ruin Khouri's dinner and kill his cook. That would be an awful lot to lose just for the sake of a joke.

Sorin rolled his eyes and set to cutting up the meat. It had been a long day already, and it wasn't even late afternoon. Tomorrow would probably be even more draining, given the new bounties he had picked up. He would need to go over those with Khouri too while they ate. A few were more dangerous than the others they had done together, so coordination would be even more important. Sorin rolled his shoulders, putting the meat aside to wipe at his brow with the backside of his hand. He hoped Khouri could handle it.

With the meat cut, he wiped off his knife and looked around the makeshift camp. Khouri had been scavenging for his herbs and bugs, and the bag near his bedroll was filled with what Sorin hoped were all wild edibles found along the way. He got up and brought it over near the fire, digging through it for things he knew for sure were good. Some tubers, some wild carrots, a few mushrooms – Sorin would be the first to admit that Khouri knew far more about wild vegetation than him, but trust was a hard thing to give when it came to the things he was putting in his stomach. He pulled out what he knew and set the rest aside, dicing up the vegetables just as he had done to the meat. If Khouri wanted to eat the rest, he could put it in once Sorin had already eaten his fill.

With everything cut up and ready, Sorin grabbed the pot and looked for the canteen. The camp really was a mess; Khouri's things were scattered around, the purchases from town still in various piles upon the ground. He managed to spot the canteen with a bit of effort, finding it buried beneath Khouri's bedroll.

Sorin frowned the moment he picked it up. A shake revealed it to be empty but for a few stray drops, not even remotely enough to get boiling for the stew. Khouri must have used all the water to make his potion refills. Sorin sighed and rose to his feet, the canteen and the pot both in hand. There was a river nearby, the Drow had said. What a pain, especially after all the walking he had already done today.

Khouri had gone east, so Sorin set off in that direction, listening for the telltale sound of moving water. The forest was growing quiet now, the day turning to evening and the sun sinking lower in the sky. Soon the dark would come. Sorin sighed, pushing past a low hanging branch. It was going to be such a pain to cook in the dark. How far was the river? Khouri probably hadn't expected Sorin to follow, so he hadn't felt a need to give a distance.

Sorin gritted his teeth and stepped over a log, ignoring the insects buzzing around his head. The the stab of frustration echoed somewhere in his chest. Khouri's words lingered in the back of his mind from before. It was good that they were learning more about each other, right? That sort of closeness was a good thing. Khouri was always going on and on about wanting to be partners, yet Sorin couldn't shake the bitterness thick on his tongue. If Khouri wanted to be so close, then why had he kept his heritage such a secret? It didn't matter much, one way or another. Khouri could be part Orc, and Sorin's job would still be the same.

He frowned when he realized there was no contract stating that Khouri had to be upfront with him. There wasn't, but Sorin still would have liked knowing. Navidae knew and hadn't cared, so why hadn't Khouri told Sorin? Did he think he would care? Perhaps they weren't close enough for that sort of sharing, he mused. They only fucked like rabbits every night.

The sound of water cut off his thoughts before they could grow any more bitter. He shoved himself through a thick patch of bushes and came out along the river bank. The river rolled sedately by, the waters as clear as crystal and the bank empty of all signs of life. Sorin furrowed his brow when he spotted Khouri's pack in the soft sand near a tree. Where had the Drow gone?

"Khouri?" he called out, making for the water. Khouri's clothes were draped over some large rocks, drying in the sun. Maybe he had swam down the river a bit more? Sorin wasn't overly familiar of this area, but he was fairly sure there weren't any river creatures to worry about.

He sighed when nothing answered him but the birds and the river. Khouri would come back when he felt like it, he supposed. Moving towards the water, Sorin knelt beside the water's edge and began to fill the canteen first. It was hard to judge the depth here with the water so clear. If it weren't getting so late, he would consider bathing himself, too. Maybe tomorrow, he thought, stoppering up the canteen and setting it in the sand. They could stand to head out a bit late for something like that, surely.

His ruminations were cut off a moment later by a pair of hands on his shoulders, a teasing kiss against his neck, and then a rough push that sent him head first into the unexpectedly deep water. It really had been stupid to assume Khouri wasn't nearby.

It took an embarrassingly long time to find the surface and even longer for Sorin to manage to stop coughing once he had managed to breach it. Sorin found his footing on the slick rocks and moved the wet hair from his eyes, glaring up at the naked Drow gloating from the river bank.

"Come to peep on me?" Khouri laughed, his voice just heard over the sound of the churning, splashing water. He cocked his head and seemed to preen beneath Sorin's gaze, stretching luxuriously in the sun, showing off every inch of his dark, tantalizing skin. There were leaves caught in his hair, and that told Sorin well enough where Khouri had been hiding. "Can't even bathe without you trying to cop a feel. What an unscrupulous man you are, Sorin."

Sorin wondered if the severity of his glare was dulled by the sight of him drenched like a bedraggled cat caught out in a storm. He started to slosh his way towards the bank, snatching up the floating pot from where it had fallen in the river. "You *brat*," he hissed, hating that Khouri just smiled prettily at him. "You're going to pay for that."

Instead of being afraid or even apologetic, Khouri just laughed again, stepping into the water. "Oh, am I?" he wondered, the water enveloping him wantingly. Sorin paused mid-step, mouth going dry as he watched Khouri's approach. The Drow's slender hands tangled in his own hair, pushing it back as he dipped below the water, wetting it so that it lay out of his eyes. It was striking how much it changed the shape of his face, painting him as something darkly seductive and mildly dangerous more than the young, pretty creature he normally was.

It took the clearing of his throat to gather the ability to say something. Sorin tore his eyes from Khouri's chest and past the soft lip caught between sharp white teeth. He forced himself to ignore everything but Khouri's dark eyes. "Yes," he grunted, feeling hot. "Don't try to distract me. It won't work."

Khouri took a step closer, his brow raised. "Distract you?" He smiled in a way that made Sorin take a half-step back. The water was up to Sorin's hips, but he couldn't care. "Why, Sorin," he breathed, letting his hands fall to his own chest, up to his ribs. "Are you feeling distracted?"

Dangerous. This was dangerous. Sorin swallowed the urge to back up, standing his ground even as the beautiful creature drew closer. The light glinted off Khouri's silky hair, highlighting notes of blue within the black. Like a crow's feathers, they shone like ink before a fire. Khouri reached him with just a ripple of water, resting his delicate hands on Sorin's chest. It was impossible to ignore the way the sunlight caught the silver of his piercings. They were peaked from the cool water, from the chill of damp skin on a breezy day.

"What do you think you're doing?" Sorin asked, hair dripping, boots soaked, and yet unable to move for the building want growing somewhere in his loins.

"I thought I was bathing," Khouri said, batting his long lashes. Droplets of water clung to them like crystals. "But I suppose now that you're here, I'm seducing you." He lifted himself onto his toes and tugged Sorin down by his hair, bringing his soft lips just a hair's breadth from Sorin's. Breath warm, eyes half-mast, he let out a pretty little sigh before looking into Sorin's eyes. "Is it working?" he whispered, speaking the words against Sorin's lips.

Sorin dropped the pot, his hands fixing themselves to Khouri's narrow hips. "Not even slightly," he tried to growl, but it came out far lower than he had meant it to. Khouri shivered at the sound, his cheeks tinting with his blush. It was completely unfair how good the Drow looked. Sorin held onto his hips tighter, making him gasp. Entirely unfair.

"You're lying," Khouri breathed, his smile so cocky. He glanced down between their bodies, seeing for himself how hard Sorin already was through the wavering, refracting water. The outline of his cock was prominent through the wet fabric, even more so when pressed against Khouri's thigh. "It's not good to lie," Khouri chastised, reaching his hand between them to fondle Sorin.

"It's not good to be a brat to the one making your dinner," Sorin returned, a shiver running down his spine. Khouri's hand was confident in its movements, stroking along the length of him with the flat of his hand. Were they seriously doing this here? Now? Dinner was going to be late.

When Khouri saw fit to pull him from his trousers completely, all care disappeared. Khouri licked his lips and hummed, his hand wrapping around Sorin and pumping him lazily. "Is that what you're doing?" he murmured, looking up with a smile that dripped with faux innocence. "I could have sworn you were peeping."

"Why would I ever need to peep when you dress the way you do?" Sorin shook his head and sighed, the pleasure heady already. Dark fingers trailed along the head of his cock, teasing the slit. A rush of heat swelled through him, barely cooled at all by the water lapping against his body. "I needed water. You used it all with your poisons."

"Doesn't look like that's all you need," the Drow teased, letting go of Sorin to rest his hands on his shoulders. Khouri brought his lips to Sorin's ear with a yank, his breath warm and just a tickle against his skin. "You got so excited. So easily, too. What a weak man you are. I don't know if I should be flattered or pitying."

"You should finish what you started is what you should do," Sorin said tightly. He gripped Khouri tightly by the hips, lifting him up to kiss a line up Khouri's bared throat. His skin was warm, fragrant in that strange, foreign way it always was. The scent filled Sorin's head and drove him faster, rubbing himself against Khouri's naked thigh in want for the hand that wouldn't come back. His nipped Khouri's pulse point and then laved it with his tongue, loving how Khouri gasped sharply in his ear.

Laughing shakily, Khouri held tighter to Sorin's shoulders. "Why should I have to when you're the one who followed me?" he asked, already hard himself.

On instinct, Sorin wanted to make some barb about it being polite, but he held back once he remembered that little was polite about the Drow. Even if Khouri had no intention of making good on the promises his body was making, Sorin knew well enough that he could still get what he wanted. He drew his hand down Khouri's body, letting his nails scratch and cut lightly into his soft skin. Khouri moaned brokenly, drunk on the pain like the little freak he was.

"Because I'll finish it myself if you don't," Sorin said, speaking the words lowly against Khouri's pierced ear. He kissed the lobe and bit down on it gently before leaving it be. His mouth was Sorin's ultimate goal, his lips parted and so temptingly flushed just an inch from his cheek. Sorin didn't care much between kissing them or fucking them, but he wanted Khouri's mouth and he wasn't going to wait to get it.

For a moment, Khouri seemed more than willing to indulge him. His dark eyes fell to half-mast, his tongue wetting his lips in a slow, seductive pass. But at the last second, Khouri turned, Sorin's lips just brushing past his cheek. The Drow smiled, teeth sharp and shiny white. "What a foolish man you are," he laughed, looking back up at Sorin. "Kissing me? I've been playing with poisons all day. Do you really want to risk it?"

Sorin swallowed, self-preservation at an all time low when knee-deep in his lust. "You can't be serious," he murmured, still rolling his cock against Khouri's thigh. "There's no way your saliva has enough of a concentration to affect me."

Khouri hummed, leaning back in to nuzzle Sorin's cheek like a tease. "Tolerance is such a finicky thing, isn't it? Who knows how much you could handle before your body goes into shock?" He drew his lips along Sorin's cheek and up to his ear, the touch tingling. "I could kill you with a kiss. Such romance. What a shame you'd only be able to experience it once."

Sorin growled, taking Khouri by the ass and squeezing like a warning. "You're lying again, aren't you? Nothing will happen if I kiss you."

Gasping prettily, his lips wet and wanting, Khouri smiled. "Awful lot to risk if I'm not," he said, batting his dark lashes.

That was their dynamic, wasn't it? Sorin gritted his teeth and stared at Khouri's lips, trying to discern the poison from the plush, wet, inviting picture he made. This was dangerous, but Sorin felt himself already addicted. Sorin cupped Khouri's cheek and stroked across his lips with a thumb. Soft. Warm. As tempting as the ripe red of toxic fruit and just as easily plucked. Sorin dipped down and paused a hair's breadth from Khouri's lips, holding the Drow in place so he couldn't pull away again.

Khouri's lips curled into a smile.

Sorin felt himself fall all the faster.

"I've risked more for less," Sorin breathed, kissing Khouri's smile without another moment of hesitation. There were worse ways to die than this. Far, far worse. The water cooled while the kiss burned, the fervor from before building up like pressure needing to blow. Khouri wrapped himself around Sorin's body, still smiling, still laughing, still loving his little games as deadly as they may be.

And when Khouri parted his lips and moaned, Sorin knew he would be content if this were the way he fell. And if it was a lie, a true lie...

There was no better time to start building a tolerance, was there?

Chapter Five

"But Sorin," Khouri whined, tugging at the human's sleeve. "Sorin, it's going to rain tonight."

Sorin let out a growl of a sigh, making Khouri wonder if the man were part werewolf or just that beastly. "And?" he said dryly, glancing down at Khouri with pitiless eyes. "We've slept out in the rain before."

Khouri leaned even harder on Sorin's arm. "Yeah, we did because there was no town nearby," he said, digging in his heels to make Sorin stop walking. "There's one near right now! Shouldn't we be proactive? Shouldn't we take up fortune's offer when presented with a better option?" He pouted up at Sorin, hugging his thick arm to his chest to keep him in place. "Please? I don't want to spend the next week walking around with wet boots."

"Would you rather we get chased out of a town then?" Sorin asked, barely sparing him a glance. "It's smarter to make camp now and settle in for when it hits, not risk being caught with nothing just because you decided to be a brat about dry boots. Of which, I might add, I don't have already after your little river prank."

Frowning, Khouri smacked Sorin's shoulder. "I fail to see how it's bratty to want my feet to be dry for once. And you got what was coming to you. Don't act like I didn't make it up to you," he sniped, pushing off the hunter's arm to cut him off instead. Khouri planted himself in front of Sorin, standing his ground with his arms crossed. "I'm offended that you have such poor faith in me and my ability to keep a low profile. I'm not incompetent, you know. I can blend in."

The look Sorin shot him was patently unimpressed. "The Elf I spoke to informed me that there's no such thing as a Drow with a low profile." He moved to walk around Khouri, but when Khouri darted over to block him, he stopped entirely. "Would you *stop*?" he snapped, his cold blue eyes narrowing.

"Would *you*?" Khouri moved closer, craning his neck to look Sorin in the eye. "You aren't scary. Growling at me and calling me names won't make me listen to you, so stop treating me like a child. Are you really so scared of being seen with me?"

Taking pot shots at Sorin's manliness only seemed to rankle him further. "People are hunting for a Drow, Khouri," Sorin said, gesturing angrily. "Do you really think they're not going to think you're the one with the bounty?"

Rolling his eyes, Khouri grabbed Sorin by the front of his shirt and tugged him in the direction of the town. The hunter stumbled after him, caught off guard enough to be easily led. "Don't underestimate me, Sorin," Khouri murmured, glancing over his shoulder at the man. "If something happens, blame it all on me. I won't even argue with you next time you order me around. But, I'm not going to sleep outside in the rain again just because you think I can't keep a low profile." He had managed long enough without Sorin at his side, and it was insulting to think Sorin trusted him so little now. Khouri stomped off in the direction of town, ending the argument there. If Sorin thought he could boss him around, he had another thing coming.

Despite Sorin grumbling the entire way to the town, Khouri felt that the day was shaping up to be something good. The wind was picking up by the time they entered the small little village, the sky churning with black clouds that promised to open up on them at any moment. Sorin slowed Khouri by yanking on his hand, pulling him back before he could break cover from the trees. A raindrop, fat and cold, plopped onto Khouri's cheek when he looked up at the hunter. The surface really was full of wonders. So much rain and so often.

"What is it now?" Khouri asked. The rain was coming faster, falling atop his head. "Come on, Sorin. We're going to get soaked."

Sorin didn't seem to care. "This is a bad idea." Gesturing with his head, he motioned towards the inviting looking buildings behind them. A peal of thunder punctuated his words, but even then, he didn't make a move to seek shelter. "These people won't hesitate to—"

Khouri frowned. "I'm well aware of the risks, Sorin," he said slowly, hoping that this time the man might understand. "You do know that I'm accustomed to navigating your kind. What I'm not accustomed to is standing out in the rain as my partner lectures me about the pitfalls of my race. *Again*."

"I'm not trying to lecture you, and we aren't partners."

Rolling his eyes, Khouri yanked hard on his wrist, freeing himself from Sorin's overly protective grip. "Whatever," he said, ignoring Sorin's angry huffs as he made a beeline straight for the nearest tavern. It was already getting dark, the sounds of laughter and bellowing voices audible from the streets even with the storm riling up. "I'm getting a drink," Khouri called out over his shoulder, throwing his hood over his head lazily. "Feel free to come get one with me once you've learned how to have a little fun."

Sorin shouted something at his back, but Khouri didn't bother listening. He pushed through the door and into the crowded, raucous bar, the scent of warm bodies and cheap ale filling his every sense. Every table looked filled, many meandering in the aisles, standing against walls or leaning on tables as they talked and laughed and enjoyed the good company. Khouri entered without much fanfare, weaving through the crowd until he reached the bar, water sloughing off his cloak as he moved. The light was low, and almost everyone looked fairly buzzed. He doubted anyone would throw a fit at the sight of him unless he did something egregious.

Waving down the red-faced bartender, Khouri had his money on the table, placed his hands at his sides, and had a smile on his face before he tried to order. "I'll have some mead, please," he said over the thrum of the bar behind him.

The bartender didn't do much more than take up his money and grab him a mug. Or at least, he didn't at first. When he moved to slide the mug over to Khouri, he must have caught sight of his face or his skin. The mead slopped over the side of the cup when he jerked it to a stop, gaping. Khouri tried to smile carefully. Non-threateningly.

"And what do you think you're doing in here?" the barkeep hissed, giving furtive looks down the line of the bar, making sure no one else had seen him. "We don't serve your kind! Get out before you cause a riot! I can't afford to refurbish the place just because you thought it a good idea to come where decent people gather."

Well, it was better than an outwardly hostile reaction. Maybe he needed to come off as anything but a threat. Khouri pouted, batting his lashes a little. Seduction usually worked where common decency failed. "Please?" he tried, leaning forward a bit on the bar. It was hard to show off his body like this, rain-soaked and hidden in his cloak as he was, but he did his best. "It's pouring outside. I just want something to warm me up before I have to go back out for the night. Just one drink is all I'm asking. I've already paid."

The barkeep narrowed his eyes, and Khouri didn't miss how they trailed down his body, pausing on his clavicles. He drummed his fingers on the side of the mug. "Just one, you say?" he verified shrewdly. "And then it's out with you?"

"I promise," Khouri said, though he meant to do no such thing. He was going to sleep in a proper bed tonight. He didn't care how he had to go about getting it.

The mug was pushed closer to him and then drawn away before Khouri's fingertips even brushed it. "And you'll keep that cloak on mighty tight, too," the barkeep stipulated, giving another look down the bar. "And sit in the back."

Khouri rolled his eyes but was about to agree when a warm, solid mass came up behind him, leaning against his back. Khouri froze. "He'll sit with me," came Sorin's low growl, his hand fixing itself to Khouri's hip proprietarily. "And he'll have as many drinks as he wants."

A victorious grin split Khouri's lips. "Oh?" he asked, looking up to take in Sorin upside down. "And will you be paying for them?"

The hand on his hip went tight. "Don't push it, Khouri," Sorin gritted.

The barkeep was anything but entertained. "Excuse me?" he said, crossing his arms. He was a large man but not as large as Sorin no matter how hard he tried to posture. "And who are you to be making rules in my bar?"

Sorin tossed down a handful of gold. It clattered loudly enough to draw more than a few eyes, and Khouri ducked behind Sorin as carefully as he could, hoping to minimize the fallout should the bar turn on them. "The Drow sits and drinks with me," Sorin repeated, his large hand covering the mug of mead easily, dragging it back over to him.

The barkeep looked ready to pop. His face was red, more from being ordered than from the stipulations. He gathered up the gold and nodded shortly, drawing it all off the counter and into a pouch on his hip. "If there's even *one* issue, I throw you both out," he said through clenched teeth. "And I better not notice any of my china missing, *Drow*. Or there will be hell to pay."

Khouri didn't have a chance to defend himself, if he even wanted to try. Sorin took him by the shoulder and turned him around, leading him through the crowd and to an empty table. "More trouble than you're worth," Sorin muttered under his breath, but Khouri knew he didn't mean it.

"Thank you for that," he murmured, glancing up at Sorin. "Not many people would have stood up for me."

Sorin grunted. "Sit down," he said, pushing Khouri into a seat with a hand on his shoulder. Sorin slid the drinks onto the table in front of him, giving the barkeep one last glare before sitting down himself. Khouri took his mead in hand and sipped the cool liquid, warmth following every swallow. "Are you hungry?" Sorin asked, meeting his eye. "We haven't eaten yet this evening."

Khouri shook his head. He was more cold than hungry, more tired than either. It was nice to be able to sit, to drink, but Khouri would have preferred being closer to the fire. Every time the door opened, a breeze blew past, chilling him and his damp clothes until he shivered. "I'm glad for the drink," he murmured to Sorin, shifting a little closer to the man. "I just... this place still isn't very comfortable for me."

"What's wrong?" Sorin asked.

"Aside from the obvious reasons? It's chilly in here with this on," he admitted, tugging a little at his soaked cloak. They were far from the roaring hearth, and Khouri knew it would take a lot more than a few drinks to make his clothes dry and his body warm.

Sorin raised a brow. "Then, take it off." The way he said it made it sound like the obvious choice.

"I can't. If everyone sees me, they'll probably start rioting." Khouri ran his fingers along the old wood grain of the table. "You remember when we first met. That's not a rare occurrence, Sorin. I've been chased out of pretty much every bar I've ever been in up here."

A warm, heavy hand covered Khouri's on the table. He looked up at Sorin, who smiled. "You weren't with me before," he said, his other hand coming up to untie the knot at Khouri's throat.

It was probably the drink that kept Khouri from protesting the removal of his cloak. That and the reassuring warmth of Sorin against his thigh and on his hand. He leaned against the table and stretched, his skin finally able to breathe. Sorin draped his cloak over another chair, his hand falling to Khouri's bare spine, soothing and warm. Khouri could feel the stares already, but there were no screams, no shouts. He laid against the table, trusting Sorin to keep it that way.

"It's nicer now, but still. I think I'd prefer changing clothes and being away from the stares. Why don't you get us a room?" Khouri asked, leaning his head on his arm to look at Sorin, letting his exhaustion show a little through his inviting smile. "You won't make me sleep out in the rain again, will you?"

"I should, considering all the trouble you've put me through. Your idea of a low-profile is very different than mine," Sorin said, taking a drink from Khouri's half-finished mead. Khouri tugged at his wrist until he gave it back, drinking from it quickly before Sorin could finish it all. "They probably won't let me rent a room if they know you're with me. Gold got us this far, but these people do have their limits."

Khouri set his empty mug on the table, warmth blooming from his cheeks to his toes. "Really? Just because you came in here with me," he said, looking out at the bar around them. A few people were staring, a few men near the far corner looking as if they weren't quite sure what to think about him being there.

Grunting, Sorin let out a breath, looking anything but eager to leave again. "This is why I told you that you couldn't be hasty," he said, crossing his arms. "If you had just kept your face hidden, I could have figured something out. This wouldn't have been an issue if you hadn't forced me to intervene. Now, we're both going to be blacklisted."

Why Sorin cared about being blacklisted from one tavern when Khouri was barred from a dozen, Khouri didn't know. But, if it were simply a matter of them being associated with each other, there were plenty of ways around that. "Well, Sorin," Khouri said, turning back to smile at Sorin. "That's easy enough to fix. Sorry in advance."

"What-?" Sorin didn't get the chance to ask. Khouri drew

back his hand and slapped the hunter soundly across the cheek, kicking back the chair to stand up.

"I never want to see your face again!" Khouri shouted, eyes dancing as he stomped his foot. "I'm not some toy for you to play with when you get bored!" He snatched up his cloak and the nearly empty cup, throwing the remaining drink in Sorin's face for good measure. "Fuck you. I don't need this."

It was hilarious, frankly, how Sorin seemed to lock up as all eyes fell on him. He gaped and held his cheek dumbly, looking at Khouri for guidance. Khouri rolled his eyes. It really wasn't that hard to see what he was planning.

"Nothing to say for yourself?" he continued with a glower, waiting for Sorin to add to it. It wouldn't be believable if he just sat there like an idiot. Sorin's lips curled into a frown. Khouri made it work. "Fine. Be that way. I'll find someone else to buy me drinks. Someone who *appreciates* me!"

All eyes were on him, Sorin's included as he stomped off, going to the far end of the bar and throwing himself down at the end of a semi-populated table. Khouri wasn't an idiot; he gave himself a wide berth from the majority of the other patrons, keeping just close enough for any curious, brave types to gather up the courage to approach him. Sorin, meanwhile, came back to life when a napkin was held out to him, a concerned barmaid no doubt asking him if he were alright.

"I'm fine," Sorin said, Khouri reading his lips. He wiped off his face with a scowl, rising from the seat to head back over to the barkeep who looked positively gleeful that Sorin had gotten what was coming to him. Khouri left Sorin to play his part, turning back to take in the eyes on him. He'd need to play his part too if he wanted the barkeep to believe that they were no longer together.

122

Putting on his most despondent expression, Khouri laid his cloak in the seat beside him and rubbed at his arms as if on the verge of tears. It didn't matter what people thought of him, of what he was. Khouri knew the prevailing belief that went hand in hand with Drow distaste, and he knew that seducing someone was far, far easier than trying to change someone's underlying prejudice. He glimpsed through his fringe at all who were staring at him, and it only took a moment to see three men off in the corner whispering to each other, the one in the center's grin nearly luminous in the dim bar.

Khouri was quick to pretend he hadn't been watching when the man's friend shoved him towards Khouri's lonely corner. On the outside, he was near tears, but internally, Khouri was already gloating. This was going to be criminally easy.

"Hey," a low voice greeted. Khouri gave a few sniffs before lowering his hands. The man before him was tall and willowy, his long hair tied up at the base of his neck in a thick braid. "I saw what happened. Can I buy you a drink?"

Wiping at his eyes, Khouri gave him a watery smile. "Oh, that's so nice of you," he said, folding his hands in his lap. "I'm so embarrassed about all of that. Please, won't you sit with me? We could drink together."

The man blinked, and Khouri realized that this man hadn't expected him to be so polite. He recovered well, nodding his head and slipping into the seat at Khouri's side. Lifting a hand, he signalled the barmaid for two drink before looking back at the Drow. "So uh, I don't think I've ever met a Drow before. I thought you were all... a lot less..." He gestured with his hand, looking to Khouri for help.

"Kind? Well-behaved? I don't drink the blood of children if that's what you're worried about," Khouri said, laughing like it was a joke though he knew that was exactly what the man was wondering. A drink was sat down in front of him, and he drank half in one pull, needing it for this next part. He could see over the man's shoulder how Sorin argued with the barkeep, how their eyes kept darting back over to Khouri's corner. "But enough about me," Khouri said, looking back to his target. "You're so kind; I should be the one asking about you."

"Oh, well, I uh…" The man's eyes went wide when Khouri leaned forward, resting his hand on the man's chest. He rallied well, grinning lecherously. "I just can't stand to see a pretty face in distress. Especially such an uh… exotic beauty like yourself. It'd be criminal."

Khouri had to take another drink just to keep himself from grimacing. "How kind of you," he said, batting his eyes. Setting his cup back down, he leaned closer, his hand moving lower now and resting on the man's thigh. "You know, I've never been so close to a human before. You're so much warmer than I expected."

A hand settled on his shoulder, the man growing confident. "Really? Not even that asshole you came in here with?" Behind his back, Khouri could see Sorin grunting something to the barkeep, whose attention was locked solely on Khouri. He wanted proof. Khouri would give him all the proof he needed. There was no way in hell he was sleeping outside tonight.

All it took was a calculated shimmy of his hips to put Khouri in the man's lap. He let gravity do the work for him, his chin hooking over the man's shoulder, his lips right at his ear. "Not even him," Khouri whispered, smiling as the stranger wrapped his arms eagerly around Khouri. Alcohol was one hell of a liberator when it came to things like this. The man had no compunctions at all about touching him, his hands lingering under the pretense of steadying the tipsy Drow. "He couldn't handle me. He didn't deserve to have me in his arms."

The man was hard. Khouri's eyes went wide at the realization. He could feel the man's dick against his thigh as hot, sweaty hands scrambled against his naked spine. "I can get us a room," the man said in a rush, pulling Khouri back just enough to meet his eyes. "I can get us a room right now, if you'd like."

"I think I'd like that very much," Khouri smiled, kissing the man on the cheek. He paused by his ear again, letting out a breathy sigh. "I'm sure you could handle me all night long."

Khouri nearly fell to the floor with how fast the man stood. He righted himself with a laugh and shooed off the suitor towards the bar. It was comical how fast the man moved, how he quickly shoved Sorin to the side to ask for a room the barkeep wouldn't give so long as he intended to sleep with the Drow. Khouri finished off the remaining drink and watched, grinning as Sorin pushed the man to the side and asked again for the room. The barkeep threw up his hands and tossed him a key, waving him off as he dealt with the new problem. Just as predicted. Criminally easy.

He met eyes with Sorin, smiling at him with a nod. "Room seven," Sorin mouthed to him before disappearing down the hall towards the rooms. Khouri sat down the mug and grabbed up his cloak, wrapping the cold, damp fabric around himself for one last jaunt outside. With one more glance given towards his suitor, Khouri was off, ducking out the door before he could be stopped or seen.

The rain was coming down much harder now. The night

125

had fully descended, and any stars or moonlight were swallowed up in the deluge. Khouri made his way around the back of the tavern and wiped the water from his eyes, counting windows. Room seven could mean a lot of things, but if he were to hazard a guess, it was probably located on the second or third floors. He touched the rough brick exterior of the building and bit his lip. It would be smarter to go to the third and work his way down on the off chance that he met someone.

Khouri was an old hand at breaking into places, but scaling the outside of a building in the pouring rain wasn't a challenge he relished. It wouldn't be hard, but it would be unpleasant. He made quick work of the slick brick with a well-aimed rope and some gloves. He scrambled up as quickly as he could, growing wetter and wetter every second he spent outside, jammed open a window, and tumbled into the hallway on the other side. Water quickly covered the floor. Khouri cursed and rush to close the window. He left it cracked a little, hoping it might explain the wetness if someone were to walk by.

With that done, he was left trying to figure out where to go. He was in a single long hallway with a few doors along it, the far way characterized by a sharp turn that he figured led to the stairs. Khouri quietly moved down the hall, checking each door as he went. Sorin would probably be in one that was unlocked since he knew to expect company.

"Sorin?" Khouri whispered, mostly to himself but hoping that he might get lucky and be heard. In a hall like this, it was going to be impossible to hide should someone come out of a room or even up the stairs. Khouri tapped carefully at the doors and tried the handles as silently as he could. The one at the end was unlocked, but what if it belonged to someone else who had forgotten to lock it?

Indecision filled him as he stood there, dripping water and worry. If he were anyone else, perhaps he could play it off as a mistake, as losing his sense of direction, but Khouri knew that if he were found up here poking around the rooms, he and Sorin both were liable to be thrown out into the rain.

Unfortunately, fate wasn't in any mood to coddle him. Khouri startled when voices echoed up the far stairway. His heart seized, and he looked around in vain for a place to hide. Should he just go back out the window? Wait for them to pass? A draft breezed past, chilling him to the bone. He didn't want to go back out there.

The voices grew louder, and he looked at the doorknob in his hand. The one door on this floor that was unlocked. What were his chances? Were they good? Khouri swallowed and saw shadows flicker against the wall at the end of the hallway. He really didn't have time to ruminate.

Khouri closed his eyes and held his breath, twisting the knob and darting inside, closing the door as fast as he could. He pressed his back against the door and kept his eyes shut, wondering which god would take pity on him should he start praying. None of the ones he knew were the type to give good luck.

"It's about time you got here," a familiar voice grunted. Khouri opened his eyes; the relief was crippling. Sorin was laid out on the bed, staring at him like he was crazy. "How did you know which door was mine? They're not labeled."

"No thanks to you, that's how," Khouri breathed, leaning heavily against the door. If he listened hard, he could hear the sound of footsteps as they passed by outside. It had been a close call. Far too close.

"You're dripping everywhere," Sorin sighed, getting up and taking Khouri's sodden cloak from him. He hung it up near the window and grabbed a towel left beside the water basin, drying Khouri's hair roughly. "Did anyone see you?"

Khouri wrestled himself free from Sorin's fretting, taking the towel for himself to dry his face. His heart was pounding but he'd calm down soon enough now that he was safe. "No one could see anything out there, so don't worry about it," he said, looking at the room around them. It was small but cozy, warm and dry and protected from the elements raging outside. He kicked off his boots and threw down his bag, brushing past Sorin with the intent of face planting on the bed.

Sorin grabbed him by the arm before he could. "Where do you think you're going?" he asked, dragging Khouri away from the bed.

"Well, it's midnight, and I just scaled a three story building in the pouring rain. So, I figured I'd reward myself with a warm bed," Khouri replied, brow raised.

"Don't you think you have something to say to me first?"

Khouri cocked his head, beginning to shiver. He wrapped his arms around himself. "Thank you for the towel?" he tried, tugging again at the hand holding him in place.

Sorin bared his teeth. "You let that man touch you," he growled, taking a step closer to loom over Khouri. "You threw a drink in my face."

Shrugging, Khouri smiled innocently. "It got the job done, didn't it?" They had a room, and no one was the wiser. Khouri had done far more for far less in the past, so why did it matter? But, Sorin didn't seem to feel the same. He took Khouri by the arms and pushed him back, tossing him onto the bed with little more than a flare of his nostrils for warning.

Khouri hit the bed with a huff of noise. "So pushy," he complained, laying back against the sheets. They weren't particularly soft, but they smelled clean at least. This bed in general was a far cry from what he was used to, his bedmate only adding to the disparity. Khouri looked into Sorin's cool blue eyes with a smile. "You really can't keep your hands off me, can you?"

"Shut up," the human grunted, crawling up to cover Khouri with his considerable bulk.

"You can't even bear the thought of me flirting with another," Khouri laughed, letting Sorin seize his hands in his much, much bigger ones. This certainly felt familiar. A shiver of anticipation licked up his spine, warm and tingly. "Don't you know, Sorin? You're the only human for me."

Sorin stared down at him for a moment, expression hard. Khouri didn't let it bother him. He knew Sorin well enough at this point to know that the man's default was typically more hostile than he intended it to be. "The only *human*?" he grunted, squeezing Khouri's wrists tightly.

Khouri smiled cheekily, licking his lips and laughing when Sorin's eyes followed. "Why, naturally," he teased, watching Sorin bring a hand down his chest to run his fingers over his ribs. "I do have a lover still. But you're different," he purred, closing his eyes as the fingers slowly stroked his skin. "I don't think I could ever find another human as good as you."

Sorin grunted. "Is that what I am to you, then?" His hand slipped beneath Khouri's cropped shirt, a warm thumb rolling over his pierced, peaked nipple teasingly. It sent another thrill of need through Khouri, reminding him so much of how Navidae would play with him. "Some sort of pet? A distraction? Someone to take care of you while you run from your lover?"

It was funny how Sorin wanted to define their relationship with his hand already up Khouri's shirt, but who was Khouri to judge? They certainly weren't the types to do things formally, if what they shared was something that could ever be described as formal. "You're..." he began, cutting himself off with a muted moan as Sorin jerked up his shirt and took his nipple into his mouth. He was going to warm up quickly if they kept on like this. "Ah, you're so much fun, Sorin. Why ruin it with labels?"

Khouri couldn't hold back his keen when Sorin took the piercing between his teeth and tugged harshly as punishment. He fisted the sheets and arched against Sorin's body, grasping weakly at the hand still holding him to the bed. As hard as it was, it still wouldn't mark. "Did I make you mad?" Khouri gasped, toes curling when the teeth eased up, Sorin's tongue soothing the sting with gentle licks. "You're never rough with me, no matter how much I beg you to hurt me."

Sorin's cool breath chilled Khouri's damp skin as he sighed. His cold blue eyes met Khouri's, pinning him in place better than his hands alone could. "I forgot how you like that sort of treatment," the human scoffed, glaring at Khouri's neck. No, not his neck, Khouri corrected. At the marks showcased by his rumpled shirt. "You're such a brat. How am I supposed to punish you when you like pain?"

Well, there were plenty of ways so long as Sorin was willing to get creative. Khouri's cheeks grew hot at the thought. "Navi would—"

"Don't," Sorin cut in, sealing their lips together before Khouri could manage to finish his thought.

The kiss was deep, probing, Sorin keeping his eyes open to stare into Khouri's with a dominance that had him shaking. Khouri parted his lips without needing prompted, moaning as Sorin took over entirely. It was what Sorin did best, wasn't it? He never shied away from putting Khouri in his place, from taking what he wanted when he knew Khouri would let him. He kissed how he lived—without quarter and with great, great patience. Nothing at all like Navidae but just as effective.

Khouri closed his eyes and surrendered to it all. His hands went limp beneath Sorin's hold, and after another minute of devouring, engulfing kisses, Sorin pulled back, a strand of saliva connecting their lips. "I won't have you thinking of him when you're with me," Sorin delivered, his piercing eyes making Khouri feel so small. How did the man not even sound winded? Khouri felt on the verge of melting, but Sorin hardly looked warm.

"Do you understand me?" he asked when Khouri failed to respond. Khouri nodded, gasping for the breath he couldn't catch. "Good," Sorin growled, letting go of his hands to begin undressing Khouri properly. "I think I've found a way to punish you."

If that was intended to make Khouri nervous, it did the exact opposite. Excitement filled him in a warm wave, pooling in his stomach until he could barely sit still while he was undressed. Tight leather and worn cotton parted from his body reluctantly, fluttering to the floor with a whisper barely heard. Khouri tugged on Sorin's shoulders, whining softly until Sorin took the hint to remove his shirt as well. "What are you going to do to me?" he breathed, staring up at the man and all of his thick muscles, Khouri's hands so dark against the white of the human's skin. He bit his lip and looked at Sorin through his lashes, praying he might finally get those muscles to treat him the way he had been craving since he left the Duskriven.

Instead of answering him, Sorin raised a brow and brought his hands to his belt, coaxing it through his belt loops slowly. "Put your hands above your head," he said lowly, and Khouri rushed to comply, grabbing onto the worn wooden headboard eagerly. Khouri's head was spinning already at the thought of being bound, of having the thick leather wrapped around his wrists and bruising him as he struggled beneath Sorin's bulk. It had been so long since he had last had that. Too long.

"You really are so well-trained," Sorin remarked, coiling the belt around Khouri's wrists and then through the slats in the headboard.

"Maybe I just know what I like," Khouri breathed, testing the tightness once Sorin was done. For a man who claimed to be unused to this sort of thing, Sorin certainly did know how to tie a knot. Khouri could twist his wrists and move his fingers, the bind not so tight that it cut off his blood flow, but tight enough to keep him right where Sorin wanted him. "You shouldn't give Navidae all the credit."

Sorin's brow twitched. "I thought you weren't to speak of him again," he growled, laying himself down along the length of Khouri's naked body. He was so warm, so mindlessly warm, and Khouri was struggling already to roll his hips against Sorin.

"Just... Come on, Sorin," Khouri huffed, trying and failing to get stimulation like this. "Is this your idea of punishment?" It was bad, but it wasn't *bad*. Not like how Navidae would punish him. Those punishments made Khouri's eyes roll back, his toes curl. They made him scream himself voiceless until all he could do was plead to his lover in gasping, wordless cries to end the beautiful torment. "You're going to bore me if all you do is hold me down."

Narrowing his eyes, Sorin loomed closer to his face. "You really want punished that badly?" he asked, cupping Khouri's cheeks in his hands.

Khouri struggled harder, biting his lip. "Yes," he whined. He had been ignoring it for the most part, but now that he was trussed up and pinned down like this, it was all he could think about. A need had been growing in him since he had left Navidae's bed, one that he didn't think he could ignore any longer.

"You're really sure?" the human asked, leaning closer, the warmth of his breath just ghosting across Khouri's lips. Like this, Sorin's hair curtained around them, hiding Khouri from the world in a waterfall of moonlit silver. "You won't begrudge me if I... *indulge*?"

The way Sorin lingered over the word, rolling it across his tongue like mead, nearly did Khouri in. He went limp against the bed and bared his throat on instinct, eyes squeezed shut as he struggled for breath. "Please," Khouri begged, wrapping his thighs around Sorin's waist to pull him closer. "Please, please, please."

"So well-trained," Sorin mused, and Khouri readied himself for the pain, for that wonderful combination of pleasure and agony that shook him to the root of his being. "I suppose I shouldn't keep you waiting if you're already willing to beg for it."

He shouldn't, Khouri wanted to scream. He really, really

shouldn't. Where would Sorin strike first? Would he rake his nails down Khouri's chest? Would he bruise his hips with his big, strong hands? Or would he take one look at the scars on Khouri's shoulders and find it in himself to add to them despite their established rule? A shiver of want curled over his skin, gooseflesh following in a wave. It would make Navidae so mad to find someone else had been there and had dared mark what was his. Khouri could see his face now, ruby eyes narrowed as he traced the unfamiliar bitemark. He would be livid. He would add a hundred more just to erase the one that didn't belong on his pet's skin.

A warm hand traced down Khouri's chest with unerring gentleness. "What are you thinking about?" Sorin asked, his fingertips caressing Khouri's dripping cock. "You're so wet already."

"You," Khouri said, opening his eyes a little to implore Sorin. "What you might do. Please, Sorin. I want it so much."

"You're such a filthy little thing, aren't you? Getting so worked up over just the anticipation. You haven't been denied much, have you?"

Khouri pouted. "You're denying me now." He whined a little, shifting beneath Sorin's weight.

"I wonder about that," Sorin said quietly, leaning forward to kiss Khouri's pouting lips.

If Khouri expected him to be rough or demanding, Sorin didn't care to play along. This kiss was mindlessly gentle compared to the first, soft and searching, deep without being forceful. Khouri whined low in his throat, wasting his breath as Sorin mapped out every inch of his mouth as slowly as he wished to go. Struggling did nothing to speed up the pace.

Sorin merely cupped his face in his large hands, holding him still. His hips rolled against Khouri but even that was sedate.

Confusion set in, and the moment Sorin broke the kiss to breathe, Khouri was complaining.

"What was that?" he demanded, breathless but working past it. "I thought you were going to hurt me."

Sorin's eyes were half-mast, his smile hungry. "I never said that," he chuckled, leaning down to kiss Khouri's neck as gently as he had just kissed his mouth. "I said I'd punish you. I can't think of a better way to do that than to make love to a masochist."

Khouri froze under the ministrations, his eyes wide, his lips parted in a gape. "Make love?" he whispered, the words nearly foreign on his tongue. His cheeks began to burn. "Do... Do you love me?"

When Sorin laughed, Khouri felt it in its entirely, vibrating through his chest in a way that made him gasp. "Of course not," Sorin chided, curling his fingers lower, brushing them teasingly against Khouri's entrance. "But, that doesn't mean I can't torture you with some tenderness. Knowing you, you've never been held like this before."

Khouri wasn't quite sure what he was feeling, but he knew it was closer to horror than excitement.

"You can't be serious," he muttered, his breath hitching. Sorin was reaching for the oil now, grinning like a loon as he dug through his own bag for some tiny vial Khouri had never seen before. "Where did you get that?" *When* did he get it? They had always used Khouri's up until now.

"Not in a very trusting mood tonight, are you? Or well," Sorin said, pouring the scented oil over his fingers carelessly, "I suppose you were a lot more trusting when you thought I was going to hurt you. I got it in town the other day. Thought I might surprise you with a present since we've been working so well together."

Khouri flushed horribly. He looked at the wall, and then he closed his eyes when Sorin took him by the chin to bring his attention back onto him. The air was fragrant with the oil, some mixture of surface plants Khouri had never before smelled. His skin felt warm where it touched, and when Sorin slipped in a finger, his eyes shot open, the warmth so much more pronounced when it was inside him.

Sorin smirked. "Guess there's something to be said about surface Elves now, isn't there?" he mused, crooking his finger to make Khouri gasp. His other hand wrapped itself around Khouri's thigh, keeping him spread. "It cost more than I'd like to admit, but I think it was worth it. You look absolutely stricken."

Khouri felt filthy. His vision was hazy, his skin buzzing with whatever spellwork was used to enhance the oil's natural properties. Sorin was only two fingers in, and Khouri already wanted to beg. He tugged weakly at the belt around his wrists, hiding his face in his arm. This wasn't so bad, though. It wasn't what he thought it would be. Sorin thought he was doing something so jarring, but Khouri could take it. It was slow, over-gentle, but nothing so out of the ordinary. So what if Sorin had bought special oil just for him? So what if he was opening him up carefully, kissing Khouri's knee?

Khouri's cheeks burned, moaning into his arm. So what if it felt so good that he thought he might die? There was no pain to distract him, nothing to curb the edge rapidly approaching.

Sorin slipped in a third finger as slowly as he could, peppering Khouri's sweaty skin with soft, open-mouthed kisses. Everything was so tender. Sorin wasn't going to rush a thing tonight, and Khouri was completely at his mercy for it all.

His eyes shot open when Sorin's lips began to travel lower. "What are you doing?" Khouri asked, voice shaking, eyes damp already. He looked between his spread thighs and watched Sorin kiss down his stomach, lower and lower and lower until his lips just brushed Khouri's cock.

Cool blue eyes met Khouri's, Sorin quirking a smile. "What's it look like?" he said, brow raised. He looked entirely too composed with his lips tracing the words against Khouri's heat. His fingers were still moving, brushing teasingly against the place inside Khouri that made him shiver.

"It looks like you're trying to kill me," Khouri muttered, knees tightening around Sorin's head when he began to move lower, his tongue lapping at the underside of his cock, following the vein. Khouri choked, body clenching around Sorin's fingers, arms jerking against the belt holding him still. He would have bruises on his wrists by morning and not for the reason he wanted.

Sorin hummed, rolling his eyes as he opened up his mouth and took Khouri to the hilt in one easy, nonchalant move. Khouri jolted as if struck, crying out Sorin's name in a broken, needy whine. Sorin pulled off him and gave him a look. "Given how much you talk about him," he began, working his fingers in a slow, mindlessly gentle rhythm, "I would have expected your lover to have at least gone down on you before."

How could Sorin be bringing this up now? "H-He does," he answered after a minute of trying to gather his breath. Bracing his heels on the bed, Khouri tried in vain to ride the fingers.

All he got for his efforts was a hand on his hip, holding him to the sheets easily.

"Shocking considering how you're reacting to me doing it," Sorin mused, his voice so level that Khouri couldn't think it fair at all. "Maybe I'm just special."

Every time Sorin spoke, his breath tickled the head of Khouri's cock, and his scruffy beard teased the skin of his inner thighs. "Maybe you're driving me insane," Khouri tried to say, his voice breaking somewhere towards the end. Navidae went down on him plenty but never like this. It was something he saved for after they had already had their fun together or as a treat for behaving. Sometimes as a punishment, but that never felt like this.

Sorin kissed the head and then down Khouri's shaft, removing his fingers completely. Khouri whined, but Sorin just held him in place and lapped at his cock, his sharp eyes never leaving Khouri's face as he worked. His large hands wrapped around Khouri's thighs, cradling him close as he pleasured Khouri to his heart's content.

"Gods, Sorin," Khouri begged, his mind going blank from the emptiness and the unbearable warmth surrounding him. He longed for the caress of sharp, pointed teeth—for something more. "Please, fuck me already."

In response, Sorin grinned and moved lower, his fingers and his tongue fucking into Khouri in a calculated effort to make him scream. Or well, try to. Khouri didn't scream. He absolutely did not scream. He closed his eyes and arched like a bow, his lips parted in a keen that had to be audible to the next room over. Sorin laughed, and it vibrated in the worst way, his tongue retracting to kiss Khouri's fluttering, needy hole like the teasing bastard he was.

"This oil really is amazing," he mused, rising up to meet Khouri's eye, licking his lips a little. "It makes you taste even better than you normally do."

Khouri's face was going to set fire to the bedding. His eyes pricked with angry tears. "That's so lewd," he groaned, his head falling back into the pillows as he arched again, desperate for something more. "Gods Below, you're an utter beast."

"Not tonight, I'm not," he corrected, moving up Khouri's body, sharing the heady, fragrant taste of the oil with him in a kiss. A kiss that made Khouri's toes curl, his body keyed up and melting. Sorin cupped his cheek in a hand and stroked Khouri's hair from his eyes, smiling at him. How a smile could look so cruel, Khouri would never know. "So, sit back and enjoy this," he said, his thumb swiping over Khouri's trembling bottom lip. "You're going to cum when I think you've had enough."

"What does that mean?" Khouri asked, eyes wide as Sorin pulled himself free from his trousers, coating his long, thick cock with the oil still on his hand. A shiver of anticipation ran down Khouri's spine at the sight, doubling when Sorin hissed in pleasure.

Seizing a thigh in his hand, Sorin spread Khouri wider, lifting him a little as he lined himself up. "It means," he began, slipping the head of his cock inside, punching the breath from Khouri's lungs, "that I'm going to take you to pieces, Khouri." He fed him another inch, Khouri's head falling back onto the pillow. "I'm going to make love to you until you understand," another inch, another overwhelmingly slow inch, "that I'm the only human, the only *man* you need think about."

If he expected Khouri to respond to that, he was going to

be disappointed. Khouri could hardly breathe, couldn't even begin to try to speak, even when every ounce of him wanted to poke fun at Sorin's obvious jealousy. Sorin pressed inside him smoothly, pinning him in place with his bulk and cock, layering kisses upon kisses as he rested there, in no rush to move at all. Khouri shook from his bound wrists down to his legs, his tongue trying to give back some of what Sorin was giving him. He was coming up short, incredibly short, but he tried. He was trying so hard.

Sorin noticed, and he smiled against Khouri's lips. His hips began to move, pulling out a little and pushing back in, the pace so slow that Khouri already wanted to complain. "You're really beautiful, Khouri," Sorin whispered, moving to his ear to kiss and lick, his teeth a teasingly cruel edge that didn't feel sharp enough. "You're a complete brat, but you're probably the prettiest I've ever had."

Khouri flushed despite himself. He averted his eyes, his belly filling with warmth at the praise. His entire body felt warm, Sorin's skin keeping the cold at bay. They were pressed so closely together. It felt... intimate. "Don't... Don't say stuff like that," he mumbled, Sorin rocking into him again, angling it to brush against him where it felt best. Khouri's eyes rolled back, and he gasped, the pleasure overtaking him in rolling waves that didn't seem to know the concept of impatience.

Humming lowly, Sorin braced himself carefully and chased Khouri's lips. His hands cupped Khouri's cheeks, their foreheads brushing as he stared deeply into Khouri's eyes. Their breath mingled. Sorin didn't move faster, didn't fuck into him harder, but Khouri swore his arousal mounted, his cock leaking pitifully against his stomach.

"You like this," Sorin observed, grinning cockily and

drawing a hand down Khouri's neck, down his ribs and thigh before hooking his leg around his waist to open him up even more. The change in angle devoured up any denial Khouri might have been able to offer. "You keep complaining, but your body is honest. Probably more honest than you've ever been in your life."

Khouri shook his head weakly, eyes staring but not seeing, his mind filled with nothing but the sound of Sorin's voice and the pleasure he was giving him. Sorin's movements were so slow and luxuriant, dragging against Khouri with no sign of hurry, no fervor or overwhelming need to be sated. "I hate this," he lied, struggling against the belt, whining when it refused to give. He wanted to touch Sorin, to hold onto him as he fell to pieces. It was scary like this. It was scary feeling so much.

"Poor thing," the man sighed, and if Khouri didn't know him, he might have thought Sorin sounded pitying. The smile on his face ruined it though, and Sorin kissed him again and then again, slower and deeper each time. Before long, Sorin's eyes slid shut, the kiss as purposeful and loving as the way he moved his hips.

It all was at odds with what Khouri knew sex to be. Sorin's kisses were so deep, flaying Khouri bare and open until there was nothing to hide. His hands were so gentle. Why were they so gentle? Khouri couldn't take it. He couldn't take any of this, but Sorin seemed dead set on making him do it regardless.

Tearing his mouth away, Khouri took in a rushed, greedy breath. "Please," he begged, nearing the point of tears. "Please, Sorin, I can't."

"You can," Sorin chuckled, rolling his hips in another dizzying thrust. How was he so deep?

141

"I can't, I can't." Tears rolled down his cheeks messily. His skin felt so hot, the pleasure debilitating. A knot of something tightened in his stomach, and Khouri tugged pitifully at his bound arms, meeting Sorin's eye. "Please," he pleaded, leaning into the hand that came up to wipe away his tears. "Untie me."

"Oh, look at you," Sorin crooned, kissing his mouth chastely as his grinned. His hips kept moving, damnably slow and mindlessly deep, and he propped himself on his elbows to tug teasingly at the belt. "Will you try to run if I humor you?"

Khouri shook his head violently, closing his eyes as Sorin's cock nudged that spot again. He forgot how to breathe, let alone speak. His lips kept moving, begging for him when his voice failed. It was laughable to think him capable of running right now. Khouri was pretty sure he'd never be able to walk again after this.

Sorin smiled against his cheek. "You're really cute when you're speechless," he mused, lifting himself up to yank the knot from the belt. Khouri bit his lip and tugged eagerly, and the moment he was free, he wrapped his arms around Sorin's neck, holding him desperately. "You're really cute when you do that, too," Sorin laughed, kissing his hair.

He rewarded Khouri with a harder thrust and then another. Khouri huffed and moaned, digging his nails into Sorin's back. Every nerve seemed to sing along to the heat between them, Sorin's every move winding him tighter and tighter like a spring ready to break.

It was all so gradual, so smooth, that Khouri was a little shocked when he finally came. In most cases, his orgasm was coaxed from him with targeted bites or rough, insistent stimulation. It would come violently and powerfully, wiping out his vision and deadening his body for minutes at a time.

But now, with Sorin, with this horrible, maddening, *awful* love-making, Khouri found himself cumming between the space of a breath and a moan, in a wash of white that blanketed him as gently as a silk sheet fluttering over his sore, singing body.

"S-Sorin…" Khouri gasped, his hands scrambling at Sorin's back only to lose the strength to stay up. They slipped from Sorin's body and rested on the pillow beside his head, his eyes closed, his breathing wrecked. His release covered both of their stomachs, but Sorin kept moving, the pace finally picking up into something measured but firm. Khouri bit his lip and hissed as his overstimulated nerves began to protest it, but Sorin didn't take long to finish.

"Gods above," Sorin grunted, coming to a stop still buried deeply inside Khouri. He rocked gently, fucking himself through his afterglow, his jaw clenched and his muscles glistening as he hovered over Khouri's shaking, boneless body. "You've no idea what you look like right now, do you?"

He didn't, but he had a feeling he looked like a complete mess. Khouri closed his eyes and hid his face in the nearest pillow. He'd be lucky if he ever caught his breath after that. "You're awful, and I hate you," he said, his voice muffled but his tone carrying through. Embarrassment burned in his cheeks, his ears, and even down his shoulders. It felt so good but so awful. He had never enjoyed a punishment less, never came so easily in his life. Exhaustion swelled in his aching body, and he fidgeted and whined as Sorin pulled out. They made such a mess of this bed. What a lovely surprise for the barkeep when he came calling to reclaim his key.

But Sorin was laughing, proving that he didn't think or care about any of that. He lowered himself along Khouri's body, snatching the pillow away easily as he kissed Khouri's trembling shoulder. "It wasn't that bad, was it?" he asked, smiling as if he had done something clever.

"It was horrible," Khouri pouted, trying and failing to snatch back his pillow. He gave up when Sorin dropped it on the floor and instead settled on looking at the wall.

"Well, it was meant to be punishment." Sorin kept up his mindless fondling, kissing Khouri's cheek and his downturned lips, his forehead, his chin. "Don't tell me you didn't feel good at all."

It was childish of him, but Khouri nodded his head. "Awful, completely awful," he said, pushing at Sorin's strong chest. "It's no wonder you humans live such short lives, fucking like that. You're dooming yoursElves with that awful tenderness."

Sorin stared at him for a beat and then laughed loudly, unabashedly. "Sure, sure," he said, rolling them over, taking Khouri with him to lay the Drow out along his chest. "And the violent bloodletting you call sex is what makes you so long-lived."

"Well, it's certainly not hurting the chances." Khouri frowned and hid his face in Sorin's neck, ignoring how he arched into Sorin's gentle touches. He kept shifting subtly, enjoying the feeling of Sorin's body hair against his sensitive skin. Drow didn't have any, and Khouri found the sensation too novel to resist. The human's hands stroked down his back in soothing passes, his cheek nuzzling Khouri's hair. It was all so warm. Khouri closed his eyes, remembering how exhausting this day had been.

The silence was comfortable, but Khouri still broke it.

144

"We'll be leaving the town tomorrow, won't we?"

Sorin sighed, his hand stalling for a moment before resuming its motions. "Yeah. There's no way we can stay here another night. After the commotion we caused in the bar, there's pretty much no possibility of us being able to do much in this town. You're too nefarious, and I'm going to be labeled as trouble."

Khouri let out a little laugh. "You *are* trouble," he mumbled, kissing Sorin's cheek sweetly.

"I wasn't before you came into my life," he grunted, his hand traveling lower, cupping Khouri's ass like a warning. "You're a terrible influence. Just look at how far I've fallen from the grace of respected society."

"You call this respected society?" Khouri snorted, stroking his fingers through Sorin's long, blond hair. It was such a pale blond, the strands so brilliant that they glistened in the wane candlelight. "Bumpkins, more like."

Sorin's hands traveled higher, leaving his ass alone to pet along his lower spine with his knuckles. He raised a brow and quirked a smile. "Bumpkins? Really. And you're so familiar with high society, are you? A brat like you?"

Khouri rolled his eyes, leaning up a bit to look at Sorin pointedly. "I'm very important where I come from," he said, trying and failing to hide his smile.

"You?" Sorin scoffed, unimpressed. "Somehow, I doubt that."

"Oh, but Sorin, it's true," Khouri swore, swooping down for a kiss. "I'm very important. Or well, my lover is. He's quite infamous in the Duskriven. Known far and wide for his work and wealth. And for me too, I suppose, since I'm rather sought after." He smiled with glee, sensing Sorin's annoyance growing. It was fun, though, so he ignored it and kept going. "I've seen decadence you can scarcely imagine, Sorin. Navi spoils me rotten. With gems and fancy food and expensive gifts. I never want for anything when I'm with him."

"Sounds like you should go back down there then," Sorin said stiffly, batting away Khouri's hand when he moved to cup the human's cheek.

Khouri smiled warmly. "I've thought about it. Navidae never makes me sleep out in the rain. That probably makes him a better lover than you," he teased, leaning in for another kiss.

The kiss never landed. Before he could so much as laugh, Sorin shoved him off his chest and back onto the bed. Khouri bounced slightly, stunned, and watched as Sorin got up and went across the room, blowing out the candles that kept the room lit. "Bedtime already?" he asked, pouting a bit. "That was rather sudden. I'm not tired yet."

"I don't care," Sorin bit, his voice unexpectedly cold.

Frowning, Khouri sat up. "What's gotten into you all of a sudden? I thought we were having fun."

The glare Sorin shot at him made Khouri feel an inch tall. "If you don't like it, then maybe you should go back to your rich lover," he bit, putting out another candle with a harsh puff of air.

What? He didn't think... He couldn't think Khouri was serious, could he? Khouri held the blankets tightly in his hands, his throat tight. "Sorin?" he tried, covering his legs with the sheets, the room growing darker and colder by the second. A draft prickled at his still damp hair, chilling him without Sorin's warmth to chase it away. "You know I'm just kidding, right?"

Sorin didn't deign to look up from the task at hand. He backed the next candle with his hand, leaning down to blow it out. "Are you, though?" he asked, his tone a forced calm. "You don't waste any opportunity to talk about him, Khouri. What am I supposed to think when you say you ran from your lover, but you never stop talking about him? In fond tones, even."

Khouri felt the tightness in his throat recede, anger winning out. "That it's complicated, Sorin," he snapped, staring down at his fists tearing at the sheets. Hadn't he told Sorin this all before? Why was he bringing this up now? "That it's frankly none of your business what my standing is with my lover. You aren't a replacement for him." For the life of him, Khouri couldn't tell if Sorin wished he were. "There's no reason for you to be so jealous."

The last candle went out before the last syllable passed Khouri's lips. He curled into himself, his eyes adjusting quickly but not as quickly as he wanted them to. Sorin hovered at the end of the bed, and Khouri could tell he was debating whether or not to lay down there or on the floor. Scrubbing at his eyes, Khouri let out a silent breath, wondering where the mood from before had gone.

"I don't want you to be a replacement," Khouri said, his face in his hand, hiding his eyes as he drew back the covers in a silent but sincere offer. "There's nothing to replace. You're you, Sorin, and I like you because of that. I like him, too, but don't think for a minute that I conflate the two of you. I'm not that shallow."

Sorin stood still, a statue at the foot of the bed. Khouri didn't try to look at his expression through the dim. He feared what he might see if he tried. So, he held the sheets up, laid back down and waited with his breath held.

Slowly, so slowly that Khouri nearly gave up, Sorin began to move towards the bed. He took the proffered sheet in hand and settled himself in the bed beside Khouri, keeping a healthy distance between them. A distance that had never existed before. Sorin said nothing, and Khouri didn't try to prod him.

It was dark with the candles out. With the mood tense, it felt all the darker. Khouri wrapped his arms around his pillow and tried not to think about the line of Sorin's spine against his own. It had just been a little fight. They had them all the time, didn't they? About Khouri being bratty or Sorin being overbearing. He rubbed his eyes against the coarse fabric of the pillow, trying and failing to make those arguments feel like this.

"I love being with you, Sorin," Khouri whispered, deafening in the darkness. "Don't forget that, okay?"

The warmth of Sorin's back shifted, and before Khouri could so much as stiffen, he felt strong arms wrap around him from behind. Sorin tucked Khouri's head beneath his chin, cradling him close, closer than they had ever slept together before.

"Go to sleep, brat," Sorin grunted, his voice warning Khouri to say nothing. To take it with grace and accept the gesture for what it was. Khouri smiled and closed his eyes.

It wasn't perfect, but it was exactly what he needed it to be.

Chapter Six

Sorin woke up to a numb arm and Khouri sleeping so close to him that he couldn't tell where one body left off and the other began. He blinked blearily at the Drow curled into his chest, at the way Khouri's silky hair flowed over his tingling arm in a river of darkest night. Khouri was still fast asleep, his lovely face relaxed and open as he dreamed. Sorin stroked his hand down Khouri's soft, naked skin, wondering in that half-wakeful way how anyone could be so beautiful.

Soft skin, soft hair, soft lips. Sorin leaned forward, brushing his against Khouri's for just a moment. Khouri wrinkled his nose and mumbled but didn't wake. If Sorin could wake up to this every morning, he might have a better temperament. The weight of the night before still sat heavily on his limbs, but it was too early to be angry. Sorin could pretend that Khouri was all his for a bit. No one else was awake to dispute it.

"Mmm," Khouri mumbled, leaning closer to his chest, his soft lips brushing Sorin's cheek as he slept on. "Mmm?"

"What is it?" Sorin whispered, wondering if he might talk in his sleep. What sort of things did he have to say? Khouri was so chatty while awake, so he probably wanted to talk Sorin's ear off now too. "Khouri?"

His violet lips parted, his teeth a teasing band of white behind them. "Sorin," he murmured, slow and elongated, savoring the sound of his name on his tongue. "'s time to go, Sorin."

Smiling, Sorin stroked through Khouri's hair. "Where are

we going?" he prompted, glancing out towards the window across the room. He had covered it during the storm to block out the lightning, but it was still open enough to show that it was early morning. Still plenty of time before they needed to get moving. "It's your turn to pick, isn't it?"

Khouri wrinkled his nose cutely. "'s time to go," he insisted, his hand curling into a loose fist against Sorin's chest. "Navi's waiting."

Sorin's smile tightened. "Who?" he asked, his voice low, his joviality evaporating just like that.

But Khouri just smiled sweetly, nuzzling his face against Sorin's skin. "Navi," he repeated, his brow relaxing in a way that told Sorin he had fallen back to sleep. His breath was gentle against Sorin's chest, almost tickling him.

Just like that, reality came crashing back in. The fight, the sickening jealousy– it all hit him somewhere below the gut, winding him in a way he didn't think he could recover from. Khouri slept on, completely unaware of it, but what was new there? The Drow didn't see anything wrong with how he was going about things, and if Sorin were a less possessive man, perhaps there would be no problem. Unfortunately for them both, Sorin wasn't.

Extracting himself without waking Khouri took more skill than he thought he possessed, but somehow, he managed it. Sorin snatched up his shirt from the floor and shrugged it on along with the rest of his clothes. Khouri's were strewn all over the floor, but he tried not to look at those too closely. Instead, he glanced at the looking glass on the mantle, taking in the dark circles under his eyes, the scruff that was rapidly becoming a beard, and the wild mane his hair had become during the night. Sighing, he combed through it with his fingers as best he could, glancing back at Khouri for just a moment more. It was stupid of him to do, but there really was no helping it.

The Drow hadn't stirred much with his absence, but he had rolled into Sorin's spot, arms wrapping around his pillow in lieu of the body that was now gone. The sheets were pooled around his waist, his dark skin contrasting beautifully against the off-white cotton. Somehow, Khouri made a cheap, used tavern bed look inviting. Sorin had to hold himself back from doing something stupid. It wouldn't help things, him acting out of a pique of jealousy. It'd just make him weaker to Khouri, and he had had his fill of weakness long before now.

There was no way he could stay in the room. Not with Khouri looking like that. Sorin leaned over the only table in the room and scrubbed at his face with water from the washbasin, trying and failing to calm his fevered thoughts. His life used to be simple before this. Work, eat, sleep. He fucked if the occasion presented itself but never with the frequency of this… whatever it was. Khouri rolled over, and Sorin was drawn to the sight like a man possessed, his eyes raking along the naked expanse of the Drow's petite figure.

Light from the half-covered window panned across his body, and just as Sorin was about to give in, he saw it. The unmistakable silver of the scars collaring Khouri's neck and shoulders. Something hot and acrid pooled into his stomach, his resolve strengthened just like that.

He held back on the urge to slam the door behind him and instead shut it softly, hating himself for caring. The hallway was bright enough to sting his eyes, the sunlight streaming in through the uncurtained windows. The day looked bright despite his mood. Sorin hated it a little bit too for that.

Instead of glaring at the sun for doing what it did best, he turned away and made off down the hall, taking the same stairs he had climbed the night before. A drink was what he needed. His stomach roiled at the thought of booze so early in the morning, but it was that sort of day and who was he to argue with his mood? He had earned it, he figured, for putting up with Khouri's fanciful ditherings for so long. He shoved open the wooden door separating the stairs from the bar, making a beeline for the counter. Thankfully, there was a different person behind the bar today. Sorin would've hated to argue for his booze while in a mood like this.

"Give me an ale, boy," he grunted, sitting himself down in the chair nearest the door. There weren't many around, the crowd from the night before long since gone. A few stragglers lingered in the corners, sipping away at potions and booze to cure their probable hangovers, a few others picking at greasy breakfasts with appetites that didn't seem to match the portion sizes on their plates. The boy, probably the barkeep's son, darted off to fill up a tankard for Sorin. He was back within a minute or so, and for that, Sorin was grateful.

Staring down into the murky, amber liquid, Sorin frowned. How long would Khouri sleep? Would he wait patiently for Sorin to come back upstairs, or would he cause more problems by coming downstairs to look for him? Sorin took a sip of the hoppy ale, letting the taste roll over his tongue. He didn't want to think of the look he'd get from the Drow if he caught him drinking this early in the day.

But then again, why did Sorin care? Khouri wasn't his. He was a *client*, and when Khouri was asleep, safe and sound and with all aspects of their contract fulfilled, Sorin was free to do as he pleased. He took another sip, kneading a bit at his eyes. He could still smell Khouri on his clothes. It filled his head, adding to the annoyance growing somewhere along his temple.

It was just a fight. He needed to stop thinking about it. Nothing had changed. Nothing that mattered. Khouri was just a client, and Sorin was just some easy dick for him while he ran wild away from his lover. Just because Sorin had grown accustomed to the company didn't mean Khouri needed him anymore than what he'd already paid him to provide.

"A bit early for drinking, isn't it?" a stranger at his elbow remarked. Sorin tried not to jump. He hadn't heard her sit down. "Rough night, then?"

Sorin barely glanced at the woman, already annoyed by the cheerful smile on her face. He didn't recognize her. Was she just that friendly, then? Sorin grunted, turning back to the ale in front of him. He didn't need concerned strangers offering up their opinions on his breakfast of choice.

"Can't say I blame you for imbibing," she carried on, tossing her long, white-blond hair over her shoulder with the air of someone who knew full well they were tromping over the boundaries of social convention and loving every minute of it. "After a storm like that, I don't think I'd be in any mood but a maudlin one. We don't get them like that where I'm from."

Grunting, Sorin drained half his tankard in one swallow. The ale was as bad as it had been the night before, but he wasn't drinking for the taste or his health. He didn't know how much longer he could keep this up. Khouri was infuriating, and he never seemed to understand just how bad it was that he kept defending his lover so passionately. He had run from the man, hadn't he? How could he still be so fond of him? Sorin wasn't desperate for a relationship. He wasn't even sure he liked Khouri in that way to begin with, but there was something so grating about being constantly compared to an invisible ideal he could never quite seem to live up to.

"Are you here for business?" the woman chimed in his ear, going so far as to lean into his personal space to make sure he heard her. Sorin jumped back, glaring hotly at her until she moved away. "You don't look like the type to take a vacation."

"And how do you know I'm not a local?" Sorin asked, wondering if she were the outlet he needed to get rid of this frustration. She looked strong, her arms well muscled where they were uncovered by her tunic. If they got into a fight, he was pretty sure she would make him work for his victory.

The woman tapped the side of her nose sagely, but there was something unsettling about the way her smile sat on her face. "No local dresses like that," she said, gesturing to his fur mantle and the thick armor fastened to his shins and forearms.

"How astute of you," he grunted, going back to his drink. She didn't seem like the type to fight in bars. Definitely not so early in the morning at any rate.

"Not quite as astute as you, Hunter Tolgrath," she laughed, moving her seat to angle towards him, her elbow resting on the counter, propping up her head. "Your reputation precedes you, I'm afraid."

Sorin stiffened. He wasn't the type to be recognized by many. He wasn't in the line of work that was aided by notoriety. If this woman knew him, she was someone either in the trade or well-versed enough with it to know who to avoid or, at worse, who to target. Sorin wasn't blind to the bounties piled upon his own head or the long list of enemies he had made earning his coin. He knew this couldn't bode well.

"And who might you be?" Sorin asked, eyes narrowing.

He tightened his hand on his empty tankard, readying himself to bash the woman's brains out if she made any move for a weapon.

He nearly did it on principle when a moment later the woman's eyes flashed a brilliant, piercing pink, something like a heat wave shimmering over her features for a split second. Her dark skin deepened to midnight black, her eyes glittering like gems. It was gone in an instant though, but an instant was all Sorin needed to know she was Drow.

"I'm an agent of someone who is very interested in your particular skillset," she said cheerfully, her false face returned as if nothing at all had changed to begin with. "My name is Alacrita. It's a pleasure, I'm sure."

"I don't work with agents," Sorin said automatically, mind racing. Who was this woman? What sort of person did she represent? Sorin didn't make it a habit to work with or for the Drow. He hadn't thought his name extended that far from his usual circles.

The woman laughed a small, chilling laugh. If she hadn't revealed herself before, her laugh might have done just as well. It was cold in a way that humans' never were. "Oh, I'm certain you'll want to hear of this job," she entreated, waving down the bartender for another round for the both of them. "Very competitive. Very challenging. The pay reflects both, and if you succeed, you'd never need work another day of your life."

If Sorin were involved with any other client, he might have said yes. He might have been eager about it too. But as it was, Sorin waved off the drink the bartender sat down, moving to stand up. "I'm not interested in taking on any more clients," he said gruffly.

He barely made it to his feet before her hand grabbed his arm, her grip so tight that it took his knees out from under him, forcing him back into his chair. Alacrita's smile was tight but still pleasant to anyone looking in. "I'm afraid I was told to insist," she said, only letting him go when the pain began to show on Sorin's face. "You'll listen to the offer first."

Sorin bared his teeth, rapidly losing sensation in his arm. "Or what?"

"Or I'll rip this arm from your body and move on to the next hunter on my list," she said pleasantly, her smile betraying nothing. For a moment, her teeth turned sharp, fangs hanging from her gums in a monstrous grin. The differences now between full and half Drow were obvious. Khouri didn't look half as monstrous as she.

"And then I'm permitted to leave?" Sorin cursed the idiotic thought that made him leave his weapon in the room upstairs. Just because they were in a slow, sleepy town didn't mean they weren't at risk. "Or will you force me to take the job regardless?"

"Oh, I wouldn't dream of forcing you to work when you hold no desire to," Alacrita murmured, holding her hand to her heart as if she felt some dismay at the thought alone. "His Lordship simply wishes to employ the best of the best, and he simply won't stand to let any of them go without hearing his most generous offer."

Sorin's anger faltered for a moment. "His Lordship?" he repeated, furrowing his brow. How had he attracted the attention of a Drow noble?

Alacrita nodded. "I'm sure you've heard tell in your circles of a Drow bounty in these parts. For the capture of a marauding Drow running loose and wild amongst the surface-dwellers?" She waited for Sorin to nod before continuing. "His lordship is the one who placed the bounty. He's lost someone quite dear to him. He simply wishes for the return of his lover by any means possible."

A block of ice began to form in the pit of Sorin's stomach. It couldn't be...

"Then why bother with the bounty?" he asked, keeping his face carefully blank. She couldn't know of last night, could she? Of the Drow he had walked in with. If she did, then why was she playing coy? "That bounty labeled that Drow as a menace. A killer. If he wanted his lover back, then why bother blacklisting them?"

Alacrita tossed her hair over her shoulder, looking at him with eyes that seemed to pity him. "So naive, you humans," she sighed, a small smile forming on her full lips. "To chase him back down to the Duskriven, of course. If he found himself unwelcome above, he would have to go back below, wouldn't he? His Lordship is rather desperate, you see. He fears his lover may never return on his own. It would be rather... unpleasant for those of us in his employ should his lover turn up dead."

She paused for a moment to shudder. Lifting her mug of ale, she drained it in a few large swallows, wiping her mouth with the back of her hand. "So that is where you come in, Hunter Tolgrath. His Lordship wishes to hire you to bring back his wayward lover. Upon delivery of him, you will be awarded your weight in gold. And, might I be so bold to say," she led, looking him up and down with a look that held no small amount of heat. "You would make off rather handsomely should you be successful."

Sorin swallowed. Her interest aside, she was right. That

would be a considerable amount of gold. A ludicrous amount were it coming from anyone but a Lord. Sorin sat back in his seat, his head abuzz with her words. It had to be Khouri. It couldn't be anyone else.

"And how would I find His Lordship's lover, should I be willing to accept this," he forced himself to ask. "You've how many others on this bounty? How come no one else has stumbled upon him yet?"

Sighing, Alacrita leaned against the bar. "Though I've never met him myself, His Lordship's lover is rather notorious," she began, blinking slowly like a cat. "Before he became the Lord's pet, he was known to be a rather cutthroat thief amongst the Duskriven's more unsavory streets. A dark beauty with hair as black as night and a smile sweet enough to pacify you as he slits your throat. The Lord anticipated he would be hard to find and even harder to apprehend. No hunter has come close to him yet, but that doesn't mean we are completely blind and deaf to his whereabouts."

Leaning down, she grabbed the strap of a bag and pulled it into her lap. Digging through it, she pulled out a few rolled slips of parchment and then a quill. Unrolling one, Alacrita set the rest aside, pointing to a spot on an intricately drawn map with the tip of her sharp-nailed finger. "We've heard tell of a Drow passing through here," she began, tracing a winding path along the very same trail Sorin and Khouri had traveled on their way here. "Remains of a camp were found here." It was the spot where they had stopped to fuck, the sketched shape of the cave rendered in poor detail. "And here." Where they had rested a week ago after Sorin's jaunt into town.

"That doesn't mean much now," Sorin heard himself say, his voice sounding a little tight. He stroked down his chin despite himself, wishing his beard were thicker if only to hide more of his expressions. "He could have run miles from here during the rainstorm last night. If he's as good as you say he is, the chances of finding prints after the storm are next to nothing."

"Ah," she smiled, waving her finger like a schoolmarm. "But you forget; the Lord's pet is rather fond of luxuries. It's impossible not to be, given how the Lord spoiled him. He is no doubt holed up somewhere in this vicinity, waiting out the storm and his pursuers."

She knew everything, didn't she? Everything except the fact that Khouri wasn't traveling alone. Sorin swallowed a mouthful of alcohol, wishing he had said no to Khouri when he begged to stay in town. Things were falling apart because of that damn brat, and now Sorin had to figure out a way to gracefully turn down the offer without arousing more suspicion. He kneaded at his eyes, trying to forget the reward. He had never heard tell of so much gold before, let alone seen it with his own eyes. Navidae was richer than he first thought, and that just soured his mood even more.

"Why... why did the lover run?" Sorin lowered his hand, staring at the woman levelly. "Was there something going on? Was he being mistreated?" It's *complicated*, Khouri had said. How complicated could it be if Navidae longed for him to come back? "If he were spoiled as much as you say, then why bother running from the lap of luxury?"

It was clear that she hadn't expected him to ask anything like that. Alacrita's eyes narrowed, and she drummed her sharp nails against the bar's scarred surface. "I wasn't aware you had moral compunctions in regards to your jobs," she sniffed, rolling the map back up carefully. "I am not a resident in the Lord's manor. I don't know the details, and we aren't in

159

the habit of making a fuss over issues like that. One does as one's position allows where I come from. That gives a person a lot of freedom to be cruel if they so choose."

"But you know the rumors," he pressed, his concern mounting with her words. Khouri had been so insistent that the scars were consensual, that he enjoyed the pain. On some level, he did, but it didn't sit well with Sorin. Drow couldn't be that different than humans.

She smiled a little. "We all do. The Lord's affair with the street thief was the topic of much gossip. Countless nobles of the highest breeding strove to be lovers with the Lord, and yet he chose gutter trash." Alacrita paused for a moment, shuddering at the thought. Sorin had to hold back the instinctual urge to defend Khouri.

Thankfully, Alacrita continued on, waving her hand dismissively. "A beauty by any means, but still, when one has no standing, one is nothing." She shoved the map back into her bag, meeting Sorin's eyes. "The lover ran for his own reasons. Any of us would be lucky to have what he had with the Lord, and from what I know, they were close. Fifty years is a long time to be committed to another, even to us. His Lordship is bereft, and that alone is enough to tell me that he wishes for his lover's return out of a place of sincerity."

Sorin's throat was tight. His temple pounded. Every instance of Khouri gushing over Navidae replayed in his mind like the most incessant of memories, growing louder with every second that transpired.

Khouri missed Navidae. Navidae missed Khouri. There was no room for Sorin, and if there was, it wasn't in any capacity he wished to occupy. He stared down at his mug, at the glamored Drow and her remaining parchment scroll.

Something told him it was a contract.

Something told him that he would sign.

Alacrita grinned, seeing it in his eyes before he could come to terms with it himself. She unrolled the contract and slid it over to him, quill slipping into his hand in the blink of an eye. "Sign here and here and then again on the other copy," she whispered, leaning closer to breathe the words against his ear. "You've a deadline of two weeks to bring Khouri Lucifin to the Lordship's manor, lest you forfeit your claim to the reward."

"And... and how does His Lordship expect me to deliver his lover to him?" Sorin asked slowly, signing his name even slower, every letter an act of struggle. The *scritch scritch* of the quill against the parchment seemed to scream at him to stop, but Sorin couldn't. The deed was done, and Alacrita swiped the top contract from under his hand, rolling it up with a bright grin. Her glamor faded for a moment in her glee, her bright pink eyes dancing like fox fire.

"In one piece, preferably," she said, gathering her things to stand. She tossed down a few coins for the drink, staring down at Sorin with a look that said she wished their business didn't need to conclude so quickly. She pulled a brimmed hat from her bag, casting it atop her head. "But be warned, I hear the pet has an affinity for poisons. Something he learned in the dredges of our fair city, no doubt. Others have tried drugging him to no avail, so I'd avoid that if I were you."

They didn't try paralytics, Sorin thought woodenly, watching the Drow saunter through the crowd, casting the brim of her hat over her eyes as she ducked out the tavern door. They didn't know to try. But Sorin did. He knew every way to incapacitate Khouri, and he had every ounce of trust necessary to do it, so long as he were willing to break it entirely.

The walk back up to the room went by in a blur, his copy of the contract folded up tightly and hidden in the palm of his sweating hand.

He opened the door to the sight of Khouri awake, something he was a bit sickened to see. The Drow perked up and smiled at him, the sheets still draped over his hips and not much besides. At some point, he had gotten up and stolen one of Sorin's shirts. It hung off his narrow frame like the worst sort of tease, somehow compounded by the wicked little daggers in his hands, a whetstone balanced on his knee.

"Oh, you're back," he greeted, blowing some of his fringe from his eyes. "Where did you go? If you were getting breakfast, you could have told me. I would've had you smuggle me some, too."

"Get up," Sorin grunted, not bothering to answer his question. He went for his pack and gathered up what he still had scattered on the floor. He made sure to bury the contract deep, tucking it in a pocket that couldn't be reached easily. "We're leaving."

Khouri's smile fell. "Sorin, is something wrong?" He sat up slowly, losing his carefree tone. "Did someone find out I was up here?"

He turned and met the Drow's eyes. Khouri was wrapped in the sheet, his eyes glossy and wide and his lips like the petals of a violet. He looked like temptation, but Sorin refused to let himself yield to it. Turning back to his pack, he knelt down and tightened the straps decisively. "Everything's fine, Khouri," he said. "Now get dressed, pack your things, and sneak down to the tree line while I settle up with the barkeep. And give me back my shirt. If I can't look in your bag, you can't look in mine."

If he expected an argument, he didn't get it. What came was the soft shuffling of cotton against skin, Khouri standing and pulling on his clothing without another word. He tossed Sorin's shirt in his direction, leaving Sorin to bend down and pick it up. Curiosity thrummed off his every move, his graceful body slipping into his tight clothes until they garbed him like a second skin. He glanced over his shoulder and caught Sorin staring, but instead of saying something, he just offered up a small, worried smile.

"We're okay, right?" he asked, hefting his damp bag onto his shoulder, his cloak looped over his arm. "You know, after last night..."

"We're fine, Khouri." If he said it with a smile, maybe the Drow would believe him. "Don't worry about it."

Khouri swallowed, looking uncharacteristically small as he held his things close to his chest. "I'll see you soon, then," he sighed, turning towards the window. He waited for a reply that didn't come and, after a moment, sighed, wedging open the window and slipping out as sinuously as a practiced thief. If Alacrita were to be believed, that was exactly what he was too.

Sorin made quick work of his own things and lifted the bag onto his shoulder, snatching up his axe too. Khouri's hurt expression seemed to be stamped on the back of his eyelids, gnawing at him like the guilt he refused to feel. Sorin was a professional, after all. He'd do this job, and he'd do it well.

A job was just a job, and far be it from him to let a bratty little Drow get between him and his weight in gold.

Chapter Seven

Something was off, but for the life of him, Khouri couldn't figure out what it was.

For the third time since that morning, Sorin pulled out the map and held it close to his chest, reading it as he walked. Every so often he would glance up at the sun and reorient them, taking them due south and closer to the humid, arid forest ahead. Khouri fanned himself with his hand, recalling all too well how disgusting it had felt traveling through a similar heat when he first had left the Duskriven. What he wouldn't give to go back to the town from before. A cold mug of mead sounded like a dream right now, one he would pay any sum to enjoy.

"As much as I adore putting my faith in your navigation skills," Khouri said, breaking the silence that had been following them doggedly for the past ten miles, "I think that avoiding weather like this would probably be better than diving head first into it."

Sorin peered over the top of the map, glaring at him without much heat. When surrounded by the wet, sticky air, there was no heat left to sting as much as the weather already did. "I know what I'm doing," he grunted, going back to whatever it was he thought he was accomplishing behind there.

"Sure, if you say so," Khouri grumbled, shifting his folded cloak to the other arm, a thin layer of sweat sticking uncomfortably to his skin. "But that doesn't mean I know what you're doing. Why don't you let me lead for a bit? Let's go back north. This heat is awful." If the humidity got any thicker, it would be like drowning with every breath he took.

"Suck it up and deal with it," Sorin grunted, in no mood to play it seemed. "I know where we're going."

"And where is that?" Khouri snapped a little, his own patience evaporating like the sweat on his dark skin. Gods, but it was hot. Did he feel it worse than Sorin, or did Sorin just handle it better? There wasn't an ounce of shade along the path they traveled, the only spot of cover in sight some far off forest that looked just as stifling with the thick heat mirage rippling along the stretch of space between them. Could there really be a town out here? How did they survive with it so oppressively hot?

"Where we need to be, Khouri, so stop harping on it." Sorin folded up the map with an annoyed air, shoving it deep into his pack without another word. He held a hand over his eyes and looked off towards the forest, orienting them towards it silently. Khouri sighed and glared at him, but if he felt it, he didn't make it known.

"You're being such an ass today," he mumbled, shifting his cloak again into the other arm, regretting not keeping enough space open in his pack to let him shove it in there so he wouldn't have to carry it. "You've been an ass since we left that other village. Did you forget your manners back there? Maybe we should double back to get them." Before he got fed up enough with Sorin to stab him, he added silently with a glare hot enough to make Sorin turn.

For a moment, it looked like Sorin might snap back at him. Instead, he took in a deep breath and looked back ahead, letting it out with a low sigh. "Just keep moving," he muttered, shifting his back higher, his own fur-lined mantle tucked under his strap to hang from the bag. The glint of his axe in the sunlight was nearly blinding. "It's too hot to argue, and we need to get into the forest before we run out of water."

Khouri groaned, wiping the sweat from his brow. He wasn't used to this sort of heat at all. The Duskriven was nearly frigid, any light that shined down there created through artificial means. The sun baked him from above, his dark hair holding the heat like a stone. How surface-dwellers put up with it, he would never know.

But in the end, Sorin was right. Once Khouri stopped complaining, he found that the walk did go faster. The sun rose and then began to list to the west, its overbearing heat easing slightly as it lost its apex. Khouri was completely soaked in sweat when they finally ducked into the trees, the shade granting some relief but not much. The humidity was even thicker here, sticky and heavy and just barely preferable to what it had been before.

"Great Gods far below," Khouri swore, leaning heavily against a tree. "I fucking hate this. I hate this place so much."

"Whining won't make it better," Sorin said, his own breathing labored, his long hair bundled up in a messy bun on the top of his head. His pale skin was flushed red, his simple shirt soaked through with sweat. He pulled the axe off his shoulder and carried it in his hands as he pressed on, forcing Khouri to keep moving.

"It'll make me feel better," Khouri gasped, stumbling behind him weakly. "Can we please, for the love of all that resides beneath our feet, make camp soon?"

"There's still daylight to burn," Sorin tried to say, but Khouri just shoved forward and blocked the man's path, chest heaving as he tried to breath in the air that stuck in his throat.

"If we don't stop soon, I am going to pass out," he said, stumbling a little in his search for another tree to lean against. "Seriously, Sorin. I don't think I can keep up this pace with it so hot."

Sorin let out an annoyed growl, but it seemed he was too worn out himself to bother arguing. He let out a breath and nodded, looking around at the wilderness surrounding them. "Let's at least get deeper in," he sighed, taking Khouri by the arm to get him moving. "We need to find a clearing, so we can make a fire."

Khouri pulled a face, his vision swimming a bit. "A fire? In this heat?" He was cringing at the thought alone.

"You want to eat tonight? It'll help keep animals away, too. Always make a fire, even in heat like this," Sorin lectured, dragging Khouri through a thick bunch of vines to deposit them into the first clearish space they had seen yet. Khouri didn't bother to yank himself free of Sorin's hand. He just shucked off his satchel and crumpled to his knees, letting Sorin hold onto his arm as he finally rested.

"Yeah, yeah, whatever," he groaned, his hand falling down beside him on the ground when Sorin dropped it. "You go do that. I'm gonna. Breathe. For a bit." Try to, at least. Gods, it was so hard to breathe here. He heard more than saw Sorin walk off to gather wood. There was plenty around them so he wouldn't have to go far, luckily. The clearing was strewn with all sorts of loose branches and the like, some dried while others looked soaked through with the moisture afflicting everything in the forest's embrace. Khouri closed his eyes and caught his breath. With the sun off him and the hike over, he could begin to cool down a little.

He opened them back up when he heard a soft sort of

167

clatter, turning a bit to watch Sorin deposit an armful of small branches into a pile. He knelt down with a handful of moss and set himself to stacking it all together, building up the fire the way he always did when they made camp. A lot of skill went into the movements. Sorin had been doing this for decades. It showed.

Sorin edged away from him the moment Khouri tried to sit beside him. "What's wrong?" he asked, scooting closer to spite Sorin. "Not feeling like talking to me now? I just wanted to watch you work."

"It's too hot to have you clinging to me. Go drink some water and leave me be," Sorin said a little harshly, a flood of sparks rising off the flint and steel to fall on the tinder bundle tucked inside the dried sticks. A few caught, and Sorin leaned down to blow gently on it, coaxing it into a small fire within a minute or two. There was a lot more smoke than there usually was, probably from all the moisture in the wood.

As weary as he was from the day's travel, Khouri figured he knew the way to alleviate whatever it was bothering Sorin. He moved closer to Sorin despite his admonishments, draping himself against the man's solid, muscled shoulder. "I know a better way to deal with the heat," he whispered, kissing Sorin's cheek, running his hand down Sorin's arm to rest over his hand. "Why don't we sweat it out together?"

Sorin stilled, his breath catching in his throat. Khouri smiled and moved his lips to Sorin's ear, teasing him with a soft gasp. "You've been so tense today," he breathed, lacing their fingers together, bringing Sorin's hand to settle on his thigh. "So on edge. Do you want me to help? Let me make you feel better."

Cool blue eyes took him in, a shiver running down

Khouri's spine. Sorin stared at his lips and then lower, following the line of Khouri's neck down to his clavicles. "It's..." His eyes closed, his jaw tightening. He pulled away from Khouri and stood up, leaving him on the ground by the fire. "No. I'm going to go bathe. I'll be back in a bit."

Khouri blinked, staring up at the hunter in disbelief. "Oh, well," he murmured, beginning to lift himself off the ground. "I'll come with you." It was so hot here. A dip in a river would be heaven.

"No, you won't," Sorin grunted, looking off into the trees. "Stay here. Finish making the camp up. I don't need you hanging on me as I wash." He turned and began to move towards the tree line. "It's hot enough right now as it is."

It stung more than it should have. Khouri crossed his arms and sat back down, glaring at Sorin's shoulders as he walked off into the woods. What was that all about? "Fine then!" he shouted at his retreating back. "Don't drown yourself!"

Sorin didn't even react, and within a few seconds, he disappeared entirely, vanishing amongst the thick foliage and hanging branches. Khouri sighed and kicked at a log half in the fire, watching the sparks rise up in a wave nearly as angry as he was. What on earth was going on with him? Khouri had been around plenty of men, but in his experience, they tended to sweeten their disposition after getting off as much as Sorin had.

"His loss, then," he muttered to himself, glaring into the crackling fire. If he didn't want to touch Khouri, then he didn't have to. It would have been nice to have been rejected in a kinder way, but Sorin had always been a rough brute of a man, so he shouldn't have been surprised.

Rubbing at his eyes, Khouri told himself to stop thinking about it. It didn't matter. Not really. Sorin was probably just irritated from all the walking and the humidity. There was no point in taking it personally. Khouri sighed. Logically, he knew that, but it was still hard not to be upset. Things had been going well, hadn't they? What a mess this had turned into. He really hoped it was just the weather. He really hoped the irritability would pass like a bad storm. Maybe it would once they got out of this forest.

But that begged the question of where they even were right now. Khouri rolled onto his knees and looked for Sorin's bag, spotting it off against a far tree. He moved towards it, digging into the bag for the map he knew to be inside. Sorin had been so cagey about where they were heading. Any attempts to pick the next destination had been met with staunch refusal to Khouri's utter chagrin. If Sorin thought he could bogart the map, though, he had another thing coming.

Clothes, whetstones, some dried jerky– Khouri rooted through it all, snagging a piece of jerky to chew as he searched for what he knew had to be inside. Gods, Sorin was a slob. Nothing was organized in here. The clothes were all wrinkled, the weapons strewn about in a manner that Khouri figured had to be dangerous. It was only after a few minutes of constant digging that his fingers brushed crisp parchment tucked inside a side pocket. Smiling victoriously around his mouthful, Khouri swallowed and yanked it free, setting it in his lap.

His smile morphed into a confused frown a moment later when he realized he had grabbed two pieces of parchment, not just one. The one on top, the thicker of the two, opened up to reveal the map. Khouri glanced at it, tracing his fingertip along the route they had taken thus far. They had been walking for a couple days since the last village, their progress directed towards the south. Traveling at Sorin's side had given him a rough estimate of distance and walking speed, and with a bit of quick addition, he gathered they were somewhere within the Berserian Forest.

Khouri bit his lip, his finger traveling a little lower over an x that marked what he knew to be an entrance to the Duskriven. That x... that hadn't been there before, had it? Khouri would have noticed it when he had stolen the map, wouldn't he? He drew the map closer to his face, the evening far from too dark for him to see through. A cursory sniff told him the ink was fresh. Much fresher than the rest around it.

Running his fingers through his hair, Khouri tried to keep the inevitable thoughts at bay. It was just a coincidence, right? Sorin had probably just marked the Duskriven entrance to make sure they steered clear of it. They were heading south because there had to be some major city he wanted to go to. A city with big bounties and a big enough crowd that Khouri could get lost in; a place where Khouri didn't have to worry about being seen or targeted.

His heart lurched in his chest when he forced himself to look back down at the map. Once the forest ended, there was nothing southwards. Nothing besides a few insignificant dots that symbolized villages too small to bother with.

A branch snapped somewhere behind him, and Khouri whirled around, breath choked and adrenaline pumping like a heady cocktail of fear and instinct. He scanned the darkening tree line. Was it Sorin? An ambush?

He jumped half a foot in the air a moment later, only to catch himself when his eyes recognized the disturbance for what it was. A squirrel ran out through the clearing, darting past him to reach the other side of the camp. Khouri let out a short gasp of a laugh, smacking his cheeks a little. His heart hammered in his chest. He needed to calm down. This was silly. This was so silly. He knew nothing at all, really. Not nearly enough to be getting so paranoid, at any rate.

"Just breathe," he told himself under his breath, rubbing at his eyes. "Just. Breathe."

A much needed breeze rolled through the clearing, cooling the sweat on his brow. The leaves whispered, and the grass answered, the parchment crinkling along, begging to be included. Khouri looked down at the other sheet, his hand stalling just above it. A feeling of disquiet filled him, only growing stronger when his touched the papery surface. For some reason, he didn't know if he wanted to look at it.

He closed his eyes, laughing at himself a little. What was he so afraid of? It was just a little piece of paper, no bigger than a sheaf from a book. He snatched up the page and opened it with his eyes still closed, taking in a deep breath, refusing to let his smile fall. Silly. So silly.

Silly as it was, he couldn't help but count to three before he opened his eyes.

Confusion greeted him first once he did. He bit his lip and furrowed his brow, the thick, ornate script a little hard to read. He ran his finger beneath the first line, parsing out slowly what was written. *Hereby that which has been agreed upon in order of His Lordship in search of the aforementioned...* Khouri relaxed a bit, realizing it was just a contract. For a bounty? Some sort of acquisition, it looked like. Was this what they were going south for? Khouri wondered who on earth could have given it to Sorin. They had been together pretty much the whole time.

Khouri cursed whoever had written this. He scooted closer to the fire in hopes that the unnecessary light might help him read the looping, cramped script easier. There should be a name on here, one that told who had ordered the bounty. So much legal-speak. It was a wonder Sorin was able to read any of this at all. He supposed that working with these types of contracts often allowed for a certain amount of proficiency. It would be a necessary skill to learn if Khouri wanted to be a hunter too.

With that in mind, he set to studying the page before him. First came a few paragraphs of various clauses, it looked like, all outlining the various rights and claims each party had. Things to protect from scams and double-crosses, a few lines here and there to account for injuries and compensations. Whoever had written this was thorough. Exceedingly so. Sorin was dealing with a professional, one who knew what they were doing and wasn't afraid of covering every single possibility that might arise.

Moving on, Khouri narrowed his eyes at the next section. His attention wavered when he was met with another thick block of text, the script all the more cramped, the words nearly unreadable. He snapped back into focus when he caught sight of a tangled *Dr–*. Could it... No, there was no way. It couldn't say Drow, could it?

It took a moment for him to realize his heart was pounding. Khouri looked down and covered his heart with his hand with a frown. He needed to calm down, he told himself. It was too early to be making snap assumptions. Just keep reading. It was probably nothing.

The next paragraph made his heart stutter. For a moment, he swore it stopped entirely. The script changed suddenly as if written in another hand. The words seemed illuminated, drawing his eye and stealing his breath from his lungs as mercilessly as a punch to the gut.

Upon completion of the outlined task, His Lordship, the renowned Navidae Marrowick, Purveyor of the Western Dusklands and the most loyal servant of the Council–

His eyes began to blur, so much so that he could barely read what remained. He didn't need to, though. He would know the hand of his lover anywhere. How many years had he sat at Navidae's side, watching him work, watching him sign document after document, ending lives with just an errant scratch of his plumed quill? Khouri sagged forward, catching himself in the dirt, something like anger flooding his veins.

What was this? How could this be? It had to be a mistake. He forced himself to look, to see past the fury, the betrayal.

Signed by the Hunter Sorin Tolgrath on behalf of his most noble Lordship in that the return of one Khouri Lucifin be made swift and punctually–

"What are you doing on the ground, brat?" an annoyed voice asked, the forest crackling and crunching in deference to his arrival. "I'm gone for an hour, and you're already making a mess of yourself."

Khouri was on his feet in an instant, the contract clenched in his shaking fist. The very air tasted bitter on his tongue, and when he saw Sorin, saw him with his shirt slung over his shoulder, his long hair wet and tossed over alongside it, as guiltless as priest, Khouri saw red. Blood red.

"What is this, Sorin?" he breathed, his body cold, his breath coming short. "What did you do?"

174

Sorin had the audacity to look confused, but it only lasted for a moment. After that, he just looked ashamed. "Khouri," he murmured, taking a step closer, reaching for him with the hands that had signed the contract. With hands that had sold Khouri out like chattel. "It's not what you think."

"Then what is it?!" Khouri shouted, eyes pricking with moisture. He threw the contract up to Sorin's eye level, reaching for a dagger from his hip. "Because from where I'm standing, it looks like you sold me out!"

The man snarled, moving into Khouri's space. "I didn't," he bit, and if he were just a touch angrier, maybe Khouri would buy it. "You have it all wrong."

"Do I?" Khouri hissed. "Then explain why you have my lover's signature on this?" He brandished the parchment, jabbing the point of his dagger at the looping name tucked so neatly into the corner of the page. "Explain why the hell you signed next to it?"

"Put the knife down, Khouri," Sorin ordered, somehow keeping cool despite the tempest of emotions assaulting Khouri. He lifted his hands placatingly, hair still dripping wetly from the river he had just come from. For a moment, the memory of him submerged in the water and spitting curses rose up in Khouri's mind, overlaying the present like a cruel joke.

"I won't," Khouri breathed, throwing down the contract, holding the dagger out in front of him. "Not until you explain yourself."

"I did it for you, alright?" Sorin shouted, his loud voice rolling through the clearing, echoing off the trees like a clap of thunder. His chest heaved, and his glare was as hot as the fire

175

behind them. "They came to me. Threatened to break my arms if I didn't hear them out. You miss your lover so much? Well, he misses you too, brat."

"What are you talking about?" The dagger in his hand shook, his feet moving him back as Sorin steadily worked his way closer. "Navidae did this? How did they find me?"

Sorin rolled his eyes. "They've been tracking us since the cave," he grunted, averting his eyes, glaring somewhere past Khouri. Khouri ached to look, to follow his gaze, but he forced himself to keep his eyes on Sorin. "There are dozens of hunters looking for you. I took the damn contract to get the information they had. To see how much they knew."

The dagger fell an inch, and Sorin matched it, moving that much closer. "How... How am I supposed to believe you?" he asked. "I saw the reward. I saw how much he was promising." It was more than enough to incite betrayal. Far more than enough.

"Because," Sorin said, his voice soft though his features were hard. "We're partners, aren't we?"

Khouri froze, his eyes wide. He wanted to believe him; every inch of him wanted to believe that Sorin spoke the truth. He wrapped his arms around himself and stared at the man before him, looking him in the eye, searching for the truth. Sorin sighed and drew ever closer, arms outstretched to embrace him.

When he wrapped his arms around Khouri, it almost felt the same as it had before. Sorin was warm. So warm. "Do you... Do you promise?" Khouri's voice was shaky, his face buried in Sorin's chest. The dagger slipped from his fingers and hit the ground with a dull thud, nerves soothed by the man's familiar scent, by his addicting warmth.

Sorin didn't answer. He held tighter, holding a hand to Khouri's head, keeping his face on his shoulder.

"Sorin?" Khouri whispered, tugging against his hold, stomach twisting anxiously.

"I'm sorry," came the low, whispered reply.

There was a sharp jab as something was stabbed into Khouri's thigh and then a dizzying rush as the world began to tilt on its axis. Khouri clung to Sorin's chest, staring up at him, confusion brimming in his eyes. "What?" he gasped, his knees giving out. Sorin caught him before he could fall, but he hid his face from Khouri, staring at the ground.

"Just sleep," Sorin's low voice rumbled, Khouri's eyes so heavy that they refused to remain open. "Just sleep, and it'll all be over once you wake."

All over? What would be? But blackness encroached greedily, devouring him completely before he could ask.

Chapter Eight

Low voices wrapped around Khouri softly, words lilting and falling in a cadence he couldn't quite understand. Where was he? What was he doing? The world was cold here, cold and dark, his skin prickling unpleasantly in the wind. Cold everywhere but some, unpleasant everywhere but some. It was warm against his cheek, soft and gentle like sun-bleached cotton.

More voices. Khouri felt a thrum beneath him, his hands hanging, his legs dangling. Sorin? Was that Sorin's voice. He wanted to look, to check, but his eyes felt so heavy. He couldn't open them.

"-don't care what he's doing," Sorin's voice murmured, muted but still angry, as if he were keeping quiet out of politeness and not much else. "Get him down here before I leave and take him with me."

"Please, sir–"

"That's *Hunter* to you," Sorin interrupted, and Khouri twitched at the tone, trying to move his fingers to soothe Sorin before he got them in trouble.

"A thousand apologies," the other voice said in a tone that was anything but apologetic. "*Hunter* Tolgrath, please. His Lordship is on his way. He is very busy seeing to his affairs, but you must understand that he is most eager to be reunited with his lover."

Something about that made Khouri uneasy, his self-preservation prodding at the base of his spine, urging him to move and do something. The darkness was too heavy though, too smothering. Khouri groaned and shifted, silencing the conversation for the moment.

"S... Sorin?" Khouri slurred, his eyelids so heavy. "What... 'm so tired."

He felt Sorin's hand stroke along his thigh. "I know, I know," the man sighed, his voice tight. "Just stay asleep, okay? We're almost done."

Done? Done with what? A job? It was so hard to think with the fog in his head and the cold distracting him. Khouri mumbled his questions, but Sorin just hushed him again. It was odd, that. Sorin wasn't usually so withholding.

"Get him here *now!*" Sorin hissed. "If he wakes up before I'm gone, I will make sure you are the one who feels my wrath."

"I cannot predict when His Lordship will arrive!" the voice hissed back, and the fog shifted a little, a face taking shape in Khouri's mind. Was that Dezik? But that didn't make sense at all, did it? What was Navidae's footman doing here on the surface? Dezik sounded mad. Sorin shouldn't antagonize him. Whatever it was Sorin needed, Khouri was sure he could get it so long as he kept a cooler head. He patted at Sorin's body in a way he hoped was soothing. It was hard to tell where he was touching. It felt a little like he was draped over Sorin's shoulder. What an odd place for him to be.

Khouri felt more than heard Sorin's responding growl. "You have one minute," he said through clenched teeth, "to bring him here or I leave."

There was silence, and then there was a tight, put upon

sigh. "Fine," Dezik snarled. "Do *not* move." Footsteps clacked against a tile floor, disappearing slowly, leaving them alone. Khouri shivered again, wondering where they were for it to be so very cold. Dezik, the cold, the strange conversation...

Why, it was almost as if he were back in the Duskriven.

In the span of a heartbeat, Khouri's eyes opened, the fog lifting in a horrible, heart-lurching snap. He struggled viciously before he knew quite what he was doing.

"Let me go!" he grunted, his heart hammering in his chest. The tile below him was familiar. The walls too. The cold, the oppressive, biting cold was the most familiar, and with horror, Khouri realized he was indeed back in the Duskriven.

Worse yet, it seemed that he was back home entirely.

"Khouri, Khouri, calm down dammit!" Sorin rasped, trying and failing to hold him in place on his shoulder. "You're safe–"

"Let me go!" Sorin lost his grip and dropped him onto the cold tile floor. Khouri hit the ground hard but didn't let it slow him down, kicking and biting at Sorin's reaching hands. The sleeping draught weighed down his limbs, but Khouri fought through it. No. *No.* He wasn't done! He wasn't ready to come back here. Pain blossomed dully against his side, spreading outwards from the impact of the fall, but it didn't matter. Nothing mattered now but getting away. Navidae was here, and Sorin had carried Khouri right back into his lover's suffocating arms.

"Ah," a horribly familiar voice sighed. "Finally. You took longer than promised, Hunter Tolgrath."

Khouri froze like a hare before a fox, and Sorin was back

on his feet in an instant, forgetting Khouri for the moment to address the Drow before him. "I'm not used to coming down here," Sorin said, and Khouri saw his eyes flicker down to look at him, something like concern or worry softening his face. Was he worried that Khouri had hurt himself? Or was he just worried that he had damaged his client's property? Khouri bared his teeth at the human. Sorin let out a sigh, looking back up. "You could have sent someone to meet me at the tunnel near the surface."

Footsteps clicked against the cold tiles, and Khouri refused to move his head to see his lover approach. But it didn't matter much since Navidae leaned over into his field of vision, smiling the same sharp, hungry smile he always wore when he looked upon Khouri. "I think given the amount you're being paid, you should have gift wrapped him along with delivering him to me. Don't complain, Hunter. You won't find sympathy from me for your efforts."

Khouri didn't know how to feel as he looked into the eyes of his lover. Everything was a blur—happiness warring it out with anger, the relief nearly smothered by blinding betrayal. Navidae was here, and Khouri was home, and a part of him celebrated it. How could it not? The days full of homesickness and yearning fell away in an instant, and for the life of him, Khouri wanted to embrace Navidae.

Then reality set in with the cold persistence of an icy draft. This wasn't okay. This wasn't okay at all.

Navidae hadn't changed a bit in the time they had been apart. He still stood tall and handsome, clothed in expensive garments that put Sorin's simple traveling garb to shame. Khouri wrinkled his nose and blinked away the drug trying to drag him under. It was obvious that Navidae had dressed purposefully today for this. He wore the fitted silver shirt that Khouri liked so much. His high-collared cloak added to his regal appearance, something Navidae usually eschewed when home and relaxing. It was the same cloak he wore when they first met, pressed and prepared in anticipation of this moment.

Khouri hated him for the gesture. It was easy to tell that Navidae thought this some grand, heartfelt reunion more than the kidnapping it really was. He rolled onto his stomach to avoid looking at him, contenting himself with the pattern on the tile and the thought that Sorin and Navidae were no doubt about to butt heads. Khouri hid his face in his arms, shivering as the tile added to the cold already assaulting his body. He had missed Navidae more than he cared to admit right now, but he most assuredly had not missed this cold.

"My pay?" Sorin grunted, and Khouri heard Navidae chuckle before feeling a warm hand rest on his naked back. Khouri startled a little at the touch. He hadn't heard Navidae kneel.

"Right down to business already? And I've only just arrived. Answer me some questions first, Hunter," his lover crooned, tracing meaningless shapes along Khouri's bare skin. "I'm so curious as to where you found him."

Khouri tried to resist the instinctual urge to lean into Navidae's touch. Navidae was so warm, and his voice so soothing. "I heard about him in a bar," Sorin lied, and Khouri lifted his head up enough to glare at him. "It wasn't hard to track him down."

Navidae made a thoughtful noise. "And he came above on his own?" he asked, his hand moving to Khouri's hair. Khouri tried to shake him off, but Navidae was nothing if not persistent. "No sign of another with him? No sign of coercion?"

Sorin's voice was hard, his desire to leave more than apparent. "None. He came above on his own. Now, where is my payment? I don't see my weight in gold in here."

"Of course, I have your payment," Navidae delivered evenly. "But, I would be remiss if I didn't assure the safety of my purchase before I gave it."

Sorin made a noise of confusion, but Navidae just laughed, gently turning Khouri over again. He smiled down at Khouri, his reddish, rust-colored hair backlit by the spelled lights above, a bloody halo embracing his handsome face. "Welcome home, my sweet blackbird," he said softly to Khouri, pushing the hair away from his eyes gently. "For every bruise and marr I find on him, I'm docking you fifty pounds of gold."

He said it with the same tone he used on Khouri, and for that reason, Sorin didn't pick up on it for a moment. But when he did, he strode closer, eyes angry and fists tight at his side. "Excuse me?" he said, looking ready to grab Navidae by the cloak to rip him away from Khouri. "That wasn't part of the deal."

Navidae looked anything but challenged. He simply raised a brow and shrugged, still combing through Khouri's hair with his long, sharp fingers. "Wasn't it?" he mused, glancing at the angry bounty hunter dismissively. "I'm afraid that if my agents failed to make mention of it, it still doesn't negate the contract you signed. Or perhaps," Navidae smiled, "you simply didn't read the fine print?"

If Khouri were in a better state of mind, he might have felt some measure of pity for Sorin. Trusting a Drow? Really? He hadn't thought Sorin so naive. But, as it was, Khouri could barely keep his eyes open, let alone care about the man who had just sold him out receiving a fair wage. Instead, he rolled onto his shoulder and shook off Navidae's hands. There was almost no chance of him reaching the door and even less of him somehow managing to navigate the dangerous streets in this state, but Khouri really would rather die than not try.

"You can't be serious," Sorin deadpanned somewhere above, the two of them so wrapped up in their posturing that they failed to realize Khouri's plan. "What are you going to do? Strip him naked on the foyer floor and count every meaningless mark you see? That's completely unacceptable."

"Is it now?" Navidae murmured, rising up onto his feet. Sorin was a large man, but Navidae was too, especially for a Drow. He stood only a few inches shorter than the human, his confidence making up the difference between them. "I fail to see how it's unacceptable to be worried about the state of my lover. You did just drop him onto the tile in front of me. What guarantee do I have that you haven't employed a similar care in handling him up until this point?"

Khouri wanted to yell at them both to shut up, but it was taking every ounce of strength he still had to keep moving. He had gone maybe a yard, and only a few more separated him from the door. His pipe dream was beginning to smoke, and he held his breath carefully, desperate to keep it alight.

"Because," Sorin bit, taking a step closer to Navidae, "I'm a professional. I do my job, and I do my job *well*. That's why your agent sought me out."

"I've met a rather large number of *professionals* in my life, Hunter Tolgrath," Navidae said, completely uncowed. "And a great many of them hide behind reputation as if it exempts them from personal accountability. You did sign my contract as is respected and understood in your profession. Therefore, it is my right to assure myself that the job you've done for me is deserving of such a large sum of money."

Khouri stopped crawling. He seethed and rolled himself onto his back, propping himself up as high as he could get. "I am not some *job* to be *haggled over,*" he cut, and both men startled away from their pissing match to look for him. "Stop talking as if I'm a piece of meat, you fucking butchers!"

Navidae's eyes went wide when he saw how far Khouri had gotten, and he was quick to close the distance between them, hefting Khouri into his arms easily. "Oh, of course not, pet," Navidae tried to soothe. "Pay no mind to us. We can always sort this out later."

It was almost funny how Sorin avoided eye contact with Khouri. It might have succeeded to be if not for the utter betrayal he had offered up. "I'm not leaving until I've been paid the promised amount," the hunter said, crossing his arms pointedly. His axe was still slung over his back, and Khouri knew well enough how fast the man could draw it if pressed.

"If that's how you want to handle this, then by all means," Navidae smiled, nuzzling Khouri's hair with his cheek. "You're more than welcome to stay as a guest in our home until a proper price can be agreed upon. Perhaps this is better anyway. I'm most eager to see to my wayward lover. I've missed him terribly."

Khouri grimaced, smacking at Navidae's chest weakly. Sorin? Stay with them? Anger aside, Khouri could think of a dozen reasons why that was a horrible idea, their affair residing proudly at the top of the list. He shook his head and opened his mouth to protest it, but Navidae kissed him soundly, silencing him, gesturing with a hand at some servant to settle Sorin. Without breaking the kiss, Navidae was walking off, leaving the hunter somewhere in the foyer as Khouri was whisked away, mouth devoured by his lover.

He blamed the drug for why he let Navidae indulge for so long. Khouri's cheeks flushed as Navidae licked into his mouth, tongue and taste so familiar that it was instinctual to accept them eagerly. Khouri closed his eyes, his hand loosening in Navidae's shirt. It felt like a dream, the kiss. Hazy and warm and comforting enough that it made Khouri want to fall asleep.

Navidae broke the kiss after a few moments, the hallways disappearing behind him in a fog of blurred color and glowing faerie lights. "That's a good pet," he crooned, peppering Khouri's cheeks with more kisses. "So well-behaved. I suppose it's the drug still, isn't it? Does it come and go? You looked so angry with me before."

"I still am," Khouri mumbled, pushing through the stupor. He was so angry. Blindingly angry. Angry at Navidae and angry at himself for wanting to forget it in favor of more kisses.

Shouldering open the door to their bedroom, Navidae smiled winsomely down at Khouri. "This isn't at all how I had imagined our reunion," he admitted, sounding mournful. "But we're together again, so isn't that what's important? Not the insignificant little details?"

Insignificant details? Like how Navidae had kidnapped him just to drag him back into his bed? He pushed weakly at Navidae's chest, drowning already in the familiar scent his lover wore. Everything around him was familiar in the worst way. The room looked as it had the day he left, dripping in luxury and scented faintly with perfume. The walls were lined with dark, expressive paintings, the floor covered in thick, plush rugs. The chest at the foot of the bed dripped with gems and inlaid gold, and Khouri made himself look away, knowing it was empty of all the jewelry it usually held. Did Navidae know? Did he know how Khouri sold the gifts he had given?

Now wasn't the time to worry about it. Navidae brushed aside the dark crimson curtains from the enormous bed, laying him down in the blood red sheets. Khouri could see glimpses of the city through the enormous vaulted window at the far end of the room before Navidae let the curtains fall back into place, hiding them from the world at large. It had been dark outside, but that didn't mean much to a realm beneath the earth.

Faux moonlight streamed inside, glowing through the thick curtains draping the canopy of the bed. How many times had Navidae taken Khouri against one of the windows? Against one of the walls? The memories were flooding him too quickly to dam, the scent clinging to the sheer, red sheets only adding to the deluge. Did Navidae still have all of his things here? Were his clothes and baubles and books still nestled away in the large wardrobe against the wall?

"I don't want to look at you right now," Khouri mumbled, fighting through the drug. He needed to stop caring. To stop thinking about the parts of this place that felt like home. He looked up at the ceiling instead, taking in the familiar shape of the chandelier hanging overhead, the focal point from which the bed's curtains hung. Its graceful curves and polished surface were almost misleading. It was made of hundreds of bones, all shiny and white and redolent of the starlight absent from this place. What on earth had Sorin dosed him with? It felt like stumbling through thick mud, his mind filled with fog. "Where's Sorin?"

Navidae hummed as he took in Khouri on the bed, seating himself on the edge of the mattress to card his fingers through

Khouri's hair happily. "Pay no mind to that human, pet. He was just a hired hand. Unless, of course, you want him for something? He is rather strapping, isn't he?" Navidae mused, kissing the corner of Khouri's damp eye. "If you want him as a pet, pet, I'm sure I can arrange it."

It took most of his strength, but Khouri managed to shove Navidae's face back with the palm of his hand. "Would you stop that?" he muttered, leveraging himself up into a sitting position. His head spun, his stomach clenched, but he gritted his teeth and kept upright, glaring at Navidae's smiling face.

"Stop what?"

Khouri narrowed his eyes. "Stop acting like you've done something worthy of praise."

"Haven't I?" Navidae asked, leaning closer. Like this, surrounded by the red curtains, his hair looked all the bloodier. "Haven't I brought you home? Haven't I brought you back to where you're loved and adored, away from the place that hated and hunted you like a beast? I don't ask for you to thank me, pet, but I expected some measure of understanding."

"Oh, I understand fully well what you thought you were doing," Khouri hissed.

"Then why do you reject me?" Navidae asked, prodding like a child fascinated by a bruise. "Why won't you let me hold you? Is that so much to expect when I've been fearing you dead?" He reached out a hand but seemed shocked when Khouri pulled away.

"Then maybe you should have thought about that before you hired Sorin to bring me back like an unruly pet," Khouri snapped, eyes pricking with moisture. He scrubbed at his eyes, hating how worked up he was, how hard it was to control himself with the drug dulling his thoughts, highlighting his pain. Navidae may have paid him, but Sorin still took it. He took the job, and he treated Khouri like a mark, like some criminal or miscreant to be dealt with and deposited for a sum. He had thought they were past that, that they were more than that. But apparently, they weren't.

Khouri was such an idiot.

Navidae leaned in closer. Khouri had to hold himself back from leaning into the comfort he knew his lover would offer. "It's alright," he cooed, resting his hand on Khouri's thigh, his long fingers squeezing gently. "Any hunter would have done it if they had the chance. I offered a large reward for your return. Only the best for you, so don't take it so personally."

"I have to take it personally," Khouri muttered, looking through his hands at Navidae's face. At his handsome, familiar face. Khouri had never been so upset with him before. He wasn't even sure how to handle all he felt. "He was... we were fucking, Navidae. How else am I supposed to take this betrayal?"

Navidae froze, his expression broadcasting his anger and shock. His fingers tightened on Khouri's thigh, his sharp teeth bared. "He fucked you?" he murmured, voice still smooth and level despite his budding fury. "Why, perhaps I should pay him even less in that case, if he were already taking his payment from you."

"Don't be crude," Khouri muttered. He was hurting, but he didn't have to be the only one in pain. "He can't take what's freely given."

His words hit just how he had wanted them to. Navidae

189

winced, his dark cheeks flushing. "So," Navidae led, taking Khouri by the chin to make him meet his eye. "Am I to assume then that you've been having all manner of fun in the world above?"

Khouri huffed out a breath. Navidae was trying to be scary, and it wasn't working at all. "That depends on your definition of fun, I suppose, now doesn't it?" he delivered. "If you're wondering if I've been sleeping around, then yes." Though, he hadn't. Not really. Sorin was the only one he'd trusted, even if that trust had been misplaced. "I'm sure you have been too."

"You'd be wrong to assume that, pet," Navidae said softly. His hand was gentle as it moved to cup Khouri's cheek. "How could I? I've been searching tirelessly for you. Do you hate me now? Is that why you let that human touch you?"

"It... it wasn't like that." Khouri tried to push Navidae's hand away, but Navidae just took it in hand instead. He laced their fingers together, bringing them up to his lips to kiss. Cheeks hot, Khouri looked away. It was awful doing this in their bed. Khouri wanted to invite his lover in, not argue with him like he deserved. "Stop making this about you. I'm not going to forgive you for dragging me back here just because you didn't sleep with anyone while I was gone. You've never cared before. I'm not the one in the wrong here."

"Is that so?"

Khouri didn't like the look on Navidae's face. "Yes, that's so," he muttered, dragging his hand away from his lover.

"So if I did strip you bare, would I find his marks on your lovely skin?" Navidae asked. He edged closer, refusing to break eye contact. "Did you spurn me in as many ways as you could up there while running from our bed?"

"No, you wouldn't, and don't even think about trying to check." Khouri glared, fists tightening in the sheets at his sides. "Why are you acting so jealous? You know I've had other lovers. I know you have as well. What makes this so different?"

Jaw tight, Navidae looked down, his eyes searing as they gazed upon Khouri's body. "You left me, Khouri. I've no idea what to think. For instance, what is this you're wearing?" Navidae asked, drawing his hand along Khouri's exposed midriff. "You've never worn such revealing things before. Not around others. Not for anyone but me. Did the surface change you, or are you just trying to hurt me more?"

Khouri smacked his hand away. "You sound so bitter." Jealousy coated Navidae's words thickly in ways he had never heard it do before. "I wasn't going to dress like some noble's pet up there. I wanted to be taken seriously."

Navidae raised a brow, looping his fingers through the laces on Khouri's thighs. "And you thought this was the way to do it?" he whispered, tugging harshly at the strings, loosening them. "I can't say I hate the look, but Khouri, the thought of those humans looking at you..."

Before Khouri could react, his reflexes so dull and slow, Navidae was on top of him, his lips to Khouri's ear and his breath hot along Khouri's chilled skin. "It makes me want to slaughter them all," he crooned, fingers tight in the laces, in Khouri's hair. "They aren't worthy of seeing any part of you. I know you're mine, Khouri, but I can still be jealous."

Khouri had forgotten this. He had forgotten how warm Navidae was, how pervasive his words, how strong his body. But the haze filling his head was wasn't strong enough to tell him that he didn't had reason enough to be angry, and

191

nothing Navidae had to say was going to assuage him. With his hands on Navidae's shoulders, Khouri shoved with all his might, throwing Navidae off him and back onto the floor. The curtains waved like pools of blood with the movement, parting an inch to let the moonlight stream inside. Their private world was sundered, rent in two.

"Get off of me!" he grunted, forcing himself to sit up, to keep from letting Navidae back on top of him again. Navidae was gathering himself up from his graceful sprawl, a frown fixed to his face. "Don't touch me," Khouri said, threading his voice with ice. "Get out. I'm not going to sit back and let you have me after what you've done."

"Are you punishing me, pet?" he asked incredulously, his hands on the mattress. "All I did was bring you back home."

"You drugged me," Khouri hissed, turning and kicking at his lover, shoving him back towards the door. The curtains split open, framing Navidae in their bloody folds. "You sent out hunters to rip me from my wandering and carried me back into your bed. You *paid* them. You paid my partner to betray me. You deserve every ounce of spite I give you, Navidae," he spat, grabbing a pillow to throw at Navidae for good measure, chasing him towards the door. "Now get out! I don't want to see your face!"

Khouri expected Navidae to argue. He expected Navidae to glare and yell and push, but instead, Navidae grabbed the pillow from the floor and tossed it back onto the bed. "You're tired. It's understandable, I suppose," he murmured, turning towards the door with shoulders stiff. "We'll talk more after you've come to your senses, pet."

"Get the hell out," Khouri hissed.

Sighing, Navidae opened the door. "I did miss you, Khouri," he said, slipping through the doorway. His ruby eyes met Khouri's for a moment, intense and piercing in a way that twisted Khouri's stomach to knots. "Rest well."

The door closed slowly, and Khouri didn't allow himself to relax until it shut completely. His heart hammered in his chest, his cheeks flushed and eyes stinging. The pillow in his hands smelled of Navidae, and Khouri punched at it weakly, cursing the drug that made him feel so out of sorts. Scrubbing viciously at his eyes, Khouri threw himself back into the bed, ignoring how soft the sheets were, how comfortable the mattress. It still smelled like them both, even after all this time. He told himself he hadn't missed it. He told himself it wasn't a lie. With a swipe of his hand, he closed the curtain again, sealing himself from the world and all its ugly, accurate truths.

Burying his face in the pillows, Khouri shut his eyes and tried not to shake. He would make Navidae regret this. Him and Sorin both.

Chapter Nine

Sorin began to regret his decision pretty much as soon as Navidae, *vile Drow Lord of the Western Duskriven Navidae*, insisted he stay a few days before his payment could be gathered. He had already felt horrible enough with the guilt eating at him, but now, he had the added stress of being a human in a den of Drow. At any moment he expected to be attacked, either by his gracious host or his spurned and betrayed lover.

You deserve it, his inner voice muttered as Sorin once again checked every inch of the guest room for traps or hidden poison caches. *After what you did to Khouri, you deserve anything coming to you.*

Frowning, Sorin let the mattress fall back into place. He deserved a lot, but thinking it like that wasn't going to help things. If only Navidae had come and met him sooner, perhaps Sorin wouldn't have had to think about this at all. He could've been up above by now, his gold in hand as he paved the way for a cushy future without a backwards glance. Now, he had to live with the guilt and the fact that he probably wasn't ever going to see that gold.

He had to live with the fact that he had betrayed one of the best things he'd found during his travels.

Sorin grimaced at the floor. Part of him wished there was some poisoned dart or bladed trap waiting for him in this room. What an ass he had been. The sooner Navidae could gather the gold, the better off Sorin would be. Khouri would escape again no doubt, and then Sorin could relax knowing that things had worked themselves out in the end.

A knock sounded on the door, and Sorin nearly jumped out of his skin. Who could that be? He reached for his knife on the bedspread, slipping it into his boot should it prove to be an assassin. Sorin hadn't seen hide nor hair of another soul since he had been shoved unceremoniously into this room after Navidae had whisked Khouri away.

Opening the door just a crack, Sorin peered out into the hallway. "Who is it?" he asked, eyes going wide as whoever it was shoved on the other side, moving him easily as if he weighed nothing. Sorin struggled to brace it shut, but his attempts were in vain. A dour-faced Drow woman stood in the doorway, looking anything but out of breath after that display of strength.

If she had any thoughts on his attempts at denying her entry, she didn't make them obvious. "The master sends for you," the servant said quietly, her nose wrinkled in distaste. Her white hair was wound into a tight bun on top of her head, her eyes a piercing red color that reminded him far too much of fresh blood.

"Does he have my pay?" Sorin asked, on edge. Did Drow not need to blink? Her gaze was disconcerting.

Instead of answering, the servant narrowed her eyes, looking him up and down as if she found him wanting in some regard. "No," she said finally, meeting his eye after one last disapproving pass. "It is time for the evening supper. His Lordship wishes for you to join him. Follow."

Before Sorin could so much as ask why, she was turning and leaving, her pace fast enough that he rushed to follow after her. He barely had the time to close the door behind him before jogging down the hall, her gait misleadingly long for how short her legs were. "Hey, what's the rush?" he grunted, catching up just as she turned a corner. Sorin tried to keep his bearings, but the harried pace and unsettling decor made it difficult.

The servant just harrumphed, holding her head high as she led him through the halls. "His Lordship shall not be kept waiting," she said, barely glancing at him as she spoke. "Tis the height of rudeness for a guest to assert himself so."

It was the height of rudeness where Sorin came from to treat a guest so abrasively. Sorin held his tongue on the insult he wanted to lob, contenting himself with the thought that as fast as they were walking, he'd soon be where he needed to be and free of her company.

He was proven right when, after only another minute or so, they came upon a pair of thick, polished doors. The servant stopped and reached out a hand, opening them with an ease that surprised Sorin. For her slight frame, he hadn't expected to see such strength, but then again, he supposed that Drow were made of tougher stuff than humans. Peering past her, he looked inside, eager to see if Khouri were anywhere to be found.

The servant let him enter first. A hall large enough for a banquet opened up before Sorin. The ceilings were high, far higher than the outside of the manor seemed to be capable of boasting, and from the very center hung an elaborate, antiquated looking chandelier. Though it held at least a hundred candles, none of them were lit. Instead, the glow of fox fire illuminated the room, glistening eerily off the polished silver plates and cutlery clustered on one end of the enormous table.

Looking back at the servant, Sorin cleared his throat. "Where is His Lordship?" he asked, noting how not a single sound could be heard throughout the grand hall. "Am I dining alone?"

The servant sniffed. "He will be here shortly. Take a seat and begin."

If she were any chillier, Sorin might freeze solid. Nodding his head, he let out a low sigh, looking back at the places set at the table. There were three places set, two close together and the other a few seats away, back to the door. Sorin didn't need to ask to know where he was intended to sit. Despite that, he still turned back to look at the servant, only to find her gone, nothing but dead air and silence in her wake. It figured, he thought, walking towards the table, that he would be left here alone to await Navidae.

At least he didn't have to wait for dinner. The table was already laden with food from dishes that ranged from whole beasts to stewed vegetables to bowls filled with all manner of things Sorin couldn't properly identify. He sat himself down in the seat meant for him, judging the food with a careful eye. It certainly smelled edible, even if some of it looked less than normal.

"Ahh, you beat me here," a voice called out, and Sorin startled a bit, whipping around in his seat to take in the man entering. Navidae made his entrance quietly, slipping through the door with a grace that seemed to belong to all Drow. He was smiling as he always seemed to do, clothed in an ensemble that looked more expensive than Sorin's axe with a neckline just as dramatic. His sharp, dark collar bones framed a pendant of turquoise, one that matched Khouri's ever-present earrings.

"Your servant was very brisk," Sorin said, watching the Drow navigate around the table and seat himself in one of the chairs across the way. "I'd be surprised if I didn't beat you here."

"Ah, well, Nvidia doesn't like to waste her time on duties below her," Navidae smiled. "You understand. How have you found your rooms? Are they to your liking?" He gestured at the food before them welcomingly. "Of course, help yourself while we get acquainted. If you are a guest here, we should be civil."

The way he worded it sent Sorin's instincts ringing vaguely somewhere in the back of his mind. "They're fine. You obviously do very well for yourself," he said, looking between the dishes carefully. "And while I've got it on my mind, what of my payment?" Sorin asked, helping himself to the food closest to him. Meat was usually a safe bet, and he took some of whatever beast it was on the platter at his elbow. Hooved feet and wings? It smelled good, at least. "You've kept me waiting for a while now. I'm inclined to believe you don't intend on paying me."

Navidae waved his hand errantly, pouring himself wine from a silver decanter. "It's being seen to," he said offhandedly, taking a sip before he bothered to serve himself any real food. "Such impatience to be paid. It's almost as if you don't trust me."

Sorin didn't say anything. He let his look do the talking for him. It prompted a laugh from Navidae, one that sounded a lot warmer than Sorin expected it to. The Drow rested an elbow on the table and stared at him, a small smile on his lips as he took Sorin in. Sorin ignored him for the most part. Whatever the meat was, it was pretty tasty. Somewhere between a chicken and a goat but tender enough that it seemed to melt in his mouth.

"So," Navidae began, his ruby eyes unsettling enough to make Sorin stiffen in his seat.

"So," Sorin parroted, refusing to be intimidated. He took another bite, brow raised.

"My blackbird tells me that you partook of his many charms while he was away." Navidae folded his hands on top of the table, hand too close to his knife to bring Sorin any measure of comfort. "I must say I'm not fond of the idea."

It took only a moment for Sorin to parse out what he was saying. The moment it clicked was the moment Sorin began to look for an exit, swallowing the bite of food far too quickly to be safe. "Did he now?" Sorin replied, wondering just how angry Khouri was if he were selling Sorin out too. As discreetly as he could, Sorin edged his boot closer, keeping his own knife within easy reach should he need it. He glanced down at his plate for a moment, wondering if it had been wise to eat so readily. Could it have been poisoned?

Navidae rested his cheek on his propped up hand, blinking slowly at Sorin like a cat debating on going after a mouse. Where Khouri's features were soft, Navidae's were deathly sharp. His cheekbones were chiseled enough to cut should someone get it in their head to try slapping him. Navidae hummed and smiled, his mood unreadable. "He did," he said, the pointed white of his teeth just visible past his grinning lips. "He was quite vehement in his rejection of me, but he found the time to make sure I knew just how... *close* the two of you had become whilst on your travels."

Was it just a Drow thing to be so damnably vague? Did he know, or was he trying to get Sorin to admit to something? Sorin wasn't going to sit here and sweat just because Navidae found it fun. "We work well together," he decided to say. If

Navidae wanted to play this game, he only had to ask. "Khouri is a good match to me. He takes direction well."

"Why, thank you," Navidae preened, leaning forward with a smile. "You should have seen how unruly he was the day he first fell into my arms. It's been a lot of work, but I am most proud of the result."

Something like jealousy pooled in the pit of Sorin's stomach. So, they were talking about sex. He sat back up but kept his boot near, just in case. "About that," he said, noting how Navidae perked up at the potential for more. "How did you come to... know Khouri? For someone so predisposed towards wandering, I find it hard to believe he settled into a life of luxury easily." Or willingly for that matter. "Half-Drow aren't typically accepted down here, are they?"

Leaning back in his seat, Navidae looked at Sorin thoughtfully. "Curious, aren't you?" he murmured, rolling his eyes. "I suppose Khouri told you enough to make you so. He is such a wonderfully contradictory puzzle, isn't he? He came to me first," Navidae said, tapping at his bottom lip as he spoke, "some odd half-century ago. I'd certainly never seen the like of him before, so I simply felt I must have him."

The way Navidae made it sound, Khouri was just a pet to him. Grinding his teeth, Sorin narrowed his eyes. "Came to you?" he prompted, recalling how Khouri had said he hadn't been born in the Duskriven, but he had ended up there. "In what way?"

Navidae visibly adored Sorin's prodding. He smiled his sharp-toothed smile and laughed a little. "In the way that most do," he said, raising a blood-red brow. "He broke into my manor, pilfered my valuables, and then came for my head. I can still remember it as if it were yesterday. He looked so beautiful bathed in my servants' blood."

200

Navidae paused there, laughing at whatever expression Sorin wore on his face. "Oh, did I shock you?" he asked, leaning forward in mock concern. "Why, did he never tell you? I'm rather notorious in these parts. My dearest blackbird heard of a reward placed on my head by a rival family and felt the need to fill his purse. It's all rather romantic if you know how to appreciate such things."

Coming from a Drow, Sorin shouldn't have been so surprised. He leaned back in his seat, eyes still wide at the thought. Caught in the middle of a grudge, huh? Khouri certainly had a way of phrasing things. "Why didn't you just kill him?" he asked. "He tried to kill you, didn't he?"

Waving his hand, Navidae scoffed. "And waste such perfection? I can always buy more servants, but a lover like that is hard to come by. It's as you said, after all," he led, eyes dancing. "Half-Drow are a rarity down here. I simply had to have him."

"And of the family that sent the hit?" Sorin offered.

Navidae's smile grew. "I'm afraid they're no longer with us," he said cheerfully, taking his wine glass by the stem to sip from it. "Of course, I had no official hand in that. Our government frowns upon such infighting, and I am nothing if not an upstanding member of our society."

Sorin snorted, taking up his own glass and drinking from it. If it were poisoned, Navidae would see to him dying even if he did abstain. "I'm sure you're the picture of civility," he deadpanned. Drow society wasn't a very talked about thing up on the surface, but Sorin had heard tell of the government or what passed as government to them. If a family were caught fighting with another, both were liable to be eradicated in the name of preserving the peace. It hardly stopped the infighting, but it meant that those who were predisposed to it were forced to work carefully to see their success met.

"That is what my government says," Navidae chimed, laughing a little. "What the rest say depends on my mood." His eyes cut to Sorin, hard and shining like rubies. "And what does my blackbird say to you of me since we are on this topic? I'm sure he has told you all kinds of cruel things to gain your pity."

"I don't pity Khouri," Sorin said, setting his glass back down. "If you're wondering if he's bad mouthed you, he hasn't." It would have been better if Khouri had. Maybe then, Sorin wouldn't have brought him back here. "If you haven't noticed, I'm not exactly his favorite person either right now. Have you ever seen him this angry before?"

Navidae let out a sigh and shook his head. He picked at his food with his fork, looking a bit rueful. "I've known him a considerable time and I've yet to see him reject my touch like he does now. Even when we first met, he was always open to my affections. I've no way of telling how long it might last or what might soothe his anger."

"Apologizing might," Sorin muttered, but it was still loud enough for Navidae to hear. The Drow set down his fork and raised a brow. Sorin stared back, figuring he wanted him to go on. "You *do* know what apologizing is, don't you? It's not just a surface oddity."

"Don't goad me in my own home, *Hunter*," Navidae said tightly. His blood-colored eyes were narrow, burning in a way that Khouri's never did.

Sorin rolled his own at the display. So easy to anger. "Oh, I'm sorry," he answered. "I forgot you're already being spurned enough as it is." Sorin's eyes widened when Navidae made a move towards his knife. Was it better to get into a fight now, or wait until the matter of his pay really became an issue? Sorin doubted he would ever make it to the surface if he wound up killing Navidae over dinner. "But, hey, come on. I'm sure he'll come around. Being together for so long has to mean something, right?"

Just as the anger had come, it went again in the blink of an eye. Navidae let his hand fall to the table, the knife untouched. Sorin breathed a sigh of relief. He was taller than Navidae, but he knew well enough that Navidae didn't get where he was now by being weak. "What do you know?" the Drow muttered, staring frustratedly at the door. "He was mine far before you thought he was yours."

The words were worded to sting, but they didn't. Sorin leaned back in his seat and took in Navidae. For a noble with the entire world at his fingertips, he looked certifiably maudlin. He remembered Khouri's words from back in the cave. *"For all he has, I think I'm the most precious thing he can call his own."* It seemed true enough. True enough that Sorin felt a bit of pity for the man.

"I never thought he was mine," Sorin said after a moment of tense silence. "I knew he was yours from the moment I first heard him say your name." As bitter as it was to admit it, Khouri had always made his claim known. Khouri had made it clear from the start that Sorin wasn't some replacement or some grand new lover for him to run away with. Sorin wasn't clear on what he and Khouri were, sure, but he knew well enough that it wasn't comparable to what he and Navidae shared.

Navidae scoffed, eyeing him warily. "And yet you still decided to take what wasn't yours."

Sorin shrugged. "I brought him back to you, didn't I?"

"Is that supposed to excuse you for all you've done up until now? I've killed dozens who did a third of what you did to my lover," the Drow delivered. "The only reason I haven't ripped you limb from limb is for fear of what it might do to Khouri's already sour mood."

"Khouri said he's had other lovers before," Sorin said tersely, sitting up straighter. "He said he can do whatever he wanted. That you weren't in charge of him. Why do you even care that I was involved with him?" It sure as hell wasn't as if Khouri thought much of their affair. If he cared at all, he might not have spoken so much about Navidae.

There was silence. Navidae seethed, the air growing heavier with its weight. When he spoke again, Sorin shivered. "What Khouri and I share," he began, eyes burning into Sorin's, "is an understanding. I no more control him than he does me. We have rules. We have things he cannot do, and things I cannot do. He can have other lovers. By all means, he can have those who remind him that there is much that no one else can give him but me. I don't care about some nameless upstart tasting what has long been mine, so long as they realize the gift they are being given and treat it as such."

Sorin opened his mouth to say something, but Navidae held up a hand, his expression so absolute that he silenced Sorin easily. "But," Navidae continued, "he *cannot* put them before me. He can't give more of himself than what he gives to me. *You*," he hissed, his glare poisonous, "have been given far, far too much. You *expect* even more."

The sound of the door opening cut off any reply Sorin might have been about to make. Sorin didn't startle, but it was a near thing. Navidae's gaze was instantly focused somewhere over Sorin's shoulder, and Sorin turned too to take in the one they had been talking so much about.

"It's lovely to see you join us, Khouri," Navidae greeted, standing graciously to hold out the seat next to him. It was almost as if a switch had been flipped. There was no sign now of his murderous anger towards Sorin. Was it an act for Khouri's benefit? Sorin didn't know, but he kept his boot close in case he needed to defend himself should Khouri excuse himself. Fear of Khouri's disapproval would only go so far.

"Hey," Sorin greeted as well, uncomfortable as anything. Khouri moved with infinite grace, his slender arms distracting, bared as they were in the lace-work top. The silvery.... was it really spidersilk? Sorin supposed it must have been, given the proclivities of the Drow. It created a beautiful contrast to his skin, his flowing skirt exposing his thighs through the open panels on the sides. Sorin let his eyes wander, hating that Navidae did the same. Something like this felt like it should only be appreciated alone, intimately. Sorin didn't want to share any part of that with Navidae.

But, Khouri didn't even look at Navidae, and he sure as hell didn't look at Sorin. He simply snatched up the plate and a fork as he moved, bypassing the proffered seat entirely to sit further off. Navidae frowned, and Sorin hid a smile. He wasn't sitting by Sorin, but at least he wasn't sitting by Navidae either. Wordlessly, Khouri began to fill up his plate, eating quietly and ignoring the eyes on him.

Navidae cleared his throat, glancing at Sorin for just a second before addressing Khouri again. "We were just talking about you," he said brightly as if that talk hadn't been about murdering Khouri's lovers. "I'm pleased to see our words summoned you like a blessing. I can't begin to say how much you grace us both with your presence."

Sorin stared at Navidae blandly. Evidently his comment on apologies was going to be summarily ignored. What an idiot. Khouri wasn't even pretending to act like he had heard, instead opting to stare at Sorin suddenly with a gaze as intense as it was surprising.

"Your knife." Khouri's words were clipped. Polite but distant.

Sorin blinked. "My what?" he asked, his mind immediately jumping to the one in his boot. Did Khouri want to stab Navidae for his attempts at flattery? He was reaching for it already, delighted by the thought. After all Sorin had just sat through, he felt he deserved watching Navidae sweat under Khouri's heel.

Khouri closed his eyes, sighed, and then opened them again. "Give me your knife. I can't cut this meat," he said, looking like every word he had to exchange pained him.

Leaning back up, Sorin flushed. "Oh," he said, taking up the knife beside his own plate. "Yeah. Sure–"

"Pet, why don't you use mine?" Navidae quickly interjected, already standing up, knife in hand. "Or better yet, I'll cut it for you–"

Khouri's shoulders tensed, and he didn't bother looking away from Sorin as he spoke. "If you don't sit back down right now, Navidae, I'm going to jab my fork in your eye." His voice was as cold and effective as ice. Sorin shivered, and Navidae froze in place, eyes wide as he stared at his lover taking the knife from Sorin.

Navidae sat back down with a muffled thud, mouth a hard line and his back stiff. "I hardly think the situation worthy of threats, pet," he muttered, glaring at Sorin for some reason. "Aren't you mad at him too? Why am I the only one being spurned by you so viciously?"

"Well, I would say he's got more reason to be angry at you, don't you think?" Sorin offered, a grin on his face as he helped himself to more of whatever it was he was eating. Knowing Drow, it was probably some horrifying cave creature, but with Khouri there, his appetite had returned in full. "All I did was my job. You're the over-obsessed lover who sent out hunters to retrieve what you thought was yours."

Navidae clasped the edge of the table so hard that the wood groaned quietly in protest. With him wound so tightly already, Sorin felt it was no surprise that he snapped with just one barb. "I would say that creatures nearing the end of their pitifully short lives shouldn't aspire to speed up the process by goading their betters," Navidae replied, his voice level in a way that got Khouri's attention.

"I'm mad at you both," Khouri said bluntly, stabbing at his food with an annoyed air. "You should stop competing for a losing title."

Sorin smirked. "Did you hear that? I think that's your place in this race."

Navidae bristled. "Oh, no," he said, gesturing towards Sorin. "That honor is all yours. You are, after all, so painfully old. It would be cruel of me to deny you of your rightful title as the Loser of Losers when you've no chance to better yourself in this lifetime."

Oh, that was hilarious coming from a creature twice Sorin's age. He readied himself to say as much but was cut off before he could even open his mouth. Khouri stood up, his chair screeching across the floor in disapproval. The air froze in place. Sorin stared at Khouri, Navidae doing the same.

"You're both unbelievable," he said, his hands resting on the tabletop, eyes frigid enough to freeze them both in place. "Absolutely unbelievable. Is this all a game to the two of you? Is my agency a joke to be laughed at?"

When he said it like that, Sorin just felt like an ass. He chewed the inside of his cheek and met eyes with the fuming, beautiful Drow. "Of course not," he said, balking a little when Khouri turned the force of his glare solely on him.

"That's absolutely *rich* coming from the man who trussed me up like a stuffed pig and dragged me back here against my will," Khouri hissed. "You've already shown how much you value my freedom since you quite literally put a price on it."

Navidae let out a soft snicker and promptly earned Khouri's undivided attention. Sorin relaxed a little when the focus shifted off of him and onto the other Drow. He half felt sorry for Navidae for what he figured was about to come.

"Don't you dare laugh, Navidae," Khouri said coldly, his gaze as frigid as an icy wind. "I'm so angry I could break something."

Sorin had never seen Khouri so angry before, and from the looks of it, neither had Navidae. The dining hall was deathly silent, Khouri glaring down at the plate in front of him. He looked as if he were half considering lobbing it across the room. Sorin got ready to move in case he did. There was no telling which of them would be the target, but he supposed if there was one sure-fire way to test who he was most mad at, it would be that.

Instead of acting on the anger he no doubt felt, Khouri

instead crumpled. His shoulders fell, and his angry frown turned into an expression of pure sadness. "It doesn't feel like I'm home like this," he whispered, his hands clenching on the edge of the table, knuckles white. "You've locked me in a cage and expected me to say thank you for it." He looked up, meeting Navidae's eyes. "We've been together for fifty years, and you still don't even know me."

For a moment, it looked as if Khouri were storming towards the door. He shoved away from the table and cut past Sorin. Or at least he made it look as if he were going to. Sorin's eyes went wide when Khouri grabbed him by the shirt instead, yanking him from his chair with a strength Sorin hadn't been expecting. "We're leaving," Khouri told him, glaring back at Navidae as he dragged Sorin towards the door. "Don't try to follow. I don't want to see you if you're going to act like this."

Navidae stood up to protest, but they were already halfway to the door. "Khouri, come on!" Navidae called out. He had the sense to stay put, at least, not moving to follow them. "At least stay through dinner!"

Khouri shoved Sorin towards the door, whirling around in a flare of silk and lace to glare daggers at his lover. "I'll eat when and where I please, Navidae," he nearly snarled. "You've lost the right to share in my company."

And Sorin hadn't? He didn't try to ask, though, not when Khouri turned back towards him. Sorin had seen kinder looking dragons than the Drow right now. He let Khouri snatch up his arm again and drag him through the heavy doors, not bothering to take a last backwards glance at Navidae as they did so.

The pace was quick and the mood smothering. "Where are we

going?" Sorin asked gently, wincing when Khouri's nails began to cut into his arm. Was it just a Drow quirk to walk so fast?

"To your room," came the simple, barbed reply.

"Can I ask why?"

Khouri snorted, turning a corner, the pace not letting up an inch. "Because nothing will sting him more than me willingly putting you before him," he replied, smiling an unkind smile that seemed to waver, already on the verge of falling. "He's... He's too self-centered to think anything different."

Sorin let that sit in the air for a moment, nearly tripping over his feet as Khouri dragged them down another hall. He was beginning to recognize the portraits now. "Are... Are you okay?" he forced himself to ask, wincing again when the nails cut deeper.

"No," Khouri said flatly, ending the conversation there before he drew blood.

Sorin was glad Khouri seemed to know his way around, but when they stopped in front of his door, Khouri didn't bother asking before he opened it and shoved Sorin inside. Sorin stumbled and caught himself before he fell, turning around to see Khouri following him inside too. A thousand thoughts tore through Sorin's mind at what Khouri could be planning. Was he going to kill Sorin himself?

The moment the door closed, Khouri's haughty, imperious mood crashed around his feet. Khouri leaned against the door and covered his face with his hands, sliding down to sit on the ground. Sorin didn't know what to do, his instincts telling him to comfort while Khouri's body language screamed to go away.

"Khouri," Sorin called out gently, approaching slowly because he had to try something. Even if it were a trap, which he was beginning to doubt more and more every second, Sorin was honor bound at this point to do whatever he could to make amends. "Do you want to be alone?"

The Drow's narrow shoulders hunched, his hands trembling in front of his face. "I *want* none of this to have happened," he answered after a moment of nothing, his voice shaking as much as his body. "I *want* to wake up and still be on the surface with a man who wouldn't sell me out and with a lover who had enough restraint to keep himself from dragging me back before I was ready."

Sorin grimaced, his guilt doubling. He hadn't wanted things to go like this. He hadn't wanted Khouri to be so miserable. Inching closer to the Drow, Sorin sank to his knees and reached out a hand, resting it on Khouri's shoulder. When it wasn't shaken off, Sorin moved closer. Khouri didn't protest when Sorin pulled him into his arms. He didn't protest Sorin stroking through his hair or kissing his head, offering what comfort he could.

"I'm sorry," Sorin said, feeling Khouri tremble. "For what little it's worth now, I'm sorry."

"Do you even know what you're sorry for?" Khouri mumbled, holding Sorin to him, refusing to let an inch of space between them.

His skin was soft where the lace left off, and Sorin stroked along his back, kissing his even softer hair again just because he could and Navidae couldn't. "I'm sorry for making you feel like this," Sorin said, meeting Khouri's eyes when the Drow deigned to glanced up at him, dark eyes liquid and as black as night. "I'm sorry for thinking that I knew best when it came to your happiness."

"You don't," Khouri whispered, lips trembling a bit. "No one knows best but me."

"I know that now," Sorin hushed, moving a lock of Khouri's hair behind his delicate ear. He really was so pretty, wasn't he? Soft lips, dark eyes, skin as smooth as the petals of a flower. Sorin held back on the urge to kiss him, knowing now wasn't the time. After all he had done to Khouri, that time might not ever come again. "I've learned my lesson."

Khouri's face crumpled, and for a moment, Sorin feared him on the verge of tears. His small form fell heavily against Sorin's chest, and Sorin lifted him easily, toppling them back onto the bed until Khouri was laid out along his chest like a small, miserable kitten. "Th-Then why doesn't Navidae?" he stammered, hiding his face in Sorin's shirt. "Why doesn't he understand what he's done wrong? I would've come back. Why didn't he just wait for me to come back?"

Because he was an idiot? Because he was selfish, possessive, jealous, controlling? A thousand answers flooded Sorin's mind, but he held his tongue. As it stood, Sorin wasn't in much better standing. He stroked Khouri's back and held him while he shivered, letting the Drow hide his face when the tears eventually began to fall. "It's okay," Sorin soothed, knowing it was poor comfort to give. "He's an asshole, but he does care about you, right? Maybe he just needs more time to realize where he went wrong."

Khouri managed a ragged laugh. Tear tracks lined his cheeks when he looked up, but he still smiled through it. "I never thought I'd hear you defending him," he said, voice wavering as he hiccuped a little. Wiping his eyes, Khouri looked around the room a little, slipping off Sorin to settle in beside him, their legs still tangled together. "Can I…" he began, biting his lip even as he fought another sob. "Can I stay here tonight?"

Sorin would be a bigger fool than he already was if he even thought of saying no. "Of course you can," he said softly, moving to get up. This was a big manor. Sorin could find some other place to sleep. He had seen some sofas in a sitting room a hall or two away. It would be a tight fit, but he had slept on worse.

Just as he was about to slip off the bed, a small, slender hand wrapped around his wrist, holding him in place. "Where are you going?" Khouri whispered, sitting up a little.

"I was going to give you my room. Isn't that what you wanted?" Khouri was still upset with him. Sorin wasn't so much of an ass as to force the Drow to put up with his company when he wanted nothing to do with him.

Khouri averted his eyes, but his grip on Sorin's wrist was firm. "You don't have to go," he whispered softly after a moment of silence. He glanced back up at Sorin, his trembling lips striving to look cocky. "Because, you know, nothing pisses Navidae off more than us sharing a room." Khouri even managed a laugh. "It would be a good punishment for him. Once he realizes I'm not back in ours."

Sorin smiled warmly at Khouri, letting him have his excuse. "It would be," he said, tugging his hand free so that he could shuck off his shirt and toss it to the floor. He paused a moment later, looking back at Khouri. "Or… Did you want me to keep it on?" There were boundaries now. New ones that Sorin had no idea how to navigate.

But Khouri just rolled his eyes, shaking his head a little as he laid back down in the bed. "I don't care, so long as you don't expect anything to happen," he mumbled, tucking himself under the fine sheets. "I'm mad at Navidae but not mad enough to go that far."

"Fair enough." Sorin pulled back the sheets and slipped in himself, Khouri's body a smooth line against his shoulder. He turned onto his side out of habit, his arm tucking around Khouri's narrow waist loosely. Freezing again, he cleared his throat, the question on his lips but Khouri already answering.

"It's fine. Just know I'll figure out your punishment soon too," Khouri whispered followed by some short, musical noise that must have been the Drow language. The lights went out a moment later, and Khouri settled in against Sorin's front, his small hands resting atop Sorin's arm. If Sorin imagined hard enough, he could pretend Khouri was holding him there.

If only that were true. Sorin held back on the sigh in his throat and instead settled for kissing the back of Khouri's neck. "Good night, brat," he whispered, closing his eyes. The day had been long and treacherous and filled with aggravation and relief in equal measure. It was well past the time to rest, and his body seemed to agree.

And if he heard a *good night* returned to him, he would chalk it up to pleasant dreams. To think otherwise would be pushing his luck.

Chapter Ten

Khouri slept fitfully and awoke to the sight of Sorin's bare chest pressed against his cheek. For a moment, he almost wondered if it had all been a bad dream, if they weren't just sleeping still in that tavern's bed, the angry barkeep none the wiser to Khouri's presence. Khouri closed his eyes and wished with all his might that it was true.

Sorin would never sell him out. Navidae would never reward someone for dragging Khouri back kicking and screaming.

It almost worked for a moment, but then the blanket slipped and the frigid air crept in, chilling Khouri in a way that only the Duskriven's ever present cold could. If he pressed closer to Sorin, if he surrounded himself in the man's warmth, he could lie to himself for a little longer. But a lie wouldn't help him. Not really. It would only prolong the inevitable, and Khouri had long had his fill of pretending. He opened his eyes and sighed, looking into Sorin's sleeping face. The man held him close despite Khouri's warning the night before. It was hard to begrudge the contact now when it was cold, but Khouri still wrinkled his nose and began the process of untangling himself from the hunter. It wouldn't do to reward Sorin for this kind of behavior. Not when Khouri was still mad at him, and not when Sorin could take it as an allowance he didn't deserve.

Carefully, arduously, Khouri extracted himself from Sorin's embrace, slipping out of the bed as quietly as he knew how. Sorin didn't stir, probably still worn out from the dinner yesterday. Khouri ran his fingers through his hair, pushing it back from his eyes to take in the room around him. This was just a guest room, so he would need to go back to his own for clothes. There was no telling what Navidae had done with his old ones, the ones he had worn on the surface, or his satchel. Sorin's room held only his own belongings, the bed, a wardrobe, and a few paintings that illustrated Navidae's unwelcoming mood towards Sorin in general.

Khouri's lips curved into a slight smile as he drew near the closest one, his fingers brushing the smooth frame. Navidae really didn't like Sorin. The picture was unsettling, even to Khouri, the portrait of some Drow with sharp, piercing eyes that seemed to follow the viewer's every move. One of Navidae's ancestors, probably, but that didn't negate the creepiness. If anything, it sent the message that even if Navidae wasn't watching Sorin, someone was.

Such theatrics. Khouri really was home.

He rolled his eyes and dropped his hand, heading to the door. The hallway was as chilly as it had been the day before, barren of all life and just as welcoming. Khouri closed Sorin's door and began the long walk back to the room he and Navidae shared, arms wrapped around his chest to keep out the cold. Navidae was probably already awake and gone, off doing his duties as a noble. If Khouri were lucky and quiet, there was a good chance he would be able to get in the room and out before Navidae became wise to his location.

The thought alone made Khouri frown. He turned another corner of the seemingly endless halls, ears tuned to any sound that might mean someone was ahead. He didn't want to see Navidae at all, not after last night and certainly not after that horrible reunion. As much as he had missed his lover, Khouri couldn't forgive him after what he had done. Not until Navidae realized how out of line he was and apologized properly for it.

Sighing, Khouri spotted the room he needed and made for

it, opening the door slowly and peering inside only to find it empty. As quickly as he could, he darted inside and locked the door behind him, heading to the wardrobe where he kept his clothes. They were all outfits that Navidae had bought for him– beautiful, expensive things that highlighted his figure or his skin, his collarbones or his ankles. They felt like woven water as Khouri skimmed his hand down the lengths of the hanging garments. He closed his eyes with a frown.

What he and Navidae had shared had always been more understood than outlined. They had had their rules for things, and they knew what annoyed or hurt the other, but aside from that, there had never been much emphasis put on communicating. There was no need when Khouri was comfortable with anything Navidae wanted to give him and vice versa. Pulling one of the outfits from the wardrobe, Khouri set to stripping and wondered when things had gotten so out of sync. Once upon a time, they had understood each other implicitly. Now, Khouri would be lucky to make Navidae understand why he had done what he had done.

"It never used to be so hard," he muttered under his breath, tossing his worn clothes to the floor and leaving them for someone else to deal with. Scrubbing at his eyes, he snatched up the new outfit, tying the strap behind his neck clumsily as he went. Navidae used to do it for him, but Khouri didn't need him. He pulled on the leggings next and closed the wardrobe with a slam, marching to the door. He unlocked it and slammed the door behind him too for good measure, making off down the hall for.... somewhere.

Where was he even going? Khouri slowed for a moment but then forced himself to keep moving. Back to Sorin's room? Sorin wasn't in much better standing than Navidae, and if Khouri lingered around with him, Sorin would no doubt try to suck up to him in hopes of making amends. Back to the master bedroom? Khouri held back a grimace. It would just be a matter of time before he ran into Navidae there, and there was no way Khouri wanted to put himself near a bed while Navidae was in the vicinity.

His cheeks warmed at the thought. Navidae was nothing if not convincing, and angry as Khouri still was, he had missed Navidae's unique brand of touch. But no. No. Khouri wouldn't tempt fate by making it easier on his lover. He looked to the left and then to the right, puzzling over his options just as an idea took root. If Navidae were working, then he would be off in his study. The library was always empty this time of day. Empty most times, in truth, since Navidae mainly kept it as a gift to Khouri anyway. The added bonus of Sorin not knowing where it was cinched it as the obvious choice.

Decision made, Khouri turned left and moved as quickly as he could down the hall past the judgemental eyes of the portraits along the walls and around the various statues and art pieces Navidae liked to clutter the place with. The library took up a sizable portion of the manor's third floor, dominating an entire wing all on its own. The heavy oak doors opened with a strong push, and Khouri slipped inside, breathing in the familiar and comforting scent of paper, ink, and dust that always seemed to linger in the air despite regular cleanings. The grime never bothered Khouri. If anything, it was nice to be in a place that wasn't quite pristine and perfect. Relatable in a way. Nostalgic in others.

Looking around the large, cavernous room told him that Navidae hadn't changed much during Khouri's absence. The shelves towered high above his head, still sitting where Khouri had left them. There was an ever-present fire in the fireplace and a thick layer of dust along the chairs nearest to it. Something tugged in Khouri's chest at the sight, but he didn't linger on the thought of why the sight of it upset him. It wasn't as if Navidae had spared all that much time to sitting and reading with him anyway. Too busy, Navidae would say. Instigating the ruling class was a full time occupation.

The thoughts made Khouri frown and hold himself tighter. Ignoring the fireplace, he looked instead to the shelves. They were as they had always been, sculpted from obsidian and polished to a deadly shine. In the light of the fire, they glistened like the darkest of ink. Reaching out a hand, Khouri trailed his fingers along the dark surface, taking in the books nearest to him. Navidae had never paid any mind to a cataloguing system, but Khouri knew them all by heart.

His fingers trailed over the titles. *In the Blackest Pit, In Mortal Fields, The Tale of Visitric, Under the Azure Sky.* There was no helping the sigh that came. They were all memoirs and tales of adventure and travel and intrigue. Khouri had read them all at one time or another, the only form of escape he had from the oppressive darkness he called home. He pulled one from the shelf and stroked the cover gently. For a moment, he had seen and felt what the books had promised. It was just a shame that his story had to end so abruptly.

Pushing the book back into its spot, Khouri moved towards the far wall out of habit, sitting down on the pillowed window sill just as he would always do on days where he felt suffocated. The glass was cold, but the cushions were warm, and when he leaned his forehead against the window, he saw that not much had changed outside either since he had left. He had only been gone a few months, which in their world was as good as the blink of an eye. Why had he expected things to look different now? Maybe the surface really had spoiled him.

The city twinkled back at him grimly, seeming to agree. Navidae was far from the shady, disgusting places where Khouri had spent most of his childhood, but that didn't mean much in the Duskriven. Practically every burrow held its own measure of danger, just in different forms. The streets were glossy black here, well-maintained and redolent of the wealth residing along its length. Arching posts hung overhead, providing light in the form of shapeless, white balls of undulating magic. What little plant life there was was painstakingly maintained to the point of artificiality, cultivated to appear as something more fetching than just undergrowth planted along the street in measured intervals. It was a shame Khouri had spent the whole trip below unconscious. He would have paid a great deal to watch Sorin try and navigate the nameless streets with the body of Lord Navidae's lover slung over his shoulder. Must have been hard to find his way around like that. No one around here would stick around long for fear of the fallout.

His eye followed the line of the street until he grew bored of it, and then he turned his sights further away where he finally noticed a spot of different among the sea of sameness. Across the way, Khouri could see the facade of another building. Unlike before, its windows were now boarded up; the sharp, wicked fence around the property was broken and fractured.

Khouri hummed, only vaguely wondering what might have happened. It wasn't an odd thing to see down here, and he assumed it had to do with politics. Navidae might have even been responsible for the demise of the neighboring family, though he would never be so brash as to publicize the fact. He would save that for later when he had Khouri in his bed or on his lap, close enough to whisper of his deeds proudly. No doubt the family that had once occupied the manor was now dead or exiled, perhaps even married off to save face and preserve what little standing they had left. At any rate, their demise presented something new to look at, which Khouri thought was nice.

He still sighed. He couldn't help but stare at the other building ruefully, wishing he could go over and explore it, perhaps check for things that might have been missed in the looting. There were always so many secret compartments and hidden mechanisms lurking behind walls and within the floorboards. Jewels, deeds, money… There was no end to the possibilities, but Khouri knew that Navidae would never allow it.

On a whim, he tugged at the window's frame. A short, fleeting zap stung his fingertips, informing him that, yes, Navidae had indeed updated his security spellwork. There would be no sneaking in or out of the manor this time.

Kneading at his eyes, Khouri brought his legs up onto the window sill as well, wrapping his arms around them as he stared forlornly out the window. It wasn't surprising that Navidae would have reinforced them after Khouri's escape. It had taken years of waiting for the charms to wear down enough to let Khouri slip away, and there was no way Navidae would let the same thing happen a second time. If Khouri wanted to go outside, Navidae would have to be the one to let him out.

He nearly scoffed at the thought. The only way that would happen would be if Navidae accompanied him. Before, Khouri had been able to come and go as he pleased so long as he gave notice and told Navidae where he was going. Khouri hadn't left much in those early days, too content with the wealth around him and the gifts and pleasure and attention as it was heaped upon him. Now, he doubted that he would ever see that level of freedom again.

What a mess it all was. The situation, his relationship, his… whatever it was he shared with Sorin. The greatest casualty of all had to be Khouri's head. His thoughts were spinning and racing like a dervish, longing for a solution to the problems before him. Perhaps time would bring answers, but for now, Khouri knew he just needed space enough to think.

The sound of the door opening told him quite tersely that space was one thing he would not be getting any time soon. Shoulders stiff, lip between his teeth, Khouri ignored the sound of Navidae entering and instead focused all of his attention on the view outside the window.

"Good afternoon, my blackbird," Navidae greeted, his voice soft and musical in the still air of the library. For a moment, Khouri was transported back to when Navidae would come upon him in here and carry him off to bed. "I hope you slept well," he added when Khouri said nothing, "wherever it was you ended up sleeping."

Khouri heard it for the question it was. He just ignored it entirely. If he ignored him long enough, perhaps Navidae would take the hint and leave him be. Just because the man knew where Khouri liked to sit didn't mean he needed to seek him out in hopes of getting Khouri to talk to him. It wouldn't work.

Navidae's frown was practically audible behind him. The Drow began to pace, his clothing whispering softly as he moved. Out of the corner of his eye, Khouri saw him pick up a book from a shelf, flip through it, and then put it back. If Khouri wasn't mistaken, it was the same book he himself had looked at. "I missed you last night," Navidae offered next, his eyes heavy on Khouri's shoulders. "After you left, you know. Meals never taste as good when you're not there sharing them with me."

Lips curling into a frown, Khouri held his legs tighter. That almost sounded sincere. It would be more sincere if followed by Navidae excusing himself for his pigheadedness and apologizing for all he had done wrong, but Khouri knew that wasn't going to happen. Not anytime soon at any rate.

"You don't feel like talking to me now either, do you?" Navidae sighed. His pacing resumed, closer this time, his eyes raking over Khouri's figure no matter how tightly he held himself. The glass was shiny, and when Navidae approached, Khouri could see him in the reflection. He looked mournful as he took Khouri in. "Your hair is longer. I guess you really have been away for awhile." Giving a mirthless chuckle, Khouri watched him shake his head a little. "It looks so much like it did when we first met. So messy and unkempt. I forgot how much I liked the look on you."

Khouri frowned and told himself to cut his hair at the soonest opportunity. He stopped looking at Navidae's reflection. He had humored him enough already.

"You aren't wearing your jewelry," he observed next, and if Khouri cared to look harder, he was sure he would find confusion on Navidae's face. "Where is your collar? Your sandals? I see you kept the earrings, but it's odd to see you without the rest too."

The silence dragged on for a minute, maybe longer, before Khouri let out a breath, realizing that Navidae wasn't going to leave without being acknowledged. "Perhaps I didn't see the need to wear them," Khouri said dismissively, eyes firmly rooted on the window. He wondered what Navidae would say if he learned that the vast majority of Khouri's gems and baubles were now occupying various pawn shops.

Navidae hummed pensively, moving around the room smoothly for want of something to do. "Could it be because I bought you those things?" he pondered aloud. "The earrings were the first gift I ever gave you, but the rest are still sentimental items, I would think. Could you really be so angry with me?"

Khouri didn't answer. He had nothing to say to Navidae. Nothing at all.

"Or could it be," Navidae went on, not hampered in the slightest by an unwilling conversation partner, "that you no longer have them?"

Despite his best efforts, Khouri stiffened. His jaw went tight, and he kept his eyes on the outside world. "What makes you think that?" he asked as flatly as he could, hating that he had to encourage Navidae with conversation just to learn what he knew.

Navidae laughed a little. "Oh, a few reasons. Would you care to hear them? I suppose you do since you bothered answering me." He sighed wistfully. "I know where you keep them, firstly, and I saw they were missing soon after I realized you were gone. They haven't been put back, and I doubt you would keep them on you but not wear them. At first, I wondered if you weren't just hiding them in that human's room, but the staff I had in there reported that there was no sign of your usual adornments within his belongings."

Khouri opened his mouth to complain about the invasion of privacy, but Navidae was still talking. "Secondly, you've gone back to wearing your usual clothes. I know what you like to wear with what. You never wear a low collar without something around your neck, and if you choose to go barefoot, you always wear your sandals. You are a creature of habit, my blackbird, no matter how much you may think otherwise. I know you far better than you give me credit for." He paced a little behind Khouri, the soft sounds of his spidersilk cloak whispering as he moved. "But then again, I suppose the most damning piece of evidence would be this."

A familiar chiming cut through the air, and Khouri turned woodenly only to see Navidae cradling the silver and ruby bracelet between his fingers. The very same that Khouri had almost sold a few weeks ago to some foul-breathed pawn shop owner but kept because of sentimentality. Navidae was smiling softly at it, and Khouri watched him glance up. The gems glistened brightly in the room, mocking him for his weakness. It only grew worse when Navidae dipped back into his pocket, this time bringing out a jeweled lace collar, one that Khouri had ended up selling to pay for Sorin's exorbitant fees.

So, Navidae knew. He knew that Khouri had sold them, and he knew that he had kept the oldest pieces, too attached to see them in the hands of another. "If you're trying to make me feel guilty, it won't work," Khouri said, finally meeting Navidae's eyes.

"I'm not." Navidae crossed his arms and stared evenly at Khouri. His fingers tapped against his silk-covered arms, almost as if he were staring at an unsolvable problem. "Did you not like them? The gifts, I mean."

Why did he care so much? "They were fine," Khouri answered. "I just needed money, and I wasn't about to pawn things that weren't mine." He looked back down to the streets below, taking in the grimy streets, the dark that loomed just out beyond the ever-present glow of the city. "I didn't think you'd notice or care much one way or another. You give me so much already."

"I don't think I cared much until I was informed that you kept the earrings and bracelet. Protected them viciously, they said. It may have been decades ago, but I still remember giving you these as the very first tokens of my claim."

Navidae paused for a moment. "They said you killed half a dozen bandits to hold on to them, and in all honesty, it just made me want you back even more, hearing that." He gave a soft chuckle. "Do you want these back, pet? They're rightly yours, your personal attachment to them notwithstanding."

Khouri just shook his head. "I won't wear them while I'm angry with you," he said dully, turning away again. "I know how much you like me wearing them. Consider it another punishment for you. Another of your own making."

The jewelry made a sad sound as it was tucked away, one that nearly rivaled Navidae's sigh. "I don't think you've ever been this cruel to me before," he remarked. "Even when I first found you. Don't you remember?" Navidae murmured, his voice lilting and smooth in the quiet of the room. "You came to me so eagerly compared to this. A half-starved creature with no master, yearning for a kind touch, though you hardly knew yourself what you wanted."

"And instead I found you," Khouri said petulantly, curling up tighter in his small window sill. He kept his eyes on the city below even though there was nothing of interest to see. It had been like that before, back when Khouri had lived on the streets, stealing and fighting to survive. His curiosity had taken him here into Navidae's palace, and then once that had lost its luster, it had taken him above.

Navidae kicked at the floor pitifully. Khouri ignored him.
Or tried to up until the man grew close enough to touch, the
warmth of his body a physical presence against Khouri's
spine. "Don't sound so bitter, pet," Navidae pleaded, hovering
his hand over Khouri's hair but hesitating to touch. Smart
of him, Khouri thought. He wasn't sure what he would do if
Navidae tried something, but it seemed Navidae wasn't quite
sure if he were ready to find out either. "You know I only
wanted what's best—"

"If the words 'what's best for you' come out of your
mouth," Khouri spat, turning to glare at his lover, "I will make
you regret bringing me back into your home."

Navidae flinched, his eyes wide. His hand fell back to
his side. "*My* home?" he repeated, a look of utter confusion
passing over him. "Since when has it just been *my* home?
Khouri, this is your home too. It's been your home for—"

He couldn't listen to this. Khouri stood up, and Navidae
backed away, letting him move away from his window
sill. Navidae rallied quickly though, following after him
incessantly. "It's been your home for *years*, Khouri," he
continued, throwing a hand towards the window he had just
abandoned. "Ever since you came through that window. You
don't belong above. You belong here where you're treasured.
Not in the arms of some *human* you stumbled upon and most
certainly not wandering around aimlessly amongst people who
would see you dead in a heartbeat."

"I… I never thought I belonged up there," Khouri said
quietly, turning just enough to glance up at Navidae. His lover
was flushed and frustrated, but the fact that he was trying
to argue at all was something surprising in itself. Navidae

227

thought himself above such things, too prideful to risk losing an argument to bother starting one in the first place. "You don't understand anything. You certainly don't understand that I'm in no mood to talk to you right now."

"It's been days since you came back," Navidae said pointedly, and Khouri didn't bother to correct him on the details of his return. It wouldn't do any good when Navidae still thought himself in the right. "You dodge my every move. You refuse even to eat with me, let alone share our bed… I fear your mood to talk is as absent as my patience to wait for its return."

"Why don't you just hire a bounty hunter then?" Khouri sniped, knowing it was childish. "Maybe then, they would bring it back for you?"

Navidae covered his face with his hand, sighing deeply. Khouri turned back around, fuming. Why hadn't Khouri thought about this eventuality? He should have prepared himself for a confrontation or at least thought of better ways to deny Navidae than just childish quips and shouting. He clenched the silk of his mantle tightly, his knuckles going white. Navidae didn't even understand what he had done wrong. How were they going to have a mature discussion when Navidae failed to even pick up on that much?

His thoughts were severed like strings hewn with a swiping blade when Navidae embraced him from behind, his approach as silent as the grave and just as insidious. Khouri didn't know what to do. He shook and stared at the floor, Navidae's familiar scent washing over him in a heady wave.

"What do I have to do to have your forgiveness?" Navidae asked, nuzzling Khouri's hair, his hands squeezing his hips. "It's utter agony having you mad at me, Khouri. Not when I just wanted you back in my arms."

"How can I forgive you of anything when you don't even understand what you've done?" he replied, hating how he leaned into his lover's warmth. It wasn't like being embraced by Sorin or anyone else for that matter. Sorin was blunt, uncomplicated. He said what he meant, and he did what he wanted because it was what he wanted to do. Nothing more, nothing less. Navidae, though… Navidae was a thousand sharp angles wrapped in silk; one wrong move would have Khouri cut to pieces.

"Oh, it's easy, my blackbird," Navidae told him, kissing lightly at the tip of Khouri's ear. "But, let's not worry about that now. Heavy topics can wait, can't they? Why don't we get reacquainted? It's been so long, after all."

Navidae's teeth were the worst kind of distraction. They conjured memories of late nights and heated touches, of unbearable ecstasy and dizzying pain. An embrace was never just an embrace. It was a chance to fall. A chance to lose entirely should he make the wrong decision. Should he be weak.

Khouri wasn't weak. He shrugged off Navidae's arms and stepped away, turning to look his lover in the eye. His cheeks were flushed, but he forced himself to ignore it. It and Navidae's hungry, eternal lust both.

"You really think you can have me again, don't you?" he asked, holding himself as he stared at Navidae. "You really don't think you've done something wrong."

"I think I've done something to make you upset," Navidae corrected, his expression falling at the rejection. "You've been upset before, and you still let me touch you. It's just a little

229

fight, Khouri. We've been apart for ages, so why won't you let me make it up to you?"

"In the only way you know how?" Khouri scoffed, his hands squeezing tight into fists. He could still feel Navidae's warmth on his skin, his teeth against his ear. He wanted it, but if he let Navidae get his way, nothing would change. Nothing would be learned. "If you want me, you have to do better than that, Navidae."

Navidae took a step closer, his eyes burning. "What do I have to do then?" he asked, coming to a stop in front of him. "What do I have to do to earn your touch? You don't want gifts; you don't want my attention. So, what can I give you to make you want me again?"

"I want to go back to the surface–"

"Anything but that," Navidae interrupted, stopping him before he could finish. "I won't let you go where I can't follow, Khouri. You belong here. Not up there."

Khouri bared his teeth, dropping his hands to his sides. Anything but that? Fine. "I want you to get on your knees," he said in a silky, pervasive tone. This time, Khouri came to Navidae, looking up at him with barely an inch between them. "I want you to get on your knees, throw away your pride, and beg me to share your bed again."

Navidae looked stricken. His nostrils flared and he stiffened. "Excuse me, pet?"

"You heard me," Khouri whispered, licking at his lips and smiling when Navidae leaned closer to him, no doubt wanting to taste. "If you want me, you have to work for it. Prove to me that you really are willing to do anything to have me back where I belong."

"I'm inclined to think you'd look better on your knees," Navidae said, his lips barely an inch from Khouri's. His hands were hovering at Khouri's arms, the warmth bleeding through the air like temptation. "Are you really so stubborn?"

Khouri smiled, pulling back just as Navidae went in for a kiss. "I think I am," he said, taking a step back, looking over his shoulder at Navidae with his eyes half-mast. He had forgotten how good it felt, this back and forth between them. Navidae had never struggled to keep up with him. That, at least, hadn't faded with the distance. "Get to kneeling, Navidae. Else, I'll go spend my evening elsewhere. In more accommodating company."

It was a heady thing, watching the want and pride war it out in Navidae's eyes. His jaw was tight and his shoulders stiff. He parted his lips as if he wanted to argue, only to think better of it. Khouri rolled his eyes and looked at his nails, letting out a low sigh. "I suppose Sorin will have to satisfy me tonight," Khouri remarked, taking a step towards the door. "A shame. I've nearly forgotten the feeling of your embrace."

"Stop."

Khouri paused, hand posed on the ornate door handle. He turned and raised a brow, watching Navidae simmer. "Yes?" Was he really going to do it?

"You really are cruel to me," Navidae muttered, averting his eyes as he sank to his knees. "Utterly cruel. I'd kill that human in his sleep if I thought you wouldn't resent me even more for it."

"That... doesn't sound like an apology," Khouri said

slowly, his hand slipping from the door. His heart was pounding, cheeks flushed at the sight of his prideful lover on his knees. Had Navidae ever been so thoroughly knocked down before? It must be hellish for him, feeling so weak.

Navidae blinked slowly, seething beneath it all. Khouri took a step towards him, waiting. "You...." Navidae looked at the wall. "You vex me in so many ways. Please come back to my bed. To *our* bed. I can't bear another night of knowing you're back but still so far from me." He looked back, meeting Khouri's eyes ruefully. "There. Will you accept me now that I've made a fool of myself?"

"If you think that is what constitutes begging for my forgiveness, I fear you'll never hold me in your arms again," Khouri delivered coolly.

"Well, excuse me if I'm not familiar with the concept of begging," Navidae snapped. "I tend to leave that to you, so unless you'd care to give me a reminder of what it looks like–"

Khouri rolled his eyes and moved back towards the door. Why had he even bothered? Navidae was as sincere as a beast and just as pushy. It had been a mistake to think he might apologize, and an even bigger one to think that maybe, just maybe, Navidae cared enough about him to show some modicum of weakness.

He was just about to step out into the hall when Navidae leapt to his feet and grabbed him from behind, dragging him into his arms before Khouri could manage leaving. He struggled and snarled, glaring at Navidae, but Navidae was big and strong, and when it came to a competition of strength, Navidae would always win.

"Get off of me!" Khouri hissed, wriggling and clawing at

Navidae's arm fixed around his chest. Navidae was so strong that he felt his feet leave the floor, his lover hefting him easily to carry him away from the door. "Put me down!"

"No," Navidae grunted, carrying him back over to the window sill and plopping him down onto the pillowed edge. He boxed Khouri in with his arms before Khouri could dart away, holding him to the seat as he knelt again between Khouri's thighs. "I won't let you go. Not until you forgive me."

"This is the exact *opposite* of how you should be seeking it," Khouri spat, shoving at Navidae's shoulders. Navidae's hands rose up to grab his wrists, stopping him from scratching like he wanted to. The cold glass of the window met his shoulders, his lover rising up to follow him back. "Navi, *stop*," he pleaded, closing his eyes. "Why don't you understand? It's you acting like this that makes me run away!"

The hands around his wrists let go suddenly. Khouri opened an eye, breathing heavily as Navidae edged away, his head cocked and eyes narrowed. "What do you mean?" he asked, brow furrowed. "You've never complained before about how I treated you."

Khouri took the chance while he had it, planting his bare foot on Navidae's chest and shoving him back enough to let him stand up. He did it fast so Navidae couldn't grab his ankle. "If you're so blind that you can't even see what's wrong with your behavior," Khouri recited, moving past him and for the door again, "then there's nothing I can do to help you."

"Where are you going?" Navidae was scrambling to his feet, the sound of his fumbling loud in the quiet of the soon-to-be-empty room.

"Back to Sorin's room," Khouri shot, already halfway

out the door. He spared Navidae only a single glance. One last look to show him just how badly he had erred in this nonsensical apology attempt. "Don't you even think of following me." His lover looked despondent. Lost.

Good, Khouri thought, shutting the door behind him. He didn't care one bit. If he thought it enough, it would probably become true. The sick feeling in his stomach couldn't last forever.

Navidae was an idiot. An utter idiot. It wasn't hard to see what Khouri wanted from him. It wasn't hard to see why he was upset, yet here he was, having to explain it to Navidae like a mother to a child. Khouri kicked at the plush carpet, scowling at the ostentatious decorations along the walls of the hall. He remembered a time when he had been dazzled by the wealth Navidae boasted in his home and on his person. He remembered being so awestruck, so delighted by every bauble he was given. But now, Khouri could hardly stomach the sight.

Was it too much to ask for, to be able to wander? Navidae delighted in calling him a bird, but this place was a gilded cage whose bars loomed closer, growing tighter every day.

When Khouri entered Sorin's room, he didn't let the human speak. He just threw himself into the bed and buried his face in Sorin's chest, wishing the covers would swallow him whole.

"I'm beginning to wonder if you even have your own room," Sorin grunted, tossing aside the daggers he had been sharpening for want of something to do.

"I don't," Khouri muttered, comforting himself with Sorin's familiar scent. It was entirely unlike Navidae's, woodsy and smokey like the fires they would light in the forest up above. If Khouri could just lose himself in the scent, maybe it would transport him back to a place where the world was quiet and where Navidae couldn't get to him. "Do you want *me* to go?"

"Do you want me to go?" Sorin asked him right back, smoothing his hand down Khouri's spine. "I can go find somewhere else to be if you just want a bed to sleep in that doesn't have him in it."

Khouri smiled against the man's shirt, lifting his head to meet Sorin's eyes. "How chivalrous of you." He stroked down Sorin's chest, biting his lip a little. "You don't have to leave. I just wanted some space. He won't come in here, so I can avoid him in peace."

Sorin's big hand carded through his hair, so gentle despite the size. "What happened?" he asked, his senses too good to fool. "Did you get into an argument?"

"What do you think?" Khouri sighed, burying his face in Sorin's shirt. "He's not understanding me. He doesn't even seem like he's trying to. It's like he's so focused on having me back in his arms that he can't see that what he did was wrong." It wasn't that complicated, was it? Was it really so hard to see why Khouri was upset? Sorin hushed him and petted him, but it didn't do much to answer Khouri's questions or assuage his worries.

"I just..." Khouri began, Sorin's hand stalling for a moment in his hair. "I just wanted to travel. I wanted to see things. Experience things. I can't be happy trapped in a place like this. I would have come back if he had just waited." Pausing, Khouri looked up at Sorin. "Is that so hard to understand?"

"I don't think it is," he said carefully. "Have you thought about... leaving?"

235

Khouri snorted, burying his face deeper. "That's what got me into this mess, Sorin," he said, his voice muffled. What good would leaving do again? Navidae hadn't been wrong in saying that the surface was no place for him. The rest of the Duskriven was no better either. "I've got nowhere to go, no one to rely on, and no prospects." And for as much as he still wanted to leave, Navidae was... he was still Khouri's lover. Khouri couldn't just forget about him, and even if he could, he didn't want to. Being with Navidae made him happy. They were good together aside from this one, monumental thing.

Sorin shifted beneath him, uncharacteristically nervous. "That's... not necessarily true," he said quietly, his hand stroking comforting shapes along Khouri's spine.

Khouri frowned, scooting higher on his chest to meet his avoidant eye. "What do you mean?" he asked, cocking his head. "You know better than anyone how limited my options are."

Sorin grumbled and pushed Khouri's face back down. "I'm just saying you aren't as alone on the surface as you think," he muttered. "I mean, if you weren't still mad at me. I'm not as young as I used to be–"

"I'll say," Khouri cut in, earning himself another scowl. "You're ancient."

"Says the brat twice my age," Sorin snapped. "You know what? Nevermind. Pretend I said nothing. You're alone on the surface. Carry on with your moping."

"Well, now you've got me curious," Khouri groused, snatching up Sorin's hand and resting it on his cheek. "Come on, tell me what you were going to say. You're getting old, so...?"

"So," Sorin bristled, his voice rough but his touch soft as he stroked his thumb along Khouri's cheekbone. "I was thinking I might need some help with my work. Collecting bounties is all well and good, but if I had a partner, I could be doing a lot more..."

A myriad of feelings filled Khouri at the word *partner.* Fear. Distrust. Anger. Hope. He averted his eyes and bit his lip, wondering how he was supposed to feel. "The last time you said that," he murmured, letting Sorin pull his attention back onto him, "you stabbed me with a sleeping draught."

"We all do stupid things." Sorin frowned, looking decidedly uncomfortable.

"You mean *you* do stupid things," Khouri amended coolly. "I just sleep with stupid men."

Sorin let out a mirthless laugh. "You really do," he said, sighing as he relaxed into the pillows. "But, the offer is there. I'm as sincere as I can be. You don't have to trust me. I'll gladly work to earn it if that's what it takes to win you over."

Khouri didn't know what to say. The idea wasn't unpleasant. It wasn't unpleasant at all. Looking up at Sorin, Khouri felt his cheeks warm. Sculpted face, piercing blue eyes, and a mouth as cruel as it was kind. So different from Navidae. Maybe that was a good thing.

Clearing his throat, Khouri let out the breath he hadn't realized he had been holding. "Partner?" he murmured nonchalantly, something like hope flooding his chest. He kept his eyes low, trying not to look as excited as he felt. "You really think of us as that?"

Sorin shrugged, embarrassed by his own admittance. "We

237

work well together," he said, brushing a lock of Khouri's hair behind his ear. "You're an utter nightmare, but I had fun with you. So, yeah," he went, meeting Khouri's eye. "If you were to come back above with me, I envisioned us as partners. Real ones. Share the map ones."

Khouri didn't know what to say. He didn't know how to feel besides elated that Sorin had enjoyed his company so much. Leaning up, he kissed the hunter chastely, stomach aflutter at the thought of them returning to normality up above. There were a thousand things standing between them and that dream, but Khouri didn't want to think of them. They could wait for later.

"You aren't off the hook," Khouri whispered, leaning in for another kiss.

Sorin's hands were gentle on his waist, doing nothing but resting there, letting Khouri lead. "I know," he said, looking into Khouri's eyes. "But I'd be a poor partner if I didn't do what I could to make you feel better now. If you'd have me."

Khouri smiled against Sorin's lips, losing himself in the tender embrace. For the moment, for the night, for just a measure of peace that he couldn't find anywhere else. Reality existed just outside the door, and eventually, something would have to give. But for now, Khouri would focus on this.

Just this.

Chapter Eleven

Khouri had to wonder if it were worth it to give in to Navidae first just to break the monotony that had become his life.

The dullness came upon him slowly but surely, and it came in the guise of a pattern that even Khouri could feel was stifling. Wake up, bathe, wake up Sorin, goad him into bringing him food, whittle away the hours by reading or sleeping or talking, and then fall into bed to repeat the whole cycle over again the next day.

By the fourth day of nothing new, Khouri felt ready to rip his hair out.

By the fifth, he was readying himself to be even more drastic. Thankfully, Sorin was right beside him through it all, still hard up about not being paid but taking it with as much grace as he could with Khouri in the room. The hunter was as supportive as he could be, given the circumstances, but even that was beginning to grate on Khouri's nerves. Sorin could be as apologetic as he pleased, but it didn't solve Khouri's problems. If anything, it just reminded him of how he was avoiding them.

"You're in peril again," Khouri sighed, his tone a little brisker than it needed to be given the game they were playing. Clearing his throat, he tried again, this time with a bit of a smile. "Maybe I need to explain the rules again to you. You don't seem to be very good at this game."

"Give me a break," Sorin grunted, staring at the piece in his hand with a glare. "I'm still picking it up. I'll beat you this time."

Khouri rolled his eyes. Again? They had already played a dozen games. "If you really want to lose so badly, who am I to deny you?" he teased, setting the board back up dutifully. "I suppose it's not like I've anything better to do with my time than trounce you at a children's game."

"I don't know; it seems like a big manor," Sorin shrugged, setting down the piece he had in his hand in the wrong spot. "I'm sure there are better things you could be doing than hiding out here with me."

With a tight smile, Khouri moved the piece to where it belonged, snorting a little at Sorin's irritated expression. "This is pretty much the only place I can be where I won't get ambushed again," he said ruefully, gesturing towards Sorin to make the first move. It was a rookie move, the same one Sorin had led with all the other games, but Khouri supposed confidence was tantamount to foolishness when it came to trying again. "That leaves my options pretty slim."

"Well," Sorin led, avoiding his eye as he spoke. "Maybe you should just get it over with."

Khouri's piece clacked against the board a little harder than necessary. "How do you mean?" he said tightly, dispatching Sorin's knight-errant with brutal efficiency.

"I *mean*," Sorin moved his next piece, this time a little less foolishly, "that it might be better just to talk to him and get it over with instead of hiding away for the rest of your life. I can tell you miss him, Khouri." Sorin's eyes were steady when he looked at Khouri, even though his voice was bitter. "You've missed him since you ran to the surface. Ass though he may be, I know you want to see him still."

Khouri bit down on his lip hard enough to taste blood. He stared at the board and took his move blindly, avoiding Sorin's knowing eye. "You don't know anything," he muttered, crossing his arms. It was chilly in here, the fire not doing nearly enough to keep him warm. Sorin was wrapped in his mantle even, but Khouri only had his sheer clothes. "Hurry up and make your move. We'll play something different after this."

Sorin pursed his lips but said nothing, knowing well enough how Khouri felt. He took his chancellor in hand and carefully judged the available spaces around him, moving her to one for a moment before moving her to another. Indecision tensed the man's shoulders, his jaw tight as he studied the board. His seriousness was nearly enough to make Khouri laugh. It wouldn't matter where he moved. Khouri already had him where he wanted him, no matter what choice he made.

They both startled when the door opened just seconds after Sorin damned himself thoroughly. One look at Sorin's face was enough to tell Khouri who it was, even without turning to look. Not that Khouri really needed to look. None of the staff would dare to enter without knocking, and the remaining one it could be was more than obvious.

"What do you want, Navidae?" Khouri asked with a sigh, keeping his eyes on the game board and the move he still needed to make. So, even this safe haven had its limits. "I'm a little busy right now."

Navidae, in lieu of asking for permission, just walked in and stood at Khouri's shoulder. "The same thing I've wanted for days now, my blackbird," he said quietly, looking down at the game board. "Just a chance to speak to you."

As if that were all Navidae wanted. "You're speaking to

me now," Khouri replied offhandedly, making his move and watching Sorin jump to make his own, even though it was pretty obvious that the human wasn't paying attention to the game any longer. He moved his piece sloppily, opening up his defenses once again for Khouri's spy. He stared at Khouri with a raised brow, his words from before still hanging heavily in the air.

"Please?" Navidae pleaded, and that gave Khouri pause. His hand froze midway from moving his spy in, and when he did deign to look upon Navidae, he saw his lover wore a look of utter resignation. "Please, Khouri. Can we speak in private?"

Khouri looked at Sorin, who held up his hands, removing himself from the situation. It made Khouri's stomach tighten with nervousness. Swallowing, he took Sorin's piece with little pleasure, even though Sorin seemed utterly shocked at the sudden and decisive victory.

"Fine," he said, standing up from the seat. Sorin was giving him a look that said he didn't have to go if he really didn't want to, but Khouri ignored it. "Let's get this over with." Prolonging things would only make them worse, and if Navidae had finally gathered the wherewithal to seek Khouri out in Sorin's room, it meant that his patience was wearing thin.

"I'd wish for you to be a little less resigned when you say that, but I suppose I should take what I can get," Navidae said, his attempt at teasing falling a bit short. Nodding to Sorin, he wrapped an arm around Khouri's waist, guiding him towards the door. "Good afternoon, Hunter."

"Have fun," Sorin grunted behind them, but Khouri didn't have the chance to say his own goodbye before Navidae had him whisked out the door and into the hallway.

"Where are we going?" he asked, shaking off Navidae's touch. It felt too warm, too comfortable. If Khouri let himself get too close, he might forget himself and fall back into their rhythm.

Surprisingly, Navidae didn't force the contact. He kept his hands to himself and seemed almost nervous now that they were in the hall together. "I wanted to go somewhere private," Navidae said, "if that's alright with you."

Khouri furrowed his brow, crossing his arms tightly. "So now you're asking?" he asked pointedly.

"Please, Khouri," Navidae sighed, hand gesturing before them, pleading for him to accept. "I'm trying. You said you didn't like me being pushy. Is this not what you wanted?"

He was... trying? Khouri stared at Navidae in shock, unsure if he had heard right. "It is..." he said slowly, wondering if perhaps something had happened to his lover. Something drastic. Nothing else would explain him being so conciliatory. "I guess that's okay."

"Thank you," Navidae breathed, sounding relieved. He settled his hand gently behind Khouri's back, not touching but guiding him forward. "I figured we could talk in our room. It's the only place the servants can't eavesdrop, and you know well enough how much Nvidia loves her gossip."

Khouri certainly did. For as tight-laced as she was, she certainly wasn't tight-lipped. He kept close to Navidae as they walked, hoping that the rest of their little fight hadn't already been passed along to the other nobles within their social circle. It had been ages since Khouri had last gone to a gala or

meeting with Navidae, but he still knew how fervently some
of the others wished Khouri to be theirs. Talk of a fight would
only rile up the rumors and Khouri's wishful suitors.

The halls were empty as they moved through, granting
Khouri some measure of relief. "So," he said, glancing up at
Navidae. "When are you going to pay Sorin? He won't leave
until you do."

Navidae raised a brow, obviously not expecting Khouri to
offer conversation willingly. "I'm not sure. I thought it might
be easier just to kill him, but then I was forced to reconsider
once I thought of how you might react to that. You profess
to be angry at the both of us, but your actions hardly say the
same thing."

They turned a corner, and Khouri held back a smile.
Sorin's paranoia wasn't totally misplaced then. "How much
fault can be given to a human for being greedy?" Khouri
asked, shrugging his shoulders. "He was jealous and stupid.
He admits to it. He's actively trying to make up for it. You, on
the other hand," he said, glaring up at Navidae, "won't admit
to anything."

Navidae stopped, and Khouri was confused for a moment
until he realized they were standing outside of their bedroom.
His lover opened the door and gestured Khouri inside, locking
it behind them once they were truly alone. "Maybe I will
now that I've had some time to reflect," Navidae murmured,
watching Khouri walk deeper into the room.

Though it had sounded fine in theory, actually being
back in the bedroom with Navidae opened up its own set
of problems. Khouri held himself tightly and looked from
the fireplace to the wardrobes to the vaulted window in the
far corner. The bed he steadily ignored. "Start talking," he

muttered, keeping his eyes on anything but Navidae. "Say it if you're going to say it."

Navidae let out a sigh. "I'm not sure what it is you want me to say to you," he began, and when Khouri looked up, he found Navidae staring at him. "Do you want me to say that I'm sorry? That I missed you? That I'm okay with letting you leave me even though it feels like utter agony to be away from you? I just want things back to how they were before, Khouri. I can't stand having you mad at me."

"You should have thought of that before you hired hunters to drug and kidnap me," Khouri said, but the words felt flat. It was hard to be barbed when Navidae looked so vulnerable.

"Evidently, I should have," Navidae mumbled. He turned towards the fire, staring into its crackling depths. The glow of the firelight glinted off his hair, sculpting his handsome features like a statue. "But I can't take back what I did. I can't even say I regret doing it. I don't, but I regret the rift it's driven between us."

Khouri held his breath. "Do you remember when we met?" he asked carefully, looking too at the fire to avoid his lover's gaze. "You wasted no time in accepting me into your bed, your home. Your life. You would let me come and go. You would wait for me to come back. At what point did that change?"

Navidae turned to take him in, but Khouri couldn't meet his eye. "Around the point where I realized I couldn't live without you, I suppose," he said levelly. Khouri flushed. "I realized I couldn't bear the thought of letting you leave and you finding something better while you were gone."

"That's..." Not what Khouri expected him to say. He

put his back to Navidae, trying and failing to school his expression. "I never would have done that," he breathed, holding himself tighter. "I always come home." This had been his home for so long that to think of another place as comparable... It just felt wrong. Navidae had intrigued him from the moment he put the blade to his neck. As wonderful as the surface was, Khouri knew where he would always return to.

Navidae wrapped his arms around Khouri from behind, hooking his chin over his shoulder to kiss Khouri's cheek. He ran his hands down Khouri's arms, lacing their fingers together gently. "I know," he said softly, kissing him again. "I should have trusted you more." Navidae felt so warm, and Khouri found himself leaning into the embrace despite his better judgement. Maybe Sorin had been right in saying that Khouri missed Navidae.

He lost his train of thought when Navidae lifted their joined hands and kissed Khouri's fingertips, his lips trailing down to bite the silk that wrapped delicately around his forearms. With a purposeful tug, Navidae slipped the cloth from Khouri's arm, letting it flutter to the floor with barely a silent whisper. Khouri sank his teeth into his bottom lip, gooseflesh rising on the newly bared skin. The same happened with his other hand, the silk leaving him easily, so very eager to be free of his flesh that Khouri felt naked already.

"What do you think you're doing?" Khouri asked, eyes rooted to the sight of his cast-off garments. Why did he let Navidae do that much? His heart was pounding, his cheeks burning. "Are you trying to seduce me?" he whispered, eyes wide.

"Why do you ask?" Navidae said softly, kissing the delicate

skin of his inner wrist. "Are you feeling seduced?"

Khouri pursed his lips and looked steadfastly at the wall, trying to get angry. While he was distracted, Navidae carefully turned him until they were face to face, his smile hungry and his eyes so confident. What on earth had given Navidae so much confidence? They had their moment of sincerity, sure, but Khouri was still a long way from forgiving him.

It only took three steps to back Khouri up against a wall. Three small, unnecessary steps to trap Khouri in his arms and keep him from running away until after he'd had his fun. "Still so sensitive, aren't you?" Navidae mused, leaning forward to kiss the underside of Khouri's jaw next. "You've always been so beautifully receptive to me."

It was dangerous to let Navidae try this with him, but Khouri felt himself flush, his knees weak and his body beginning to ache for all that Navidae promised with every word he whispered. He clutched at Navidae's sleeve, forcing himself to keep his eyes open and expression stern. "Seducing me won't make me stop resenting you," he said, his voice sounding weak to his own ears.

"But, it would make you mine again," Navidae said, laving his tongue along Khouri's sensitive ear. "It would put you back in my bed where I could at least pretend you were still beholden to me. I've missed you so much, Khouri. Please. Please don't turn me away."

Khouri shivered enough for Navidae to feel it too. A teasing sharpness caressed his ear. Navidae's teeth trailed along the tapered edge with a dizzying slowness, pausing just for a moment to kiss the earrings he had given Khouri so very, very long ago. Khouri couldn't breathe, and when the warm, insistent hands began to tug at his clothing, he lost the fight with his common sense to tell Navidae to stop. It felt so good. He didn't want to end it now, even though he knew he should.

"Just look at you," Navidae breathed, leaving Khouri's ear alone to take in the mess he had made of him. It only took a careful pull on the knot at the base of his neck to bare Khouri's shoulders, another to guide the top down around his hips. "You are so beautiful. You've haunted my dreams ever since you left. Even now, I feel as if I'm dreaming."

Khouri leaned heavily against the wall as Navidae trailed his knuckles along the old scars on his neck and then down his chest, caressing his skin reverently. "Navi," he whined, closing his eyes when he felt the hand pass his navel and settled on the single tie that held the last of his clothing to him. They were already in the bedroom. It would fall, and so would Khouri. "You're teasing me."

"Will you forgive me?" his lover asked, pinning Khouri to the wall with his warm, hard body. His hands closed around Khouri's wrists, holding him in place as if Khouri were in danger of moving at all. "It's been so long. I want to make up for all the time lost between us."

What could that mean? Khouri's mind rushed to think, a thousand acts filling the space behind his eyes. Navidae had already had him in every way imaginable. The idea of any of them right now made Khouri feel so weak. He wanted it all. And Navidae knew it. He knew Khouri had given in because he was already kissing along his neck and tugging him away from the wall, pulling him towards the door at the far end of the room.

"You'll let me spoil you, won't you?" Navidae sighed, loosening the final piece of clothing from Khouri's hips as

248

they moved. The billowy trousers slipped easily to the ground, and Navidae helped him step out of them before leaving them behind completely. "Gone so long, wasting away in such poor company. You must be starved of your comforts."

Khouri was starved of something all right. Of his sanity, his common sense. His willpower was utterly gone, and he was certain that nothing Navidae had to offer him would bring it back. The hand on his lower back was hot enough to burn his skin, guiding him through the door into the warm, humid air of the private baths Navidae kept. Khouri knew this room well, having bathed in the mineral waters more times than he could count. Navidae would pamper him plenty. The thought alone was enough to make Khouri's legs go weak.

Navidae caught him before he could drop more than an inch. "You always were so weak to the steam," he chuckled, guiding Khouri effortlessly to one of the many ornate chaises that littered the expansive room.

How many times had Navidae taken Khouri on one of them? Khouri's thoughts weren't helping ground him. He whined a little when Navidae didn't sit beside him. "What are you going to do to me?" he asked, watching his lover settle between his legs, a large, warm hand wrapping around his ankle. Khouri hadn't been shy about his body in quite some time, but the distance or the time apart seemed to have erased what defense he used to have against Navidae's steady gaze.

Smiling, Navidae brought his fingers to Khouri's legs, to the silk wraps he had coiled around his calves. "Everything," he promised, finding the clasp that held them in place with an accuracy that was unnerving. It wasn't surprising, though. Navidae had bought him these clothes and adornments. Picked them out just for Khouri. Of course he knew how to take them off. "Are you scared?"

Khouri shook his head, watching coil after coil of wrapped silk flutter to the ground. When that leg was bare, Navidae gave his ankle a kiss before moving on to the next. "I've never been scared of you," he said softly, biting his lip when Navidae looked up from his work. His ruby eyes were piercing.

"You haven't, have you?" Navidae smiled, shaking his head a little as he let go of Khouri's ankle. Leaning up, he kissed Khouri deeply, cupping his head in his large hand. "My fearless little songbird," he murmured against Khouri's lips. "You make me want to break your wings."

The words alone made Khouri tremble with want. He settled his hands on Navidae's broad shoulders, losing himself in a kiss for as long as he could. The steam was filling his senses, blocking out everything that wasn't Navidae. It was too much. It was all too much, and Khouri felt himself give up the last bit of resistance he had left. It felt too good, too familiar to refuse.

Navidae broke the kiss before Khouri could let the black overtake his vision. He stared down at Khouri happily, brushing back his hair to see his eyes. "I think I'll have you in the bath before I have you in our bed," he mused so casually that it nearly passed Khouri by entirely. "Your skin always smells so good after you bathe. I barely need the perfume."

Blinking slowly, Khouri leaned into his touch. "Carry me?" he asked, feeling lethargic. It would feel so nice to be in the warm waters, Navidae at his back, touching him so gently beneath the water. They rarely got to indulge like this together, even before. And wasn't this nice? Navidae was setting aside his work for him, pursuing him like a priority. The Khouri of few months ago would have leapt at this opportunity. The

Khouri of now couldn't quite refuse it either.

Smiling, Navidae lifted him easily beneath the thighs, committing to the decision for him. "Oh, Khouri," he frowned, hefting Khouri a bit higher. "You've lost weight, haven't you? I knew that beast wasn't providing for you."

Khouri shook his head, his arms looped around his lover's neck. "It's from the walking," he explained, sighing lowly as Navidae settled him into the warm, frothing waters. "I eat plenty, so don't go bothering Sorin about that." He looked up as Navidae pulled away from him, still standing on the ledge beside the waters. Navidae was still dressed, soaked up to his elbows but otherwise untouched.

Scoffing, Navidae moved over to a stone table and selected from the assorted vials the soaps and oils he wished to use. "I'll blame him for every little blemish I find on your perfect body, pet," he said, holding a deep blue crystal vial up to the light. His ruby eyes cut over to Khouri, his expression stern. "You're mine to mark. No one else's."

"Hmm. Are you going to strip anytime soon?" Khouri asked, watching Navidae expectantly. He rested his arms on the edge of the inground pool, chin propped on his forearm. "I'd hate to bathe alone."

"Impatient. I love it." Navidae sighed with a smile, bringing his choices over and setting them down beside Khouri. "I want to treat you, so let me at least make sure I'm using the good stuff." Khouri picked up one of the bottles and watched out of the corner of his eye as Navidae cast off his shirt and kicked off his shoes, the expensive garments falling to the damp floor in an uncaring heap.

"You're so wasteful," he murmured. The bottle in his hand

was indeed the good stuff. Just an ounce of it cost more than Khouri's entire wardrobe, and if he knew Navidae, which he did, he knew they were about to waste the whole bottle. He was going to complain, but Khouri's cheeks darkened when he finally looked at his lover properly, taking in the broad, muscled expanse of his chest, the cut physique he wore cockily. Navidae's hands dropped to his waistband, slipping the silk belt from the loops until they were loose enough to step out of.

Khouri tried and failed to tear his eyes away, his mouth dry and his body hot all over. Navidae's cock was hard, of course, thick and heavy between his strong thighs.

"Suddenly shy?" Navidae asked, brow raised as he slipped sinuously into the warm waters. "Sweet blackbird, you're so cute when you're skittish."

Khouri shoved the vial at Navidae's chest blindly, his cheeks on fire. His attention was jerked back though when Navidae grabbed his wrist, dragging him into his lap easily. "I'm not shy," he tried to say, looking anywhere but at his lover. His knees settled on the bath's built-in ledge, comfortably submerged up to his chest in the warm water.

"Somehow, I doubt you," Navidae teased, kissing along his neck as his hands explored beneath the water. "But don't stop, I beg you. You remind me so much of our first time together when you get like this. Do you remember it? I do, fondly."

"That was decades ago," Khouri muttered, resting his forehead on Navidae's strong shoulder. He heard the pop of the vial's lid and then felt a stream of cool liquid roll down his back, the enchanted oil staying put even beneath the water. He gasped as it filled his senses with warmth and the heady scent of decadent fruit and sex. "We were a lot different then."

Navidae hummed, rubbing the oil into his skin reverently and massaging his tired muscles. "Not so different," he said, letting a single hand slip down the line of Khouri's ass. He rolled a finger against his entrance. Khouri went stiff, but Navidae didn't go further. "You were still beautiful; I still wanted to ruin every inch of you."

Khouri shivered, the teasing passes of Navidae's finger not enough. He leaned up to kiss and mouth at Navidae's ear, spreading his thighs wider as subtly as he could. "I wanted to kill you back then," he whispered like a secret that he knew Navidae already knew.

"Not so much anymore, then?" Navidae's finger pressed harder, slipping past the ring of muscle. The oil coating it made Khouri burn inside, his body sweating as his need grew. "What about now? After I dragged you back into my arms so rudely?"

Gasping, Khouri couldn't reply. Navidae pressed deeper, opening him up with an almost lackadaisical care. For a moment, it was all Khouri could do to hold onto the upper ledge, his hips up and bearing down on Navidae's finger greedily. He wanted more. He wanted more, but he didn't want to ask for it, not when Navidae should be the one begging Khouri to let him.

"You look like you want to say something," Navidae observed, his lips curved like he knew every thought running through Khouri's fevered mind. "Did you want some more? I could stop if you hate it."

The thought of stopping was unbearable. Khouri shook his head, kissing Navidae's cheek desperately. "Please don't stop," he said softly, the rippling water louder than his voice. "I want more."

"Then let me give it to you, pet," his lover crooned, turning his head to catch Khouri's lips in a kiss. He began pressing in another finger; his free hand soothed Khouri when he began to tremble. The pace was as gentle as the water rolling against them, and Navidae moved his attention to Khouri's neck, his breath almost cool in the overwhelming heat of the room.

Khouri knew it was coming, but he still flinched when Navidae sank his sharp teeth into the crook of his neck. The grip on his hip tightened, keeping him from jerking away. Khouri gasped and went boneless against Navidae's smooth chest. The warm, scented water muddled the pain until it all felt good. It was the most familiar thing so far, this dizzying pain and rolling pleasure.

"You really did miss me, didn't you?" he murmured, wincing as the teeth pulled away; the hot blood trickled down his skin slowly. "It must make you so mad that most of your marks have faded."

Navidae gave an appreciative hum, too busy lapping up the blood to bother answering. His hand couldn't seem to settle on a place to stop, running down Khouri's thighs and back, his arms and chest as if Navidae needed to reacquaint himself with his wayward lover's body. The fingers fucking into him paused, removing themselves to Khouri's utter dismay. But, he didn't have much control anymore. He understood that. Khouri was making it too easy for Navidae by sitting in his lap like this. Too easy to fall back into how they had been before.

This time, the teeth hovered over Khouri's shoulder. He shivered as Navidae kissed the spot tenderly, his warm breath the worst kind of tease. "I haven't forgiven you, Navi," Khouri whispered, hiding his face in Navidae's neck.

"And why not?" his lover asked, his hands cradling

254

Khouri's hips lovingly. His cock was hard between Khouri's spread thighs, brushing against his leg every time he shifted. "How could you begrudge me for bringing you back home where you belong when you missed me too?"

Khouri was spared from answering by Navidae taking another bite. The pain swelled and sharpened, tingling from his cheeks to his toes. The water below began to tinge pink with drops of red, dissipating slowly just like Khouri's resolve. He held Navidae's head to his shoulder, begging silently for him to bite harder.

It wasn't a lie to say that Khouri missed Navidae. He had. He really, really had. Sorin was all well and good, something different from the monotony of Khouri's everyday life, but Navidae. Navidae knew how to hurt him, and that, more than anything, made Khouri sing. Navidae smiled against his shoulder, bloody lips nearly burning as he tore his teeth from Khouri's skin. He went in for a kiss that Khouri didn't refuse, passing the taste of cold iron on his tongue with a skillful press, a dizzying dance that always left Khouri gasping for breath.

"You do belong here, Khouri," Navidae breathed, pulling back just to make Khouri chase his lips. "You just need to be reminded of it every now and again."

It probably had been a mistake to let Navidae get this close again. It had probably been a mistake to kiss him, touch him, speak to him like this. Khouri wrapped his arms around Navidae's neck and tangled his fingers in the thick, rust-red hair at his nape. Such an odd color down here, but it suited Navidae like nothing else.

"Remind me all you want," Khouri whispered, lapping up the remaining gore from his lover's lips. "I will still want to fly."

Navidae let out a shudder of want, his piercing ruby eyes narrowing into thin slivers. "Oh, Khouri," he growled, rolling Khouri's name on his tongue like a song. The grip on Khouri's hips turned mean. "I really did miss you."

There was nothing teasing about the kiss that Navidae offered up to him. It was deep, commanding, and passionate enough to burn. Khouri whined into it, closing his eyes as Navidae licked into his mouth and reacquainted himself with all he had gone without during Khouri's absence. Blood tinged their saliva, the taste growing stronger when their tongues skimmed pointed teeth haphazardly. Khouri clutched at Navidae's hair and plastered himself to his lover's chest, their cocks rocking together with an almost frantic urgency.

When Navidae stood, he took Khouri with him, holding him by the thighs. He brought them out of the water and hefted Khouri easily onto the waiting ledge. "I want to take you in our bed, my blackbird," Navidae crooned, his voice husky and deep as he spoke against Khouri's ear. "I pray you won't run from me if I try."

This had definitely been a mistake. Khouri brought his hand to his mouth to stifle his broken cry for more. Navidae was gloating. He could see it in his every move, in how Navidae lowered himself to lap at Khouri's cock, in how he probed at Khouri's entrance with fingers that knew just how to move to make him melt. Khouri fought to prop himself up when Navidae's mouth went lower, his tongue fucking into him mercilessly alongside his fingers. A mistake. It had been a mistake to think he could do this without letting Navidae drag him right back to where they had left off.

"You're terrible," Khouri moaned, covering his face with

his wrist. His body felt so alive, his legs trembling with their need to wrap around Navidae's head and make him go deeper. "Awful. You think you're so good, but I didn't miss this at all."

The pleasure stopped but just for Navidae to smile up at him, his mouth a mess of oil and saliva. "Liar," he said, his voice a little softer than Khouri expected it to be. His big hands smoothed down Khouri's thighs, and then Navidae looked down at the patchwork of scars he had left on them over the years, his eyes hardening. Before Khouri could ask what was wrong, Navidae was hefting himself out of the bath, dragging Khouri up by the wrist and onto his shaky, unsteady feet. He didn't have to stumble long, though. Navidae lifted him into his arms, making for the bedroom door with an intent in his eyes that couldn't be misconstrued.

The bedroom was cold compared to the baths. Khouri curled into Navidae for warmth, kissing his neck as he was carried to the bed and deposited onto the soft, welcoming sheets. Unlike the bed from the tavern, this one felt comfortable, clean, large, and built from the most expensive materials available beneath the earth. Khouri rolled along the silken sheets, grabbing for Navidae impatiently. He was tired of waiting and resisting his lover. There would be time to be angry later, but for now, all Khouri wanted to do was be welcomed home in the best way he could imagine.

It was all too natural, falling back into this familiar rhythm. Navidae covered him easily with his body, searching for his lips in a kiss that dominated everything. They had been caught in each other's ebb and flow for decades, this give and take a neatly choreographed dance by now. Navidae would take him here or against the wall, fucking him open with his fingers first and then his cock. He would bite Khouri a few more times, whisper in his ear how he belonged to him, and then

257

Khouri would cum, as caught up in the moment as Navidae. It would feel divine, and Khouri ached to have it all once again.

Khouri lifted his hips and arched his spine, spreading his legs like his part required, but to his surprise, Navidae didn't respond. He just kept kissing Khouri, his eyes closed and his hands almost gentle now. Khouri squirmed, rolling against Navidae's hard cock, but Navidae simply moaned into the kiss, ignoring his own desire in a way he never, ever did.

Pulling away, Khouri looked at Navidae breathlessly. "Is something wrong?" he asked. "You're never this sedate with me." Teasing, yes, but never like this. This was almost chaste, and Navidae was certainly *never* chaste.

"Is sedate bad?" Navidae asked, opening his eyes. They were darker now, blown with lust that was still carefully checked.

"Sedate is weird," he decided, untangling his arms from Navidae's neck. "What are you planning? If you're still mad, there are better ways to take it out on me."

Navidae's hands were warm when they stroked down Khouri's arms, his smile small and almost self-conscious if that were ever a word Khouri would use to describe any part of Navidae. "Do you like it when I'm rough with you?" he asked casually, so casually that it had to be purposeful. He met Khouri's eyes carefully, too restrained in his actions to put Khouri's nerves at ease. "I'm never gentle. I rarely ever ask your opinion on it. Does that bother you?"

"Why are you asking me now?" They had been together for years, fucking like this for years. Khouri shifted impatiently, biting his lip when Navidae didn't table the discussion for later. "It's a bit late to be worrying about that now, isn't it?"

"I've been worrying about it endlessly," Navidae said through gritted teeth. "Ever since you ran away from my bed. Just answer the question, Khouri. Does it bother you? Is that why you resent me? I can see all of you like this. You didn't let that human of yours hurt you."

His fidgeting stopped. Khouri frowned. "Do you really think I ran away because I got sick of you being rough with me when we fuck?" He pushed at Navidae's chest, making a move to get off the bed and reach for the clothes still littering the floor. "What I do with Sorin is none of your business." Navidae was such an idiot. He had to be trying to get inside Khouri's head to make him feel guilty about leaving. If that was his game, then there was no reason for Khouri to entertain him any longer.

He made it nearly to the edge of the bed before he was stopped. Quick as a whip, Navidae grabbed his wrist and prevented him from fleeing completely. The tight, careful look from before was gone. In its place sat desperation. Worry.

"Well, what else could it be?" Navidae asked, looking lost. "Haven't I been good to you? You've never wanted for anything here. It had to be me, right? It was either that, or you were stolen, and your hunter already vouched that you left on your own. So, what was it?" he asked, looking into Khouri's eyes desperately. "Was I not available to you enough? If I wasn't satisfying you, I would have done more; you didn't have to run off and find another lover."

He really didn't understand at all. Khouri was stunned by the realization, enough so that it made it easy for Navidae to drag him back into his arms and pin him back down onto the luxurious bed they had shared together for nearly fifty years. "Did I… hurt your feelings?" Khouri whispered, cupping

259

Navidae's cheek in his hand. It wasn't an act. Even in a lie, Navidae would refuse to give up his pride. This was the truth laid bare and vulnerable at Khouri's feet. The purest kind of supplication. "You were really worried you had done something wrong, weren't you?"

Navidae leaned into his touch, nearly pouting. "What else was I supposed to think?" he muttered, avoiding Khouri's eyes. "You left without a note. Without any sign of why or when you would return, if ever. And then, I bring you back, and you're in the arms of some human, even after you knew he sold you out to bring you to me. It doesn't make any sense." He paused, hiding his eyes in his fringe. "I know... I understand that I can be a bit much sometimes, but I thought that you were happy here with me."

The guilt Khouri had avoided for so long swelled in his chest. He combed through Navidae's hair with his fingers before tugging him down and embracing him. "I was happy here," he whispered. "So happy. And I still am."

"Then why did you leave me?" Navidae asked, hiding his face against Khouri's shoulder.

"I've told you before," Khouri said, rolling them over so that he could lay across Navidae's chest and meet his avoidant eye. It was hard to get Navidae to stop fighting him, but he managed by taking his lover's chin in his hand. "I want to travel. I want to experience things."

"So you had to just, just *leave* me?" Navidae interrupted, narrowing his ruby eyes. He batted Khouri's hand from his face, rolling them back over to pin Khouri to the bed. Khouri didn't fight it, knowing it made Navidae feel better, more in control. "I *worried* about you!" he said accusatorily as if it had been a hardship and something he never wanted to do again.

"And *you* sent bounty hunters after me," Khouri shot back, meeting Navidae's glare head on. "I don't expect you to understand, Navidae. That's why I didn't bother saying anything. You would have stopped me because you don't understand. I would have come back on my own, but you were too impatient to let me do that."

Something in Navidae seemed to die, either the fight or his will to feign apathy. He frowned and avoided Khouri's eye again, letting out a sad huff of breath. "But what if you didn't?" he asked quietly. "What if you had fallen for that insufferable human and forgotten all about me? So what if you don't love the Duskriven? This is a horrid place, so that's understandable. But what of me?" He met Khouri's eye carefully, looking far more vulnerable than Khouri had ever seen him be before. "You're all I have down here, and unlike you, I'm in no position to run away to the surface to follow you."

Khouri sucked in a breath, holding it for a moment and then letting it go. His chest felt tight. Navidae was a lot of things but upfront about his needs? His vulnerabilities? Never. Khouri brought his hands to his lover's warm shoulders, stroking down his smooth skin. "I never said I wasn't being selfish," he whispered, dragging Navidae down on top of him so he could hide his face against Navidae's neck. "But I'm back now, aren't I? You know it wasn't your fault, and even though I'm mad at you for the way you did it, I'm still glad to be home."

"You mean that?" Navidae asked, holding him close, kissing along his ear and the earrings he had given him, the ones Khouri had killed a man to protect.

Khouri smiled a small smile. "I'm in our bed again,

aren't I?" he answered, drawing his hands lower and digging his nails in a little to elicit a shiver from his lover. Kissing Navidae's shoulder, he stopped hiding, biting his lip with a flush on his cheeks. "Where you always want me."

There was no mistaking the heat in his lover's eyes. Navidae wore lust like a second skin, one that clung to his muscled body and refused to be parted from him until Khouri lay spent and breathless, wrecked and bloody and singing with pleasure. It took Khouri's breath away now to see it. Navidae leaned in for a kiss, licking into his mouth with the confidence of someone who felt entitled enough to lay his claim without question.

"Are you sure?" Navidae asked once they broke apart, holding Khouri's small hand to his cheek.

Khouri nodded, spreading his thighs and baring his throat. "I want you," he said, "so don't make me wait anymore."

He began slowly as if he needed to familiarize himself with Khouri's body. Kissing down his chest, Navidae licked and sucked, his teeth gentle for the moment though that wasn't likely to last for much longer. Khouri sighed and combed his fingers through his lover's thick hair, the warmth from before returning gradually until he was fidgeting and whining for more.

"You're being so gentle," Khouri breathed, closing his eyes as Navidae lapped at his nipple, rolling and tugging the other between his fingers with a care that was almost dizzying. Khouri could remember the night Navidae had pierced them so clearly. It had felt so good. Khouri's toes curled in the silk sheets, the feeling of the smooth fabric against his naked skin almost like an embrace in itself.

Pulling off his treat, Navidae blew warm breath across the damp surface of his skin, making Khouri gasp. "I know," he said, kissing down his sternum and over his hips. Though he occupied himself with Khouri's body, his eyes were locked on Khouri's, almost as if they were looking for something in Khouri's expression that Khouri couldn't name. "Do you hate it?"

Khouri shook his head, letting go of Navidae's hair with one hand to fist the sheets above his head. "It's so weird," he said, breath ragged. This was more like how Sorin made love than how Navidae fucked, and for the life of him, Khouri didn't know how to process it. The dissonance was heady though. He couldn't bring himself to complain or tell Navidae to stop.

"I know," his lover repeated softly, kissing the head of Khouri's cock briefly before disregarding it entirely. The denial, at least, was familiar. But then Navidae paused by his thighs. He eyes flicked up to meet Khouri's, asking for permission for something he had never questioned before. "Can I...?" he led, trailing off to lave his tongue along Khouri's inner thigh. His teeth were gentle when they nipped his skin, showing rather than telling what he wanted to do and where.

"Don't ask," Khouri gasped, clutching at Navidae's hair with his fingers. "Don't ever, ever ask. Just do it. I want you to do it. Make me hurt. I want to hurt." He trusted Navidae with this. There was no need to question anything, not when it came to things like pleasure, pain, and the heady combination that Navidae knew how to deliver with just his mouth, his hands. Navidae sank his teeth into Khouri, and Khouri let out a loud cry, throwing his head back as tears formed in the corners of his eyes. His thighs trembled, and his cock leaked pitifully.

He wanted more. He wanted everything he had missed during his absence from Navidae's bed, and he wanted it now.

Navidae let go of his thigh, blood coloring his lips like macabre lipstick. "It's infuriating how beautiful you are," he sighed, kissing his way up Khouri's body, leaving a smear of red as he went. "Do you know how much I worried when you disappeared? I thought you'd been taken from me. The thought blotted out all else. I was filled with rage."

"T-Taken?" Khouri gasped, shivering and sweating while Navidae took his time. His lover's fingers dipped inside his entrance, fucking into him gently, teasingly, making him arch his spine as Navidae entertained himself with Khouri's body.

"By another," Navidae sighed, his voice carrying none of the desperation Khouri felt now. "By one of my rivals or one of your countless admirers. I tell you after every function we hold how many of the others approach me, asking how much it would cost to get me to part with my lovely pet." His fingers crooked then, spearing Khouri mercilessly in the spot that made his vision flood white. "I thought someone might have grown tired of my refusals," Navidae said, eyes hard, his expression angry and jealous at the thought.

"What would you have done?" Khouri laughed breathlessly, fucking himself on Navidae's fingers. The memory of the shuttered, empty manor across the way flashed through his mind, a smile curling onto his lips. They were back in familiar territory now, and that was what Khouri wanted. It all felt so good. His thighs burned, his shoulders stinging as he sweated. "What would you have done if I had been taken? If you had gotten word of me laying in some other noble's bed?"

"I would have slaughtered the entire palace," Navidae delivered slowly, teeth bared, eyes as bright as poison. "I would have made them suffer for taking what's mine."

Khouri moaned, clutching the pillow beneath his head as Navidae took back his fingers and spread his thighs wide to make room for what came next. Finally. He had finally realized what Khouri wanted and how he wanted it. "And if I was happier there?" Khouri asked, opening an eye to smile at his vicious lover. "And if I enjoyed their touch more than yours?"

There was no warning given for when Navidae thrust inside Khouri, muscles bulging in his arms as he held himself over Khouri, shaking with the urge to move, to fuck into him like an animal. Khouri arched his spine in a perfect arc, lungs devoid of air, mind devoid of thought. Navidae bent him in half and bit at Khouri's ear, his voice nothing but a rough, lust-darkened growl.

"I'd kill them in front of you," he promised, sinking his teeth into Khouri's shoulder again. It wasn't deep this time, but it hurt. It hurt beautifully. "I'd slaughter them all and fuck you in the mess until you changed your mind."

It was better than Khouri could have imagined. Sorin hated being goaded, but Navidae welcomed the excuse to lose control. Khouri let loose of the pillow to grab Navidae's sweaty hair, forcing their mouths together. The kiss tasted of blood and obsession and notes of utter truth. Navidae lost his hold on holding back and his hips connected with Khouri's in a quick, hard rhythm that punched the air from Khouri's lungs. The slap of skin against skin filled the air, every thrust dragging against Khouri's bitten thighs. Navidae's name fell from Khouri's lips in a litany, the pain and pleasure mixing until there was no distinguishing the two. It all felt good. It felt so right.

And somehow, inexplicably, Navidae had the breath to keep going. He laughed darkly in Khouri's ear, soothing the sting his teeth had made. "Do you like that?" he asked, changing the rhythm to something slower, almost teasing in its pace. "Do you like the idea of fucking in the blood of the dogs who mounted you? Of coming apart just inches from their lifeless husks? Of letting their dead eyes watch you writhe on my cock?"

Khouri didn't know how he expected him to reply when he could hardly gather the breath to cry out, let alone speak. Tears fell from his eyes, his hands scratching at Navidae's muscled arms. "They don't deserve to see me," Khouri gasped, feeling Navidae stop completely at that. Blinking through the wetness, Khouri managed a smile, so hard that it was beginning to hurt. "Isn't that right?"

Navidae's answering smile was positively vicious. His eyes glistened behind his messy fringe, his sharp teeth bestial in the low light of their bedroom. He grabbed Khouri's wrists in one of his hands, pinning them above Khouri's head with a low laugh. For a moment, Khouri wished they had taken the time to fetch the leather restraints from the chest at the foot of the bed. "You're perfect for me, Khouri," Navidae decided, shaking his head as he chuckled. "No one could satisfy me like you."

"Please," Khouri huffed pitifully, tugging at his wrists just to feel the power his lover commanded. "Navi, please. I can't take it." His thighs were trembling at being denied. Navidae's cock was so hard and hot inside him. Khouri clenched desperately, and Navidae stopped holding back.

"Pretty blackbird wants to sing for me," Navidae whispered, thrusting in hard enough to make Khouri keen. He held onto Khouri's wrists so tightly that Khouri knew escape was impossible. "Do it, pet. I haven't heard your voice in so long."

He felt so exposed like this with Navidae's eyes roving over his body as if it were his to do with as he pleased. Khouri licked at his lips and let out another moan, the pace overtaking him easily. Navidae's body was strong, built for power and dominance, and he used every ounce of it to make Khouri submit. Closing his eyes did little to hide from it. Khouri let his voice out as beholden to the pleasure as Navidae was to him.

"Navi," he cried messily, squirming and clenching, doing all he could to get Navidae to move faster and touch him where he need to be touched. "N-Navi, please. Let me cum. I need it so much-"

He didn't get to finish his pleading. He was caught up in Navidae changing angles, directing every thrust against the spot that made his toes curl. Khouri parted his lips, but nothing came out but a breathless, choked cry. He stopped seeing. He stopped thinking. Khouri wrapped his burning thighs around Navidae's waist and gave in entirely. His mind was gone to the pleasure.

The hand binding his wrists went tight, and in the next instant, Navidae stole the breath from his lungs in a hungry, dominating kiss. Khouri's cock was trapped between his stomach and Navidae's abs, the stimulation too much all at once. Khouri came with a broken sob, the sound swallowed up in the kiss. His body tensed; his spine arched. Navidae broke the kiss to bite down hard on Khouri's neck and came inside him in thick, hot bursts.

As tired as he was, as messy as he was, Khouri could only smile up at the ceiling, his vision awash with white and dancing lights, with pleasure and pain, and a pure, inarticulate sensation that felt so familiar, so intimately right, that he never wanted to come down. It had been so long since he had last been here surrounded by warmth and the scent of Navidae and blood and sweat and the passion they made when their bodies came together. Khouri closed his eyes and let his legs slip from Navidae's waist, his body boneless and lethargic and utterly content. This, if nothing else, had been worth being brought back for.

"Don't fall asleep so soon, pet," Navidae crooned, brushing Khouri's bangs from his eyes. He leaned in to kiss Khouri's lip, his hands still so explorative after all he had already touched. "I'm not even close to being done with you yet. The toys missed you as much as I did. It would be so cruel to make them wait any longer."

Khouri whined, closing his eyes to arch as the fingers dipped back inside him to play with the mess Navidae had left behind. It wasn't perfect, this tenuous give and take, these barely defined rules they had played by for decades. But as Navidae kissed down his chest, as he worshipped and kissed and took, Khouri felt at peace. It didn't matter right now how long he planned to stay. It didn't matter that Khouri had ever left in the first place. It felt like home for the moment, and Khouri was content to bask in it for as long as Navidae wanted.

Chapter Twelve

Sorin didn't worry himself when Khouri didn't come back to the room. There were a lot of reasons why the conversation could be dragging on, he figured. Another argument perhaps, or maybe Khouri had succeeded in getting through Navidae's thick skull. Sorin nearly laughed at the thought as he cleaned up the game board, slowly examining every piece before he put it back in the silk bag it had come in. It was probably the former in all honesty. Navidae was an idiot, and no amount of conversation could help that.

So, no. Sorin didn't worry when Khouri still hadn't come back after an hour. Or even two or three. As the day wore on, Sorin grew impatient, but worry wasn't a part of that. Not at all. If he peered out into the hallway every so often to listen for voices, he would say it was due to concern. If he paced the room once the faux night descended, it was due to irritation but not worry. Never worry.

Eventually, the hour grew late enough that Sorin was forced to sleep, and still, Khouri was gone. The bed felt too big, the sheets too cold. Sorin gritted his teeth but sucked it up, closed his eyes, and forced himself to ignore it. Khouri had his reasons. If it were taking him this long to sort out his problems, then Sorin should give him the benefit of the doubt. He had made his offer already. It was up to Khouri to take it.

But when morning came and there still was no sight of Khouri, Sorin began to assume the worst.

Did it really take that long to figure out their issues? Sorin went through the daily motions he had become accustomed to making while under Navidae's roof. He got up, washed his face, partook of the breakfast that was sitting out in the parlour near his room, and set himself to maintaining his weapons, though he hadn't had an opportunity to use them yet.

The further along he got in his routine, the lower his mood fell.

Sorin wasn't a fool. For every hour that Khouri was away, the realization of what the two Drow were doing became more and more likely. Grinding his teeth became harder to avoid. Sorin chewed the inside of his cheek as he sharpened his knife for the tenth time. Every instance of Khouri praising Navidae rose into his mind unbidden, reminding him once again that Khouri had a history with the man, and that history wasn't nearly as unpleasant as Sorin might have wished it to be.

So when the door knob rattled and cracked open, Sorin was hardly in a good mood to entertain the Drow that poked his head inside. Khouri came in despite it, a tired smile on his face and dressed in something far different than what he had worn the last time Sorin saw him. The implications grew, especially when Sorin caught sight of the new wrappings around Khouri's neck. The bandages were a stark white against the Drow's dark skin. Sorin's jaw tightened at the sight.

"I see you two made up last night," Sorin said, hating how bitter the words came out. It was idiotic to think he had any claim on Khouri. Not when he wore Navidae's so proudly already.

Khouri hummed tiredly, gliding into the room in a gown of soft grey. Sorin's eyes were drawn to the sight of his collarbones, the deep neckline plunging down, down, far past the rules of common decency. Soren's mouth went dry at the sight of a thin silver chain hanging against his chest like a necklace strung from between his pierced nipples. He forced himself not to dwell on it for his own sanity. A jeweled collar rested against Khouri's throat, the ruby glistening like blood in the conjured light of the room. Sorin wondered if that had been a gift. An old one or a new one? Neither answer settled the discontent rising in the pit of Sorin's stomach.

"You would think that, wouldn't you?" Khouri mumbled, padding across the plush carpet in his bare feet. Upon closer inspection, Sorin found they weren't quite bare. Delicate silver chains wrapped around his ankles, draping over his feet prettily. They chimed gently as he walked, music following him wherever he went. The effect was arrestingly charming, so much so that Sorin felt a ripple of heat wash over him. But Khouri caught him staring, forcing Sorin to look away. "You don't mind if I sit, do you? I'm so tired," the Drow asked, looking a little confused and more than a little flushed.

Sorin just inclined his head, expecting him to take the seat across from him. Instead, Khouri pushed aside Sorin's hand from his thigh, seating himself in his lap as if he were entitled to the contact. "What's wrong? Didn't your lover give you enough attention last night?" he asked a bit harshly. For all of his bitterness, he didn't even try to refuse the Drow. Khouri's hair and skin were fragrant with some heady scent, his robe nearly dripping off his body from its sheerness. Its embroidered trimming seemed to weigh the fabric down, the gold conspiring to bare Khouri entirely.

Sorin forced himself to look away. "Where is he, anyway?" Sorin asked, either to remind Khouri of the lover he already had or to see just how alone they really were right now. "I didn't think he'd let you come keep me company when he could have you warming his bed."

271

The Drow in his lap gave a soft, tired laugh. "You sound so jealous," Khouri replied, not bothering to rise to the bait. His slender hand rested on Sorin's chest, his dark eyes laughing silently as they peered up to meet Sorin's. God. He looked like he had only just come from being fucked. "Would it make you happy to know that you made Navi jealous too? He accused you of treating me better than him, citing that as the reason why I ran away."

It was petty and childish, but it did make Sorin feel better. He would've felt even better though if Khouri hadn't called him Navi. Sorin raised a brow and covered Khouri's hand with his own, bringing it to his lips to kiss. Whatever Navidae had done to Khouri's skin had made it irresistibly soft. "And what did you say to those accusations?" he wondered, running a hand down the line of Khouri's flank. If he tugged just a little harder, Khouri's gown might slip off completely. It might slip off and let him see those piercings for himself.

"I said that he treats me just fine. That I don't mind a little pain when I play." Khouri looked down and followed the hand as it explored his thigh. "But, that doesn't mean I like to play when I'm exhausted," he said flatly, plucking Sorin's hand from his leg and depositing it back on his hip. When he looked at Sorin, it was with tired warning. "I told him why I left, and then I left him so he could mull it over. I assume he's off doing that right now or seeing to his duties as a noble."

Sorin tried not to look put out that his advances had been rejected. He fixed his eyes on the gem hanging from Khouri's slender throat instead. "And what about this?" Sorin asked, nodding curtly towards the collar. "I hadn't thought you the type to accessorize past your earrings." Which were also a gift from Navidae, if Sorin wasn't mistaken. The thought alone made him burn.

272

Khouri raised a brow and looked down at the collar he wore. "Don't like it? It's worth more than your life," he said plainly. He brought his fingers up to play with it, the ornate lace of the collar itself blending beautifully with the color of his skin. "It's an old gift," he confirmed after a moment of thought. "I sold it on the surface, but as it turns out, Navi's hired hunters bought it back for him."

"But *he* gave it to you, didn't he?" Sorin said, glaring at the piece. "He bought it back and put it on you again."

"*He* gave me everything, Sorin," Khouri answered, his humor obvious. "Everything I have. A home, affection." He leaned in, lips at Sorin's ear. "It bothers you so much, doesn't it? That I wear his marks and his gems."

It did. It bothered him endlessly. Sorin closed his eyes and gripped Khouri's hip in his hand. A shiver crawled down his spine when the lips began to kiss and nip at his ear. It hardly seemed fair that Navidae got to lay his claim in so many ways and Sorin with nothing at all to show for himself. He wanted to mark Khouri. He wanted to sear his name into that damnably perfect skin until the whole world knew that Sorin had been there, that Khouri was his to touch.

"Do you want to mark me too?" Khouri whispered, reading his thoughts easily. "Are you wondering why I never let you before?"

Sorin growled, hating that he was being riled up so easily. "Why didn't you?"

"Because you don't need to lay your claim upon me," the Drow said, kissing Sorin's cheek teasingly. His hands traveled down Sorin's chest; the brush of his hair was so soft against Sorin's neck. "You've done it with just your hands on my hips.

Navi is *that* jealous, after all."

He was, wasn't he? Sorin would be a liar if he said the thought didn't please him. He squeezed Khouri's hips and watched the pretty Drow sigh, his soft lips parting, his long lashes kissing his cheeks as he blinked slowly. It really was unfair how attractive Khouri was. Everything about him invited Sorin closer, like poisonous berries hanging from a beautiful wreath. This had to a trap, but to what end? Sorin was tempted to play along just to see how far it got him and how much it earned him. He had eaten of this tree before, so surely the toxin couldn't hurt him much.

"Ah, Khouri," Sorin grunted, torn from his thoughts as the Drow's hands ghosted over his trapped length. "What are you doing?"

Khouri smiled against his skin and laughed a little laugh, unlacing the ties that kept Sorin's trousers closed. "I can see how much you want me right now, Sorin," he whispered. "You're not very subtle about it."

Sorin gritted his teeth. "That's not what I meant, you brat." But Khouri was dipping his hand inside, pulling him into the cool, open air. He clutched the armrest with one hand and Khouri's narrow hip with the other. "Won't Navidae throw a fit if he finds you touching me?" If they had made up, then why was Khouri still bothering with Sorin anyway? He hadn't thought of himself as much more than a distraction while they worked things out.

For all of Sorin's worry, Khouri didn't seem to hold even an ounce of his own. He nuzzled Sorin's neck and began to stroke, skimming his thumb over the head of his cock. "You act like he's allowed to have a say in the things I do," the Drow huffed before nipping Sorin's skin gently as a punishment.

274

It was getting harder to concentrate or to worry. Sorin sagged into the chair and tugged Khouri closer, his hand moving to the Drow's ass. It really was as if Khouri were wearing nothing, the gown so thin that the smooth lines of his body were made painfully clear. His eyes alit on the soft shape of Khouri's cock. A wave of heat washed down his spine when he saw the slender ring locked around him. Khouir's small, perky nipples were practically visible with the fabric pulled taut, and when Sorin gave his ass another squeeze, he felt the smooth hardness of a plug brush his fingertips. So, he really had just come from Navidae's bed. Trussed up and told to wait for him to return, no doubt. But Khouri had come looking for him instead.

Sorin held back a laugh. Khouri didn't want to play when he was tired, but it looked like he wasn't allowed to play at all either way. What would Navidae do if he found out? This was getting so dangerous, but Sorin would be damned if he stopped now.

"Isn't that how it usually goes, though?" he asked lowly, lifting a hand to roll his thumb against one of the nipples. Khouri had some strange necklace-like chain strung between them, looping around his neck and body. "Someone willing to pay so much to bring you back doesn't seem like the type of person to be interested in sharing."

Khouri threw his other leg over Sorin's hips, straddling him properly. It put his ass firmly in Sorin's hands, his mouth close enough to kiss. His violet lips split into a cheeky smile, eyes dark with mirth. He moaned so gently against Sorin's cheek. "You don't know the first thing about Drow, do you?" he teased, dipping forward into the barest brush of a kiss.

"You're not even full Drow," Sorin grunted.

"Half seems to be more than enough to have you at my

mercy." Khouri licked a stripe along Sorin's stubbled cheek, laughing softly in his ear. His voice fell like rain, soft and musical and soporific atop the mounting pleasure. "I can do whatever I want, Sorin. You're no threat to him. You're mine, but that doesn't mean I'm not still his."

It was getting harder and harder to make sense of Khouri's words. Sorin wanted to pretend it was because of the cryptic wording, but he knew it was just an indication that he was nearing his end. He clutched Khouri's hips and ass tighter, grinding against the gorgeous Drow. "You're insatiable is what you're saying," he managed to say just as Khouri cupped his balls and twisted his hand around his shaft, sending him over with a low groan. He spilled in Khouri's hand, his head resting against a slender shoulder. The perfume from before filled his every sense, dizzying when coupled with the afterglow.

Khouri combed through Sorin's long hair with his clean hand, laughing his small, pleased laugh. "I might be," he whispered, bringing his cum covered fingers to his mouth to lick them clean. "But Sorin, I think you may be too."

The sight alone made Sorin want to collapse. His chest heaved, and his hands cradled Khouri's hips loosely, watching him lap at the mess on his hand. "What are you doing here, Khouri?" he forced himself to ask, staring into the Drow's dark, dark eyes. This couldn't be just whimsy. Sorin wasn't nearly lucky enough for it to be anything but calculated, and with Khouri making no move to work himself off, it seemed like it had to be just that.

"Can't just enjoy me for the moment, can you?" Khouri breathed, leaning into his chest. He wrapped his arms around Sorin's neck, purring when Sorin held him back. "Did you think I'd forgotten about you?"

"I thought you had your lover back where you wanted him."
He hadn't thought Khouri forgot about him, but he certainly
hadn't thought he figured much into Khouri's interests
anymore.

"Oh, I do," Khouri assured, kissing Sorin's cheek. "But
I couldn't just leave my *partner* all alone, now could I?" He
smiled at the word as he said it, making it sound lewd.

It sounded lewd, but Sorin was more confused than enticed.
"Partner?" he repeated, giving Khouri's ass an appreciative
squeeze. "After you've made up so… tenderly with your
lover, you still want to talk about being my partner?" One of
them was being led on, and Sorin had a startling notion that it
wasn't Navidae.

Khouri sighed, moving to kiss Sorin properly. It was deep
without being rushed, just a gentle press of tongue and lip that
relaxed Sorin despite his frustrations. Slowly, Sorin closed his
eyes and held Khouri closer, loving the taste of the Drow and
the feel of him in his hands.

"The two don't have to be mutually exclusive," Khouri
murmured once he pulled away, his dark eyes all the darker
for the ember of want within them. Sorin's breath came up
short the longer he looked at him. Khouri's beauty was almost
blinding. "I'm sure we could work something out, don't you
think? So long as everyone's happy, there's no reason why we
can't all get what we want."

It couldn't be that easy, could it? Sorin opened his mouth
to ask what he had in mind only to be cut off by the door once
again. Both of them looked as it opened, and Sorin was more
surprised than Khouri when Navidae let himself in again, a
sated look on his face that Sorin knew came from something
more than just finishing whatever work he had been doing.

The expression fell once Navidae caught sight of them together, Khouri curled up in Sorin's lap and Sorin's hands holding him in place. Navidae wrinkled his nose but didn't say anything. "There you are," he greeted, not bothering for an invitation before he walked inside. Khouri looked up from Sorin's shoulder, smiling at his lover. "If you were so lonely, you could have sent for me. No need to... *bother* the hunter."

Whether from the orgasm or just his own jealousy, Sorin felt emboldened. He let his hands move lower on Khouri's hips, squeezing pointedly. "He wasn't bothering me at all," Sorin said, playing with fire and loving it. "I'm more than happy to keep him entertained while you're off doing whatever it is you do."

"Play nice, you two," Khouri murmured, reaching for Navidae with an insistent hand. "Are you done with your work?" There was an almost desperate edge to his voice as if he couldn't wait much longer.

"For the moment, yes." Navidae cupped Khouri's hand in his own, traveling down the delicate arm until he could wrap his arms around Khouri completely. He glared at Sorin but hid it when Khouri turned in for a kiss. "Are you ready to come back to bed, my blackbird?" he whispered after indulging Khouri with a chaste kiss. If he tasted the cum on Khouri's lips, he didn't show it.

Sorin frowned when Khouri fell into Navidae's kiss easily, their embrace effortless in a way that spoke of long, committed habit. For a moment, Sorin clutched at Khouri's hips tighter, rejecting the inevitable separation. Khouri broke the kiss and looked at him, smiling gently.

"Yes," he said, leaning in to kiss Sorin again just as easily as he had kissed Navidae. Against Sorin's lips he spoke, soft and beautiful and everything that Sorin had ever wanted. "I think I'm ready to go back to bed."

"Then let's be off," Navidae said, lifting Khouri up and into his arms easily, pulling him from Sorin's lap the way one would pick up a lazy, sleepy cat. Khouri wrapped his arms and legs around Navidae welcomingly, tangling his fingers in his lover's hair. Navidae held him close and looked down at Sorin with something almost like acceptance in his eyes. "Thank you for occupying him, Hunter," he said, his voice a bit cool. "He can be a handful if left on his own."

"It was my pleasure," Sorin returned, smiling when Navidae furrowed his brow. "He's a delight."

Navidae hummed, and Khouri laughed. "Why aren't you agreeing, Navi?" Khouri huffed, leaning up to kiss his lover's pointed, pierced ear. "I'm delightful, aren't I?"

"Of course you are, pet," Navidae soothed, meeting Sorin's eye just to roll his own, a smile on his face. "Let's get you back to bed. Enjoy the rest of your day, Hunter."

"I'm sure you'll be enjoying the rest of yours," Sorin said, watching the Drow turn and make off towards the door. A flicker of envy smoldered in the pit of his stomach at the thought, but it was muted. Manageable. His eyes widened when Khouri shifted higher in Navidae's arms, peeking over his shoulder to look back at Sorin with eyes full of mischief.

Khouri hooked his chin over Navidae's shoulder, smiling his mysterious little smile as he was taken towards the door. "Think about it," he mouthed to Sorin, waving tiredly with his still-messy fingers. "Partner."

Sorin swallowed, slumping into the chair the moment the

279

door closed. He wouldn't be able to stop thinking about it after all of that. That was probably Khouri's intention, and Sorin would be damned if it wasn't a compelling argument.

Chapter Thirteen

Khouri wasn't sure what woke him, only that he was awake and desperately wishing otherwise.

The circumstances weren't as bad as they could have been. He was in bed surrounded by the red curtains that shielded him from the faux light he could just make out through the thick fabric. Navidae was a warm, dozing weight at his back, arm still slung over Khouri's waist, his legs still tangled with Khouri's beneath the thin sheets. There was no reason to be awake, but he was.

"Navi," he whispered, peering over his shoulder at his lover's sleeping face. "Navi, are you awake?"

When Navidae didn't stir, Khouri sighed. It figured. They had been up for most of the night after all, so it stood to reason that the morning would be spent sleeping. Or, Khouri thought ruefully, it should have been. What had even woken him up? The room was as silent as the grave; the only break in the quiet came from Navidae's soft, steady breaths.

The hand around his waist tightened, and Khouri's eyes went wide when a moment later Navidae rolled against him, a hard, insistent surprise nudging him against his lower back. "N-Navi?" he whispered, thinking him awake. "I know your stamina is impressive, but come on!"

Instead of an answering laugh or a sharp-toothed smile against his neck, Khouri received another measured breath, another sleepy nuzzle. Navidae was still fast asleep, though his body didn't seem to feel the same.

Khouri let out a small laugh, rubbing against the insistent cock with a wiggle of his hips. Well, this was certainly a surprise. Was this what woke him up? Usually, it was Navidae who woke up first and not the other way around. Khouri wasn't quite sure what to do with himself. Should he wake Navidae up? Should he just ignore it? Something like that wouldn't just go away on its own, and it seemed such a waste to let an opportunity like this slip away.

He held tighter to his pillow, frowning. On the other hand, what had Navidae done to deserve a treat like that? He certainly hadn't earned it with his refusal to see Khouri's side. They had barely discussed things at all, and falling into bed so quickly hadn't helped things in the slightest. The cock against his back was insistent, though, rubbing and grinding against him, every so often moving lower to thrust against the curve of Khouri's ass. Gods, but it felt good.

Memories flooded him in a wave. He had only been in this position once or twice before. Catching Navidae asleep wasn't an easy thing to do, and chances like this came only once every few years. Khouri blushed at the thought, but he was already moving lower, unwilling to let something like embarrassment or a grudge stop him from doing what he wanted. When it really came down to it, Khouri just wanted it in his mouth, Navidae earning it be damned.

Turning to face Navidae brought Khouri face to face with a sight he rarely ever got to see. Even looking at Navidae's body made Khouri flush. His lover was laid out in a casual sprawl, his hand above his head while the other lay in Khouri's abandoned spot. His rust-red hair was fanned out along the pillow, a halo that emphasized the sharpness of his face and the wicked curve of his lips. A pang of want stabbed Khouri somewhere in the pit of his stomach. Navidae went on and on about how beautiful Khouri was, but he didn't seem to understand just how much he affected Khouri with a body and face like that.

"It's so unfair," Khouri muttered, tugging the sheet still clinging to Navidae's hips away to bare him fully. Strong, muscled arms, strong, muscled thighs. His cock was half hard from whatever dreams he was having, and Khouri laid himself out along the bed, taking it in hand to coax it fully to life. It barely fit in his hand, thick and long and as perfect as the rest of him. Khouri had never met Navidae's kin, neither his sires nor siblings, but if he had, he might have thanked them for the care that was put into Navidae's conception. His sires obviously knew what they were doing when they married.

Khouri glanced up to watch Navidae's face for any sign of him waking. An errant brush of his thumb over the head of his cock earned Khouri a muted hum, Navidae's hips rolling into his hand gently. "You like that?" he murmured, smiling a little at the moisture now glistening the tip of Navidae's cock. He leaned forward and trailed his lips against the shaft, kissing along the length as he kept up his gentle stroking.

Warmth greeted his lips, the cock pulsing and twitching, kissing him back in the only way it knew how. Navidae let out another noise, this one a low moan. His hands tightened in the sheets and pillow, but still he slept on, a thin sheen of sweat breaking out along his skin. Khouri laughed to himself and opened his mouth, taking in just the head. He gave a gentle suck and closed his eyes to savor the familiar taste. This was so much fun. There was so much to miss about Navidae, and this had to be near the top of the list. But gods, Navidae was big. Khouri's jaw was already beginning to ache, saliva dripping from his chin as he bobbed his head slowly. He used his hand for what he couldn't swallow, pulling off a bit to lave his tongue along the head. Navidae's thighs trembled against his sides. The sounds were getting louder now, and Navidae's breath more ragged.

He would wake up in another moment or two. Khouri smiled around his mouthful. If he were going to wake his lover up, he intended to make it something memorable.

With his hands on Navidae's thighs, Khouri pulled off completely and caught his breath, watching Navidae twitch and whine. So beautiful. Khouri kissed the dripping head and sucked in a lungful of air before taking him down to the hilt, swallowing around him as rhythmically as he knew how.

Like clockwork, Navidae awoke with a choked moan, his ruby eyes blinking rapidly through the pleasure. "What?" he mumbled, dragging a hand through his hair to move it from his eyes. His hips were moving despite his confusion, his cheeks flushed as he stared down at Khouri with growing amusement. "Couldn't wait for me to wake up?" he asked, biting his lip when Khouri pulled off, catching his breath for a moment.

"Maybe you're still sleeping," Khouri gasped, rocking his own hips against the sheets, painfully hard already. He went back down on Navidae, taking him in about halfway, letting his throat rest. The taste was sharper now, Navidae dripping precum more and more.

"Such a sweet dream you are, then," Navidae sighed, curling his fingers through Khouri's hair. There was no yanking or pulling or even an insistent press to move Khouri lower. Navidae smiled down at him gently, basking in the pleasure he was being given. It made Khouri's cheeks burn to watch.

Navidae noticed. He always did. His laugh was warm and musical, his hand cupping Khouri's chin to pull him off his cock. "But you aren't a dream, are you?" he asked, his thumb chasing the path of Khouri's tongue along his bottom lip. "You're my blackbird, finally come home."

Khouri furrowed his brow and parted his lips, on the verge of correcting Navidae, but the thumb simply slipped past to settle along his tongue, stopping him from speaking. Navidae chuckled and pressed down lightly, playing errantly with his mouth as he looked at Khouri with eyes full of mirth.

"You don't need to berate me, pet. I'm aware of the truth," he said, his other hand brushing a lock of hair behind Khouri's ear. "But you're still home. You're still here. You're mine to hold again. Every morning has been misery. Waking up alone, you vanished from my side." He removed his thumb and guided Khouri higher. "It's been torture. Utter torture." Khouri went without complaint, laying himself out along his lover's strong body, kissing him once they were close enough to do so.

"And now?" Khouri asked, sighing as he rolled against Navidae. "How do you feel now?"

Navidae groaned, closing his eyes for a moment as he savored the feeling. "Khouri, my sweet," he said, his bright eyes opening as he gave a lazy, hungry smile. Hands fixed to Khouri's hips, he looked utterly content. "I feel as if I could fall for you all over again."

"Is that so?" Khouri kissed him again, just a chaste press that Navidae chased after when he pulled away. The hands on his hips tightened, and Khouri tangled his fingers in Navidae's thick red hair, brushing it back from his eyes. "You're that weak to me, aren't you?"

"Of course," his lover said, rolling them over easily, sharp teeth glinting as he smiled. "I'm utterly in thrall."

The sheets were warm against Khouri's bare skin, warmed as they were by Navidae before him. He arched against the bed and towards his lover, leaving his hands to rest on the pillow above his head. "What a dangerous pet I must be," he sighed, closing his eyes as Navidae's lips fell to his bared throat, "to hold my master in thrall."

Khouri felt the teasing twinge of Navidae's teeth against his skin, softened only by his lips as he grinned. "You could ask me anything, and I'd be hard-pressed to refuse you. Not with you so sweet beneath me," Navidae breathed, moving lower and taking his time to kiss every inch of Khouri's skin that he could. "Not with you yearning for my touch." He kissed Khouri's clavicle. "My heat," he breathed, meeting Khouri's gaze with half-lidded eyes. "My mark."

The pain blossomed beautifully when Navidae punctuated his words with a bite, Khouri's toes curling and his fingers grasping the pillow weakly. Blood flowed sluggishly down his collarbones but only for a moment. Navidae's tongue lapped it up greedily, cleaning him in slow, stinging licks that felt like blessed agony.

"There's only one thing I want," Khouri sighed, wrapping his arms around Navidae's neck, combing through his hair as he played with the mess he had made. He let out a muted cry when Navidae took another bite in response. Navidae really was in a rewarding mood. Sometimes, he made Khouri beg before he bit him twice.

His lover's lips were painted red when he pulled back to look at him. They curled into a smile at whatever he saw. "Tell me what it is," he ordered softly, dipping down to share the taste of Khouri's submission in a kiss. "Tell me what you want, pet. I want to spoil you."

He would do it too. Khouri knew he would. If he asked for it, Navidae would make him arch and writhe and cum with barely a moment's hesitation. If Khouri just asked, Navidae would level cities. He would take him in a bed of gems and jewels as the heads of their enemies watched on from pikes. Navidae would do it if that was what Khouri wanted.

"Let me go," Khouri breathed, vision so hazy, the red of the curtains bleeding into the red of Navidae's hair. Everything felt so soft, so wonderfully intangible. "Just let me go."

"Let you go? But Khouri," Navidae chuckled, the laugh playing out against his throat as he leaned down, lapping up the blood that still flowed. "You're holding me too tightly for that."

Khouri shook his head, but it did little to alleviate the wonderful weightlessness the world seemed to have taken on. "Above," he clarified, whining when Navidae froze, his tongue pausing mid-lick. "Let me go back up."

Navidae pulled away with a tense frown on his face. He wiped the blood from his lips and loomed over Khouri. "We've talked about this already," he said stonily. "I won't give you that."

The pleasurable haze was fading fast, and Khouri frowned, longing for it to come back. "You mean you've talked about it," he muttered, looking at the curtains angrily. "You must not be very devoted if your generosity comes with stipulations."

"Khouri, don't be like that. You know very well why I'm saying no." Navidae let out a sigh, the mood between them ruined. He peppered Khouri's turned cheek with kisses, trying and failing to turn things back into what they had been before. "I'd burn the world for you," Navidae promised, his eyes as earnest as they could be. "Isn't that enough?"

His sincerity stung. "But you won't let me go out in it," Khouri sighed, bringing his fingers to Navidae's cheek. "You won't let me take in the sights and sounds and pleasures it has to offer me. You'd see it in flames before you would see me out in it without you by my side."

His lover's face fell. "Well, what could it offer you that's better than what's here?" Navidae sat up, moving himself free from Khouri's hands to gesture at the opulent room around them. It was just a shame Khouri couldn't see it for the curtains in the way. "What could it offer you that I can't?"

Khouri snagged his hand from the air and kissed it. He trailed his lips along the palm, taking in Navidae's defeated expression. He really didn't understand. He didn't understand at all, and Khouri wasn't sure he could make him. "This isn't about you," Khouri murmured, hating how Navidae stiffened. "This isn't about filling some gap that you can't fill. It's about me being who I am."

"I thought I knew who you were," Navidae mumbled, staring off at the curtains.

"You do. You know me better than anyone." Khouri kissed his hand again, drawing his attention back. "You know that I've always been like this. You know how I would leave for a time and then come back. You have to know that I'll come back from this too."

Navidae's expression was unreadable. His eyes settled on their joined hands, on Khouri's lips brushing along his knuckles. He dragged their hands back and leaned in, kissing Khouri with a passion he hadn't expected.

When they broke, Khouri was breathless. His eyes were struggling to stay open as his lover tangled his fingers in his hair. "What was that?" he asked, trailing his hand down Navidae's chest, the touch of his warm skin addicting after a kiss like that.

For a moment, there was nothing. Nothing but the sound of their shared breath and Navidae's avoidance. Khouri kissed him again, just a chaste kiss to the corner of his mouth. "Are you being shy?" he asked, leaning up to nibble Navidae's ear. "Do you feel like you don't have any control?"

Navidae swallowed and settled his hands on Khouri's hips. He didn't need to answer. Khouri already knew. Perhaps it had been a bit much to expect Navidae to handle this sort of talk all at once.

Pulling himself away, Khouri pushed down on Navidae's shoulders, making him lie flat on the bed. Navidae grunted a little. "What are you doing?" he asked, watching Khouri turn around.

"Giving you a break," he answered, straddling Navidae's waist to present his ass to Navidae. "Be rough with me. Tell me what to do. Get comfortable again before we come back to it all."

He leaned himself down to lap again at his lover's cock, and that seemed to bring the life back into his lover. Navidae's strong hands settled on his hips and yanked him down lower, the ghost of a sigh teasing Khouri's sensitive skin. "You've no idea what you do to me, pet," Navidae said, kissing his entrance slowly, his tongue slipping inside with a confidence that seemed unshakeable.

Khouri had an idea. He had several. A shiver tore down his spine as Navidae added his fingers in alongside his tongue, working the spot inside that made his thoughts go white. He dropped to his elbows and took Navidae in as deeply as he could, thighs shaking more and more the longer Navidae worked. Khouri could turn Navidae into a raging beast at the wave of his hand. It was the most powerful feeling in the world, submitting to a man like him.

But suddenly, too soon, the fingers pulled out, the tongue following suit. Navidae took him by the hips and tugged Khouri off of him completely. "Straddle me properly," Navidae ordered, voice a little rasped, husky in a way that made Khouri shiver. He yanked Khouri back around, and then into place when he moved too slowly for him. Khouri blushed as he was lined up, hovering just above Navidae's hard, wet cock.

"Navi," he whispered, thighs trembling with the effort of holding himself up. His lover's eyes were intent, roving along his body with a hunger that neared desperate. Khouri felt the same. He ached to lower himself, but he knew he had to wait. He couldn't give in until he was allowed. With his hands braced on Navidae's chest, he pouted and looked into his lover's eyes. "Navi, please. Please let me."

Navidae gripped his hips tighter, holding him in place. "Do you know what I did to bring you back to me?" he asked quietly, his tone serious in a way that seemed out of place given what they were about to do.

Khouri squirmed, biting his lip. "Yeah, I know already," he said, wriggling but getting nowhere. "Do you really want to remind me of that right now? We don't have to talk about it this minute, Navidae."

"That's not…" Navidae trailed off, closing his eyes for a moment. When he opened them again, he tightened his jaw and dragged Khouri down, impaling him on his cock in one swift move. Khouri threw back his head and scratched Navidae's chest, the overwhelming fullness too much all at once.

When Navidae spoke again, his voice was tight and his grip tighter on Khouri's hips. "That's not what I meant," he said through clenched teeth, a bead of sweat rolling down his cheek. He held Khouri in place, refusing to move. "I sent hunters, but I had no idea you were on the surface when I did. I searched the Dusklands for you, Khouri."

Khouri could barely find his voice. "A-And?" he managed to gasp, leaning forward for a kiss. If he could just distract Navidae, get him off this topic, maybe he would fuck him the way he needed.

"And," Navidae continued, turning his head so that Khouri only caught his cheek, "you've no idea the things I've done to find you. You've no idea how many houses I laid to ruin in hopes of finding you within."

What?

Navidae laughed, looking off over his shoulder. "You had no idea, did you? I thought you had been stolen from me, Khouri," he said, "because what else would explain you disappearing on me?"

Realization filled Khouri, but Navidae saw it too. Before Khouri could gather the breath to say something, Navidae thrust into him to make sure what little air he had was wasted on a moan instead.

"N… Navi," Khouri whined, the pace too fast to allow for conversation. His thighs moved of their own accord to meet Navidae's thrusts halfway. "T-The house… across the street–"

"Yeah," Navidae grunted, grinning a little at whatever look Khouri wore on his face. "I started there. Didn't know if they might have spied you from your little perch and decided to covet what wasn't theirs."

"Started?" Khouri closed his eyes and moaned, Navidae driving into him brutally. He could see it now. The ruined manor, the broken, jagged fence– Navidae had gone through a list of names and destroyed them all just on the off chance that Khouri might be somewhere within those walls. How many had Navidae killed? How many had been exiled? Khouri's cheeks burned at the possible numbers, his cock aching at the thought alone.

Navidae saw his pleasure, and he laughed. "Do you like that?" he asked, slowing down to torture him a little. "I thought it rather cruel myself since it was all for naught. I would have felt better if someone *had* stolen you. At least that way I could imagine you hadn't left my side willingly."

The pleasure outshined the guilt Khouri felt, and for that, he was grateful. He leaned down for another kiss, one that Navidae didn't shy away from. Their tongues met, and Khouri let Navidae lead, nearing the edge all the faster for the low groan that rumbled through Navidae's chest.

"P-Please," Khouri begged, breaking the kiss. "Navi, please. Let me cum." He spoke the words against his lover's lips, gasping greedily, stealing the breath from Navidae's lungs since that was freely given.

"You think you deserve to cum?" Navidae asked, his voice a laugh. He gripped Khouri's hips and slowed down the pace even more. "You think you deserve it after all those nobles lost everything for the idea of you?"

"Would you hate me if I said yes?" Khouri smiled, moisture pricking his eyes as he looked down upon his handsome lover. They both knew full well how those nobles envied Navidae. Every gala Khouri went to was one suitor after another begging him to part with Navidae in favor of them. They had gotten what they deserved, even if it had been under false pretenses. Khouri couldn't weep for their loss. It was simply their just due for trying to covet what would never be theirs.

When Navidae laughed, Khouri felt it from the tips of his ears down to his toes. "You really are perfect, aren't you?" he mused, lifting Khouri by the thighs and dropping him down in one targeted move. "Touch yourself for me," he ordered, turning the pace punishing. "I want to see you cum like the needy little pet you are."

Khouri made a broken sound, grabbing his cock with a hand that shook. Too good. It all felt too good. His thighs burned from the effort of moving, Navidae's hands only urging him faster rather than taking the weight for him. His breath came short, his vision hazy. "I'm so close," he whined, listing forward, his head bowed from the effort of staying upright.

"Then do it," Navidae ordered, his voice a growl, his hands tightening. "Do it, Khouri. Cum. Now."

He never could resist an order, especially when Navidae gave it so commandingly. Khouri came half in his hand, half on Navidae's chest, his vision white and his breath lost somewhere in the mix. It didn't take much for him to lose the battle of keeping upright, and he fell against Navidae in a heap, ass still bouncing to work off the cock inside him.

"Navi," Khouri wailed, wrapping his arms around his lover's neck, missing his lips as he kissed his cheek, his chin, his throat. Every thrust made his body twitch, his nerves aching and raw but still so desperate for more.

Navidae kissed him to swallow his moan, his nails digging into his ass to keep the pain a constant reminder through the pleasure. Khouri shuddered and shook, clenching harder, working his lover off quickly so that he could share in the bliss too. He was rewarded a moment later with a low grunt and Navidae's bruising grip driving him downwards, his cock pumping him full of his release. Khouri gasped in his ear. His hips were numb, his neck still bleeding.

"So perfect," Navidae murmured, taking him by the chin and dragging him up for a kiss. Khouri tried to keep up with it but found himself falling short. Navidae smiled against his lips and let him go, combing through hair with his fingers. Khouri let his head fall to Navidae's chest, listening to the slowing of his lover's heartbeat, feeling the wet mess drip down his thighs once Navidae gathered the willpower to pull out.

The silence fell like a warm blanket around them, Khouri sighing happily. It felt so good being like this. Good enough that he could let himself shelf the conversation for a bit longer. His body sang with the echo of Navidae's touch, and even if things weren't perfect, that certainly still was. The heat dissipated slowly, but wrapped in Navidae's arms, Khouri hardly felt the returning cold. It had been such a long night already and now an even longer morning. Slumber teased Khouri like a soft touch, and with Navidae sated and quiet, perhaps it was time to give in.

"How long?"

Khouri opened his eyes, snatched from the edge of sleep by the sudden question. "How long?" he repeated, blinking tiredly at his lover. He should have expected Navidae to prefer fucking over talking about the things they desperately needed to talk about. It was a shame Khouri's body couldn't keep up with the demand. "Give me an hour or so. I want to sleep at least a little bit today."

Navidae frowned, his expression tight. "Not that," he muttered, avoiding Khouri's eye. "How... How long would you need above? How long would you leave me for?"

He was up and awake before the words had time to fade. Khouri stared at Navidae in shock, hardly believing his ears. "Are you serious?" he breathed, hands settled on Navidae's broad chest. "You'd really let me go?"

"You'd go whether or not I let you anyway, wouldn't you?" Navidae posed, his frown all the deeper. "I just... If I agree to this, I just want to know how long. Where you'll be. If you're really safe. It's dangerous up there for you, Khouri. I can't just let you go without being sure."

Khouri swallowed the instinctual urge to wrinkle his nose at the promise of more rules. It was fair, though. Exceedingly fair given how he had run off last time without so much as a goodbye. "I will be safe," he said, dipping down to reward Navidae with a kiss. "I'll travel with Sorin. He's strong, and he knows the surface."

Navidae's hands were warm on his hips, holding him there as if he never wanted to let go. "I'm... I'm not fond of the idea," he sighed, meeting Khouri's eye reluctantly. He rolled his eyes when he saw Khouri about to protest. "I don't care about other lovers. I care that he can touch you when I can't."

There wasn't much of a line between those two things, but Khouri supposed it was monumentally different to Navidae. "But is it really the same as when you touch me?" Khouri asked, kissing him again, rewarding him for being so forthcoming to discuss this at all. "He doesn't mark me. He doesn't play with me the way we play together. You're the only one I let hurt me. Isn't that enough to assuage your jealousy?"

The hands went tight on his hips. "It's better than nothing," he said, narrowing his eyes. "If he ever leaves a mark on you, I *will* kill him. If he ever tries to take more from you than what's been graciously allowed, I'll kill him. If he tries to *keep* you…"

"You'll kill him?" Khouri prompted, smiling gleefully.

"Oh," Navidae murmured, rolling them over, "I'd make him wish I had."

"Sounds fair enough," Khouri laughed. "What other ground rules do you want?"

Navidae hummed, tracing his lips against the raised scars he had carved into Khouri's shoulder. "I'm not sure," he admitted. "We aren't used to talking about these sorts of things."

Truer words had never before been spoken. Up until his escape, Khouri had been content to let Navidae do as he pleased. It had always worked out for the best when it came to sex. Looking back on it, that was probably more due to luck than anything. If they hadn't been so compatible in bed together, there was no telling what sort of issues would have arisen from their decided lack of communication.

"Maybe that's where we went wrong. It probably would've saved us a lot of anger over all of this if we had," Khouri murmured, savoring the teasing kisses while he could. "But, I suppose I should just be happy you're so willing to do it now." Better late than never, especially when it came to something as important as this.

Ignoring the barb, his lover let out a huff. "Let's start with my first question," Navidae offered, his frown softening into a smile the more they spoke. "How long? I can't bear to be without you for ages. It'll be easier since I'll know where you're going, but I do have my limits too."

Khouri bit his lip, wondering how much would be too much. They needed time to get any distance away from the Duskriven, but factoring in a return time would also eat up days and days. "A few months?" he posed, judging Navidae's expression to see if it were too much to ask for. "Six, ideally. Half the year above, half the year with you."

Navidae's smile was rueful. "I was thinking more like two," he admitted, rolling himself onto his shoulder so they laid side by side. "Six is…"

"It's the blink of an eye for us, Navi," Khouri reminded him.

"When it's misery being parted from you for a minute, let alone a month, it's not." Navidae sighed. "Three months."

Khouri raised a brow, recognizing the tone Navidae was using as the one he used when dealing with matters regarding price and the government. So, they were haggling now, were they? "Five, and I'll spend another month here before I leave," he said, leaning closer to his lover to touch his chest gently.

Navidae took his wrist before his could, seeing through his act easily. "You're staying here a while yet longer regardless, pet," he said firmly. "I won't let you leave me any time soon. Not until I've been assured that everything I want is in order before you go."

That was probably fair, but Khouri didn't have to like it. "See it from my side, Navi," he tried. "I have to travel on foot. If you don't give me time enough to account for that, I won't be able to make any good distance. I won't be able to see all I want to see. Sorin's work requires that, so I need at least five months."

"I'll get you horses," Navidae said firmly.

"You know I don't know how to care for one," Khouri scoffed.

"Then I'll send servants with you," he insisted. "Footmen, stable hands, a whole retinue."

Khouri grimaced, shaking his head so hard he saw stars. "Absolutely not. Sorin would never agree to that, and I wouldn't either. We travel on foot, and we travel alone. I won't have you monitoring everything, and if you've got ideas of following us with more hunters, I'll kill them on sight." From the way Navidae's nostrils flared, Khouri could tell he had been planning exactly that.

Before Navidae could argue, Khouri covered his mouth with his hand. "Do you trust me, Navi?" he asked, meeting his eye evenly. "Do you trust that I'm able to defend myself? Do you trust that I'll come back?"

"It's not you I distrust," Navidae said, pulling his hand down and holding it against his cheek. "It's everyone else in the world."

"They're not so bad," Khouri tried, rolling closer to kiss him soothingly. "They're pigheaded and rude but nothing I can't handle. I've dealt with worse here, and you know it." He ran his hand along Navidae's muscled arm, looking up at him through his lashes. "And just think, you won't have to pay Sorin at all if you consider allowing him my company to be reward enough."

"It's not fair when you get like this," Navidae breathed, kissing him again but deeper. "Does he know about that, or is that a little surprise for him later?"

Khouri shrugged, smiling. "He still needs to be punished for what he did. It would suit him right if he went through all of this for nothing but the pleasure of my company."

Navidae laughed against his hair, holding him close, his lips brushing Khouri's ear like a tease. "I'd give anything for that," he said softly. "I'd give anything to be able to travel at your side so long as it meant we were together. He has no idea how lucky he is."

A wave of wistfulness flowed through Khouri, and for a moment, he wanted that too. "You love your life too much here to give it up," Khouri said softly, burying his face in Navidae's neck. "I wouldn't make you give it up just for me."

"Even if it's just for three months?" Navidae chuckled.

Khouri nipped his skin with his teeth gently. "I thought I said five," he mused. "Funny how you heard three. Greedy, aren't you? Or maybe you're just growing hard of hearing in your old age."

Navidae frowned and held him tighter. "Four months," he tried, but from the tone of his voice, Khouri could tell he knew he was fighting a losing battle. "Four and I send a hunter for weekly updates."

"Five months," Khouri said firmly, kissing Navidae's lips and then his cheeks and then his eyes. "I'll leave here a month from now, and you can expect me back in exactly five. I'll send letters if I'm able. I'll visit if I'm homesick." He smiled and put himself against Navidae's ear, kissing the lobe gently. "I'll let you strip me bare and check for marks when I come back. You can fuck me in the foyer, and I won't complain. In front of every noble you hate, if you want."

Navidae's protests were strangled in his throat at the words. He pulled back and looked at Khouri with wide, lust-darkened eyes. "If it's even an hour more–"

He laughed, kissing Navidae again. "I'll let you drag me back with a thousand hunters if it is," he promised, nuzzling Navidae's neck. "You can send one every month for a progress report, but any more than that and I start sending them back sans eyes." He could see it now, the wild life before him. Sorin was sure to love the rules, but Khouri was sure he would warm up to it once he recognized all the perks it would afford him. Endorsed by a Drow noble like Navidae, Sorin's reputation would become the thing of legends. It would more than make up for the decided lack of gold. Or make up for it enough.

"Don't think for a moment I won't," Navidae said, wrapping his arms around Khouri to hold him tight. He hardly looked happy, but that was to be expected. They were fair terms that didn't favor him as much as he would like. Khouri leaned up to give him a kiss, rewarding him for putting up with it.

It didn't surprise him when Navidae deepened the chaste kiss into something heated. Khouri parted his lips and accepted it eagerly, warm from his fingers to his toes. A hand stroked down his waist and hip, tugging him closer to Navidae's firm body. Were they going to do it again? It had been a fair bit less than an hour, but after all of the conceding Navidae had done, Khouri supposed that another rough round was fair.

Breaking the kiss, he took in a ragged breath, tangling their legs together. "You feel so good, Navi," Khouri murmured, shivering a little when Navidae's warm breath rolled across his wet lips. "You make coming back down here bearable."

"Is that what encourages you to come back?" Navidae laughed a little, dragging Khouri by the hips until he was laid out on top of him. His cock was hardening, sliding wetly against his hip as they rolled together in a long established rhythm. Forward, back, forward, back– Khouri let out a breath of a moan and wrapped himself around Navidae like a vine. "I guess I'll have to fuck you enough to make up for every moment you're away."

He punctuated the statement with a firm squeeze, Khouri arching as Navidae's fingers dug into the fresh bruises covering his hips. The pain came swiftly and smoothly, ghosting over his body like a phantom touch. "Such lofty promises," he laughed, feeling drunk on this alone. "Do you really think you can make good on them?

Navidae found his lips in a kiss, one that was short but nowhere near chaste. "Well, how else will I make sure you come back?" he asked, staring at Khouri as if he were the sun, the moon, and every star they couldn't see this deep below the earth. It made the decision to leave harder than it should have been. There really was nothing above that could compare to Navidae's touch. To his adoration.

"I'm your blackbird, aren't I?" Khouri whispered, his heart skipping a beat when Navidae smiled. "I'll always fly home."

Chapter Fourteen

"So let me get this straight," Sorin said in a quiet, pedantic whisper. "You *volunteered* me to be your babysitter? And I'm not even getting paid for it this time?"

Khouri shared a look with Navidae and frowned a little. "Do you think he knows he's still in trouble?" Khouri asked, settling his cup of tea in his lap. It was going to grow cold at this rate, but he could always get more, he supposed. The perks of having servants. "I think being paid should be the last thing on your mind, Sorin. And anyway, wasn't it you who offered me the partnership? Last I checked, partners didn't need to pay each other for their company."

"As if you should ever pay another for their company, pet," Navidae scoffed. He gave Sorin the same unimpressed, barely contained glare he had been leveling the hunter with since they sat down to this semi-hostile tea. "Do you not grasp the gift you are being given? Be grateful, Hunter. A night with my blackbird is worth far more than your weight in gold. He so graciously gives you *five months* of his time, and yet you think it permissible to sneer."

"Navi, calm down," Khouri huffed, setting his tea on the table to cross his arms. "Sorin, I told you already that I was working on your proper punishment. Are you really going to look me in the eye and tell me you think you deserve the gold after all you've done?"

Sorin rolled his eyes and leaned back in his chair, his own cup of tea looking comically small in his big, scarred hands. "It'd be nice," he muttered, shooting a glare at Navidae. "Especially after putting up with him and his ice manor. Do you Drow really not understand the concept of warmth?"

"We understand the concept of setting recalcitrate houseguests on fire when they complain," Navidae shot right back, his teacup creaking worryingly in his hands. The drink had been meant to calm nerves and offer some level of civility to the parlor room, but as it was, Khouri was more worried for the cups than preserving a mood that was never there to begin with.

Khouri sighed, and all eyes drew to him, the others looking as if they were ready to compete for his hand even now. It was the last thing he wanted, but maybe that was the only way to get them to behave and talk to each other while in the same room. Children, he thought. Absolute children, the both of them.

"The next person to squabble gets nothing from me for a month," he said flatly, smiling when Sorin balked and Navidae paled. "Not a kiss. Not a touch. Not even a word. I suggest you get along for the rest of this meeting if you don't want to be caught out in the cold."

"Pet, there's no need for threats," Navidae blustered, reaching out a hand to pet Khouri in hopes of sweetening his mood. "We're just playing. It's just harmless fun."

Khouri leveled him with a look that told Navidae exactly how much he believed that. "It's about as harmless as you pretend to be when meeting with the Council," Khouri replied, watching Navidae fidget. "And we all know how genuine that is. I'm not asking for much here. Don't you want to see me happy?"

"Of course I do, my blackbird," Navidae murmured, his hand resting on Khouri's knee. "I just want you to be happy here. With me. And not him," he finished, shooting an obvious glare Sorin's way.

"Right back at you, *your esteemed Lordship*," Sorin glowered.

Khouri frowned, picking up Navidae's hand to drop it back into his own lap. "See, it's this sort of behavior that worries me. You can't argue like this if we're going to make this work. Something like this requires communication," he said, hoping they might agree. "If we have concerns, we should discuss them before they become bigger problems down the road." Like what had happened with him and Sorin. They certainly didn't need another miscommunication like that again.

Neither looked eager. Khouri furrowed his brow. "I know you have worries about this, Navi," he said sternly, meeting his lover's avoidant eye. "Why don't you air them and we can talk about it."

Navidae grimaced. "Any concerns I may have can be discussed in our bed later," he said, sneering at Sorin.

Sorin bristled. "I have nothing to say to him," he muttered with a glare.

"Well, we got into this fiasco because we failed to use our words," Khouri said icily. "So, I suggest we fix that. Together. Who would like to go first? I promise that neither of you are leaving until we talk."

Navidae and Sorin glared at each other from across the table, almost daring the other to go first.

Khouri sighed. Nothing was going to get done like this. "Navi, why don't you begin? I know you have things you're worried about. Why don't you tell Sorin what they are and we can see about sorting them out?"

"Yes," Sorin grinned, crossing his arms. "Why don't you go first? Let me know all about your worries. I'd love to assuage your fears."

"My *fears* aren't going to be fixed by you," Navidae snarled. His eyes were burning, his jaw tense in a way that Khouri didn't like.

"You don't know that, Navi," Khouri said slowly, unsure of how to handle this. It was so far out of his purview, and it wasn't as if he and Navidae were in the habit of discussing things like this.

"Yeah, you don't know that, *Navi*," Sorin parroted, enjoying this far too much.

Khouri glared at Sorin, but it wasn't enough. Navidae was nearly vibrating with frustration. "Do you really want to know?" he said in a tight, quiet tone.

Sorin smirked. "Please, enlighten us," he said. "I'm just dying to know."

"Where do I begin?" Navidae hissed. "Should I start with my endless issues with you? With your attitude and intentions and the fact that you think it permissible to insinuate yourself into our affairs as if it's your right? Or should I begin by listing off the glaring problems I see in this plan of yours to take to the world above?"

Khouri cut in before Navidae could continue. "What problems?" he asked. He had thought they had discussed this all before. Navidae was naturally going to have issues with

Sorin—that was a given—but the rest…

"It's all just so unknown! Where are you going? How would I contact you if something were to happen? How would *you* contact *me* if something were to happen?" Navidae tossed up a hand and glared at Sorin. "What guarantee do I have that this hunter isn't planning on stealing you from me? How do I know he won't sell you off for another bounty? He had no compunction in doing it when I paid, so what if someone offers more? You know how sought after you are, Khouri."

Khouri blinked, a little shocked that he had held all of that in for so long. "I already told you that you could send a messenger once a month," he began, but Sorin was too impatient to wait his turn to speak.

"Do you really trust us so little?" he growled, hands clenched tightly to the seat's armrests. The wood protested meekly, but its cries went ignored. "Why would I do any of that? Why would you think I'd let anything happen to him? You've been with him for fifty years; a little trust is the least you can give us."

"Trust is a little hard to give when I've spent the last three months thinking my lover kidnapped by my political enemies," Navidae hissed. His eyes were burning like bloodstones, his sharp fangs bared in warning.

"It was only two and a half," Khouri said quietly, only for his words to be swallowed up by the oncoming argument.

"Nothing will happen to him," Sorin insisted. "He can take care of himself for one thing, and there's no way in hell I'd let anyone touch him, let alone some sleaze bag who thinks they can buy my complicity in letting them."

"I don't want *you* to touch him," Navidae spat.

"Well, I don't want *you* to touch him either," Sorin snapped back. Both had their teeth bared, their hackles raised like two dogs about to fight. Khouri buried his face in his hands and held back a groan before standing up, moving between them before they could make good on their threatening stances. Children, the both of them.

"No one will be touching me if you keep acting like idiots," he announced, a hand on each man's chest to force them back into their seats. "Navi, you know we aren't exclusive in that way, and you know well enough that Sorin isn't planning on stealing me away from you. Have some faith in me that I wouldn't be tempted if he tried."

"Exactly–" Sorin began, but Khouri just covered his mouth with his hand, stopping him before he could goad Navidae any further.

"And you," Khouri said, directing the next part at Sorin. "Would you stop antagonizing him? You know very well that I'm not running off with you to leave him, so stop acting like I am."

Both men looked anywhere that wasn't Khouri or each other, Sorin suddenly fascinated with the pattern on his teacup and Navidae entranced with the rug beneath his feet. Khouri sighed and let them sulk for a moment before bringing their attention back where it belonged. It was obviously taxing for them to talk like this, Navidae more so than Sorin. He needed to be gentle with them. Khouri needed to coax them into doing what he wanted. He had to make them want to talk.

It was just a shame that Khouri had no idea how to go about doing that.

Trying to goad them into talking obviously wasn't working. They were both far too headstrong to put aside their egos to come to a compromise, and Khouri had his own interests to see to as well, which made it all the harder to mediate. He looked at Sorin and his fidgeting hands and then at Navidae who looked as stiff as a board, his discomfort dripping off him like a miasma. Khouri didn't know Sorin's history with things like this, if he had any past experience at all, but he knew Navidae intimately. He knew that there was no way his lover was likely to do more than snap when backed into a corner like he was now.

"Navi?" he murmured, catching his lover's attention. "Would you go first?"

"I don't have anything to say to him," Navidae huffed, crossing his arms and looking at the far wall. "You'll just do what you want regardless, won't you? You've already made your decision."

Biting his lip, Khouri reached for Navidae. He remembered how Navidae had responded in bed, how he had needed to feel in control again before he felt comfortable enough to talk. "Please?" he whispered, slipping into his lover's lap to wrap himself around Navidae. "What's bothering you? Just tell me. Don't think about him."

Navidae looked a little distrusting, but he didn't hesitate to take Khouri in his arms the moment he could, nuzzling his neck eagerly. "I already told you my concerns," he muttered, probably shooting Sorin another glare as he sought out Khouri's ear, tracing his lips along the pointed shell. "I don't trust him. How could I? You say you do, but he's betrayed you once. What's to stop him from doing it again?"

Khouri's breath shook when he exhaled, struck by how deft

309

Navidae was at finding his every sensitive spot. "He wouldn't. He only took your bounty because he thought I wanted you more than him. He wanted to give me back to you." He sought out his lover's cheek, kissing it sweetly. "He would never do that for anyone else. He's too enamored with me to give me up."

The hands on his hips went tight, Navidae's brilliant red eyes pinning him in place easily. Khouri felt his body loosen, his head tilting back on instinct to bare his throat. A hand came up to loosely collar him, Navidae's thumb pressing down gently to hitch his breath. "So am I, pet," he whispered. "I won't have him thinking you belong to him. I won't have him thinking he can steal you from me. I'd see him dead first."

It was hard to speak when every part of Khouri told him to submit. He forced himself to look over his shoulder regardless, meeting Sorin's heated gaze. "He knows I'm yours," Khouri said, shivering at the look of pure want in the hunter's eyes. "Don't you, Sorin?"

For a moment, there was no response. Sorin just stared, his hands gripping the armrests tightly. Khouri let out a small noise as Navidae nipped his collarbone, and that seemed to break the man from his reverie. Sorin blinked and cleared his throat, shifting in his seat with a flush on his cheeks that was unmistakable. His complexion really did give away everything on him.

"He's made it hard to forget," Sorin muttered, no doubt referencing the countless scars Khouri wore so proudly.

"See?" Khouri turned, eager to make his point, but before he could continue, Navidae was kissing him. Khouri made a muffled noise of surprise that was swallowed up easily, his eyes falling to half-mast. This wasn't really the sort of thing they should be doing right now. They needed to keep talking.

It just felt so nice like this. Really nice.

Sorin cleared his throat again, and Khouri jolted, turning his head so that Navidae kissed his cheek instead. "I take it you're not worried about that anymore, then," he gasped, so breathless already. The hands on his body were utterly shameless. They roved along his back, sneaking beneath his clothes easily to touch his skin. "What... What else is there, Navi?"

"You may trust him, but I only trust you, pet. I want you outfitted properly," Navidae insisted, kissing him between every word. His hands held so tightly to Khouri's waist that he wondered if he would be let go when it came Sorin's turn. "I want my hand-picked smith to arm you, and I want to outfit you with the best armor money can buy. I won't let you wear that outfit again, pet. If I can't be there to see to your safety myself, I'll do it in any way I can."

Khouri nodded along dumbly, a bit drunk from the kisses. Navidae's hands were dipping beneath the hem of his leggings, squeezing and fondling him as if they weren't in the middle of a sitting room with Sorin a foot away. "No chainmail," he managed to get out when Navidae moved his lips to Khouri's neck, laving his tongue over his marks. "No plate. Nothing heavy. I can't carry that much weight."

Navidae made an agreeing sound, nipping sharply at his throat. "Wouldn't suit your lovely curves anyway," he murmured. "Don't think I'll extend the same kindness to you, Hunter," he said sternly, speaking to Sorin over Khouri's shoulder. "I'd rather you die, so this harebrained scheme ends before it can begin."

"I wouldn't accept it even if you had offered," Sorin muttered, sounding decidedly stiff as he watched them touch and embrace. "And I won't die so easily. Get used to me,

Navidae. I don't plan on leaving anytime soon."

Navidae bared his teeth. Khouri was quick to take his cheeks in hand to move his attention back onto him. "Play nice, Navi," he whispered, pulling away from his lover's lips before he got carried away. They still had another side to hear before they concluded things. He took Navidae by the wrists and pulled his hands off his hips, shifting in his lap to slide into Sorin's. Sorin accepted him eagerly, dragging him into his arms before Navidae could get a good enough grip to keep Khouri in place.

"And what about you?" he asked softly, kissing Sorin's cheek sweetly to make his scowl soften. "What do you want?"

Sorin's big hands were heavy on his waist, his thumbs fitting against Khouri's hipbones. His cool blue eyes lingered on Khouri's chest, no doubt seeing through his sheer top. "Besides you?" he growled lowly, not bothering to hide his words from Navidae behind them. "I'd prefer not having some blasted agents following after us. I'm not in the habit of letting others track my whereabouts. I don't like it."

Navidae was glaring. That much was obvious when Khouri's skin began the prickle. He leaned forward and looped his arms around Sorin's neck, plastering himself against the man's broad chest. "Don't think of it like that," he murmured, kissing his ear teasingly. "They're just there to appease Navi, and you know how to hide your tracks, don't you?" He made sure to pitch his voice low, too low for Navidae to hear. "Think of it like a game, Sorin. Wouldn't it make him angry to learn you've outrun him?"

Khouri smiled against Sorin's ear when his hands went tight on his hips. There was a content rumble that rolled through Sorin's chest and into his own, a shiver running down

Khouri's spine at the sensation. "I guess it's not so bad when you put it like that." He chuckled. His scruffy, untrimmed beard was rough against Khouri's cheek. It had grown so long in the time they had been down here. Khouri loved it dearly.

"See? It's all a matter of perspective." Khouri chanced a glance over his shoulder, smiling at Navidae. This really was the best way to get the both of them to put aside their anger and talk, even if it did involve getting fondled territorially. He reached out a hand towards his lover and laced his fingers with Navidae, coaxing him to scoot his chair closer so he could nuzzle his lover's hand. "I even promise not to talk about Navi while we're having sex," he laughed, staring his lover in the eye. "Since you had such a problem with that before."

"You spoke of me, pet?" Navidae looked hungry, almost proud to hear that he had invaded their intimate moments in such a way.

"Never shut up about you," Sorin grunted tersely.

"He found it emasculating," Khouri teased, earning himself a rough grope to his ass. Navidae moved even closer, his hands looping around Khouri's waist to hold him. Like this, there was nowhere for Khouri to go. He was bracketed on all sides, caught between the Hunter and his lover. It would be a lie to say the thought didn't excite him. It would be an even bigger one to say he didn't wish for more.

Sorin looked ready to argue with him, so Khouri leaned forward and kissed him before he could, parting his lips to let the man take control as he was so wont to do. Navidae didn't protest to it. Khouri shivered when he felt his lover kiss his neck instead, his solid chest pressing against his back as a reminder that Navidae was still there and that there would be no ignoring him. Gods, what Khouri wouldn't give to have

313

them both intent on him. It wasn't likely to happen any time soon, but Khouri could dream.

He forced himself to break away before things got too heated. That wasn't what they were here for, sad as it was to admit it. Khouri caught his breath against Sorin's shoulder, clutching at the man's shirt when Navidae's teeth traced his scars. "I think this is the best you've gotten along together," he laughed breathlessly. "Do you feel a bit more comfortable with things now?"

Sorin hummed, and Khouri lifted his head in time to see the two men exchange a look. They looked a bit more at ease now, neither trying to glare holes in the other. "I think I can live with the terms," Sorin said quietly, "so long as he doesn't try overstepping his bounds and interfering with my work."

"And I suppose I can suffer your absence with dignity," Navidae echoed, speaking his words against Khouri's ear. "Just don't get any ideas, Hunter. Know your place with us. You won't take what is mine."

Sorin looked ready to retort, but Khouri wasn't about to let this tenuous peace fall apart. He carded his fingers through the man's soft hair and pulled him in for another kiss, this one a reward. It was hard for Sorin to stay tense and angry for long, and Khouri smiled against his lips, happiness welling up inside him. This was great. Better than great. Something miraculous had just happened. Khouri couldn't help but be proud of himself for seeing it through.

Breaking his kiss with Sorin, Khouri turned back to face his lover, a smile on his face and a hand reaching out to cup Navidae's cheek. He was so proud of Navidae. A few months ago, he never would have thought this sort of compromise possible. It was amazing what conversation could allow. "I think we have a deal, then," he murmured, kissing his lover just as he had done to Sorin. It certainly wasn't conventional, but nothing about them was.

"You sure about this, brat?" Sorin asked quietly behind him, stroking along his back with a warm hand. "Bounty hunting isn't easy. Life won't be as kind to you up there as it is down here."

Khouri opened his eyes and turned to let Navidae kiss his cheek and ear. "He's right, you know," his lover crooned, his teeth just teasing the tip of his ear. "Are you sure this is what you want?"

It was hard to say if what lay above would be better than what he had down below. It was harder to think that traveling would fill the void within his bones begging him to see and do more. Khouri closed his eyes and let the two men hold him, their warm hands gentle against his bare skin. There was no telling how difficult the road ahead would be, but that warmth was reassuring.

"Yeah," Khouri smiled, opening his eyes. "I'm sure."

Epilogue

"I can't believe I let you talk me into agreeing to this," Sorin complained for the fourth time that morning. His bag was slung over his shoulder, his axe over the other, and despite the filling breakfast and restful night they had just enjoyed, he still held the air of someone being dragged around against his will.

In his defense, the dragging was also literal.

"Quit complaining," Khouri chided, holding tighter to the hunter's sleeve in case he got it in his head to try and make a run for it. "This is the least of what you deserve after all you put me through." Khouri could understand Sorin's antsyness. The temperature was growing warmer the closer they got to the surface, and the need to chase it seemed infectious. Even the chilly, damp tunnel couldn't lower Khouri's mood. Not today. His smile was so big it ached. It was hard to believe this was really happening. He'd had too many dreams just like this to fully believe it all was real.

At least Sorin's attitude was a good reality check. Sorin let out another put upon sigh, letting himself be dragged through the low chamber. He was bent forward, far too tall for the Drow-made tunnel. "Couldn't have at least let me keep the money?" he grumbled, glaring a bit. "I think it's fair compensation for you making me stay in this damp hellhole for so long."

"I think you're lucky to leave with your life." Khouri looked back at the hunter with a smile. If Khouri had wanted to, he could have done much worse than make Sorin stay. "Don't get greedy now. It won't change my mind."

"Nor will it change mine," Navidae murmured up ahead,

leading the way with a dogged determination that Khouri had to commend. He looked over his shoulder with a look that was patently unimpressed, made even more so by the handful of fox fire he wielded like a torch to light their way. There were guides for this sort of thing, but when it came to his blackbird, Navidae insisted on doing the work himself. "You think you deserve more than what I've already given?"

"I think I deserve more than just being saddled with the brat," Sorin muttered, glaring down at the wrist trapped in Khouri's hand. He gave it a tug to test Khouri's grip, and Khouri rewarded him with a tighter one. Sorin frowned. "At least give me some money too. Don't trust him with all of it."

And let Sorin spend it all in a town Khouri couldn't go into? Yeah, that was definitely going to happen. "Play nicely, you two," Khouri chastised, rolling his eyes. The bickering had lessened over the course of their preparations, but it was far from being gone entirely. He let go of Sorin's wrist, trusting him to follow now that the exit was in sight. "We all did agree to this, so let's try to pretend we're happy with it."

"That's easy for you to say," they both mumbled in varying degrees of synchronicity. Navidae glared back at Sorin, who met his distaste head on the moment they realized what they had done. Khouri couldn't help it. He laughed, the sound echoing through the tunnel. What a group they would make if Navidae were able to come with them. Sorin would probably slit his own throat before agreeing to *that*, but the thought was enough to lessen the stab of want jabbing insistently into Khouri's chest.

"Are we almost there?" Sorin asked with a groan.

"Whining already? Who's the brat now, Sorin?" Khouri dodged the swipe directed at him artfully, darting up to hide behind Navidae's arm. Khouri stuck out his tongue and laughed when Sorin glowered.

"Still you, brat," the hunter growled, stomping after them with an angry toss of his head. "You can't hide behind him forever. I'll get you once we've left this hellhole. Then, you'll be in for it."

Khouri's eyes widened when an arm wrapped around his waist. "You'll do no such thing," Navidae said, pulling Khouri flush to his side, which couldn't be all that comfortable given the thick leather armor covering Khouri from neck to toe. Holding out a hand, Navidae gestured them forward with his face turned towards the ground. "There is the exit," he murmured, looking up just to glare at Sorin when he charged past, no doubt eager to be free of the underground. "Don't let the earth shatter down on top of you on your way out, Hunter."

"Oh, don't you worry about me, Your Lordship," Sorin snarled, shoving aside the faux rock doorway. Sunlight streamed in brightly enough to blind. "I don't plan on letting anything get me down now."

"He really is an utter beast, isn't he?" Navidae sighed.

Khouri shrugged, smiling. "It grows on you." Navidae really was holding tight to him. It took a moment to free himself and then another before he could follow after the human. Navidae rolled his eyes in disbelief, muttering under his breath in their language what he thought about Khouri's taste in lovers. Whatever. Let him pout. Navidae would be fine just as soon as he got over his knee-jerk jealousy.

A rustle of paper sounded at the mouth of the entrance, and Khouri looked forward to see Sorin unfurling the old map with a flourish. "Where do you want to go first?" Sorin called out, his eyes narrowed as he read in the low light. "Tuskina? Jalen has some good markets, but you've never seen the sea, have you? We could try for Reblin if that was something you wanted to see. I'm sure Mastha could suffer our company for a week or two..."

The names flowed past his ears like honey. "It doesn't matter where." Khouri closed his eyes as the sun bathed his face in warmth. The chill in his bones began to thaw the more he imagined what all these names might be like. What all they might hold. He couldn't wait to be surrounded in the light of the day, experiencing it through something more than a book in a chilly library. "I want to see it all, so anywhere is good to me."

"See, you say that, but I'm the one who has to figure out everything else." Sorin grumbled and fussed with the map, the light reflecting brightly off his pale hair. Khouri smiled at his partner's shoulders. As grouchy as he was acting, he could tell that Sorin was just as excited at he was.

What all would they see? What all would they do? The possibilities were as endless as the clouds he could see just beyond the mouth of the opening. Khouri took in a deep breath and let it out slowly, already feeling the warmth on his cheeks and the wind in his hair. His bag was full of supplies, his money pouch heavy with all Navidae had thrust upon him. They could go anywhere like this. They could do anything.

"Khouri?" a voice called out, breaking him from his thoughts. Khouri turned and saw Navidae hiding in the shadow of the opening, his thick cloak pulled tightly around his shoulders and the hood drawn over his head. Though he was hidden from the touch of the sun, Khouri could see how it bothered him regardless. "Could you come here for a moment?" he asked, wearing an awkward smile. "I can't imagine how you can bear this light."

Khouri smiled, patting Sorin's arm apologetically as he

climbed down the steps, joining his lover in the shadows. "It's not that bad once you get used to it. And Navi, I thought we already said our goodbyes," he teased, folding himself easily into his lover's warm embrace. "I know you still want to imagine I'll change my mind, but a desperate look doesn't suit you."

"Don't tease me, pet. No amount of goodbyes will make your absence weigh on me less," Navidae murmured, holding him tightly, kissing his head. "Do you really have to do this? Do you really have to leave?"

Pulling away, Khouri looked into his lover's eyes, smiling with as much assurance as he could. "I do," he said, cupping Navidae's cheek in his hand. So warm and so handsome. He was trying not to show his sadness, but he couldn't fool Khouri. "You'll be okay, Navi. You'll barely notice I'm gone."

Navidae scoffed, leaning into Khouri's hand. "A lie tastes the same no matter how sweet the face, my blackbird. Come back if you miss me at all. Even a little. Know that I'm longing for you every moment you're away." He leaned closer and met Khouri in a gentle kiss, one that was too chaste to sate. "You'll long for me too, won't you?" Navidae whispered, ruby eyes half-mast, his breath a tease against Khouri's lips.

Khouri pulled away before he could do something stupid like stay. His cheeks felt warm, his thoughts a little hazy. "You know I will," he breathed, giving Navidae's cheekbone one last stroke before he let his hand fall back down to his side. "Thank you again, Navi, for understanding."

"Don't thank me, pet. If it were up to me, I'd keep you with me." Navidae sighed and managed a smile despite his obvious mood. "But this is what you want, and I was always terrible at being withholding."

"Don't take it so hard," Sorin called out from his spot near the opening. His arms were crossed, and he had a foot propped up against the wall behind him, looking impatient and uncomfortable at playing audience to their tearful goodbye. "I think we've both been duped into going along with the brat's whims."

Navidae smiled, laughing a little under his breath. "Take care of him," he ordered, summoning himself up to his full height to pretend he wasn't as upset as he was. "Die before you let a single ill befall him."

"He can take care of himself," Sorin said, smiling despite himself. "But I'll do my best to return him in one piece."

Navidae hummed, not quite pleased but unable to say more with Khouri staring at him so pointedly. He managed a rueful smile. It was tight, but it was still sincere. Khouri was thankful for the effort. It was more than he would have expected to get a few months ago. All of this was far beyond anything he had ever hoped to imagine then.

A patient—if albeit so—lover. A partner who was ready and willing to show him the world and all that which laid beyond it. And above all, an open path with the sun shining, beckoning them forward.

"Ready to go?" Sorin asked, settling his hand on Khouri's shoulder.

Khouri broke away from his thoughts to smile at his partner. "Yeah," he said, taking his first step into the sun. "I think I am."

THE JOURNEY CONTINUES IN

AQUIVER,

COMING 2018.

For more information, please visit:
tdcloud.tumblr.com
facebook.com/tdcloud94

Made in the USA
Monee, IL
14 April 2022

94149404R00194